"*The Indebted Earl* is both beautiful and engaging, as the reader embarks on an adventure full of unexpected twists and turns. A diverse cast of new characters, and the return of a few we fell in love with in *The Gentleman Spy*, makes this is a must-read for historical romance fans."

GABRIELLE MEYER, author of *Unexpected Christmas Joy*

"Erica Vetsch has penned a captivating tale that stirred and satisfied my love of Regency from first page to last. With winsome characters, heart-tugging romance, and a dash of intrigue, readers will adore this final installment in the beloved Serendipity and Secrets series."

AMANDA BARRATT, author of *The White Rose Resists*

"Vetsch's impeccable research and compelling Regency voice have made Serendipity and Secrets one of the strongest offerings in inspirational historical romance in years. The compulsive trilogy comes to a wonderful conclusion in a tale that packs as much adventure as it does heart. High emotional stakes, love lost and found, and an intelligent treatment of duty and honor will delight established fans while sweeping newcomers off their feet."

RACHEL McMILLAN, author of *The London Restoration* and *The Mozart Code*

"What do you get when you mix an injured naval captain with a grieving young woman and three orphans? A poignant love story filled with action, adventure, and heartwarming moments, that's what. *The Indebted Earl* is going on my keeper shelf for sure!"

MICHELLE GRIEP, best-selling author of *The House at the End of the Moor*

"*The Indebted Earl* is a marvelous book. I love the way Erica Vetsch creates characters I care about. Get them deep into trouble, and in the end, loyalty, bravery, love, and faith save the day."

MARY CONNEALY, author of *Braced for Love*, book one of the Brothers in Arms series

"Thoroughly researched with genuine, well-wrought characters, *The Indebted Earl* is a don't-miss read! Vetsch's rich writing and carefully crafted story sweep the reader into Regency England with all the delights of this fascinating genre. This third volume in her Serendipity and Secrets series brings a satisfying resolution to the trilogy."

JAN DREXLER, award-winning author of *Softly Blows the Bugle*

Praise for *The Lost Lieutenant*
Serendipity & Secrets Book 1

"An enchanting tale, *The Lost Lieutenant* was quick to capture my heart and engage my hopes. A wounded hero meeting a heroine on the run is always a perfect recipe for romance; throw in a spy for good measure, and you've got Erica Vetsch! This is a Regency novel that will have fans begging for more."

JAIME JO WRIGHT, Christy Award winner of *The House on Foster Hill*

"A riveting Regency read, with captivating characters that will tug at your heartstrings."

CAROLYN MILLER, best-selling author of the Regency Brides series

The Indebted Earl

SERENDIPITY & SECRETS

The Lost Lieutenant
The Gentleman Spy
The Indebted Earl

SERENDIPITY & SECRETS

The Indebted Earl

ERICA VETSCH

The Indebted Earl

Published by Kregel Publications, a division of Kregel Inc., 2450 Oak Industrial Dr. NE, Grand Rapids, MI 49505.

Published in association with the Books & Such Literary Management, 52 Mission Circle, Suite 122, PMB 170, Santa Rosa, CA 95409-5370, www.booksandsuch.com.

Scripture quotations are from the King James Version.

Library of Congress Cataloging-in-Publication Data
Names: Vetsch, Erica, author.
Title: The indebted earl / Erica Vetsch.
Description: Grand Rapids, MI : Kregel Publications, [2021] | Series: Serendipity & secrets
Identifiers: LCCN 2020048880 (print) | LCCN 2020048881 (ebook) | ISBN 9780825446191 (paperback) | ISBN 9780825476020 (epub)
Subjects: GSAFD: Love stories. | Regency fiction.
Classification: LCC PS3622.E886 I53 2021 (print) | LCC PS3622.E886 (ebook) | DDC 813/.6--dc23
LC record available at https://lccn.loc.gov/2020048880
LC ebook record available at https://lccn.loc.gov/2020048881

978-0-8254-4619-1,print
978-0-8254-7602-0, epub
978-0-8254-6780-6, Kindle

Printed in the United States of America

To Peter, as always.
You're everything, and more.

And to the Seeker Girls.
I love doing this writing life with you.

Chapter 1

Military Hospital
Oporto, Portugal
June 15, 1814

If it got any hotter, the Royal Navy would have to ship him home in a flask.

Captain Charles Wyvern dabbed the sweat from his temples with his already-soaked handkerchief as he entered the military hospital. What wouldn't he give to be aboard his vessel, palms braced against the rail, taking the sea breeze full in the face?

Those days were still a fair bit off, but he *would* experience them again. He fisted his hand around the square of cloth, his mouth firming. It would take determination and patience, but those he had in abundance.

First he must recover fully from his wounds, get to London, and finally appeal to the Admiralty to give him another command. Formidable tasks, but he was making progress on the first one, at least. Charles entered the ward where he had so recently been a patient, and halfway down the crowded row of billets he found the bed he sought.

Guilt settled like a twelve-pounder in his gut as he inhaled the cloying scents of orange blossoms and dust, carbolic and sweat. Though he had been discharged nearly a week ago to complete his recuperation in the officers' quarters in Oporto, Charles faithfully returned to the hospital every day to attend his friend Major Richardson. For weeks they had lain side by side, sharing the miseries and camaraderie of military hospital life. Major Richardson had led the Royal Marines aboard Charles's last command.

But each had been tacking on a different course since arriving at the hospital. As Charles had improved, Richardson had declined. Again Charles felt the sinking weight of guilt. It was his fault Rich was here at all. If only he hadn't been complacent, had followed through on protocols, most likely neither would have been injured and Rich wouldn't now be dying.

He reached Richardson's cot and pulled up a chair. The young officer's hollow cheeks, his taut, yellowed skin, and the way his body seemed sunken into the bedding all spoke of his waning condition. The chair creaked as Charles sat, and Richardson stirred, his eyes fluttering open.

"How are you faring today, Rich?" Charles kept his voice quiet. The way his comrade looked, even a whisper might cause him pain.

"Still here, Captain."

The rasp in his throat had Charles reaching for the water pitcher, and he dipped the corner of a towel into the water and let a few drops dribble into Rich's mouth. Charles smiled that Rich, though given permission weeks ago, couldn't quite bring himself to call his captain by his first name. It wouldn't be proper, he'd said. He wouldn't want anyone to think he was trading on their friendship and treating the captain cavalierly.

"Thank you." A weak smile touched Rich's cracked lips.

"What else can I do for you?" Charles didn't wait for Rich to ask, easing him up in order to flip his pillow. Though the coolness wouldn't last, it had to feel better for a while.

Rich grimaced as he lay flat again. "How are you, sir?" His voice was as thin as a frayed rope.

"I'm coming right." Charles rolled his shoulders slightly, wincing as familiar pain—though much reduced—arced across his shoulders. He'd received a rather nasty slice from a cutlass during the capture of a French vessel, and the injury had taken far too long to heal.

Charles didn't know how to tell Rich he'd received the all clear to head back to Britain. An anchor lodged in Charles's chest every time he considered leaving the dying marine behind.

After all, Rich had saved Charles's life at the expense of his own.

Charles had thought Rich would have passed on by now, and yet he lingered. Day after day his body fought to keep its tenuous grip on this world, retreating in protracted increments. Though he had fought valiantly, he would soon have to strike his colors and raise the white flag.

Charles shooed away the incessantly buzzing flies and touched Rich lightly on the shoulder. When they had first been transported together to the hospital in Oporto, the major had been hopeful. He'd taken a musket ball to the right side, and though in considerable pain, had remained cheerful and expectant of restoration to health. He'd maintained that hope, holding on to the thought of all he had to return home to in order to keep his spirits up.

"Sophie?" Rich asked.

"Of course." Following their well-worn routine, Charles opened the sea chest under the table beside the cot and withdrew a packet of envelopes. "I'll read the latest."

He unfolded the letter dated two weeks before. One nice thing about being on the beach, the mail arrived regularly. Charles received no mail, not having anyone left to write to him. When he had first gone to sea, his mother had penned a note twice a year, but when she passed away, his mail had stopped. Any news from home was welcome aboard ship, and it was common to hand letters around the officers' mess, or at least read aloud snippets of a less personal nature.

Clearing his throat, he read to the major:

Dearest Rich,

Summer has *finally* arrived in Oxfordshire. The gardens are a riotous glory of color, so heartily greeted after the drab and cold winter refused to take the hint it had overstayed its welcome.

Is it wrong that I love the informal gardens, bursting with flowers run amok, far more than the parterre garden at Haverly with all the box hedges perfectly trimmed and every sprout consigned to its well-planned spot? The more serendipitous garden at Primrose Cottage suits my temperament better, I think, allowed to roam and bloom and burst forth when and where it pleases.

Mother would say it is my undisciplined ways leading me

to embrace unruly flower gardens, but I prefer to think of the blossoms—and my ways—as adventurous rather than rebellious. Spending time in the informal gardens speaks to my soul, and I find peace and inspiration there. After all, it is our special place, and I long for the day when we will wander its free-spirited paths once more.

Our darling Mamie is well enough. She occasionally drifts into a sort of twilight of thought where she appears to see memories from the past with more clarity than her current surroundings, but then she is back, not realizing she's been gone. The physician assures me this is normal for an aging person, though perhaps on the early side for a woman of Mamie's years. He says I am not to worry. Have you noticed how often people tell you not to worry, even when there is something definitely worrisome occurring? Still, the doctor is a dear man, and he is so gentle and kind with Mamie.

Mother is still not resigned to me fulfilling my promise to you of caring for Mamie while you are gone. She doesn't understand it is so much more than mere obligation. I truly love Mamie, and I am honored you would put your dear mama into my care until you return.

Marcus and Charlotte have arrived from London to inhabit the manor for the summer. Charlotte is now in "a delicate condition." Why can't we just say she's going to have a baby? Why must we be coy, with little side glances to invite people in on the secret we all know? So silly. I prefer plain speaking myself, but then again, you know that as well as anyone. My brother smiles indulgently when I speak my mind, but Mother gets a pinch-mouthed look that says she wishes I didn't vex her patience so much. You have always encouraged me to share what I'm thinking and feeling and wondering about, and you never quash me or tell me to spend less time talking and more time listening. It's one of the many reasons I love you.

In addition to Marcus and Charlotte, Mother and Cilla and little Honora Mary have returned from London. They are living in the dower house. I do wonder about Cilla, whether she is content to live with Mother for the rest of her days. I hope a handsome and kind man will someday stride into her life and love her and Honora Mary the way they deserve and take them away from Haverly so she can live her own life Not that she seemed unhappy wed to Neville. But he was so much like Father, reluctant to show emotion, more consumed with his role as the heir than anything else.

Honora Mary has grown, no longer content to sleep in her cradle for much of the day. She has too much exploring to do. Though she cannot yet crawl, she has discovered a talent for rolling that brings her closer to the item she wishes to investigate. I have a feeling that when she can walk, we'll all be required to chase her about to ensure her safety. She looks so much like Neville, it almost hurts. Cilla says she is glad because she has something tangible to remember her husband by. I think I can understand how she feels.

There are times when I wish we had given into impulse to marry in haste rather than listen to Mother and wait until your next extended leave. Even now I might have a little one underfoot with your eyes and my thirst for adventure.

Another change has occurred at Haverly Manor. Mother and Charlotte have embarked upon a campaign of reform, and you'll never guess. They've brought a coterie of ladies from the city to train as domestics in the main and dower houses. The ladies are former Cyprians . . . there, another delicate euphemism. They were prostitutes, Rich. Charlotte hopes to help women leave that life and find better ways to support themselves, and she will give them letters of character when they complete their training. Many are the dependents of killed or wounded veterans, which makes their plight all the more tragic. I can only imagine what it must be like to be in their situation.

I wish Charlotte every success in this endeavor. It has actually relieved my mind somewhat, because Mother has decided to champion these efforts, and as a result, she's too busy "redeeming" these women to fuss overly about me. She has only mentioned my leaving your home and Mamie and returning to Haverly a handful of times since she arrived.

You've instructed me not to fret about you, nor to ask after your recovery, and yet I find that quite impossible. So many soldiers are arriving home since Paris has fallen and the war on the Peninsula is won. Now that Napoleon has been defeated and will be exiled from France, the entire country is in quite the uproar. I wish you were here to experience it. There are celebrations everywhere from St. James's Palace to the local public houses. People can hardly believe the war is finally over. After so many years, I wonder if Britain will know how to exist without the danger.

But it is you I worry about, especially since this Captain Wyvern has taken to writing your letters for you. Are you still unable to put pen to paper yourself? Not that I am unappreciative of the captain's efforts, and please do tell him so. Though his penmanship is difficult to decipher. It has become a sort of code-breaking exercise Mamie and I thoroughly enjoy, even going so far as to employ her quizzing glass when we encounter a particularly scrawling bit. Don't tell the captain. I would not like him to think we make sport of him or do not appreciate his efforts on your behalf.

We miss you terribly, and we long for the day when you will come walking up the drive. We have been making a few small preparations for your homecoming here at Primrose Cottage. Mamie instructs Mrs. Chapman every day to be ready to bake your favorite plum duff dessert. For myself, I anticipate the moment when I will look into your eyes, press my hand to your chest to feel the steady beat of your heart, and know all is right in my world again.

Charles glanced up. The major's eyes were closed, his chest barely moving as he breathed. Had he heard the words read to him?

Heaviness weighed Charles's wounded shoulders at the thought of the woman who had written this letter receiving the news she would never again see the man she loved and had pledged to marry upon his return from battle.

War was most cruel.

While Charles felt it wrong that Rich wouldn't allow anyone to tell his fiancée the truth about his condition, he respected his friend's wishes. But he did so regretfully, resisting the temptation to inform her privately, hoping to somehow soften an un-softenable blow.

For weeks Rich had held on to hope that he would recover, and thus hoped to save Sophie's worrying over nothing. When it became more and more apparent that he would not heal from his wounds, he feared Sophie would try to come to him in Portugal. As the sister of a powerful duke, she might have prevailed upon her brother to see her safely to the Peninsula now that peace had been won, and Rich would not have Sophie see him in such a state. "She must remember me as I was."

Though he should have folded the letter and returned it to the chest now that Rich had fallen asleep, Charles hesitated. He scanned the pages until he found again the place his name was mentioned. Lady Sophia wasn't wrong when she noted his poor handwriting. He'd received a fair few complaints from the Admiralty on the subject over the years when he'd turned in his logbooks after each voyage.

Lady Sophia Haverly. A duke's daughter, a baron's fiancée, a true English rose.

Dare he admit how much he had looked forward to mail arriving aboard ship and here at the hospital? Richardson had been generous in reading portions of her letters aloud in the wardroom aboard the *Dogged* over the months. Charles suspected half the officers on the ship nursed a *tendresse* for the major's fiancée. Or at least the idea of her, with her quick wit and breezy writing style.

Not that he himself had succumbed to the charming missives beyond a mild interest. They were always sunny, always encouraging, bits and bobs of life in their Oxfordshire village. The concepts were mostly foreign to Charles, who had known no other life but the sea since he was a child. He'd joined the Royal Navy at twelve, making his way up from powder monkey to captain over the span of twenty-four years. As such, he was almost a foreigner in his own country when he found himself ashore in England.

Here in the hospital, as Rich's condition had worsened, the major had asked Charles to read the letters aloud, and eventually to pen the replies. The last letter Charles had composed had been almost entirely his own creation, Rich being too weak to contribute much to the epistle.

Charles had described the flowers outside the hospital, the orange blossoms' overpowering scent from the grove near his billet, and the bustle of the port—anything he thought might interest the young noblewoman. Was it lying not to reveal Rich's true condition? A bond existed between Charles and this woman he had never met, for they both cared for Rich. Charles had never written a letter to a young lady before, and he wasn't sure if he was executing the task correctly. He felt odd ending the letter with an endearment or two, hoping he could put into words what he knew Rich felt for his lady.

He sighed. If it weren't for him, Rich would be hale, hearty, and most likely walking up that drive in Oxfordshire, ready to resume his life as a baron and marry Lady Sophia.

Charles's fingers brushed the signature on the letter. Unlike himself, Lady Sophia Haverly wrote a beautiful hand, and her name was as feminine and appealing as her correspondence. Her words and the images they created set up an odd longing in his heart that he didn't quite know what to do with, making him homesick for a place he had never been. As a battle-hardened sea captain, full of salt and tar, he shouldn't be interested in the words of a young woman he'd never met, a woman more than a decade younger than himself, and most importantly a woman betrothed to a dying man who was his friend.

Such thoughts were both frivolous and unworthy. He shook his head, reminding himself he had no attachment to this young woman in her bucolic village. He was a mere conduit at this point, taking dictation to send to her, reading her words aloud to her intended. Her letters were a pleasant distraction from the tedium of hospital life, a bit of a novelty in his seagoing experience. Anticipated and enjoyed now but soon forgotten once he was aboard ship once more.

Even as he told himself this, he knew it wasn't true. He would not forget Lady Sophia, nor the light she had brought into the lives of himself and his officers through her words.

Tucking her letter into its envelope, he placed it with the others back into Rich's sea chest—locker, he supposed it was called on land. The movement caused tightness across his shoulders but not the agonizing searing of previous weeks. The long wound had needed two separate surgeries to open, clean, and drain, but he had finally reached the point where every movement wasn't torture.

He checked the clock on the opposite wall. If he had been aboard his beloved HMS *Dogged*, the duty officer would be sounding the changing of the watch. Sadly, with the injury to her captain, the *Dogged* had been turned over to another's command. By this time she was probably berthed at Plymouth or Portsmouth with only a skeleton crew, the rest of his men ashore and scattered.

Would he get his ship back, or, with the cessation of hostilities, would he be set ashore as well? If he were beached for any length of time, what would he do with himself? His life was at sea, and it was all he wanted.

The surgeon entered the ward. Why did the man always appear to have been dragged through a gun port backward? Hair on end, clothes rumpled, instruments spilling from his pockets. Nothing shipshape about his appearance. He'd soon find himself on the wrong side of a disciplinary hearing if he were in Charles's chain of command.

"Good day, Captain." The surgeon consulted a small notebook. "I didn't expect to see you here now that you've been cleared for release back to England."

Charles shot a glance at Rich, but the major didn't appear to have heard. "Pettigrew." He dipped his chin in greeting.

"I was thinking of you earlier today as I performed a procedure on a cavalry soldier who isn't progressing as well as I had hoped. He, too, had a saber slash, but on his chest. I had to reopen him and extract a piece of his uniform embedded deep in the wound. Now the debris is removed, I can only hope he heals as well as you have."

Charles quelled a shudder. Lord willing, he would never have to endure such medical treatment again. The second surgery to drain and clean the wound had nearly done him in. It had been all he could do not to disgrace himself by crying out during the procedure.

"I envy you returning to Britain soon. I shall be posted here until the last man either recovers or passes on, I suppose." The surgeon heaved a martyred sigh that set Charles's teeth on edge. "What wouldn't I give to be home right now."

Home. The word set up a restlessness in Charles that he didn't know how to sort. His home was at sea aboard whatever ship he served. There was the ancestral estate in coastal Devonshire, but he had never been there. And the old earl, his uncle, wouldn't want to see him anyway. In a few days, Charles would arrive ashore in Britain, a stranger in the land of his birth, with no plans beyond trying to get back to sea as quickly as possible. Pray the good Lord would show favor and have him commanding a deck again soon. This lack of direction was most disturbing.

The doctor moved to Richardson's side, his expression grave. Lifting the man's wrist, he felt for a pulse. The major's breaths were shallow, barely enough to stir the sheet across his chest.

"Has he awakened at all today?"

"I gave him a sip of water and read a bit of one of his letters to him not long ago."

After consulting his notebook once more and jotting a few lines, the doctor stuffed it into his bulging pocket and dragged his hands down his face. "I expect to receive notice he's slipped away every time I make my rounds. He's got a tenacious heart, but his systems are shutting down. It won't be long now. Probably tonight or tomorrow."

When the doctor left, Charles sat quietly beside his friend, his thoughts drifting like flotsam on the tide as he listened to Rich's quick breathing and shooed away flies. When an orderly wheeled the dinner cart down the row of beds, Charles stirred. Long hours had passed with barely a notice from him.

"Sir?" The orderly raised his brows. "The night doctor doesn't like visitors staying into the evening." He spoke hesitantly, his eyes moving between Richardson and Charles.

"Understood." Charles made no move to rise.

The orderly dithered, tugging at his earlobe.

"Corporal, if the night doctor has a problem with my presence, send him to me." Charles made up his mind he would stay with his friend until the end. He owed the young man that and so very much more. If the sawbones posted to this ward didn't care for his presence here, it would be too bad for him.

The orderly nodded. "Very good, sir. Can I bring you anything?" He inclined his head to Rich's frail form. "I'm glad someone will be with him, sir."

"A pitcher of fresh water wouldn't go amiss, Corporal. When you've time."

The man knuckled his forehead and pushed the dinner cart down the row.

Rich's hand fluttered, and Charles touched the paper-dry skin.

"Yes? What is it?" Charles asked softly.

"Promise me . . ." The young major's throat lurched, and his tongue darted out to touch his cracked lips.

Charles gave Rich a few drops of water, their heads close together. He startled when Rich's eyes flew open and bored into his from such close range. With a surprisingly strong grip, the marine grasped Charles's wrist.

"Promise me . . ." He stopped, clearly gathering his wherewithal for one last charge. "Promise me you'll go see Sophie. Tell her . . . what happened to me."

Go see his fiancée? No. Charles wanted no part of that. Rich wouldn't let him tell her via letter, and now he wanted Charles to go see her? How could he possibly? If he faced her, he would have to tell her the truth . . . that Rich had lost his life protecting him.

But Richardson wasn't finished. Gasping, as if determined to speak his piece before it was too late, he said, "Promise me you will tell her how much . . . I loved her. Take her my things . . . and tell her I was thinking of her when I died."

No. Please, no. Don't ask it of me. If you ask, I will be honor bound to say yes.

Despite being parched as an old gunnysack, tears formed at the corners of Rich's eyes and slowly rolled toward his ears.

Then he fired the shot that hit Charles amidships and holed him below the waterline.

"Promise me you will take care of her after I've gone. She always tries to take care of everyone else, but promise me . . . you'll look after her. I trust you, Charles. You've always been a good friend to me. Be a good friend to Sophie . . . Take my place . . ."

His eyes pled with Charles, his hand shaking. How could Charles refuse his friend's dying request? And yet how could he fulfill it?

"Rest easy, Rich. I promise I'll call on her. I'll do whatever I can for her."

The words had barely escaped Charles's lips when Rich's eyes closed, his grip slackened, and he let out one last, long breath.

Lady Sophia Haverly shook the vicar's hand, barely seeing him through her black lace veil as they stood on the steps of the little chapel on her brother's estate.

It had been decided the memorial service should be kept small, with only a handful of mourners, and Sophie was thankful. She couldn't have borne it if the chapel had been crowded with the merely curious.

Sophie descended the stone steps, not feeling her shoes on the treads. Sunshine filtered through the oak trees, creating dappled patterns on the crushed-stone path leading toward the lych-gate into the cemetery. The lych-gate where no bier would be placed. Rich had succumbed to his wounds in Portugal, and he had been buried there.

They had no body to commit to the ground here in England.

As a Royal Marine, Rich had done his fighting mostly at sea, and she had known the war could take his life at any moment, and if that occurred when he was aboard ship, he would be buried at sea. That there would be no graveside service for his mourners. She had thought she was prepared for this.

She had been wrong. Nothing had prepared her for this.

Sophie felt as if her insides consisted of a carefully assembled house of whist cards, and if she moved too quickly or even stepped too firmly, the cards would tumble and flutter away. Since learning of Rich's death, she concentrated nearly every minute of every day on not letting the cards tip.

The rest of the mourners filed out behind her, Mother and Cilla, Marcus and Charlotte, and Mamie. Each dressed somberly, careful of what they said so as not to cause more pain.

Sophie didn't know if more pain was possible.

Mother stalked forward and embraced Sophie awkwardly. She was not one to show physical affection, but Sophie appreciated the attempt.

"I hope you'll soon give up this nonsense about staying on at Primrose." Mother stepped back, adjusting her veil to frame the gray curls clustered around her face. "There's no need to continue living there when you have a family to look after you."

"Thank you, Mother. I am content where I am for now." Sophie couched her refusal as kindly as possible.

With a concerned frown, Mother turned to her carriage. Cilla sent Sophie a compassionate look and a small wave before following her mother-in-law.

Charlotte was next, and she hugged Sophie tight, a gesture that nearly did Sophie in. "I'll call tomorrow. Try to rest." Charlotte's jade-green eyes were full of words she wanted to say, but she was kind enough not to let them out just now. Sophie squeezed her fingers and nodded, blinking hard.

She took Mamie's hand, tucking it into her elbow, and walked toward the carriage her brother had provided for the day. Black paint gleamed, the horses' black hides too, and the ostrich feathers fastened to their bridles were black as ink. And yet the sun shone and the wind rustled the leaves overhead. Water splashed in the distance, where it tumbled over the mill wheel. How could the rest of the world go on when hers felt like it had ended?

"I remember when we brought him here for the first time." Mamie, her shoulders bowed under her shawl, took small steps, and Sophie shortened hers to match. "The baby I thought I would never have. I was well past forty, after all. But then God answered my prayers, and there I was, old enough to be a grandmother, bringing my newborn son to this chapel for his christening." Her voice held no sorrow, only memory. "It was a warm day, like this. Warm enough it rained in the afternoon, and all the guests scurried inside the house like chickens into a coop."

Her soft lips twitched, and her blue eyes, faded now but reminiscent of Rich's, sparkled. "I wasn't sorry Lady Gainsford was the last into the house. Her hat was properly destroyed by the rain. She kept asking all day, wasn't I just mortified to be having a child at my age and didn't I think it a bit irresponsible of me? The woman hadn't an inkling how long I had prayed for a baby of my own, and how I had given up hope of ever being a mother. That woman always had something spiteful to say, though she phrased it as concern."

Sophie squeezed Mamie's hand. "How could anyone be spiteful to you, pet? And thank you for telling me about Rich's christening. I hadn't realized it had taken place here. Mine did too, you know. Not that I remember it." She smiled, though she didn't want to. She carefully raised her heavy veil—provided by her mother for the occasion—and draped it back over her bonnet and away from her face. She took a deep breath. Or at least she tried to. It seemed she hadn't been able to breathe properly for days.

When the news had come—brought by her brother, Marcus, the Duke of Haverly—Sophie had known before he spoke what he would say. The look in his eyes was enough. Her tears had started before a word was said. Marcus had taken her into his arms and held her tight, his chin resting on her head. Rich would not come home. All their plans were shattered, as was her heart.

Over the past few days, Mamie had fluttered and gripped Sophie's hands until they hurt, staring into her eyes, searching for reassurance and clarity. She spent much time in silent grief, remembering, and some retelling stories of Rich's childhood. Sophie worried the sorrow would have her retreating from reality into those shadowy places where she couldn't remember the present and lived solely in the past.

As a result, Sophie determined to carry her sorrow inside, to not let Mamie see her distress. She would allow Mamie to relive her happy times, and she would carry her own grief quietly. Sophie had promised Rich she would take care of his mother, and she intended to keep her promise. Her responsibility didn't end with Rich's death. If anything, it was greater now.

The gravel crunched behind them, and Marcus caught them up as they reached the carriages. "Are you going to insist upon returning to Primrose Cottage?" Brotherly concern laced his words.

"We've been through this, Marcus. I don't know who is more strident on the matter, you or Mother." Sophie kept her tone patient and calm.

He raised one eyebrow, tilting his head in mock censure. "There's no need to go that far, comparing me to Mother. I am aware we've discussed this several times, and yet you still remain obstinate. Your rooms are ready at Haverly, and Charlotte wants you to come to us." He spread his hands in appeal. "How can I convince you? Tell me what to say to make my argument, and I will say it."

"You're a dear, Marcus, but my place is with Mamie, and Mamie's place is at Primrose. I gave my word. You must understand that."

Mamie's head came up at the mention of her name, and her eyes, so innocent and childlike, searched for Sophie's.

Sophie patted Mamie's arm gently and nodded to the footman who stood ready to help her into the carriage. "Why don't you get in, and I'll join you shortly."

Sophie turned back to her brother, tucking her arm through Marcus's, pressing his elbow into her side. "Thank you for being such a rock. I don't know how I would've gotten through this week without you."

Her brother pulled her into his embrace, his chest rising on a deep breath. "I wish I could do more. I wish you didn't have to walk down this path at all, and I wish you wouldn't insist upon walking it alone. I wish you would come home where I can look after you properly." He spoke into the top of her bonnet, hugging her as if he would take her pain upon himself if he could.

She chuckled, her laugh shaky. "That's a lot of wishes."

"You know you could bring Mamie with you."

She leaned against him, drawing strength, as she had so often over the years. Before Rich had stolen her heart, Marcus had been the center of her world: brother, best friend, confidant, partner in crime. The two of them, second and third children of the Duke and Duchess of Haverly, had relied upon one another for affection and attention, since little was forthcoming from their parents. Eight years apart, Sophie had needed Marcus more than he did her. When he'd gone to university and then into the military, she had ached with the loss.

Then she had met Rich, the boy who lived next door to the Haverly estate, and in him she had found a kindred spirit. Her loneliness had vanished, and their friendship had blossomed into something more.

Son of a baron, he had not been her mother's idea of a suitable match for a duke's daughter, but when Sophie refused to be moved on the subject, the duchess had raised her hands in surrender. Father hadn't cared much one way or the other, happy enough to have her future settled.

"I shall be fine, Marcus." She eased out of his embrace, not sure she spoke the truth. "Thank you again for all you've done."

"At least come back to Haverly for one night. Or for luncheon."

She shook her head. "You will only try to prevail upon me to stay. I do appreciate your offer, but I must be with Mamie at Primrose. It is where she feels most comfortable. It is her home, and now mine too."

Marcus squeezed her tightly once more and brushed a kiss on her forehead. "You always were a stubborn child." He cupped her shoulders for a moment and then helped her up into the coach. Closing the door, he rapped on the side, and the coachman put the horses into a walk. It was unseemly for the carriage to hurry under the circumstances.

Sophie leaned back against the squabs and closed her eyes. *I don't think I've ever been this tired. Yet every time I lie down and close my eyes, my mind won't let me sleep. There are so many things to see to yet.*

"It was a lovely service, wasn't it? The vicar said such nice things about my boy." Mamie stared out the open carriage windows, a faraway look in her eyes.

"It *was* a lovely service. And everyone has been so kind." Sophie kept her voice even and pleasant so as not to upset sweet Mamie, but she wanted to leap from the slow-moving carriage and run all the way to the haven of Primrose Cottage, where her memories of Rich were the most vivid. She wanted to curl up in her bed and reread his letters, cry when she felt like it, and not have to be strong for anyone.

The coach plodded on. As they approached the cottage, the sound of the horses' hooves dulled. The gardener had spread straw on the gravel path to deaden the noise.

Mrs. Chapman met them at the door. "I've lain on tea in the drawing room." The housekeeper raised her arm and barely refrained from putting it around Lady Richardson, a breach of protocol that would be unprecedented and probably embarrassing for both parties.

Sometimes Sophie hated protocol. It kept people from being natural with one another.

"Thank you, Mrs. Chapman." Sophie removed her hat and gave it to the housekeeper. "It was a lovely service."

"Donnie and I and the girls had a moment of silence when they rang the bells." She sniffed and touched the corner of her eye with her little finger. Donnie was the gardener, and "the girls" were the laundress and the upstairs maid, who came in daily from the village.

Sophie led Mamie into the drawing room. Everywhere she looked, there were mementos and memories of Rich. His seashell collection, gathered on various holidays to visit his mother's family on the Devon coast. A cricket ball on the mantel, trophy of his school's triumph in some match or other. His favorite books. A painting he'd purchased because he had liked the look in the dog's eyes.

But they were more than possessions. Sophie had worked so hard to keep Rich present for herself and for Mamie while he was deployed, it was as if he were still here. Not a spirit or ghost. Sophie didn't believe in such things. It was all the memories, the hope of his return, the promises for the future they had made that still seemed current. As if nothing had changed, and yet everything had.

She was both comforted and cast adrift.

Mamie eased into her favorite chair. "Thank you, Sophie, dear."

"You're welcome, Mamie, but for what?" Sophie knelt beside the older woman, taking her hand. Had the day been too much for her?

"For taking care of me. For trying to make all this easier for me, which makes it harder for you. You've shouldered all the burdens while Rich has been away, and now he's gone, you're still carrying the load." She raised her other hand, soft and plump, and caressed Sophie's cheek. "I know I am not much help. I can't always remember . . ." She frowned. "It's such a relief to know you are in control of all those matters I can't look after any longer."

"You're no trouble at all, Mamie. I love living with you, and I promise, no matter what happens, I will take care of you." She rose and kissed Mamie's gray curls. "Have your tea, and don't worry your head about anything."

Later, when Mamie was in her room resting, Sophie slipped outside to the back garden. Daisies bobbed in the breeze, butterflies flitted amongst the nigella, and bees bumped and buzzed through the scented stock. Color ran riot on the slope behind the house, and Sophie wandered to her favorite spot. Surrounded by dahlias and sweet peas, she sank onto the open square of grass, wrapping her arms around her knees and lowering her head.

Lord, why? Why did You have to take him from me? You could have kept him safe, could have healed him from his wounds, but You didn't. All my plans are in ruins, and You seem very far away. How could this be Your will? This isn't fair.

Tears wouldn't fall. Somehow the sorrow was too deep. On this spot, just over three years ago, Rich had taken her into his arms and asked her to marry him.

He could have surrendered his commission and stayed in Oxfordshire, but he hadn't. Just a little longer, he'd promised. The Royal Marines needed him; his men needed him. When he'd made that promise, he couldn't have known how long it would be and that he would never return.

Mother had suggested . . . commanded . . . because of the whirlwind nature of their courtship and betrothal, that they wait until Rich returned from his next stretch of duty before they wed. Sophie hadn't wanted to wait, and neither had Rich, but when the duke, her father, had waded in, they had acquiesced. They had their whole lives ahead to spend together. A few months or even a year wouldn't matter much. They would honor her parents by giving in to their request.

How joyful Sophie had been to be loved by Rich, and proud of him in his uniform, proud of his sense of duty and honor. Of course she would wait for him—forever if necessary. Of course she would move to Primrose Cottage and care for Mamie until he fulfilled his duty.

And now it was all ruined. He wouldn't be coming home to claim her as his own. They had put off their happiness for three long years, and now none of their plans would come to fruition.

She had been able to bear the loneliness when she thought there would be a happy ending someday, but how would she endure it now?

Everything she had thought was God's will had been dumped on its head. All the promises made were fallen to bits. She had no idea what to do next.

The sobs finally came, and her carefully constructed house of whist cards blew away on the storm of tears.

Chapter 2

Charles had never seen so many epaulettes and bicorns all in one place. His heart sank like the barometer before a storm. He had known it would be challenging, but these odds were decidedly longer than he had anticipated.

He ascended the steps into the Admiralty, removing his cover as he passed through the doors and tucking it properly under his arm. Officers crowded the halls, their voices low. Each set of eyes that met his were troubled.

These men had a head start on him, for they had not languished in a hospital in Portugal for nearly three months. When peace had been declared, they had been cast upon the shore to make their case to the Admiralty for a new command, while he had been stuck on the Peninsula.

Charles edged through the officers until he reached the department he sought. The small foyer was standing-room only, with enough gold braid to gild a church altar.

"Excuse me." He waited for a narrow opening to form as men jostled to create space for him.

"No good butting in. You'll have to wait your turn like the rest of us," one man muttered. "Who do you think you are?"

Charles didn't answer. The man had a right to be testy. Peacetime could be trying to a battle-hardened sailor. He reached the clerk's desk.

"The back of the line, sir." Without looking up from the papers on his small table, the clerk raised his hand in the direction of the far end of the hall. His voice dripped with boredom. Half a meat pie lay on a greasy paper on the corner of the desk, and the man's collar was unfastened. The papers before him weren't personnel records but a rather lurid-looking broadsheet. What had the navy come to that slackers like this were employed at the Admiralty?

"Sailor." Charles used his "command voice," the one he employed on high seas when the crew needed guidance.

The man's head snapped up, and several others turned as the sound echoed off the groined ceiling.

"On your feet, man."

The clerk jumped up, gulping, and organized himself to attention.

"When was the last time you were aboard a ship?" Charles's stare pinned him in place as he took a sounding of the man's depth.

Charles made a circle in the air with his forefinger to take in the occupants of the crowded anteroom. "Sailor, every one of these men has served bravely for more years and more battles than you can count. They have endured hardship, peril, inclement weather, and privation all in the name of the Royal Navy. While you have been growing calluses on your haunches, clerking for an admiral, these men kept Old Boney from marching up Pall Mall and planting the French flag at St. James's Palace. It would behoove you to show a modicum of respect, for these men, for the Royal Navy, whose uniform you wear, and for Admiral Barrington, whom you serve."

"Charles, are you scolding my staff?" The voice came from the office doorway, and everyone snapped to attention. Admiral Barrington flicked a glance at his aide and then around the crowded room. "I can't say that it isn't warranted. Seaman Phipps, Captain Wyvern has an appointment, if you will check your ledger, and he's exactly on time. While I speak with him, perhaps you can do something useful and organize some benches or chairs for the men who've come calling today?"

He stepped back and invited Charles into his sanctum, closing the door and shutting them in. Papers, books, charts, and maps littered the desk and meeting table, and more crammed the shelves.

"Have a seat, if you can find one. Someday the broadsheets will announce I have been killed in an avalanche of paperwork. If it isn't the Chancellor of the Exchequer wanting reports down to the last grain of gunpowder, it's Customs and Excise wanting to know what the Royal Navy is going to do about the rampant smuggling along every coastline in Britain. As if this was a navy problem. We've just finished fighting the most glorious naval war in our nation's history, and the Revenue wants to turn us into constables on the coast. They should sort out their own problems." The admiral rounded his desk and dropped into his seat while Charles moved a stack of logbooks from a Windsor chair. "And before you ask, no, I don't have a command for you. Not for you nor for the scores of other officers who darken my door each day."

"What about the *Dogged*? Return me to my ship and I'll be a happy man."

"The *Dogged* is docked in Portsmouth with most of the fleet, and that's where she'll stay. There are no orders for her and no need of a captain, though if there was such a need, there are others in line ahead of you. Officers of higher rank and lengthier service will receive commands first."

"Surely there must be something? It doesn't have to be a frigate. I'd take a sloop. At the moment, I'd take a leaky row boat." Desperation tinged his voice, and he sought to quell his feelings. "Just give me anything afloat."

"I know." Barrington planted his elbows on his desk, denting the papers as he rested his chin on his clasped hands. "But there are decorated men with more experience and better connections at the front of the line. Men who are not coming off months in hospital, recovering from nasty cutlass wounds. How are you feeling, by the by?"

"Never better. A paltry cut that is fully healed." This wasn't strictly true, but near enough. The wound had healed, though he suspected he would always have some stiffness and restriction of movement.

Barrington, who had captained the first ship Charles had been assigned to as a boy of twelve, nodded, his eyes sharp as sail needles. "Glad to hear it. Have you any idea the complications of drawing down our navy now that we've won the war? Not even the Admiralty can agree on what size our fighting force should be, and there are so many backroom deals being done for who gets to command the remaining ships, it resembles a cross between the London Stock Exchange and a boxing bout."

"Then how can I get one of those deals made for me?" Charles hated the politics involved in the navy, especially when it came to handing out positions to people who were unqualified but had the right connections. In his case, he was both the nephew of an earl and an experienced commander. He wouldn't be shorting the navy if they gave him another ship. He had earned his way up the ranks and had experience and intelligence. Though he hated trading on the family name, especially since his uncle wanted nothing to do with him, he would at least explore that option before he submitted meekly to being put on indefinite shore leave. "Do I need to rely on my pedigree to get a command? To whom should I speak to see it done?"

Barrington slumped in his chair and pinched the bridge of his nose. "There's a bit of a complication with that, I'm afraid."

Charles straightened. "What complication?"

"It seems your family is *persona non grata* at Whitehall these days. Having a cousin who tried to assassinate the Prince Regent is a bit of a blight on the family tree. Only your exemplary service record and the need for experienced ship captains kept you in command this long."

Arthur Bracken, the black sheep of the family. The man who had attempted to assassinate the Prince Regent, failed spectacularly, and been shot trying to escape. Charles's relationship with the former Viscount Fitzroy wasn't common knowledge amongst his navy peers, but those in power in the Admiralty knew.

"I had nothing to do with that. I hadn't seen Arthur in ten years at least. He was a child the last time we were face-to-face." Charles crushed his bicorn on his lap, then tried to relax his hands. When word had spread that Viscount Fitzroy, heir to the Earl of Rothwell, had tried to stab the Prince Regent, Charles had been ashamed and appalled. He hadn't mentioned the familial tie to his crew lest he be tarred with the same brush.

"I'm afraid you're guilty by association." Barrington frowned. "Not guilty as such, but having that swirling about you when the discussion of who gets a command and who doesn't means you're always going to be moved to the back of the queue. Especially as you are now Viscount Fitzroy yourself."

Charles wanted to snap that it wasn't fair, but he knew how childish that would sound. "Very well." He rose. "I hope you will keep me in mind should something arise."

"Now, Charles, don't be like that. I'm doing my best for you. You've had a long time in service. Maybe it's time for you to retire. You've certainly got the means, what with all the prize money you must have amassed since taking command of your own vessel. Will you go to the family estate? I'm sure the earl would be glad to see you. You are his heir now, after all."

I am equally sure he would not be glad to see me. He would have to renege on many a tirade in order to welcome the "spawn of his slattern sister and that baseborn sailor she married."

"I may be the heir at the moment, but I still have hopes that my uncle will marry and produce a child of his own and relieve me of the title. He's getting on, but other men his age and older have begotten children. Now that he knows the title is set to go to me, I suspect he'll be only too eager to procreate. I am not his favorite nephew, though I am the only one remaining. I imagine he has long hoped some French bullet or cannonball would take care of the problem for him. No, I won't be calling upon my uncle. Beyond that, I have another errand that will take me to Oxfordshire. If there is anything I can do to further my cause, you'll let me know?"

"Of course. What takes you to Oxfordshire? That's as landlocked as can be."

"I must visit the late Baron Richardson's mother and his fiancée. I must repay a debt I owe." He bowed and spun on his heel, wanting only to remove himself from the Admiralty so he could reassess.

All the way down the crowded hall, he met the eyes of those who stared at him, looking for any indication that his petition had found favor. He hoped his face gave away nothing.

Once outside, he settled his bicorn on his head, points fore and aft, and squared his shoulders. If the path to another command was blocked for the moment, he would have to face it. He must discharge his debt to Major Richardson. Perhaps by the time he accomplished the deed, a position aboard ship would have opened up for him.

Nearly a fortnight after the memorial service, Sophie hurried up the gravel drive, clutching a handful of condolence letters and cards close to her chest in an attempt to keep them dry. Rain, a few drops at first and then a deluge, plunged from dark-bellied clouds in a headlong dash to hurtle into the ground. The wind whipped and gusted, tearing at Sophie's skirts as she gained the front steps.

Once inside the house, she flicked through the damp letters. Though she knew it was foolish, she couldn't quell the futile hope that there would be a letter from Rich. It had been a habit for so long, waiting for Thursday, hearing the coach, hurrying to the front gate full of anticipation. How long would it take for the ingrained response to the weekly mail delivery to diminish?

Mamie came from the back of the house, over her arm a trug laden with flowers. "I'm glad I finished before the rain started. Mrs. Chapman is bringing a vase. Aren't they beautiful? The scented stock is almost too strong, but I love it." She set the basket on a side table. "I thought having something bright and happy in the house might cheer us up."

Sophie forced a smile. "What a lovely thought."

"Were there letters?" Mamie's voice held hope too.

"Several from friends. A few from addresses I don't recognize." Somehow Sophie would summon the strength and will to answer them all. No one had told her that grief was so exhausting. Her body felt battered and her mind drained before she even got out of bed in the morning.

"Do you mind if I arrange flowers with you in the drawing room? I can take them to the kitchen if you'd like. I don't want to disturb you." Mamie took a few steps toward the rear door.

"Of course not. I'll read the cards aloud while you work, and you can help me answer them."

They spent a quiet hour responding to the letters until Mamie flagged.

"You go upstairs and rest, love. I'll finish the last of these. There are only two, and I know both the senders." Sophie returned a card to its envelope.

"You're a dear. I don't know what I would do without you here." Mamie rose and touched the flowers she'd gathered, releasing the heady aroma of summer and sunshine even as the rain continued and the sun hid behind sullen clouds.

Sophie kept on with the writing, repeating the same phrases on the black-edged stationary. *Thank you so much for your kind note. We cherish his memory and are grateful that you do as well.* She had just replaced the stopper in the ink bottle and checked the condition of her quill when wheels crunching on the drive drew her attention.

Her shoulders drooped. Had the vicar decided to call? Or was it Marcus and Charlotte, come once more to convince her to move back to Haverly? Sweet as they were, she wouldn't give in. Her place was at Primrose with Mamie. It was right, and she was at peace with her decision, if not with her circumstances.

Please pray the visitor wasn't Mother. Sophie didn't have the energy to deal with the dowager today. She often had to remind herself that Mother's overbearing, pedantic nature came from a place of care and concern . . . and a wee bit of bossiness. If Mother didn't care, she wouldn't meddle. At least that was what Sophie told herself.

She parted the curtains and peered through the raindrop ribbons on the window glass.

A carriage and four entered the gate and headed up the drive. Her fingers curled on the drapes. Bags under a canvas cover were fastened atop the coach. Whoever it was, they had come a fair distance. Perhaps they were lost and needing directions?

Please, Lord, let this visit be brief. At least it was nearly teatime. Refreshments would help the visit pass more easily, and whoever it was could be on their way shortly thereafter.

Sophie hurried to the door. Primrose boasted no footman or butler. In an effort to keep expenses down while Rich was away, Mamie had not filled the post when the butler retired. They would have to be even more parsimonious in the coming days, though Sophie's allowance from the Haverly estate would help. She kept their financial situation from Marcus's notice, knowing he would swoop in with aid and she would feel beholden.

Her independent streak might someday be her downfall, according to her mother, but it was sustaining her through this difficult time. Sophie couldn't muster a smile for company, but she hoped she had at least a neutral expression. Marcus teased her often about how she should never play cards for money, because her every thought shouted from her face as loudly as a town crier. Mother said much the same thing, but without the indulgent humor.

A tall, austere-looking man in a dark cloak emerged from the coach, putting on a bicorn as he stepped to the ground. A bicorn meant navy, didn't it? His eyes locked with hers, and she felt an odd sensation. Though she was sure they had never met, there was something familiar about him.

He paused on the bottom step, rain pelting his shoulders and hat. He had a narrow face, a longish nose, and fine blue eyes. His hair appeared to be brown, but with some gray at the temples and a touch of unruly curl. He must be her senior by a score of years or better. Older even than Marcus. His cloak parted, and she glimpsed gold braid on blue wool. Definitely naval. Was this a courtesy call or an official visit?

Sophie stepped back. "Please, sir, come in out of the rain. And tell your coachman to pull around to the carriage house. No need for him to wait in the elements. If he comes to the back door, he'll find warmth and refreshment."

The officer motioned to the coachman, who touched his hat brim and shook up the reins. Without a word, the navy man gained the threshold and stepped inside. With a practiced hand, he removed his bicorn and fished beneath his cloak, removing a card. "Captain Charles Wyvern, milady."

Sophie's fingers went numb, and she fumbled the card. It fluttered to the floor. "Oh dear. I'm sorry." He retrieved the card, and she took the bit of stiff paper once more as a stab of pain shot through her.

Captain Charles Wyvern, who had commanded the ship on which Rich had served. Who had been billeted next to him in hospital in Portugal. No wonder she had half recognized him. Rich had described him in detail when first being posted to his ship and had mentioned him frequently. The captain looked exactly as she had imagined he would, though older and more drawn.

She gathered herself. "Please allow me to take your cloak. Do come into the parlor. We can lay a fire if you're chilled. It's not a pleasant day for traveling. I never expected you to call upon us here at Primrose. I hope your journey was pleasant in spite of the rain. We'll have tea soon." Sophie stopped short. She was babbling. The captain hadn't moved, as if waiting for her to pause so he could speak. He glanced to where she had his card clutched to her chest, and she lowered her hands. Her nerves had been stretched taut for so long, it seemed any little thing would upset them.

Even a visit from a . . . stranger? Was Captain Wyvern a stranger? He didn't seem like it, and yet he was. Marcus would quiz her, if he were here, about how she could bounce from full spate to woolgathering in the same breath.

With long, tapered fingers, the captain released the frog closure at his throat and removed his cloak. Water dripped in a circle on the stone-flagged floor, and he held the garment away from himself. "I apologize for calling unannounced. It is most presumptuous of me, but I needed to speak with you."

Mrs. Chapman's quiet footfalls sounded, and she stopped a few feet away. "Lady Sophia, I'll take the gentleman's cloak. Shall I bring in tea right away?"

The captain handed the housekeeper the cloak and his hat with a small nod.

She leaned in close to Sophie. "Should I wake the mistress?"

Sophie shook her head. "Let her sleep. If you wake her, she's liable to be upset and foggy."

"Yes, milady."

Sophia moved across the hall. "Please, sir, come in and be comfortable." She led the way into the drawing room. Halfway across the rug, she realized she'd left something out. "Oh, forgive me. I'm Soph—" Her mother's chastisements rang in her ears. "I'm Lady Sophia Haverly."

The captain, with movements that could only be described as punctilious, bowed with a small click of his boot heels and moved to the wing chair in front of the fireplace. A jab struck Sophie's heart. Rich's favorite chair.

As the captain was waiting for her to take a seat before he did, Sophie adjusted her skirts and settled into the corner of the sofa.

He straightened his white breeches, his shining black Hessians gleaming and dotted with raindrops. "Lady Sophia, I came to express my condolences." He pressed his lips together, and his Adam's apple lurched on a swallow. "Major Richardson was an excellent marine, and an excellent officer, and an excellent friend. He served his country and his ship honorably. On behalf of myself and the crew of the HMS *Dogged*, you have our heartfelt sympathies."

Pride and grief clashed in Sophie's breast. And jealousy. This man had spent more time with Rich over the past three years than she had. They had shared meals, laughter, danger, duty. Even pain and suffering.

"Rich spoke highly of you, Captain." Sophie clenched her fingers in her lap. "Thank you for writing to us on his behalf when he was not able to pen words himself."

Mrs. Chapman entered, gripping the handles of a large tray. Sophie moved a stack of books on the low table between them to make room.

"Thank you, Mrs. Chapman. Have you seen to the captain's coachman?"

"He's eating scones as we speak. Donnie is tending the horses." Mrs. Chapman held Sophie's gaze. Would their guest be staying for supper? Possibly for the night? What arrangements should she make?

Sophie gave a small shrug and shake of her head.

When the housekeeper had gone, Sophie poured a cup of tea, inhaling the fragrance and dropping in two spoonfuls of sugar before handing it to the captain. His brows arched as he took the cup.

A smile, the first she'd felt like issuing in a long time, tugged at Sophie's lips. "I must have remembered from one of Rich's letters how you take your tea. He remarked often how supplies would run short and you would bemoan the lack of sugar for your tea." Rich had portrayed the expression on his captain's face in quite a humorous manner, and now that Sophie had met him in person, she could see it clearly.

He nodded, shifting his shoulders and wincing, though he tried to hide it.

Was it good manners to ask after a man's war injuries? Was it bad manners not to? "I hope you are recovering from your wounds?"

"I am managing well, thank you." He took a sip from his cup, rested it on his knee, and looked at the floor. Then he raised his chin. "It's because of my injury that I am here."

Sophie set the teapot down. His injury? Was he seeing a specialist in the area?

"I first must make my confession to you." His expression became bleak, his eyes far away, as if remembering something painful. He sat at attention even though he remained in his chair. She imagined he would look much the same if facing a firing squad. What had he to confess?

He took a fortifying breath and set the teacup back on the tray. "I must apologize, because I bear responsibility for your loss. If it weren't for me, Rich would still be alive and would be home with you now." He gripped his knees, the skin taut over his knuckles.

Stunned at this admission, Sophie shook her head. This man was Rich's friend. He couldn't possibly have caused Rich's death.

"Sir, I am sure you are mistaken. We understood that Rich had been shot. Are you saying you are the one who shot him?" Was that it? And if so, how was she going to bear it? It must have been an accident. But . . . surely God wouldn't take Rich from her by accident? *If You are sovereign, nothing happens by accident, right?* Sophie dreaded what the captain would say, yet she longed to know.

Captain Wyvern shook his head. "I'll start at the beginning. Our ship, the *Dogged*, was stationed off the coast of France. On April twelve, the same day Wellington was capturing Toulouse, we spotted a sail on the horizon. A *Téméraire* class, the *Bravoure*."

As if he could no longer sit still, he rose and went to the window, legs braced apart, hands clasped behind him. She could envision him aboard a ship, commanding, issuing orders, watching the horizon.

"The *Dogged* is a swift vessel, and it was natural we should give chase. It is a tactic of French ships to show themselves and then race for the coast and the protection of the batteries there. However, with favorable winds and a well-trained crew, we were able to reel in the *Bravoure* well before we would be in any danger from the coastal guns. A brisk battle ensued, and though we had taken some damage, we were able to draw alongside and batten the *Bravoure* to the *Dogged*."

Sophie listened intently, but it was as if he wasn't really speaking to her. In some ways it was like listening to Mamie spin yarns about her childhood. Far away and vague on some points, piercingly accurate on others.

"When the grappling hooks were shot across, that was the signal for the marines to board the *Bravoure*. Major Richardson . . . Rich . . . was always the first to advance in those situations, and his men followed. I remained in command aboard the *Dogged*. Though the fighting was fierce, Rich soon had the French crew disarmed and assembled on the deck. The

French colors were struck, and the enemy ship was ours. The men cheered. It was our third such battle in as many weeks, and each time we had been victorious. I suppose it was our run of wins that caused our . . . my . . . complacency. After assessing the damage to the *Dogged* and issuing orders to begin repairs, I boarded the captured vessel. I should have checked that a thorough search of the ship had been done, that all the prisoners had been accounted for, but I did not."

For long moments, the only sound in the room was the rain washing down the window glass and the ticking of the ormolu clock on the mantel. A chill, slithery feeling invaded Sophie's insides.

At last the captain stirred, rousing himself to finish the tale. He turned and faced her, not flinching, though the task clearly pained him.

"I was lax in my duty, and two French sailors burst from their hiding places on the foredeck. One had a cutlass and one a pistol. The one with the saber swung with the intent to take off my head, and if it wasn't for the quick actions of Rich, I would be dead now. Rich launched himself toward me while firing his pistol at the swordsman, causing my assailant's arm to drop at the last instant, and I suffered a slice across my back."

Again he twitched his shoulders and grimaced. "Because Rich was intent upon saving me, he neglected to save himself. The Frenchman with the pistol fired and caught Rich in the side. By the time the rest of my crew understood what was happening and apprehended the enemy, Rich and I both lay on the deck with severe wounds."

Sophie's fingers came up to cover her lips. Rich had been wounded saving his friend's life. And the captain admitted that it was his fault. He should have made sure the captured ship was secure before relaxing his guard. His admission floated in her head, shock making it difficult to attend to the accompanying emotions.

Deep creases etched into his cheeks, his mouth a grim line. "We were taken to the military hospital in Oporto. Rich apologized over and over, but it wasn't his fault. The ultimate responsibility lay with me, and I failed him. It is a burden I shall bear for the rest of my days."

Sophie's emotions bobbed on a rough sea. If he had seen to his duty, Rich would be alive? And he had the gall to show up here expecting her to . . . what? Say that she forgave him? Tell him she bore him no ill will?

Anger flared through her, and she turned away lest her face should declare her feelings. She wanted to rail at him, shout that it wasn't fair. Shake her fists and demand why. She wanted answers, and not just from the captain.

Why, God? Why did You allow this to happen? How can this possibly be Your will? She focused on Captain Wyvern's guilt. For a moment it felt good to have someone tangible to blame, somewhere to put her anger.

The captain waited, shoulders braced, face grim, anguish plain in his eyes. No doubt he was prepared for her recriminations. But what should she say?

What would Rich want her to say? By the captain's own admission, Rich had tried to take the blame for the incident that had cost him his life.

No, it couldn't possibly be Rich's fault. He wouldn't be so foolhardy when he knew he was coming home to her.

Yet in her heart she knew Rich would have sacrificed his life if it meant saving another. The fire went out of her, and she took a short breath, sinking once more into sorrow and exhaustion.

Was she better off knowing the circumstances of Rich's death? It changed nothing, other than that she was now forced to make a choice.

A choice that offended her sense of justice. But she could see Rich, compassion in his blue eyes, asking her to do the right thing.

After a moment, she rose and crossed the room. Captain Wyvern stood his ground, hands once more behind his back. "Captain, I appreciate what it took for you to come here." She spoke kindly even though she didn't feel kind. "I am certain Rich did not hold you at fault. He would not wish me to blame you either." She didn't say she forgave the captain, because she believed in speaking the truth, and his admissions were too new, too raw for her to process just now. Hopefully, emotion would eventually follow action.

The captain took a deep breath, his eyes bleak. "I understand. The major was a good man, and I wish God had chosen to take me instead."

Sophie needed to free herself from this tangle of feelings. She hadn't worked through her thoughts on God's role in Rich's death, and she wasn't ready to lay all bare now, especially to this man. "Captain, it is nearly dark. Have you accommodations for the night?" Rich would want her to offer him hospitality, and Mamie would be distressed if she learned he had been here and she had missed his visit. "You are welcome to stay here with us."

"I had planned to find lodgings at an inn." His brows knitted. "I do not wish to impose."

"Please accept the hospitality of Primrose Cottage tonight. If you have no obligations calling you away, we would be pleased to have you as our guest."

"That is most kind, Lady Sophia. I am grateful."

Though he looked pained as he said it.

Lady Sophia was both more beautiful and younger looking than he had expected. Which was odd, since Rich had shown Charles a miniature of her, and Charles had known her approximate age. But meeting her in person, he caught a hint of the restless vitality that her letters portrayed and Rich's stories had told. He felt like a mossy-backed sea turtle in comparison to her fresh-faced youth. Though she was subdued by her loss, her grief did not dampen the intelligent sharpness in her blue eyes.

The miniature had been a good likeness, yet it didn't do her justice. Especially now, in the glow of the candles on the dinner table. Though she wore a simple black dress trimmed with plain black ribbon, her skin glowed and her eyes mirrored the candle flames. Light raced across her dark-brown hair and created shadows along her collarbones. Lady Sophia sat directly opposite him, with Mamie at the head of the table, and he couldn't stop looking at Lady Sophia.

He had not asked for her forgiveness, because he could not forgive himself. And she had not offered forgiveness, at least not in so many words. Was it because she could not forgive either? She had tried to hide her feelings, but he had read several emotions on her face: anger, longing, grief, doubt, resignation. Each had played across her features in succession, recognizable because they had mirrored his own. She had said Rich would not hold him at fault. Therefore she would not either. The two had been so in tune that their actions mirrored each other's. Charles had never had that kind of relationship with anyone, much less a woman he loved. Again that faint pang of yearning struck the corners of his heart.

In spite of whatever misgivings she might have, she had offered him hospitality. Was that too done from a sense of duty and recalling what Rich would have wanted, or was it a demonstration of a generous nature?

Lady Mamie Richardson had welcomed him as if he were a long-lost son. Her delight had seemed genuine, and to his utter surprise and discomfort, she had hugged him. The warmth of her gesture had thickened his throat and roughened his voice. As she squeezed him, she had even whispered in his ear how thankful she was for his coming. When was the last time someone had embraced him? He couldn't recall.

"What are your plans now that peace has been declared?" Lady Richardson toyed with her lorgnette, twisting the attached ribbon idly. The elderly woman hadn't eaten much of the dinner, but she seemed in control of her mental faculties. Charles hadn't known what to expect of Rich's mother based upon Lady Sophia's letters, whether she might be doddering and vague. But this woman was kindness itself, even when he repeated the story of how Rich had suffered his wounds. "Will you see your family?"

Her reception and forgiveness heaped coals of fire upon his head.

"I will return to London and continue to assail the Admiralty to give me a new posting. I have family in Devonshire, though we are not close."

His cousin, the jackanapes, had all but scuttled Charles's naval career from afar. What had possessed him to try to kill the Prince Regent? Their uncle must be nearly apoplectic to have such a scoundrel as a nephew. The earl's view of Charles had always been derogatory, but at least Charles had never attempted regicide.

Be that as it may, the odds of him getting a captaincy anytime soon were bleak. It was probably wrong to pray for another outbreak of war, but war seemed to be the only path back to a command.

"If you don't get a ship, what will you do?" Lady Sophia asked. Her demeanor to him was perfectly proper but a trifle distant. He didn't blame her. He doubted he would be as composed in her place.

"I will probably apply to the East India Company for a captaincy of a merchant vessel." Though it would be a last resort. He was a navy man to his core. He had worked every day for over two decades to reach his current rank, and he wouldn't quit without a fight. Captaining a merchant vessel would seem a flat end to a fine career.

"Have you no prospects on land? I would think you would have had enough of the navy and war. Rich felt it his duty to serve his country, but he intended to come home the moment peace was declared and never take up arms again." Lady Sophia placed her hand on the stem of her goblet, rotating the glass and watching the lamplight wink off the ruby liquid inside.

Had she any idea what a picture she made?

Charles shrugged. "I've known no other life since I was a lad. I put to sea at twelve. Through study and experience, I made my way up through the ranks. It was a difficult climb, and I hope my career isn't terminal at captain."

"To sea at twelve?" Lady Richardson shook her head. "So young. Did you run away to join the navy then?"

"No, madam. I am the son of a sailor, and it was both his expectation and my wish. I am most comfortable at sea." He paused, looking around the pleasant dining room. "However, your hospitality has its appeal. The food is better, and the company excellent." He raised his glass to them, dipping his head a bit. It would be unkind to make them think he wanted to be elsewhere, though he most fervently did. He hadn't discharged his full duty to Rich yet, and he wasn't certain how to go about it.

When the meal concluded, the ladies offered to leave him to after-dinner port and cigars, but he didn't like port, and he didn't smoke. "I'll join you, if I may. Or I can take myself upstairs to my room if you'd rather be on your own this evening?" He stood first and pulled out Lady Richardson's chair.

"We won't banish you unless that's your preference." Lady Sophia picked up the candelabra from the table. "It is our custom to spend our evenings with some reading and conversation. You may join us if you wish."

He offered his arm to Lady Richardson and followed Lady Sophia across the hall to the drawing room. The candlelight created shadows that danced and jumped with Lady Sophia's movements, and in her wake Charles could smell a light lemony perfume. Far removed from the smells aboard ship, to be sure.

As he settled Lady Richardson into a chair, he knew he should stop shilly-shallying and do the thing he had been tasked to do. It wasn't in his nature to shirk a duty, and putting this particular one off as long as he had chafed. "Ladies, I had a threefold reason for visiting you. The first was to express my condolences and sorrow for your loss. The second was to relay to you how Rich came by his fatal injuries. The third still remains."

Lady Sophia had placed the candelabra on a side table and now used one of the tapers to light the wall sconces. She paused, looking over her shoulder, the soft golden light making her eyes appear larger. She seemed to be begging him to say nothing more that would hurt her.

If only he had that option. He was honor bound to fulfill his promise to Rich. If only his friend had not given him this duty.

Charles swallowed and took a breath in through his nose. "When Major Richardson passed away, he left in my possession his sea chest. He charged me with returning those things to your keeping and delivering a final message."

Lady Sophia's hand lowered, and she paused before placing the candle back into its holder. "A message?" Each word was trimmed in pain but also eager longing. "I would have any word from Rich that you possess."

"Major Richardson asked me to tell you that he was thinking of you, Lady Sophia, when he left this world. He asked me to tell you that he loved you very much."

She inhaled sharply, her hands pressing against her midriff. Her lips trembled, and she blinked hastily, looking away.

He hated causing her more grief. Perhaps once the sharpness of her pain subsided, she would be comforted by her lover's last words. Later she would no doubt be glad she had Rich's things, but for now they would probably only remind her of what she had lost. "My coachman brought Rich's sea chest to my room. Would you prefer me to bring it downstairs?"

Lady Richardson studied Lady Sophia, and when she didn't speak, shook her head. "I think it would be best if it was taken to Sophie's room. She'll want to look through it in private." Her smile was kind. "You can see to the chore when we head upstairs for bed."

Lady Sophia nodded. She had subsided onto the arm of the settee next to Lady Richardson, and the two held hands, as if drawing strength from one another. The younger woman's face was as pale as a topgallant in the moonlight, and he had the oddest urge to put his arms around her and shield her from pain. Which was ridiculous. He had no notion how to comfort a woman, and as he was the cause of her pain, she would surely reject any solace he might offer.

He stood before the fireplace, his back to the mantel, his hands clasped behind him. "I must ask, is there anything that you, Lady Sophia and Lady Richardson, need? Any way that I may be of service to you?" He wouldn't mention the promise Rich had begged of him, as he didn't want them to think he inquired only out of duty. He would have asked in any case. He owed them that much and more.

The ladies looked at each other, and Lady Sophia shook her head slightly.

Lady Richardson nodded. "Captain Wyvern, that is most kind of you, but we need nothing." She reached into a small basket at her side and withdrew yarn and needles. "We are most content here at Primrose."

"Perhaps your finances? I am a wealthy man. Captains are given the lion's share of any prizes taken at sea, and the *Dogged* was a successful hunter. Is there someone in charge of your finances to whom I might speak?" It was bad manners to speak of money, but for Rich's sake, he must.

Lady Sophia's back stiffened. "Captain, if we needed any help in that quarter, my brother, the Duke of Haverly, is more than capable of assisting us."

Her voice could have come straight from the North Sea. The spark of indignation in her eyes relieved his spirit. That independent streak would be of good use to her in the coming months.

"I mean no offense." He wished there was range in the drawing room to pace. This room with all its feminine furnishings hemmed him in as neatly as the gunwales of a rowboat. If only he could stride the quarterdeck of the *Dogged* with space to think and breathe. "I feel it my duty to aid you in whatever way I can. I am indebted to Major Richardson and to you." He spread his hands.

"How are you indebted to us?" Lady Sophia asked, still stiff. "You owe us nothing. Rich absolved you of debt, and we can only do the same."

Heat crept up above his collar, and he shifted his weight. Dare he say that her letters had been the only bright spots in many months of sea duty? That her epistles had kept him sane while in the hospital? How much he had looked forward to hearing even the bits that Rich chose to share in the wardroom?

"You have offered hospitality and welcome where I didn't expect it. Though from your letters, I should have."

"My letters?" Her delicate brows rose, accentuating the heart shape of her face.

"Lady Sophia, I read your letters to Rich . . . Major Richardson . . . when he could not read them for himself. And before that, he shared from them occasionally aboard ship. He described you as warm and generous, willing to extend grace and constantly caring for others." He stopped, lest he give too much away. "I do not think the major's assessments were wrong."

Lady Richardson nodded, reaching over to pat Lady Sophia's hand. "That describes you beautifully, dear. A treasure."

"It's you who are the treasure, sweet Mamie. You find good in everybody." Lady Sophia squeezed Mamie's hand and rose from the arm of the settee to take a seat in a chair before the fire.

Charles cleared his throat, trying to nudge the topic back to his aiding the two women. "Surely there is some way I might serve you?" How could he fulfill his promise to Rich to look after them if they wouldn't take anything he had to offer? How could he do right by the woman whose letters had meant so much, who had sacrificed for her country as surely as her betrothed had, if she turned aside his efforts?

Late that night, as he lay awake in Rich's house, having eaten at Rich's table and conversed with Rich's mother and fiancée, he chided himself. What had he thought would happen? That he would roll up in his carriage, dispense condolences and cash, and then depart with a clear conscience, debt discharged?

He reached for a small object on the bedside table. Even if that had been true, he had foregone a clear conscience in one impulsive moment tonight. Before he had carried Rich's sea chest to Lady Sophia's room, he'd opened it and removed one item.

The rain had ceased, and before he'd climbed into bed, he'd opened the drapes. He held up the item now, turning it so the moonlight fell full upon it.

The miniature of Sophie that had been Rich's most treasured possession.

He'd been wrong to take it. It didn't belong to him. He'd known it the moment he'd removed it from the chest. The stain on his integrity robbed him of sleep. He should return it to her, though he couldn't imagine how without causing much embarrassment.

He could just leave it on the bedside table and let it be a mystery as to how it had gotten there. But that was the coward's way out. And for all his faults, he was no coward.

Tomorrow he would front Lady Sophia, beg her pardon and forgiveness once more, and hand her the painting. He would then depart and never see Lady Sophia again.

He was a fool. His thoughts chased one another, doubling back and circling, but always returning to the same point.

His future and Lady Sophia's lay far apart, and try as he might, he would never be able to repay all he owed her.

Chapter 3

Was she ready to open the lid—literally and figuratively—on that part of Rich's life?

Sophie lay on her side, awakened early, as sunrise filtered into the room and cast a warm glow on the wooden chest. The box sat in the middle of the rug, scarred, dented, the metal latches in need of a polish.

Rich's sea chest. All that he had taken with him or accumulated in his days at war. His name, rank, and company stenciled on the chest, though faint from wear.

Captain Wyvern had brought the chest to her room last night.

Captain Charles Wyvern.

He was exactly as Rich's letters described him. Punctilious, proper, and reserved. A man of order and duty. He was well mannered for all that he'd been brought up aboard ships, but he didn't seem at ease. Of course, how could he be when he carried such burdens?

How was she supposed to feel? Was the captain really at fault? He hadn't fired the bullet that killed Rich. And if the captain's telling of events was to be believed, Rich had admitted that he should have been the one to clear the ship of combatants.

If she believed in the sovereignty of God, was there any such thing as an accidental death? Was it God's will that Rich die?

And how did that fit with her belief that God was good? If God was indeed good and God was sovereign over all, why did bad things happen to His children? Where was justice if good people died for nothing?

She pushed the covers aside and swung her feet out, burying her toes in the rug. She wasn't ready to work her way through that particular mental maze, and she would also leave the chest unopened for now. The contents belonged to a Rich she hadn't known well, the military man, the Royal Marine. She would rather hold close the memories of Rich as she knew him, the dashing, handsome neighbor, always laughing, who had loved her and appreciated her and asked her to be his wife. She didn't want to overlay those memories with whatever the chest contained.

Hefting the handle at one end of the trunk, she pulled it over to the bed and pushed it underneath. She had the long days, months, years here at Primrose to deal with the past. For now she needed to dress and go downstairs to see that breakfast preparations were underway.

Captain Wyvern would be leaving this morning, and she and Mamie would see him off properly—as Rich's friend. Yesterday's revelations had been a shock, but she would behave as the gracious hostess she had been trained to be and do her duty by their guest.

Sophie needn't have worried about breakfast. Mrs. Chapman had everything under control, and the housekeeper shooed her out of the kitchen. "Go and fetch the captain for breakfast. He was away outside nearly an hour hence."

Reluctantly Sophie ventured out the back door, inhaling the heady scent of wildflowers and dew on the grass. In spite of her heavy heart, the freshness of the morning buoyed her spirits. Though it was most unladylike, she stretched her arms above her head, rolling her neck. More than loosening her muscles, her spirit seemed to stretch and relax a bit.

"It's more colorful than I imagined from your letters. And wilder."

The captain strode down the path toward her, his hands in his pockets, hatless. The breeze had tousled his hair, making his visage less severe. His coat was tucked into the crook of his elbow, and the wind fluttered his white shirtsleeves. As if suddenly aware of his casual dress, he shrugged into his navy coat and fastened the buttons.

Part of her resented his venturing into the back garden, her special place. Some of her most precious memories of Rich had been created here, and she didn't want to share it with anyone, especially Captain Wyvern.

He stopped beside her, looking up the hill at the riotous hues waving and bobbing. "I don't know the name of a single bloom, but they were friendly enough to greet me anyway."

He shrugged as if embarrassed to share something so frivolous, but Sophie liked the sentiment, in spite of herself. The flowers were friendly and no respecter of persons. It took nothing away from her to share them. A bit of chagrin tinged her thoughts at being so churlish as to want him away from there.

"I don't know the names of all of them myself. Mamie is the one you should talk to if you want to be educated about flora. She planted most of these." Sophie brushed a stray hair from her cheek. "If you are prepared to break your fast, everything is ready."

He offered her his arm, and she took it, surprised that for such a thin man, he was well muscled. Perhaps wiry was the word? She supposed a life at sea kept one fit.

The table was set for two, and as the captain seated her, she said, "Mamie has a lie-in most mornings, and Mrs. Chapman takes up a tray for her."

"You take excellent care of Lady Richardson." The captain cut his ham in precise squares. "You are a credit to Rich."

"Mamie takes excellent care of me, and it is no trouble to be her companion."

"Still, not many young women your age would wish to be tethered with the responsibility of an elderly woman. It's admirable."

Sophie shook her head. "She's my family. Though the tie that bound us, that would have made us legally relatives—" She set her toast on her plate. "Though that is no longer possible, we're still family. I consider her my mother-in-law, and I love her. Duties are not burdens when they are performed out of love."

The captain nodded, then took a decisive breath, as if making up his mind about something. "Lady Sophia, there's something I must tell you before I take my leave." He reached into his coat pocket, color climbing his cheeks, and withdrew his fist. "I fear I gave in to impulse last night—"

The front door banged open, and footsteps clattered in the hall. He stopped, his fist resting on the edge of the table.

Frowning, Sophie pushed back her chair. The captain rose to his feet, placing his hand back into his pocket and then withdrawing it. More footsteps echoed on the flagstones, and loud voices.

"I'll see who it is. Please finish your meal." Only her mother would barge into the house as if she owned the place, though by the sounds of it, she'd brought an army with her. Sophie girded up her mind for the confrontation.

But it wasn't her mother storming through the hall. A man and a woman stood there, eyeing the murals, running their hands along the banister, shaking the newel post. The woman's bonnet framed her face, crowding her curls around her cheeks as if she'd been stuffed in there, and she carried a furled parasol under her arm like a baton. The man, thin of legs and arms but portly about the middle, had a bit of duck about his walk, exuding self-importance.

What on earth? Who had the temerity to barge into the home of strangers?

"May I help you?" Sophie crossed the hall.

Before they could answer, a herd of children banged the door open again, sending it rocketing back to smack the wall, and pelted into the house. Shouting, half wrestling, they tumbled to an ungainly halt of arms and legs.

"He hit me."

"Did not."

"Did so."

"You hit me first."

"You there," the man said, flicking his finger at Sophie, speaking over the melee. "Are you the housekeeper?"

"She's clearly the parlor maid," the woman in the impressive bonnet said, her tone as lofty as a belfry. "See her black dress? Though she should be properly attired with a cap and apron. Things truly are more lax in the country, aren't they? Well, we will soon raise the standards."

The boys continued to tussle, elbows and shoulders flying.

Sophie stood still, bemused. This rather uppity couple and their wild band of offspring were clearly in the wrong house.

"Boys, if you don't stop . . ." The mother put her hands on her hips. "Go outside before I give you the rough side of my tongue."

They ignored her. One pair fell to the ground, grappling like angry stoats, while the tallest pointed to a painting of a Richardson forbear and laughed. "He looks like he just sat on a thistle. Pucker face!"

"The décor *is* dreadful. It will all have to go. And this flooring. Nobody has stone anymore. It looks like it belongs in a monastery." The woman ran her hand along the top of a gate-legged table. She inspected her white glove, but there was no dust there that Sophie could see. Still the woman sniffed. "This furniture is awful. So out of fashion."

"I'm more interested in the grist mill and the farm. And the bank accounts. Once I know the balances, we can talk about renovations." The man narrowed his eyes, as if calculating sums. He seemed to remember Sophie at that point. "You there, young woman. Go fetch your mistress. We've much to discuss."

Stunned at their brazenness, Sophie didn't move.

The man and woman exchanged an arch look. "I say, if this is the standard of obedience for servants in the country, they will be put on notice immediately. Woman, do as you are told, or you'll find yourself turned out without a character. When I issue an order, I expect to be obeyed forthwith." He punctuated each word with a tap of his cane on the flagstones.

Stung, Sophie stepped forward. "Sir, I don't know who you are, but you are seriously in error. I am not a parlor maid, but even if I were, your behavior would be shameful. Barging into a stranger's house and ordering people around. This is the house of the late Baron Richardson and his mother, Lady Mamie Richardson. This is her home, and you are not welcome here. You may keep your opinions about the décor to yourself as you go." Sophie didn't know whether to be satisfied or aghast that she sounded so much like her mother at that moment. *I've learned from the best how to give a setdown.*

The man harrumphed, and the woman blinked, stepping back a pace and shaking her head, as if stunned by such an outburst.

"Well, you can hardly blame us for the mistake. You're dressed like a parlor maid." She sniffed again, stacking her hands on the handle of her parasol.

The brawling boys rucked up the rug and nudged a table, causing the vase atop it to totter. Sophie reached for the flower arrangement at the same moment footsteps sounded behind her.

The captain strode into the fracas, grabbing youthful collars and hauling the boys upright.

"Ow, say, what's this?" The eldest of the children rubbed his shoulder and scowled. He managed to get in a sly kick to the next youngest boy.

"Batten your hatches." The captain straightened the youngest two, who appeared to be twins. "This is not Gentleman Jack's boxing establishment, nor is it a dockside pub for brawling in. Now, stand there and don't make a sound."

His voice held such authority, Sophie found herself straightening. He managed to sort the melee into four separate boys.

Captain Wyvern turned to the adults. "Sir, madam, I do not know the customs where you are from, but I was to understand that it is common practice in these parts to knock and wait to be invited inside before barging into a home. And it is also advisable to control one's young when visiting another's residence. You have neither introduced yourselves, nor have you respected the privacy of this household. Surely you could not have missed the black crepe on the door? This is a house of mourning, and it would behoove you to remember that. Lower your voices, state your business, and then be on your way."

He kept a firm hand on the shoulder of one of the smaller boys, who scowled but stood still. Sophie was taken aback at his commanding tone, though she supposed he'd had years to perfect it. In his naval jacket with the gold braid and brass buttons, he looked impressive.

"Perhaps it is you who misunderstood." The strange man puffed out his chest. "I'll have you know you're addressing the *new* Baron Richardson and that I own this house and property. This cottage, the farm, and the mill now belong to me. If I choose to perform a clean sweep of the contents and start fresh, that's my business. I can burn the place to a pile of cinders if that is my choice. And my children are welcome to behave how I see fit within my own domicile."

"Perry, is that you?" Mamie asked from halfway up the steps. She gripped the ends of her shawl around her shoulders with one hand and the banister with her other. "And Millicent?"

"That's right, Aunt Mamie. I'm sorry about Rich and all. I thought you might invite us to the funeral. We waited what we felt was a decent amount of time, and now we're here to inspect the property."

Mamie descended the stairs carefully, and when she reached the bottom, she went to Sophie's side, tucking her hand into Sophie's elbow. "My dear, this is Perry. Peregrine Richardson, Rich's second cousin, and his wife, Millicent."

Rich's second cousin. And he claimed to be the new Baron Richardson?

A decent amount of time? The man had to be joking. It had been barely any time at all since the memorial service. If he was indeed the new baron—and why hadn't she considered that possibility?—then his haste in coming to Primrose seemed more like the behavior of carrion birds than a compassionate relative.

"And you are, sir?" Perry asked, turning from the women as if they were of no account.

The captain removed his hand from the boy and bowed slightly. "Captain Charles Wyvern, Royal Navy. Guest of Lady Richardson and Lady Sophia."

A coachman entered the front hall, bowed under the trunk on his shoulder. "Your pardon, sir. The baggage coach is 'ere. Where ya want us to put yer things?"

Another man followed, laden with bags. Sophie's eyes met the captain's. This was a proper invasion. How long would they stay?

"Mamie, would you like me to sort rooms? It appears Mr. and Mrs. Richardson and their children will be our guests for a day or two," Sophie said. *Pray it won't be any longer than that.*

"That's Lord and Lady Richardson," Millicent snapped. "We're not the guests. As my husband said, since he has inherited the title and the property, you are *our* guests." She handed her parasol to the coachman, who grappled with it and the trunk. "I will sort out the rooms myself when I go upstairs. For now, I'm perishing for a cup of tea." She sent Sophie a pointed stare, as if challenging her to disagree.

Bristling, Sophie inhaled, ready to hoe in, but Mamie put her hand on Sophie's arm. "Perhaps you might inform Mrs. Chapman?"

The captain cleared his throat. "My belongings are packed. I shall remove them to make space for the . . ." He stopped and then waved his hand at the new arrivals. He edged past Sophie on his way to the stairs, and as he brushed by, he reached out and squeezed her elbow.

The contact surprised Sophie. Her eyes clashed with his, and he looked hard into her face, as if bracing her up before this new onslaught.

"I want my own room. I'm not sharing with Geoffrey." The boys went pelting upstairs, streaming around the captain, who marched up with dignity and a straight back.

Millicent Richardson followed, a sneer marring her face as she observed the paintings on the stairwell wall. She spoke over her shoulder as she went. "Conducting this conversation in the hall is hardly appropriate, Perry. Go into the drawing room. I'll do a quick inspection of the upstairs and be with you soon."

Sophie didn't want to leave poor Mamie alone long with the pompous Perry, so the minute they went into the drawing room, she dashed into the kitchen.

"Mrs. Chapman, company has arrived. Actually, they don't wish to be called company. It's a relative of Mamie's, and he says he's the new baron and that he owns Primrose now. They intend to stay on, at least for a little while." She paused for breath. "There are four children—boys who don't seem to know the difference between a front hall and a gymnasium—and I fear the lady of the family will be difficult to please . . ." Sophie stopped as several expressions crossed the housekeeper's face, mirroring her own feelings on the subject.

"Six people? A new baron? Where will they stay? Primrose doesn't run to that many bedchambers." Mrs. Chapman wiped her hands on her apron. "Where's Miss Mamie?"

"She's in the drawing room with the new baron, and I must get back there. I know it's still early, but will you prepare a tea tray for five adults, and I suppose another for those boys. Perhaps some bread and butter for them, since we've nothing much prepared in the way of a sweet. As to the bedrooms, I'll move in with Mamie for the duration of the stay. That will leave my room free." She was rambling. Her mind skittered like a sheep on ice.

"What about the captain?" Mrs. Chapman asked as she checked the kettle and swung it over the fire.

Sophie's hand came up to cover the spot where he'd squeezed her arm. She could still feel his slender fingers and the strength they conveyed. "He's gone upstairs to retrieve his belongings. That will leave another room free."

The housekeeper sighed, her keys jingling as she searched for the one that unlocked the tea chest. "Too bad. It was nice having a gentleman around the place again."

In spite of herself, Sophie agreed. Though it hadn't been easy to hear what Captain Wyvern had to say, and she still struggled with his role in Rich's death, he had been kind, especially to Mamie. For that alone, she would have counted his visit welcome.

She hurried back to the drawing room, and in an instant knew something was terribly wrong. Perry Richardson stood before the curio cabinet, picking up and setting down shells, his back to the room. Sophie wanted to smack his hand. Those shells belonged to Rich. Nobody touched them.

Mamie was drawn into herself, a small figure in the corner of the settee. Her eyes had a bewildered, faraway look. Sophie went to her, putting her arm around the older woman.

"What is it?" Sophie bristled and steeled herself. If he had been rude to Mamie, she was going to forget her manners and give him the tongue lashing he deserved.

Mamie studied Sophie's face. "He says we have to leave Primrose?" She asked it as a question, as if seeking confirmation.

Perry cleared his throat, tossing the last shell onto the shelf and turning around. "This house is the country seat of the barony. It comes with the title. I'm sure you understand. It belongs to my family now."

Thuds and thumps came from overhead, and a crash followed on the heels of a yell from one of the boys. Millicent Richardson's voice could be heard like a nail on glass as she scolded her sons. At the rate they were going, Primrose would be a pile of rubble within a fortnight.

Anger flickered like hot tongues of fire across Sophie's skin. A tremor went through her, a little flash of recognition that she was about to say something she might regret. The brashness of the man, parading in like a field marshal and setting down demands.

"Sir, that is the most ridiculous thing I've heard uttered. You cannot possibly throw Mamie Richardson out of Primrose Cottage. It's her home. You must have lost your reason."

"It *was* her home. Now it is my home." He shook his head. "Come, come, woman. Do not become hysterical. I'm not intending she should be destitute. I'm sure there is a small cottage in the village where she can live out the rest of her days. I'm not completely callous. She is my relative, after all." He narrowed his eyes. "You have not explained your presence here, however. Just who are you? A paid companion, I assume? Well, you may keep your position as long as your wages are not exorbitant."

Mamie's hand fluttered, and she murmured, but Sophie spoke first. "I am not a paid companion. I am Lady Sophia Haverly, sister to the Duke of Haverly, who happens to be the overlord of this property. Mamie's son, Baron Richardson, was my fiancé, and he charged me with caring for Mamie and Primrose Cottage until his return from war."

Perry flinched when she gave her title and relationship to the duke. Then he rallied. "I am sorry for your loss, but that loss does mean the barony passes to me. Your duty to Aunt Mamie ceased when Rich died. I will see that she is taken care of, installed in a reasonable cottage in the village, and has a pension for her needs. I'm not a monster. I should think you would be grateful to have someone take her off your hands."

"She's not a stray dog. I have no desire to be freed of the pleasure of looking after her." Sophie tightened her hug around Mamie's shoulders. How could this be happening? It felt as if everything was being ripped from her.

Surely this couldn't be God's will. *God, You wouldn't take Primrose and Mamie from me, would You? You've already got Rich and the future we'd planned together. Please don't take this house.*

"Whatever your title or position, the truth remains—this house is mine, and you will need to vacate it. Sooner rather than later. My wife is most eager to begin the renovations, and she has no desire for relics of former barons to hang about. I shall go into the village to search for a suitable cottage for Aunt Mamie. If you choose to stay on there, be advised you will contribute to the household expenses. It's one thing to pension off a relative, but I won't be responsible for your upkeep as well. Though I suppose, as a daughter of a duke, you have some means . . ." He appraised her. "In any case, I expect you to be out of the house tomorrow at the latest."

Heat charged into Sophie's cheeks, and again that tremble that told her to bite her tongue rippled through her bones. The gall of the man.

A movement caught her eye. Captain Wyvern stood in the doorway, bicorn in hand, cloak over his shoulder. How much had he heard?

"Lady Sophia, Lady Richardson." He bowed as he came into the room. "I must thank you for your gracious hospitality. I could not have asked for more welcoming hostesses." His voice was as dry as pillow ticking. "You are kindness personified. Before I take my leave, I must renew my offer of assistance. Are you certain there is nothing I can do for you?"

Mamie rallied at his strong voice. "Captain Wyvern, it appears we are in need after all. Would you consider staying on to help us sort things out?"

Sophie wanted to protest. They had asserted that they were not in need of the captain's assistance. But if Mamie wanted the captain to stay, Sophie wouldn't contradict her.

It wasn't as if they needed him though. Sophie had family to aid her, and not just anyone, but a duke. With one word of assent, they could accept Marcus's offer to live at Haverly. It wasn't as if they would be homeless.

Though that would feel like admitting defeat. Of surrendering her independence and her future. Still, if that was what was best for Mamie, she would do it. Mamie at Haverly Manor was much better than Mamie shunted off to some cramped cottage in the village.

"We will accede to your demands, Baron Richardson. We shall pack and be away quickly. There is no need for you to seek a pensioner's lodging for Mamie. She will accompany me." Sophia hugged Mamie once more. "Come. We'll gather our things."

Mustering her dignity, she stood and drew Mamie up with her. They would not be cowed by this uncouth, acquisitive pomp of a man. They would withdraw from the field of battle with grace.

Even as she led Mamie from the room, her heart was breaking. How could she leave Primrose Cottage? All her memories of Rich were here.

Charles resisted the urge to put his fist through Perry Richardson's supercilious face. Evicting a widow from her home? Tossing a grieving fiancée out of her residence? And so soon after their bereavement? What was the British aristocracy coming to when such a lack of chivalry was openly displayed?

How he longed to be away from these entanglements, aboard a ship, where right was right, wrong was wrong, and order maintained at all costs. It made his teeth clench to think of such a lesser man inheriting Rich's title and properties. He felt the need to step in, but how and what was the right way?

Mrs. Chapman arrived with a heavy tea tray, and Charles approached her. "Thank you. If you will inform my coachman that he will be needed to carry some baggage outside, I would be most appreciative." He took the tray—knowing the teapot and cups now belonged to the intruders made him want to drop it from a height onto the low table—and forced himself to place it down gently.

When he joined Lady Sophia in the hall, high color rode her cheeks, and her eyes were bright. Not with tears, but he suspected with anger. And rightly so. This was a cruel blow on top of all she had dealt with. "We would appreciate if you would take us to Haverly Manor. It is but a few miles. We will pack quickly so as not to delay your departure by more than a few hours at most." Her voice was as bleak as the Baltic Sea in winter.

He thought he understood how she must feel. He, too, had been removed from his home and cast into a foreign place. He had been forced to surrender both command of his ship and the only life he knew.

Mrs. Millicent Richardson swept down the stairs, calling out to her husband even before she entered the drawing room. "Perry, that back garden is a positive thicket. We're going to have to burn it before it can be properly planted. It's been allowed to go completely to seed. As for the house, every room will need to be taken down to the plaster. It's as if nothing's been changed for half a century. I cannot imagine living in such antiquated surroundings. It's positively provincial."

A small cry came from Lady Sophia's lips, and her hand went to her throat, but she didn't protest. Instead, she leveled a stricken look at Mamie.

"Well?" Millicent snapped. "Surely Perr—Lord Richardson explained things to you. This is our house, and we have the right to do as we wish with it."

"Millicent, please, there's no need to carry on so." Mamie's hand fluttered.

"Don't tell me what I need to do or not do."

Lady Sophia moved to place herself between Mamie and the rude woman accosting her. "Lady Richardson, you have no need to concern yourself about me or Mamie from this moment on. We'll be gone from this house before noon. If you can please refrain from gutting the place until we've departed, we would be most appreciative. Though perhaps you should confer with my brother, the Duke of Haverly, before you make too many changes to the house. As overlord, it does ultimately belong to him, after all."

The baroness gaped like a flounder, and it was all Charles could do not to raise his fist and shout, "Huzzah!" Good for Lady Sophia, putting that woman in her place.

Mrs. Chapman, who hovered in the hallway near the kitchen door, raised her apron hem to her chin. "Leaving, milady? Where will you go? Whatever shall I do?"

Lady Sophia took a breath, as if to fortify herself. "For now we'll go to Haverly Manor. Beyond that, I don't know. You are welcome to come with us, Mrs. Chapman, or you may stay and work for the new family. You are free to choose."

"Of course she will stay here. What would we do without a cook and housekeeper?" Millicent put her hands on her hips. "You cannot steal my staff."

"Steal?" Charles asked, keeping his tone dry. "I do not believe you own Mrs. Chapman, nor anyone else who may live and work here. The housekeeper is free to come and go as she pleases."

Another crash and thump came from upstairs, accompanied by a yell.

The apron came down, and determination firmed Mrs. Chapman's crumbling visage. "I'll not stay in the house with this lot. It won't take me but a moment to pack." She glared at Millicent, her chin high, eyes gleaming.

Charles hid a smile. Mrs. Chapman reminded him of a warrant officer. Warrant officers ran the navy, whatever the commissioned officers might think.

With a nod, Lady Sophia guided Lady Richardson toward the stairs. "When you're finished, Mrs. Chapman, if you'll help Mamie pack her things, I would be grateful."

The morning flew by, with Charles carrying boxes and trunks and bags out to the front steps. Lady Sophia maintained her composure throughout. Mamie Richardson put items into crates thoughtfully, as if silently communing with each one.

Mrs. Chapman, on the other hand, stormed about, packed with vigor, and muttered under her breath. Charles had visions of a dragon, fire and smoke exuding, and he did the woman's bidding with alacrity.

Midmorning, he realized there would be more belongings than his carriage could hold. Time to make an executive decision. He headed for the small stable out back.

"Where is the driver of the baggage wagon that arrived here this morning?" he asked his hired coachman, who was preparing the carriage.

"Headed to the village pub, looking for a load to Dorset, where he come from. Didn't want to waste the trip back if he could find something that needed toting." Charles's coachman led one of the horses out of the small stable to hitch him up.

"Trot round there and tell him I have work for him. If he's already gone, find a wagon to hire."

"Very good, sir."

"'Scuse me, sir. Is it true?" An elderly man with a seamed face and pale eyes tugged his forelock, coming out of the shadows of the stable. "Pardon for interrupting. I'm Donnie, what does the gardening here. Is it true that new folks have come and they're forcing the ladies out?"

"I'm afraid so." Charles felt as grim as he sounded.

"And Mrs. Chapman is going with them to Haverly?" He twisted his cloth cap in his gnarled hands.

"That's correct."

"And them new folks isn't nice at all?"

"Not in my brief experience." Why wouldn't the man get on with it? Charles had things to do.

With a sharp nod, Donnie slapped his hat against his leg. "That tears it. I'm coming too. If there's no work at Haverly for the likes of me, I'll find something. But I won't work for them new folks if they're that hard of heart to be so cruel to the ladies."

Charles clapped him on the shoulder. "Good man. You can help with the baggage."

"I'll do that very thing, sir."

When Charles reentered the house, he discovered Lady Sophia in the drawing room, removing shells from a cabinet. The new owners were nowhere to be found, thankfully. She placed the seashells carefully in a small rosewood box and fastened the clasp. Her head was down, and the sunlight from the window caressed her glossy brown hair. Her shoulders had a defeated tilt, and her long lashes flicked suspiciously fast.

"Lady Sophia?"

She straightened and sniffed. "I'm almost finished."

"I've sent my coachman into the village to procure transport for your things. Also, the gardener has announced his plans to accompany you and Lady Richardson to your brother's home. I hope this is acceptable?"

"Oh, Donnie—I forgot all about him." Her hand went to her throat. "Of course he must come if he wishes. He should be retired long since, but he's so stubborn. There will be something he can do at Haverly. I'll talk to my brother about him."

"Are you nearly finished with your packing?"

With a nod, she surveyed the room. It was mostly unchanged, but Lady Richardson's knitting basket was gone from beside a chair, and the cricket ball from the mantel. Everything they were taking from this room fit in one box, with space left over. He picked it up.

"Do you need more time? It's ridiculous to expect you to be out in only a few hours. I would be happy to speak with the new baron."

"No. I don't wish to linger. 'If it were done when 'tis done, then 'twere well it were done quickly.'"

Charles paused, the box halfway to his shoulder. "Is that a quote?"

"Shakespeare. *Macbeth.*" She shrugged. "Mamie enjoys Shakespeare. We read his sonnets, but she especially likes his dramas. We talked of going to see one of his plays performed once Rich returned."

The wistful thread in her tone smote Charles in the chest.

If only Charles had made certain that Rich had cleared the ship of combatants. If only he had been more alert. If only Rich hadn't tried to save his life.

By noon the baggage coach was loaded and Mrs. Chapman sat beside the driver, her bonnet firmly in place and her Bible in her lap. She stared straight ahead, as if ready to embrace whatever lay before her with courage.

Charles handed first Mamie and then Lady Sophia up into his carriage. He couldn't help but admire her resilience. She hadn't wilted under the blows coming her way. Beautiful and strong, just as she had shown in her letters.

The new baron and his wife stood on the top step of Primrose Cottage, their offspring tumbling about them like a pack of foxhounds waiting for the horn to sound.

He touched the brim of his bicorn to them but remained silent. He would not beg their leave, not after the way they had come in like a tide and swept Lady Sophia and Mamie Richardson out.

He instructed the driver as to their destination and climbed inside, sitting across from the ladies.

Mamie pressed her fingers to the glass, craning her neck to keep the house in sight for as long as possible, but Lady Sophia had her eyes closed. Her lips moved. Was she praying? If so, for what? Courage? Strength? Lightning to strike the cottage and deprive the new occupants of the pleasure of living there?

Small talk under the circumstances was impossible. He held his council as the carriage jostled along the road.

As Lady Sophia had said, it was not a protracted journey. Before long they turned up at a massive pair of gates and stopped. The keeper strolled out of the gatehouse, spoke briefly to the driver, and opened the carriage door.

"Oh, milady, I didn't know it was you." The man bowed, lifting his hat.

"Would you open the gates, Canby?" Lady Sophia's voice was kind in spite of their circumstances. She might be retreating from battle with her sails furled and her rudder broken, but she was sailing under her own colors.

The drive curved through open meadows and copses of old trees. How had these magnificent oaks been spared the axe when nearly every tree in

Britain had been felled to build the fleet? Haverly must have some pull with the government.

They passed a large stone house. "Did we bypass the manor?" he asked.

Lady Sophia shook her head. "That's the dower house, where my mother and sister-in-law live."

If that was the dower house, what must the manor be like? Charles hadn't long to wait. They turned a corner, and there she was, floating on a sea of gardens like a flagship in full sail. Warm red brick, white trim, and more windows than he could count. The place must run to sixty rooms.

Lady Sophia had grown up here, a daughter of this house. This mansion was as familiar to her as the *Dogged* was to him.

And he had offered her financial help? When her brother owned all this? What a fool he had been. Major Richardson had rarely mentioned Lady Sophia's family, and certainly not that they lived in such splendor. Had she been laughing up her sleeve when he inquired after her financial well-being?

As they pulled to a stop, he composed his wits. He would deliver the women into the keeping of the duke, renew his offer of help in any way he could, even though he could see she needed nothing from the likes of him, and be on his way.

He had fulfilled his duty to Rich as much as he was able, and he would have to be satisfied with that.

Though he didn't feel satisfied. The debt he owed Lady Sophia was large, and simply carrying a few boxes and handing her off to her brother didn't seem enough.

He helped her from the coach and turned back for Lady Richardson. As Lady Sophia mounted the steps, one of the huge doors opened and a somberly dressed man appeared.

"Hello, Rodbury. Is His Grace at home?"

"Lady Sophia. What a pleasure. I regret His Grace is not in residence at the moment, though he is expected to return before dinner. The duchess is within, however." The very proper servant bowed. "May I take it that you'll be staying?" He indicated the baggage wagon.

"We've come home. Tell Tetford we will need a room prepared for Lady Richardson, and we've brought Mrs. Chapman with us. Oh, and would you find a place for Donnie? In the grooms' dormitory or one of the gardeners' cottages?"

The butler raised an eyebrow at Charles, who stood at the base of the steps with Lady Richardson on his arm, feeling as exposed as a cannonball on a cricket pitch.

"Rodbury, this is Captain Charles Wyvern. Please have Tetford prepare a room for him as well." Lady Sophia nodded to Charles. "It's much too late in the day for you to be setting off. I know my brother will want to meet you."

When they entered the house, Charles felt even more out of place. This must rival Carlton House or Brighton Pavilion for splendor. An atrium four stories high ended in a dome intersected with skylights that bathed the open space with sunshine. A chessboard of black-and-white marble covered the floors, and the walls were an understated pale green with gilded white trim.

Their footsteps echoed in the massive space.

"Come into the drawing room, Captain. Rodbury and the footmen will bring in the baggage." Lady Sophia untied her bonnet, handing it to the butler.

The drawing room was no less grand than the foyer, with pale-blue walls and rich, golden upholstery and drapes.

"Sophie." A striking blonde woman rose from a sofa, a heavy book in her hands. "I didn't know you were coming to visit. I'm delighted." She crossed the room quickly. Remembering Lady Sophia's letter, Charles deduced this must be her sister-in-law, the Duchess of Haverly.

"Charlotte. I'm afraid it's a bit more than a visit." The two women embraced, and Charles heard a hint of tears in Lady Sophia's voice.

As Charles seated Mamie, Lady Sophia gave the duchess a brief summary of the morning's events.

"They marched right in, gave us an ultimatum, and began speaking of all the things they hated about Primrose and how they were going to renovate everything. We were allowed to bring our personal belongings, but the rest they declared their possessions. And they have a wild brood of boys who were completely unchecked. I estimate they will have broken everything of value within a fortnight."

"That's outrageous." The duchess squeezed Lady Sophia's hands, but she cast more than one quizzical glance Charles's way. He remained standing, his hands on the back of Mamie's chair.

Lady Sophia intercepted the look and put her hand to her forehead. "I am such a dolt. Please, let me introduce you. This is Captain Charles Wyvern, who was the commander of the HMS *Dogged*, Rich's ship. He came to express his condolences. He happened to be at Primrose when the new baron and his family arrived, and he escorted us here. I hope you don't mind. I've invited him to stay at least the night."

Understanding smoothed the lines of the duchess's face, and she smiled warmly, transforming her entire countenance. She had remarkable green eyes. "Of course you must bide with us. We are in your debt for helping Sophie and Mamie. I'm glad you can stay over. I know my husband will want to express his thanks as well."

Charles nodded. "You're most kind, Your Grace."

He chafed a bit under the delay, though beyond returning to London to haunt the halls of the Admiralty, he had no clear objective.

Staying one more day wouldn't change much.

Sophie couldn't believe she was back at Haverly Manor. Her room looked the same as when she'd left it three years before to move in with Mamie—just as spacious, just as grand. Polished, mahogany furniture, thick rugs, tasteful artwork. Everything exactly as her mother had designed it before Sophie was born.

Haverly hadn't changed. It was Sophie who was different. She'd grown from a girl to a woman at Primrose, and now it felt as if, in returning to her childhood home, she was trying to slip into a pair of shoes too small for her.

Sophie nodded her approval to the maid who had dressed her hair for dinner. It had been months since Sophie had gone to the trouble of changing into formal garb for the evening meal, but things were different at Haverly Manor, and her mother would be attending tonight. Standards must be maintained.

Unpolished jet beads decorated the neckline of her black dress, absorbing the light. The decoration, even though black, could be considered her first emergence from deep mourning. In a week or two she would begin wearing grays and lavenders.

Though her heart would still be grieving, Sophie had no intention of going about in full mourning garb for months as her mother had done when Sophie's father and brother had been killed in a carriage accident the year before. Rich would not want that, and it would distress Mamie. Sophie's mother still wore unrelieved black, wanting the world to know of the loss of her husband and her elder son.

A tap sounded, and the door opened a crack. "May I come in?" Sophie's sister-in-law, Cilla, eased into the dressing room, her daughter on her hip. The baby gnawed on a string of large wooden beads, drool making her fingers and the beads shine. "Honora Mary wanted to say good night. Her nurse is taking her back to the dower house to put her to bed."

Sophie reached for her niece. "Child, you are growing like a well-watered weed." She turned Honora Mary around to sit on her lap, and the baby girl leaned back.

Cilla took a seat. "Charlotte told me what happened at Primrose. I'm so very sorry."

Sophie nodded. "It's all been a shock. It hardly seems real. I keep thinking I'll wake up soon. It's the same way I feel about Rich being gone. He's been away so long, it's hard to remember sometimes that he won't be coming home. Though being evicted from Primrose is driving the point home fairly well."

"Life can change in a moment, and it can be hard to catch up." A shadow passed over Cilla's face. She had pure alabaster skin, delicate, patrician features, and golden hair that captured any light and threw it back with interest. She had suffered great loss and come through as sweet and gentle as ever. Though she never let her distress show, Sophie wondered if her fragile-looking sister-in-law ever cried when she was alone.

"What are you going to do? I know Charlotte will be thrilled to have you and Mamie living at Haverly." Cilla leaned forward and tugged on Honora Mary's foot, making the baby gurgle and kick.

"I don't know." Somehow the thought of living at Haverly, though they would be welcome, and she loved her family, made Sophie feel as if she were suffocating. Her childhood here had been lonely and isolated once Marcus went off to school, and boarding school had been a relief. But where else could she go? She had Mamie to consider as well. "Everything has happened so quickly, we haven't discussed it."

"I met Captain Wyvern downstairs. He's quite dashing, isn't he?" Cilla asked.

Sophie blinked. Dashing? She hadn't considered it. He was quite a bit older than she and so stiff and reserved.

Though, if Cilla thought him dashing . . .

"You think so, do you?" She sent a knowing, teasing look to her sister-in-law. "If you even breathe that notion in the direction of Mother, she won't be able to resist matchmaking. She's been eager to marry you off for quite some time. Though I don't know if she would deem a ship captain a suitable husband." In fact, before Marcus had wed Charlotte this past spring, Mother had insisted he should marry his brother's widow. A daft notion, and they would have had to go outside the country to have the ceremony performed. Marcus and Charlotte were perfect together, and Cilla, though sweet and kind, would never have suited Marcus.

Cilla colored, but she shook her head. "I'm not at all interested in the captain. I just thought he looked fine in his uniform. I wondered if you had noticed." She stood and reached for her daughter. "Come, love. Time you were abed."

Sophie waited until Cilla had handed over the baby to her nurse for the brief journey back to the dower house, and together they went downstairs.

"Sophia, dear," Mother said the moment Sophie entered the room. "I know you're disappointed, but it all worked out for the best. You're home now." She tilted her cheek, and Sophie dutifully went over and kissed it. "The Lord works in mysterious ways."

Which was a phrase Mother only used when she felt the Lord's ways lined up with hers. Sophie also dropped a kiss on Mamie's cheek. "You're looking well. Did you get a chance to rest?"

While they waited for everyone to assemble to go in to dinner, Sophie studied Captain Wyvern covertly, sizing him according to Cilla's description. He was resplendent in naval dress, gold braid gleaming, white breeches, waistcoat, and cravat pristine. Dashing? It was hard to consider a man of his years dashing. He must be all of thirty-five, at least. And he had gray hairs at his temples. Of course, Cilla was a few years older than Sophie, so it stood to reason she might find the captain attractive.

Marcus entered the drawing room with Charlotte on his arm. He was bending his head close to hear something she whispered, and Sophie felt a lance of pain. They were so much in love, so much a picture of all that was possible in marriage.

Exactly what she had hoped for with Rich.

Would everything forever remind her of him and what they had lost?

Her brother hugged her tight. "I'm sorry you had to leave when it wasn't your wish. And I wish there was something that I could do about it. I might be the overlord, but I cannot forestall the laws of primogeniture. However, I am glad you came home where I can keep an eye on you." He tweaked her nose and winked, and she made a face at him.

"I'm not a child, Marcus. Will you forever treat me as one?" she chided.

He squeezed her hands. "I do miss your childlike exuberance. Circumstances have caused you to lay it aside for a while, but I hope it isn't gone forever. The way you see the world and share your joy with others is a true gift. I know it will take time, but I hope the light will shine in your eyes and your heart again."

Uncomfortable with his scrutiny and aware that everyone was listening on, Sophie changed the subject. "Marcus, may I introduce Captain Charles Wyvern, late of the ship HMS *Dogged*. He was a friend of Rich's, and they were hospitalized together in Oporto. Captain Wyvern, my brother, the Duke of Haverly."

The two men shook hands, sizing one another up.

"My wife tells me we are in your debt for providing assistance to Lady Sophia and Lady Richardson. I thank you for seeing them safely to Haverly."

"I was happy to provide aid, little as it was."

"With Lord Richardson stationed aboard the *Dogged*, I naturally kept up on her exploits. You've made quite a name for yourself. Well done. I should like to hear of some of your tales firsthand."

Mother rose. "Let's go in to dinner, shall we? It's been a long time since we were all together."

The captain held Sophie's chair for her and took the seat next to her at the table. Mamie sat across from her, looking lost and weary. Mother held court through the first two courses before Marcus asserted himself.

"Captain Wyvern, now that you've recovered from your wounds, what are your plans? When I was in London last, the Admiralty was full to the rafters with naval officers. Will you join those ranks, or have you other endeavors?"

"I confess, I have put my name in for a command, should one arise. Until then I will need to find lodgings and weigh my options."

Marcus leaned back as the footman took one plate and set another before him. "Will you be journeying to your family estate to visit your uncle?"

The captain lowered his fork, a crease forming between his brows. "I was not planning to."

He cast a wary glance at Marcus, which sparked Sophie's curiosity. She wasn't surprised Marcus knew of the captain's family. Her brother seemed to know most things about most people. He always had.

"I miss Devon." Mamie spoke for the first time. "I was born and raised there, on the coast. I miss the sounds of the sea, the wind, the waves, the seabirds. I never thought I would leave there, but then I met my late husband, and he whisked me away to Oxfordshire. When he passed, I thought I might like to retire to a cottage by the sea in Devon."

Such longing infused her voice that Sophie wanted to hug her. She'd never mentioned missing the sea before or wanting to retire to a cottage on the coast.

"I understand your homesickness for the sea, madam. I find it difficult to get to sleep here on land without the sound of the waves, or the creak of the rigging, or the piping of the watches." Captain Wyvern smiled ruefully. "I confess, sleeping in a bed that doesn't rock is a bit difficult to accustom myself to, and I have more than once considered hanging up a hammock so I could get some rest."

After dinner, Mamie took Sophie's elbow, pulling her into a corner of the drawing room, away from the conversation.

"How long are we going to stay here?"

Sophie searched Mamie's eyes, trying to discern how aware she was and seeing only clarity there. "I don't know. Our options are few, I should think. It's either stay here at Haverly, which wouldn't be my first choice but is awfully convenient, or do as the new baron suggested and find a cottage in the village."

"There is something else we might do. Somewhere else we might go." Mamie twisted the ribbon on her lorgnette, a wistful cast to her features.

"Where? Is there some other property the Richardsons own?" Sophie's heart lifted.

Mamie shook her head. "No, not to my knowledge. It's just . . . speaking of it at dinner brought it all back."

"Brought what back, dear?" Sophie intercepted a pointed glance from her mother, indicating they were being rude whispering in corners.

"I miss the sea. What if we were to take a journey to the coast? I would like to spend some time by the open water before I depart this world." Mamie shrugged. "And if we happen to find a nice cottage with an ocean view that might be to let or to purchase . . ." She let her voice trail off, but the longing was unmistakable.

Sophie's mind bobbed and tossed like daisies in the breeze. A trip? To the ocean? Away from Primrose and not having to endure watching the new tenants remake it to suit themselves? Away from the hovering, smothering, albeit caring attentions of her family?

An escape held great appeal.

"That's an interesting idea, Mamie. Let me give it some thought." Though even as she said it, she knew she wanted to go. After so many years of waiting for Rich to come home, fearing he wouldn't, of waiting for her life to really start, this call to adventure, however small, appealed to her nature like nothing had in a long while

Of course, she would have to convince her overprotective brother and bossy mother that a trip was just the thing.

Chapter 4

Sophie awoke the next morning, and for the first time since receiving word of Rich's passing, felt a stirring of interest in what the day might hold. Mamie's notion of taking a trip had occupied her mind into the wee hours, and it wasn't until she'd committed fully to the idea that she'd been able to sleep.

Thanks to her brother's well-trained staff, Sophie's clothing had been unpacked and put away. She had wondered how her brother and sister-in-law's venture of training former prostitutes to be domestic servants would work, but seeing the gently steaming can of water by the hearth told her things were progressing well. With only Mrs. Chapman on staff in the house at Primrose, Sophie had taken to doing many household chores herself, an occurrence that would have her mother reaching for her smelling salts, no doubt. The daughter of a duke didn't wait upon herself.

Rich's sea chest and box of personal treasures remained unopened at her request.

A tap on the door had Sophie shrugging into her wrapper and tying it quickly. "Yes?"

"Milady, I'm so sorry to wake you, but . . ." One of the young maids spoke softly as she opened the door. Her head poked in, her mobcap askew. "It's Lady Richardson, milady."

A throb of panic shot through Sophie. "What's wrong?"

"She's crying, milady. In her room. She's most upset."

Relief and concern collided in Sophie's chest. "Is she ill?"

"No, milady. I found her in an upstairs hall, lost and near frantic. I told her where she was and that she was safe as can be, and I brought her back to her bedchamber, but she's that distressed." Furrows marred the young girl's pretty, freckled face. "She don't seem to be in her right mind. I left the tweeny with her, but Gracie is scared of the lady, and she might not stay."

Sophie was away before the maid finished, running down the hallway in her bare feet, her nightgown and wrapper flying. Poor Mamie. Waking up in a strange place. She'd had such a good evening, Sophie hadn't given it a second thought that she might become disoriented.

She skidded to a halt outside the open bedroom door to get herself under control. It wouldn't do to discomfit Mamie further by appearing anxious. Smoothing her hair, making certain her belt was tight, she plastered a smile on her face.

"Good morning, Mamie. You're up with the sun today." She breezed in, motioning that the tweeny could go.

With a grateful bob, the youngster scurried away, her eyes wide. A feeling of misgiving settled into Sophie's middle. It would be all over the manor that Lady Richardson should be shunted off to Bethlehem Hospital before cook finished preparing breakfast.

Mamie huddled in the window seat, her hands trembling, clutching a handkerchief. She squinted at Sophie, eyes full of tears. For a moment only confusion was there, but then recognition came, and her shoulders slumped.

Sophie knelt beside her and put her arms around the older woman, leaning her forehead against Mamie's temple. "It's all right, dearest. No harm done. You're safe and sound, and Sophie's here to look after you."

Mamie sniffed and dabbed her nose. "I got lost. I didn't know where I was when I woke up, and when I went out into the hall, I couldn't find my way back. I feel like an imbecile. Why is this happening to me? What if I 'go away' in my head one day and I don't come back? What will happen to me then?" She clutched at Sophie's hand, swallowing hard.

"Shhh. Don't distress yourself. You're found now. And you're not alone in being a bit disoriented this morning. I needed a moment or two to sort myself and my surroundings when I woke up. It's been a long time since I awoke at Haverly Manor." She eased her hold on Mamie and sat back on her heels. This was the first time Mamie had indicated she knew anything was amiss, and it broke Sophie's heart. Gently she smoothed Mamie's hair away from her face and squeezed her fingers. Mamie responded with a trembling smile.

Sophie avoided the question of why Mamie was "going away" in her head. And what might happen if she didn't come back to them. The doctor had warned the episodes would come more frequently, and they would last longer. Eventually, Mamie wouldn't be able to remember anything that had happened to her recently and would become fixated upon the past, things from her younger days, until finally she wouldn't remember anything at all.

And along with this, physical frailties would increase.

But he had assured Sophie the process was long and gradual and had suggested she not alarm Mamie with what would happen in the future.

Stroking Mamie's shoulder she asked, "How was your sleep?"

A smile touched Mamie's lips. "I dreamed of the ocean. Of birds calling, and a fresh breeze, tangy with salt."

Sophie hadn't been to the seaside since she was a girl. The vastness had made her feel small and a bit afraid . . . until Marcus had taken her hand and walked with her along the sandy shore, letting the cold water break over their bare feet.

Pushing herself up, she took Mamie's hand. "Let's get dressed and breakfasted and see about making a plan. I would love to see where you grew up, and maybe we can find that little cottage on the shore and stay for a while."

She played the part of Mamie's maid, as she often did, helping her dress and fix her hair, and then Mamie did the same for Sophie back in her room. By the time they were ready to descend for breakfast, Mamie was calm and clear of mind.

"I loved taking Rich to the shore when he was a boy, but he did make me nervous." Mamie took her time making her way down the main staircase, holding on to the rail. "Never a care for his safety. I found him halfway up a cliff, trying to reach a colony of guillemot, when he was but five summers old. Though what he expected to do when he got to the birds' nesting place, I never found out. If he wasn't climbing the cliffs, he was sneaking into the fishermen's boats. I seemed to spend half my holidays trying to keep him safe."

Sophie tried to imagine her dashing fiancé as a small boy, breeches stained with dirt, hair windswept, nose sunburned. The boy had become the man, adventurous, brave, with no care for his safety.

It was hard to think of all that restless energy and courage gone.

They entered the breakfast room, and Marcus and Captain Wyvern rose.

Charlotte said, "Good morning, ladies. I hope you slept well."

"Yes, thank you." Sophie seated Mamie. "I'll bring you some breakfast."

"Please, be seated, both of you, and allow me to fetch you each a plate." Captain Wyvern remained standing, his serviette in his hand. "Your brother keeps a fine table. Much better than a breakfast aboard ship. I've already partaken of more than wisdom dictates."

He filled plates from the chafing dishes. Sophie surmised that he didn't overindulge often, being so lean. She met Charlotte's eyes, which were speculative. Sophie hadn't mentioned the true reason behind the captain's visit. It was too private, and she still didn't know how she felt about it. He clearly felt obligated to her and Mamie, and she could wish things were different, but it made little sense to dwell upon it.

"Thank you, Captain. Has my brother been able to prevail upon you to stay for a while longer?" Sophie unfolded her serviette and spread it across her lap as he set a laden plate before her. "Goodness, I'll never be able to eat all this."

"You should try," Marcus said, crossing his fork and knife on his plate and sitting back. "You're too thin these days."

Sophie took a calming breath. He meant well, he really did, but if he felt the need to keep an eye on her, it implied that he thought her incapable of doing the task herself. She didn't need someone to care for her. She was the one who cared for other people.

Like Mamie. The dear old woman picked up a triangle of toast and bit off one corner.

"The duke and duchess have been most kind, extending the hospitality of Haverly Manor, but I fear I must decline." The captain drained his coffee cup. "I will be making my departure today."

Mamie's chin lifted. "When do you think we should leave as well, Sophie? I suppose it's a blessing in disguise that we had to pack everything so quickly yesterday. It won't take long today to get everything ready for our trip."

"What's this?" Marcus asked. He looked to his wife, but she shrugged and shook her head. His eyes found Sophie's. "You've only just arrived. You're not thinking of escaping, are you?" Though his tone was light, his words hit Sophie in the chest.

She *was* thinking of escaping. She'd been thinking of it most of the night. Living at Haverly, watching the deconstruction of Primrose from afar while fending off the mother-hen cluckings of her family as they wrapped her in cotton wool, would be unbearable. She would suffocate or go mad. *Escape* was the right word for what she needed.

She dabbed her lips with the corner of her serviette and prepared to stand her ground. "Mamie and I are desirous of taking a journey together. To the seaside, as it happens." She held up her hand when Marcus looked ready to protest. "Mamie grew up on the coast of Devon, and she wants to see her home county. We both feel a trip comes at just the right time. We need a change of scenery." Excitement flickered in Sophie's mind. She'd not traveled much, but if she was going to go, she intended to make the most of the experience.

"I quite agree."

Heads swiveled to Charlotte, who held her teacup in both hands, her elbows resting on the table in a fashion that would have earned her a reprimand from the dowager had she been present. Sophie shot her sister-in-law a grateful smile.

"Marcus, before you argue, hear me out." Charlotte set down her cup and reached for her husband's hand on the tablecloth. "As much as I would love to have Sophie and Mamie stay with us, I've tried to imagine what it would be like to be either of them. They've been removed quite abruptly from the home they cherish, and so soon on the heels of their bereavement. Though we welcome them with open arms, the temptation is for us to ask—far too frequently, I am inclined to think—how they are feeling, what we can do for them, are they going to be all right? By the middle of the first day, I think I would be ready to throw a few vases and dinner plates." She nodded, raising her eyebrows to Sophie to see if she were in agreement. "They're not proposing to venture to the Pacific Islands for the rest of their days. It's just a trip to the coast for a few weeks. Two or three months at the most."

"Exactly." Sophie leaned forward, grateful that Charlotte had chosen to be her ally in this. "A change of scene for us, and a chance to breathe and think away from all the memories and sadness. A chance to make plans for the future. The sea air will be bracing, and Mamie can show me her childhood haunts."

"I haven't time to take a holiday with you to the shore. Things are too busy here at the estate." Marcus leaned back but kept hold of Charlotte's hand. "And we've got Charlotte's health to consider." He glanced at his wife's slightly rounded middle, where their firstborn grew. "In a few months she'll be nearing her confinement. She can't travel then, and I can't be away. I'm sorry, Sophie, but it's impossible. Maybe next summer."

"It might surprise you, Marcus, but I never considered you might want to accompany us." Sophie kept her voice light, but desperation took hold. If her brother closed the door on the idea, it might very well stay closed. "Mamie is free to come and go as she likes, and I do believe I have earned the same privilege. I am twenty years old and of independent means. Anyway, while I love you dearly, having you on the journey would defeat the purpose of getting away from family. Your place is here at Haverly with Charlotte."

He studied her, his face somber. Her heart beat against her ribs, and she realized just how much and how quickly she'd set her hopes on the idea of a trip to the sea. As the head of the family, it would be optimal to have Marcus's approval and backing.

Mamie pushed her plate back. "I didn't mean to start a row. It was just an idea I had." Regret and longing lengthened her face, and she blinked rapidly. Marcus looked abashed at having made the older woman cry, and he sought Sophie's and Charlotte's pardon with his eyes.

"And a jolly good idea it is." Sophie wasn't ready to acquiesce, and she needed Mamie's support. "We're only a few days' journey from Devonshire. We'll have the time of our lives. Seeing the countryside, meeting new people. It's the perfect prescription. And if we get into difficulties—though we won't—Marcus could be at our side quickly."

"You cannot go unaccompanied. The risk of highwaymen, foul

weather, lack of accommodations . . ." Marcus shook his head. "No, dear Sophie, it's unthinkable. Even if I was inclined to let you go, Mother would have several conniptions at the very idea of you traipsing across the landscape unchaperoned. I know you've always been given to flights of fancy and thirsted for adventure, but this is too much."

The flicker of excitement died, doused under Marcus's cold reasoning.

"Oh, darling, isn't there some way we could make it work?" Charlotte asked. "Perhaps we could send Partridge along with them? No harm would come to them with Partridge present."

Sophie straightened, nodding. "Of course. Mr. Partridge would be an excellent protector." The man was built like the Tower of London. He had been in Marcus's employ a long time, though what he actually did for her brother remained somewhat of a mystery. Guard, messenger, man-of-all-work?

But Marcus was already shaking his head. "I can't spare Partridge at the moment." He sent Charlotte one of those private looks that spoke volumes to her but merely left Sophie puzzled. "No, it's quite impossible. You cannot go on your own, and I cannot spare anyone at this time."

"May I interject?" Captain Wyvern cleared his throat. "If it is merely the lack of a male chaperone that is causing difficulties, might I offer my services? I would be pleased to accompany them to Devon and see them ensconced in a cottage at the seaside. If Mrs. Chapman could be convinced to join the excursion, I'm sure the ladies would be safe enough and well looked after."

Travel with Captain Wyvern?

She wanted to refuse. The journey was an effort to get away from unpleasant associations. How could she do that if the captain went with them?

Marcus pursed his lips, narrowing his eyes. He hadn't rejected the offer out of hand.

Clapping her hands softly, Mamie almost bounced in her chair. "Captain, that would be most kind of you."

"I am at your service, madam." He bowed to her, but he looked across Mamie's gray curls to Sophie.

His eyes were a singular shade of blue, and sharp as hatpins. A zip of awareness caught her off guard. In that instant, she caught an inkling of what Cilla had seen. He *did* have a dashing air about him.

"That is most generous of you, Captain, but we wouldn't want to impose." Sophie put her hands in her lap. "I'm sure we can find our own way to the coast without putting you out."

"It is no imposition. As I told you before, I am at your disposal, and nothing would make me happier than to assist you in some way." He refused to look away, and Sophie couldn't break his gaze either. "Out of respect for Major Richardson and all he meant to me, please allow me to perform this small service."

"Of course," Charlotte broke in. "What a perfect solution. Don't you think so, Marcus?"

Her brother raised one eyebrow, staring shrewdly at his wife, as if wondering if he were being coerced into something against his better judgment. Then looking from one face to another around the table, he threw up his hands. "I can't stand against all of you." He put his palms out to stop anyone from speaking. "Provided you can earn the blessing of the dowager and that you will promise frequent communications while you're gone."

"Yes, yes, of course." Sophie pushed her chair back. "I'll write every day if that is what it takes to alleviate your mind." If the only way to go on the trip was in the company of the captain, then so be it. He would escort them to the shore, then he would go away, and she could breathe and think and heal in peace.

"Once a week or so should do. But before you start packing dresses and bonnets, you have Mother to convince. It's not that I think you need her blessing in order to have a happy trip—it's that I don't want to be trapped here at Haverly all summer if she's not in favor of your journey. Living with her would be unbearable under those circumstances."

Sophie ignored his cautions and flew round the table to hug his neck. "Thank you, dear brother. You don't know how happy this makes me. We'll be fine. Mother will give her blessing." She said this with more confidence than she felt.

He returned her embrace, and when he released her, she noted the smile playing round his lips. "You'd best hope so. Take the captain round to the dower house and introduce him as your minder. She was quite mannerly and subdued last night, but today will be a different story. For all his battle experience, the captain hasn't faced a foe as formidable as our mother."

An hour later, with Mamie safely in the care of Charlotte, Sophie tugged on her bonnet and gloves in the front hall. The captain waited patiently, his bicorn pinned under his arm, hands clasped behind his back.

"Thank you, Marcus." Charlotte's voice came from the morning room, where she and Mamie had retired after breakfast. "I know you have your reservations, but this is the most excited I've seen Sophie since we got word that Rich had been wounded. She's been far too subdued of late, especially for someone of her exuberant temperament. Perhaps this trip will set her up for winter and allow her to put her mind on things other than her loss."

Heat swarmed up Sophie's neck and into her cheeks. Though she hadn't heard anything ill of herself, it was still odd to discover others talking about her. And in the presence of someone else.

"I hope you're right, dear. I can see the benefits, but it feels wrong to let her go when she's in such a fragile state of heart. I know she won't go alone, but I don't like it."

The captain pretended not to hear, for which she was thankful.

A footman held the door, and when they went outside, the captain put on his hat and offered his elbow.

He had gentlemanly manners, which should appeal to her mother.

"I feel as if I'm about to face a court martial." He looked up at the blue sky, as if testing for incoming weather. "You expect your mother to strongly oppose the journey then? Is she so formidable then?"

"Marcus says if the War Secretary would only have put Mother in charge of the military, Napoleon would've been routed in a fortnight." The gravel crunched beneath their feet, and the scent of roses drifted from the parterre garden like a beautiful memory. "But I wouldn't have you think ill of her. She has very definite ideas about things and isn't short of speaking her mind, but she does care, and she has a kind heart underneath all the posturing and pontificating." And dealing with the dowager had become much easier when Sophie realized that a lot of her mother's blustering came because she cared so much about everything. "She loves pomp and being important and having something to occupy her mind.

Like all of us, I suppose she just wants to be needed and thought important to someone."

"I shall endeavor to be my most austere. I hope you are not too discomfited by my offer to accompany you on your trip. I shall attempt not to intrude." He walked almost as if at attention.

Did he ever truly relax? Somehow she couldn't see him lounging on the grass at a picnic or sprawled on a settee with the daily papers strewn about. Was he only comfortable when on board a ship?

Though she did remember him yesterday morning in his shirtsleeves striding down the back garden slope. Of course he'd hurried into his jacket and returned to his formal ways quickly.

"I should have thanked you for your offer straightaway. I'm afraid I got caught up in the moment and overlooked your generosity." Casting back, her response had been rather abrupt and ungrateful.

"Perhaps this, in some small way, will begin to repay my debt." He stared straight ahead, his voice bleak.

The man was positively fixated upon this supposed debt, though she had tried to disabuse his mind of the notion. Did he think a few gestures of generosity would make up for the loss of her beloved Rich? It would be easier if he would cease reminding her of the past.

They made the rest of the short trip to the dower house in silence. As they reached the stone structure, a happy laugh caught Sophie's attention. Cilla had Honora Mary on a blanket under the trees at the north end of the house, and the baby's giggles were undeniable.

Even the captain chuckled. The occurrence softened his features for a moment.

Cilla spied them, scooped up the baby, and came to the edge of the drive. "Good morning. I hadn't thought to see you again, Captain. Not that I'm complaining, mind you, but I understood you were to depart today. Has something come up to change your mind?" She looked at Sophie.

Honora Mary leaned out of Cilla's embrace, holding up her arms to Captain Wyvern. The captain backed up a step, puzzlement in his eyes. Honora Mary's face crumpled, and her lower lip quivered.

"Honestly, she's never met a stranger." Cilla moved closer and handed the baby to the captain, who took her as if she were a bomb with a lit fuse.

The baby hung in his hands, his arms straight out, her face split with an adorable smile. A gout of spittle rushed over her lower lip as she squealed and kicked.

"She appears to have sprung a leak." Furrows lined the captain's brow beneath the forepeak of his bicorn.

Cilla laughed and dabbed at the baby's chin. "She's teething."

"She won't break, will she?" he asked. "I've never done this before."

Sophie smiled. "You look as if you're the one about to shatter. Let her sit on your arm, and hold her against your chest so she doesn't fall." She helped him, but even with Honora Mary on his arm, he still looked as if he were holding an explosive. The man had lived through war, and he was flummoxed by a tiny girl.

Sophie wanted to laugh, the first such impulse in a long time. Something in her chest eased a bit, like the moment when you first took off your stays at night and drew a deep, unfettered breath.

The captain cleared his throat, his hand cradling Honora Mary's back. "I know nothing of children, especially girl children, and certainly not one as young as this. I've never actually held a baby, and I suspect I'm doing it all wrong."

"All it takes is a little practice," Cilla said. "Have you come to see the dowager? She's writing letters."

When they entered the morning room a few moments later, Mother was indeed at her writing desk. Head bent studiously, her pen flowed over the paper. A small stack of cards and envelopes stood along the edge of the desk, evidence of her morning's work.

"Mother, I hope we're not interrupting?" Sophie went forward to place the customary kiss on her cheek. "What are you working on? Are those invitations?"

Mother wiped her pen and placed it in the holder. "They are. I'm having a small dinner party for some neighbors. A chance for the new help to practice serving during social functions. The girls are coming along, though they require quite a bit of guidance. I'm inviting the vicar, the magistrate, the Bellows, and the Fotheringhams. And of course your brother and Charlotte. I suppose it's no use asking you to attend. You never want to come to my parties."

Sophie tried to ignore the martyrdom in Mother's voice and put a bright smile on her face. "I'm sure it will be a lovely dinner. You're doing good work helping the ladies learn skills that will aid them in leaving their former lives behind. I'm afraid you're correct though. I won't be able to attend your party. I'm afraid I won't be here." If she presented the situation as *fait accompli*, perhaps Mother wouldn't put up too much fuss. "Mamie and I are planning a trip to the seashore for a few weeks. We're leaving as soon as possible. By tomorrow, if we can."

When she realized she was rushing her words and twisting her fingers red, Sophie forced herself to relax. "You may wish to invite the new baron and his wife though. It would give you an excellent chance to study them, and I'm sure they're curious about you as well. What do you plan to serve? Isn't it nice that so many things are in season at the moment? Is Cilla going to help you with the flowers? She has such a nice touch with arrangements."

Mother held up her hand. "Stop Sophia. Don't try to bury me in words. What's this about a trip? With Mamie? Surely Marcus isn't dropping everything to take you to the shore?"

"No." Sophie said the word slowly. "Actually, he's given permission for us to travel under the care of Captain Wyvern."

The dowager's sharp eyes went to the captain, who stood near the door. He wore his most commanding and haughty expression, and for some reason, Sophie wanted to giggle again. She'd mentioned that Mother loved pomp, and he was certainly providing that.

In spite of his demeanor, Mother shook her head, her tight curls bouncing on her cheeks. "Ridiculous. I forbid it. Get this notion out of your mind, Sophia. I won't have my daughter traipsing about the countryside like a traveling minstrel. I'm shocked that Mamie, at her age, would even consider such a journey. You should both be content to stay at Haverly until your mourning period is over. Once that is completed, I shall begin the search for a new marriage partner for you."

"No. No." Sophie blinked, shaking her head. "No." Why did she seem to be able to say nothing else? A new marriage? Unthinkable. She had already met the love of her life, and she had lost him. There would be no other. She backed up a couple of steps, grazing the mantel with her shoulder. "I do not wish to marry anyone."

"You say that now, but you're young. Once you get over the romance and the tragedy of it all, you'll see that a sensible match is the best thing for your future. I always suspected I could get a better husband for you if you would have allowed me to conduct the search instead of accepting a mere baron's proposal. Now, don't get in a snit. Rich was a nice boy, and I liked him, but you have to admit, as a duke's daughter, you could have had your pick of suitors. Certainly a marquess or an earl. Possibly even a duke." Mother melted a bit of wax from the end of a stick onto the flap of an envelope and pressed her seal into it as it hardened. "I know what's best for you. I shall begin casting my eye about, and this fall we can host a house party. It will be a bit on the early side, considering that Rich only passed away this summer, but it won't hurt to look around. That way when the Season starts, we'll have some ideas."

Sophie couldn't imagine the prospect of enduring a London Season as an eligible woman. She had foregone that ritual by becoming engaged to Rich before she had to make her society debut, and she had not regretted it for a moment, though her mother had moaned that she'd been done out of bringing a daughter out. Time to get back to the subject at hand. She would deal with Mother's matchmaking schemes when she had to, but for now it was the trip that must be settled.

"Mother, Mamie is desirous of seeing her birthplace before she is no longer able, and I wish to accompany her. Marcus has given his blessing, provided you are also amenable to the idea. I feel a trip to the shore will be beneficial to me as well, a chance to get away from unpleasant memories and the changes that are bound to occur at Primrose and settle my mind to what lies ahead." Mother might think that included a betrothal and marriage, but she would be disabused of that notion soon enough. "We will be under the watchful eye of Captain Wyvern, who has graciously offered to see to our protection and comforts."

"Madam." He bowed, clicking his heels together as he did so. "I assure you, the ladies will be safe in my care. I shall provide escort, see to their lodging and safety, and not leave their side until they are ensconced in suitable quarters. I shall make it my duty. And as you know, an officer's duty is sacred." He actually put his hand over his heart.

Sophie looked quickly out the window to hide her smile. Mother pushed her chair back and stood, all but floating over and presenting her hand. Did her lashes actually flutter?

"Captain, I am sure you would be a more than suitable chaperone for Lady Richardson and my daughter, but surely you can understand a mother's misgivings? Sophia has never traveled on her own before, and she's in such a fragile state of mind, what with being so recently bereaved. I'm afraid it's quite impossible that she should leave home at this time."

Sophie's hopes sank. She should have brought Charlotte along to help her convince Mother.

But Sophie hadn't counted upon the captain.

He took the dowager's hand and led her to the settee. "Madam, I understand your concerns. I know it might be difficult to imagine, but as a captain, I have much the same feelings toward my crew, especially the younger ones. But . . ." He sat beside her, not relinquishing her hand. "When the time is right, one must let the younger ones fledge. I have to trust in the training I have instilled in my crew. I know you must have trained Lady Sophia very well indeed, and no matter where she goes, she will be a credit to you. She has matured under your guiding hand, and now, when you visit London together, you will be able to testify to your peers that you have a daughter with a mature, caring heart, who through your guidance and training is both loyal to her promises and capable of seeing them through. She cares so much for others, through your fine example, that she would even forfeit her own time of heartache to see that Lady Richardson had an opportunity to fulfill her fondest wish. I imagine your peers in London will be both envious of your fine efforts in Lady Sophia's training but also quite admiring of your relationship with your daughter."

Mother blinked, her mouth opening a fraction, and was that pink suffusing her cheeks? Sophia had never seen the like. The captain had unplumbed depths. And he wasn't finished.

"I give you my word as an officer of the Royal Navy that neither Lady Sophia nor Lady Richardson will come to any grief under my care." He stared so intently into the dowager's eyes that Sophie found herself nodding.

Then his gaze broke away from Mother and found Sophie. His look sent a tremor through her. It was almost as if he believed the things he was saying to Mother about her.

"That's all very nice, Captain Wyvern, but my answer is still no." Mother folded her hands in her lap. "While I am quite certain you are capable of protecting Lady Sophia and Lady Richardson, you are not a fit companion for them, being merely a sea captain. I'm sure you understand."

Sophie wanted to protest, but Mother would entrench herself deeper into her stated position if Sophie breathed a word against it.

Chapter 5

He'd been so certain that the dowager duchess would agree, her refusal set him back on his heels. Not to mention the crushed look in Lady Sophia's eyes. He'd failed her.

Again.

How could he change the dowager's mind? Or should he advocate rebellion and offer to take the ladies without gaining permission? It was quite ridiculous that a woman of Lady Richardson's age and position asked leave of anybody for anything.

The return to the manor house was accomplished in silence.

Rodbury waited at the front door. "Captain Wyvern, sir, there is a gentleman in the parlor waiting for you. An Admiral Barrington."

Thoughts of the dowager disappeared. Barrington was here? Did he have a command for Charles? But why would he deliver new orders in person? Charles vaguely remembered telling Barrington that he would be visiting Lady Richardson, but the admiral must have followed nearly on his heels to arrive so soon.

"I'll leave you to your meeting." Lady Sophia walked toward the stairs with her head bowed.

"Please, I'd like you to meet the admiral."

He entered the parlor and snapped to attention, saluting smartly. "Lady Sophia, may I present Admiral George Barrington."

The admiral had risen when Lady Sophia entered, and he took her offered hand, bowing over it. "Milady, may I express my sincere condolences on your loss."

"Thank you."

She sounded quite composed, but Charles caught the strain in her voice. Was it the mention of her grief, or was it her disappointment in her mother's stance on the chance to travel?

"If you gentlemen will excuse me, I'll have refreshments sent in." Lady Sophia paused at the door. "Admiral, I do hope you will be able to stay? I am sure my brother, the duke, would wish to meet you."

"Thank you, milady. Most kind."

When she'd left, Barrington stared at the closed door for a moment. "Well, Wyvern, she's as lovely as I had been told." He seemed to realize Charles was still at attention, and shook his head. "At ease, sailor. Come. Sit." He beckoned to the chair opposite. "We've much to discuss."

"I didn't imagine you would deliver orders in person, sir." Charles flicked out the tails on his coat as he sat. "Surely a factotum could have performed the task."

Barrington dug in his pocket and produced a silver toothpick. He clamped down on it, tucking it into the corner of his mouth. "I've not come with orders. I've come with news. I am sorry to have to tell you that your uncle has departed this mortal world."

Charles's chest heaved like it had been hit by a rogue wave. "He's dead." He felt no sorrow, because he hadn't known the man, had never laid eyes on him.

"I'm afraid so. Your hope he still had time to marry and beget an heir has come to nothing. He died nearly a week hence. Heart, I believe. As his legal successor, you are now the Earl of Rothwell." Barrington bowed his head slightly. "My lord."

The title sent a cold, stark wind through Charles. His mind thrust away the notion of a title. He neither wanted nor needed it. He was a sea captain, not an earl. His uncle had wanted nothing to do with him since before his birth. He had shunned his sister—Charles's mother—and her husband, forbid them to return to the family home, and settled all his attention on his elder sister's son, Arthur Bracken. The earl and his sister's hopes had died with Arthur after he tried to assassinate the Prince Regent. Even then the earl had wanted nothing to do with Charles, and Charles felt the same. He had ignored his future inheritance as effectively as his uncle had.

"What about a command?" He held on to a thread of hope.

"For pity's sake, man, I just informed you that you've become a peer of the realm. The last thing on your mind should be trying to find a command. Your place is in Devonshire at your estate. Gateshead, I believe it's called? It's time to come home from the sea and take up your position as landed gentry." Barrington slapped his thigh. "Do you know how many men under my command would give their last farthing to be in your position?"

Charles knew Barrington spoke the truth, but still he resisted. His life was aboard a ship, sailing into the horizon, not in a manor on the coast, weighed down with decisions about crop rotation and livestock pedigrees.

The ropes tightened around him as surely as if wound on a capstan.

All he wanted was to return to the sea. Why was God trying to keep him on land?

With the admiral staying the night, Mother had invited herself and Cilla to dinner at Haverly. Sophie took the chair the captain held for her. The lines beside his mouth had deepened. The admiral must have brought bad news.

Marcus, at the head of the table, said grace, and Sophie looked from one bowed head to the next. Mamie, across the table, looked as if she wanted to curl into a ball.

She hadn't cried when Sophie broke the news that the dowager had refused her blessing on the trip. A small nod, a tightening of the mouth, and some quick blinks were enough to break Sophie's heart . . . and begin the first stirrings of mutiny.

Why did she need Mother's permission anyway? Especially if Captain Wyvern would be kind enough to escort them? How did one honor one's mother when she was so unreasonable and controlling? How did one honor the woman who would have been her mother-in-law when doing so meant defying one's mother?

"Milady?"

Sophie started. The prayer was over, and Captain Wyvern leaned to the side so the footman could serve her.

"So, Barrington, is the Admiralty still awash with naval officers?" Marcus asked.

The admiral, seated at the far end of the table next to Charlotte, nodded. "Filling up the scuppers. Bringing the ranks down is going to be a challenge. Some are mustering out, some are taking jobs on merchant ships, and some are even accepting postings to man the cutters patrolling the shores for smugglers. But most are waiting for new postings."

"Is that what you're doing, Captain Wyvern?" the dowager asked. "Or do you have other plans now that the war is over?"

"He surely does." Admiral Barrington took a sip from his wineglass. "That's the reason I came up from London. To bring the news that his uncle, the Earl of Rothwell, has died, and the title is now his."

Everyone stopped eating and looked at the captain.

He was an earl? The Earl of Rothwell. Sophie hadn't known he was a member of a peerage family. He'd grown up in Portsmouth, gone to sea at twelve. How could he be an earl?

The dowager leaned back in her chair and eyed first the captain and then the admiral. "Are you sure?"

"Am I sure the old earl is dead? Yes. Am I certain Charles is his heir? Again, madam, yes."

Marcus toyed with his fork. "I had heard Rothwell was ailing. I was waiting for you to mention the fact that you were his heir, Captain Wyvern, though I perhaps know why you didn't."

What passed between them in their looks? Marcus's was challenging, while the captain's was wary. Had he secrets to hide?

"I was never meant to inherit. That honor belonged to my cousin. I am content to be a naval officer and never looked for anything else."

"So now it will not be out of your way to escort Sophie and Mamie to Devon, since you will no doubt be heading that direction yourself anyway?" The corner of her brother's mouth quirked, and he nodded to her.

Sophie's stomach muscles tightened. "Actually, we will not be able to accompany the captain. Or should I say earl? Mother has forbidden me to go."

"Oh, now, that's all changed." Mother sputtered and dabbed her lips.

"I had no idea the captain was also a peer. As the Earl of Rothwell, he's more than welcome to escort Sophia and Lady Richardson."

The captain grew white about the mouth, and his hands tightened on his fork and knife. "Is that so? You realize, madam, I am exactly the same man I was this morning when you turned down my offer to see your daughter to a cottage by the ocean? *Nothing* about me has changed."

"But it has. Surely you can see that it has. You're a titled gentleman now." Mother smiled and nodded. "Much more acceptable to chaperone the daughter of a duke, don't you know?"

When Charles dropped his cutlery onto his plate and leaned forward, Sophie surprised herself by putting her hand on his arm. The muscles were bunched, as if he were tensed like a cat to spring.

"She won't understand, and it's no good reasoning with her," she whispered. "Please."

He looked down at her fingers on his sleeve, going completely still. But as she withdrew her touch, his arm followed her a few inches, as if wishing to prolong the contact.

"Sophia, I shall help you pack, and we'll decide upon an itinerary for you." The dowager was away with her plans, but Sophie didn't much care. "If I wasn't so needed here, I would go with you."

Sophie's mind balked at the thought of a holiday with the dowager.

She could already see the oceanside cottage, down a sandy path between sea grasses to the shore. Mamie would walk along the beach with her, arm in arm, breathing in the salt air.

With seabirds crying and the shush and scrape of the waves rolling in, perhaps Sophie could release some of her grief and begin to mend.

But in the background of her image, the captain stood staring out toward the horizon, as if waiting for a ship to emerge in the distance.

Which was silly, because after they found their seaside cottage, they would most likely never see Charles Wyvern again.

Traveling with women in tow was vastly different from journeying alone. The amount of baggage staggered him. A separate wagon had been required, driven by one of Marcus's grooms, who would return as soon as they were safely delivered to the coast. Mrs. Chapman agreed that her place was with Lady Richardson, no matter where they went; therefore the carriage was crowded. Lady Richardson and the cook sat on one bench, and Lady Sophia sat beside Charles.

Under normal circumstances, Charles supposed most men would choose to ride beside the carriage on horseback, but as a sailor, he sadly lacked the skills of horsemanship. If he was indeed to be consigned to a life on land, he probably should look into acquiring some ability on a steed.

Not that he was complaining about the close quarters. Rocking along with Lady Sophia wasn't the most arduous of duties, in spite of the warm day. It was just that everything took longer when women were involved. For a period of time, he thought they might not escape Haverly Manor at all. Between the hugging, the instructions, and the well-wishes, Charles had been ready to slip the mooring lines and shove off long before the women.

Then there were the stops. It seemed at least once an hour one or the other of the ladies needed to "stretch her legs." Not having spent time around the female of the species, he didn't know if this was normal or not. All he knew was that progress by carriage seemed infinitely slower than aboard ship.

Mrs. Chapman kept her hand on the basket wedged between herself and Lady Richardson. The woman seemed to think there might not be provisions available outside Oxfordshire and had stuffed a hamper full of victuals to stave off starvation. And she pressed food upon anyone who accidentally met her eye.

"Would you like some bread and butter, Captain?" she asked, her face hopeful.

"Thank you, no." He'd already had his fill, merely to be polite. The warmth of the day had robbed him of appetite, and he wished he could yank off his cravat, pull off his coat, and roll up his sleeves. Yet another obligation of traveling with ladies. One must remain properly attired at all times.

Lady Sophia looked as fresh and pretty as when they'd set out hours before. And for the first time since meeting her, she wore something other than black. Her dress was a dove gray, trimmed with darker gray ribbon.

Still somber, but the bonnet framing her face had a brilliant sapphire lining that brought out the blue of her eyes.

She alternated between looking out the window and poking her nose into a slim volume that the Duchess of Haverly had pressed into her hand at the last minute.

"What are you reading, if I may ask?"

"It's Robert Herrick's *Hesperides*." She flipped the book closed, her finger marking her place, so he could see the title on the spine. "I love Herrick, don't you? He seems so approachable and not puffed up with his own importance. Herrick and Burns are my favorite poets. Charlotte thinks one should never travel without at least a book or two."

Charles's education had consisted mostly of geometry, astronomy, and mathematics, taught to him by whatever first officer had held the post on the ships he served. His knowledge was sorely lacking when it came to literature. He doubted he had ever read a poem by either of the authors she mentioned, and the only rhymes he knew were sea shanties he would never utter in the presence of a woman. Learning to navigate by the stars, calculate speed, and anticipate the weather had seemed a more prudent curriculum.

Though it pained him to admit his ignorance, he could not bluff his way into making anyone believe he was deeply literate. "I fear I am not familiar with Herrick. Perhaps you could read one of his poems?"

She pressed her lips together, studying him, and then nodded. "Rich first introduced me to Herrick when he quoted part of a stanza to me." She smiled, her expression going to another time as she leafed through the pages. "I had just burst into the parlor at Primrose, talking before I was even in the room, and I suppose my appearance was a bit disheveled. I seemed always to be in haste back then, with so much to say. As if I needed to cram as much as possible into our short time together before he returned to the marines."

Which matched everything Rich had told the crew about his Sophie. That she filled every day to overflowing with her joyous life. Would Rich have been disappointed at the new maturity she now showed, or was her somberness solely a result of Rich's death? Had he not died, would she still be the same effervescent romp of yesteryear?

Lady Sophia held the book to catch the late afternoon light and began reading:

"Delight in Disorder"
By Robert Herrick

A sweet disorder in the dress
Kindles in clothes a wantonness;
A lawn about the shoulders thrown
Into a fine distraction;
An erring lace, which here and there
Enthrals the crimson stomacher;
A cuff neglectful, and thereby
Ribands to flow confusedly;
A winning wave, deserving note,
In the tempestuous petticoat;
A careless shoe-string, in whose tie
I see a wild civility:
Do more bewitch me, than when art
Is too precise in every part.

Charles mulled the words and the images the poetry created. His entire world was one of order and discipline, routine and tradition. However, this Herrick fellow might be on to something. He could envision Lady Sophia just as this poem described.

Seated among the wildflowers, her hair blowing in the breeze.

Lady Sophia waited for his response, and he could feel the housekeeper and Lady Richardson looking at him as well. He cleared his throat. "Most interesting."

At Lady Sophia's sigh, he knew he'd disappointed her. He couldn't feign knowledge he didn't have and wax lyrical over literature. If her heart lay deeply with the poets, their paths lay far apart.

That gave him pause. Their paths lay far apart in any case. Though their contact had been extended for a few days by this journey, after he saw them into a cottage near Lady Richardson's birthplace, he would take his leave and trouble them no more. Common interests had nothing to do with it, and he would do well to remember that.

Charles paid the tolls and decided to stop in Newbury if the lodgings should be of a good standard. When they reached the coaching inn, he thought "good standard" might be a stretch, but Lady Richardson had begun to flag, and pressing on was out of the question. The inn, such as it was, would have to do.

"Allow me, madam." Charles assisted Lady Richardson. Mrs. Chapman followed, and then he reached up to help Lady Sophia. Her fingers brushed his, and the touch of her skin sent awareness thrumming along his veins. The moment her shoes graced the cobbles, she released his hand. He took a moment to get his bearings.

The coachman jumped down as hostlers emerged from the stables. "The baggage cart is a fair way back. I can bring in the bags atop the carriage, and you can let me know what else the ladies need for the night." He stretched his back and shook first one leg, then the other. "Stiff as starched iron. Must be weather coming in. Here," he shouted. "Be easy with that off fore. He's skittish." He nodded to Charles and hurried to where the lead horse sidled and jerked his head. "Let me do that. You'd think you'd never seen a horse before."

Charles turned away and headed into the taproom. The windows and doors were thrown open to catch any breeze that might wander by, and the fireplace was dark. Lady Richardson sat on a bench beside the long table, and a handful of men around a table had stopped playing cards to stare at the women. Or rather, one woman.

Lady Sophia knelt before Lady Richardson, chafing her hands, smiling encouragingly. Mrs. Chapman had her basket over her arm, one hand clenching the opposite wrist, staring balefully at the group around the card table.

An old woman with a dried-apple face stood behind the counter. She was thin as a stick and short enough to walk through a gun port without bumping her head. "You needin' rooms?" Slap! A wet cloth smacked the counter, sending droplets flying. "I got two. That's all."

By his count, they needed three, if he was to have space for himself. One for Lady Sophia and one for Lady Richardson. Perhaps Mrs.

Chapman would sleep in one of their rooms. Plus they would need a place for the baggage driver and the coachman.

"There's bunks in the barn for your driver and the like."

He grimaced. However, he'd slept rougher in his time, and one night wouldn't hurt him. "Fine. If you would get some refreshment for the ladies, we'll take the rooms and meals." He looked about the taproom. It hardly seemed the place for ladies to dine. There was a bit of the rough element about it.

"Perhaps you would care to dine in one of your rooms?" He didn't like the hard stares of the cardplayers, and with evening coming on, the taproom was sure to fill up.

"No need," the crone behind the counter said. "I got a private room for when swells visit. You won't hafta rub shoulders with the likes of these blaggards."

"That's no way to talk about your best customers." The oldest of the quartet rose with his pewter tankard and made his way to the counter. Amazing that he didn't collide with the furniture, since he never took his eyes off Lady Sophia. "Gimme another, and mind your tongue, you old harpy."

The wrinkled woman took the mug and turned the spigot on a keg behind her. With a quick twist, she stopped the flow of ale just before the tankard overflowed. "There, Paul Pipkin. Put that down your gullet. It's the only way to stop your gob."

Lady Sophia straightened and sent Charles an imploring look. "We'll take that private room, if you please." She lowered her voice. "Mamie is very tired."

Later that night, Charles surveyed his sleeping quarters with a jaundiced eye. Men lay on the straw like forgotten piles of cargo, snoring and snorting, scratching and shuffling. Most were soaked in ale.

Charles dropped his bag on the floor, and by the light of one weak lantern, withdrew a precisely wrapped canvas parcel. Taking stock of his options, he chose two stout columns and affixed the ropes of his hammock to them, testing that the knots would hold against the queen posts. With his bed sorted, he shrugged out of his coat and yanked at his cravat. He'd find water to wash and shave in the morning. For now, he just wanted sleep.

Stuffing his necktie into his coat pocket, his fingers brushed something smooth and cold. With a jolt he realized he still carried the miniature painting of Lady Sophia. He had intended to return it to her the morning after he'd "borrowed" it, but he'd been interrupted by the arrival of the new baron and baroness to Primrose Cottage. In all that had transpired since, it had slipped his mind.

He withdrew the oval, letting the flickering light play over the likeness. Guilt and pleasure mingled in his chest. She was beautiful of face, but he'd also seen she was beautiful of heart. Her care of Lady Richardson, her acceptance of him as the bearer of bad news, and her kindness to all, no matter their class, were things he admired even more than her beauty.

How to return her possession with as little embarrassment and fuss as possible eluded him. Having once girded himself up for the admission, he now felt more reluctant than ever to expose his sin. Might it be possible to slip the painting into the baggage without ever mentioning that it had been taken?

It might be the coward's way out, but at this point it also seemed the best way to avoid giving Lady Sophia additional hurt.

Chapter 6

Sophie studied Captain Wyvern—Earl Rothwell—across the small carriage space.

Ever since learning of his inheritance, the man acted as if someone had informed him he was about to be deported to Botany Bay for a life of penal servitude. Most men would be giddy at the prospect of a peerage and property. Why wasn't the captain?

Rich had never mentioned that Captain Wyvern had also been heir to a title. Had Rich known? Perhaps not. It didn't seem as if the captain enjoyed talking about his past.

As they rocked along the coastal road, she tried to ease her stiff back without drawing notice. Though the journey had been pleasant, aches and jostling and confinement had taken their toll. Last night they had stayed in Lyme Regis, and Sophie felt the bloom of adventure wearing off. Now that they were in Devonshire, with glimpses of the sea out her window, she was ready to settle in a cottage.

First they were going to the captain's new property, Gateshead. The estate was only a few miles from Lyme Regis, but they had arrived in the town so late last night, the captain thought it best they find lodgings rather than press on.

Or perhaps he was that reluctant to get to his destination.

"When was the last time you visited the estate?" Sophie asked, to break the silence in the coach.

The captain stirred. "I've never been there." He studied the rolling fields out his window.

Mamie leaned forward. "Never been to your family's home?"

His mouth thinned.

They were prying. An unforgiveable breach of protocol. Discomfort was writ plain on his face. He owed them nothing, certainly not explanations. Though she could admit to herself she was curious beyond what was considered proper, and her mind populated all sorts of reasons why he might never have laid eyes on Gateshead.

"You don't have to tell us. Your reasons are your own, and we don't wish to invade your privacy." Sophie winked at Mamie to let her know there was no harm done.

He didn't speak immediately, and then he shrugged. "If you're going to stay in the region, some version of the story will reach your ears eventually. Better it should come from me. My mother's brother was the previous Earl of Rothwell, recently deceased. My uncle never married and was the youngest of three children. The eldest, Eliza, married a diplomat and courtier named Nathaniel Bracken, and she had one son, Arthur Bracken, known as Viscount Fitzroy."

Sophie's mouth fell open, and she blinked.

"Yes, that Arthur Bracken. It turns out in addition to being a less-than-competent assassin, he was also not the legitimate son of my aunt Eliza. Nathaniel Bracken and Aunt Eliza passed him off as her son, though his real mother had been Nathaniel's first wife, a Frenchwoman he met in Normandy. They hid Arthur's origins by disappearing into the country for a period of time, and because our family was estranged, no one was the wiser. Portraying Arthur as an Englishman ensured he would be the next in line to inherit the earldom and would sidestep the awkwardness of being French in a country that was at war with France. All of this came to light after the investigation into the assassination plot earlier this year."

Sophie pondered this blackest of black sheep in the Rothwell family line. No wonder Captain Wyvern did not wish to discuss it openly. Her brother, Marcus, had been involved with the capture of Arthur Bracken, having been a guest at White Haven estate last year, where the assassination attempt on the Prince Regent's life had been made. Though she had tried to worm details out of Marcus, Sophie hadn't been able to crack his reticent defenses. What she knew of the affair she'd gleaned from the newspapers and her mother's gossip. Unreliable sources, to be sure.

Captain Wyvern let out a sigh. "As for my never having been to the estate, that's easily explained. There was a rift in the family before I was even born. My uncle disowned my mother when she had the audacity to marry for love, well beneath her station. She eloped with my father, an able seaman, and she set up house in Portsmouth, while my father continued to serve in the Royal Navy. They had me, sent me to a day school for would-be sailors, and when I was twelve, I enlisted in the navy. My mother had been forbidden from ever returning to Gateshead, and when my uncle learned of my birth, he issued the same command regarding me, even though I was his heir for a time, before Arthur came on the scene."

"That's dreadful. What a terrible man your uncle must have been." Sophie couldn't imagine making such a decree against a child, who had no part in his parentage, nor shunning a sister merely because she married for love.

Sophie felt a kinship with Charles's mother, though she hadn't suffered the same extremes. The Duchess of Haverly hadn't been thrilled with Sophie's selection of a husband either, thinking a baron too low on the register for a duke's daughter, though she'd resigned herself eventually. A chill went through Sophie as she recalled that her mother had plans to reopen the marriage discussion when Sophie returned from her trip to the seaside.

Why couldn't Mother understand that Sophie had no plans to fall in love again? And Sophie would never marry for less than love.

They passed through a village, shops, houses. A church flashed by. Faces stared as they made their way.

"That's Gateshead Village. According to the stories my mother told, you must go through the village to get to the estate on the peninsula." Charles supplied the information, but his voice was devoid of emotion. Was he excited? Uneasy? In his place she would be filled to the brim with expectations and adventure, and perhaps a bit of vindication?

The carriage traveled along a lane bordered on one side by a long hedgerow, and it slowed, turning through a pair of gates to a long, winding road that led south toward the sea.

The captain shifted in his seat, his back straightening. "The estate comprises the entire peninsula. There are steep cliffs and a cove where boats shelter." Half a coat of arms glinted on the gate. When closed, the gates must form the entire shield.

Odd that he was coming to a family home he'd never seen before, and now he owned it. Not just owned it, but was the titled lord of this manor. What must he be thinking?

The road serpentined around the low hills. Stone walls bordered pastures and fields, and here and there a copse of trees nestled in the cleft of a small valley. Crofters' cottages and barns dotted the fields. The estate certainly looked large and prosperous.

They topped the last rise, rocked down a slope, and turned in an arc that took them along a circular drive. Sophie couldn't see much of the house, being on the far side of the carriage when it came to a stop. Stone, a row of windows, a heavy door. On her side of the coach, in the center of a circle of grass, a fountain sat dormant. From the middle of the fountain rose a moss-splotched statue of a young boy raising his hand to feed a bird perched at the tips of his fingers, wings outstretched.

But the fountain itself was choked with debris, stagnant water filling a few inches of the pool.

A shame it had been so neglected. It was quite lovely. Perhaps it could be restored.

Captain Wyvern climbed out of the carriage, and punctilious as always, helped the ladies. When Sophie's feet hit the gravel, the breeze off the sea tugged at her skirts. She put her hand atop her bonnet and looked up at the house.

Stark came to mind. Cold gray stone, dark slate roof tiles, peeling white trim around the windows. A forest of chimneys rose into the sky, and the dark, heavy front doors looked as if they belonged on a Spanish prison.

The house appeared solid enough, but it had an air of abandonment about it, sitting like a stodgy rectangular block, with no trees or gardens or even ivy to soften its bulk.

Mamie adjusted her dress, blinking in the sunlight. "This isn't a cottage. I thought we were going to a cottage."

Sophie tucked her hand into Mamie's elbow. "It's all right. We're visiting Captain Wyvern's new home first. We'll get to a cottage soon." She should probably call him Lord Rothwell now, but through Rich's letters she had known him for so long as Captain Wyvern, she could hardly imagine him as anything else.

He put his hat on and clasped his hands behind his back, rocking on his toes as he surveyed the house as if assessing a new command. His frown deepened.

With a squeal of protest, the massive front door opened, and a pair of sharp brown eyes skewered first Sophie and then Mamie, before his stare fell on Mrs. Chapman. "Who's there and whacha want? We don't need no maids around here. The staff is full."

Mrs. Chapman, who had been adjusting her lace cap, jerked her chin.

Before she could retort with the sharp side of her tongue, the captain stepped forward. "I am Captain Charles Wyvern." He paused. "And the present Earl of Rothwell."

The man blinked rapidly, his tongue darting out to lick his lips, something calculating in his eyes. "Your lordship. We didn't know you were coming." He tugged his forelock and bent at the waist in a sharp bow, going from belligerent to obsequious in a flash.

"And you are?"

"Halbert Grayson, sir." He gripped the edge of the door as if the ground had shifted beneath his boots. "I've been steward here for six years." His head bobbed with each word.

"Perhaps we might be allowed to come inside?" The captain's voice was dry as attic dust.

"Of course, of course." The short man stepped back, making ushering motions.

"Ladies?" Captain Wyvern indicated they should precede him.

Their footsteps echoed on the wooden floor. In ages past, the floor had been painted, but now it bore the scuffs and scrapes of much use, the wood grain showing through the leaves and flowers that had been stenciled on the planks.

Dark paneling covered the walls, and tapestries much in need of cleaning hung from a picture rail. The entire place felt gloomy and untended, as if it had been closed up since the reign of George I.

The steward yanked off his cloth cap, and with a swipe, removed a layer of dust from the table in the middle of the hall.

"Place is a bit done in at the moment. The old earl was a bit of a Tartar, and he ran the housekeeper and maids off a few months before he met his end. Wasn't nobody but me left when he died, and I can't take care of everything." He spread his hands. "I woulda left too, he was that mean, but I couldn't abandon him."

"I thought you said you had no need of maids?" Mrs. Chapman dragged her finger along a ledge and showed the dark smudge to the steward. "I could employ a dozen girls for a solid week here and still not finish the job."

"I can't be spending his lordship's money or hiring people without leave. The magistrate said I had to wait until he heard back from London about who would be taking over the place before I made any transactions. Haven't even been able to draw wages myself. Now you're here, sir, you can set things right." He held his hat against his chest. "Things haven't been right at Gateshead for a long time, not since the old lord got sick, but with your leave, I can start getting the estate back on a good footing."

His eyes pleaded. He ducked his head, the picture of humility. He must have been worrying whether he would catch the blame for the condition of the estate and whether the new earl would keep him on. Sophie could sympathize with his position, but something about the man made her wary.

Charles removed his hat, smoothed his hair, and tucked the bicorn under his arm. "Very well. For now see if you can find refreshments for the ladies. They will be my guests for the next few days."

"Guests, sir? This isn't your countess then?" He motioned to Sophie.

"No." The captain was quite curt and offered no explanation. "Where is the drawing room?"

"Through there." Grayson pointed across the hall.

"I'll see to the tea and biscuits, sir." Mrs. Chapman folded her arms across her chest. "If this man will show me to the kitchens. No telling what state they're in. And I'll fetch my basket from the coach. I had the innkeeper stock it this morning."

The parlor was in better shape than the front hall, appearing only to suffer from the need for a good dusting. Heavy paintings coated with aged varnish covered the walls, narrow-nosed, be-ruffed ancestors glaring from the canvases.

"It isn't too bad." Sophie tried to put a bright face on things. "A little attention and it will be a fine house again."

"It feels like an anchor roped to my boots." The captain dropped his hat on the sofa and went to the south-facing windows. He jerked the heavy drapes apart. Clouds of dust swirled out, and he coughed, putting his forearm over his mouth and squinting. Beyond the fly-specked windowpanes, a furlong away, the level ground ceased, and far in the distance, the sky met the sea. "At least the view is decent."

"It will be even better from the upper floors." From what Sophie could ascertain, there were at least three stories to the manor house and probably rooms under the eaves. Not as large as the Haverly estate house, but still sizeable.

"That must be an abrupt cliff. I wonder if it's stable and how far it is to the water below. I'm surprised there isn't a hedge or fence to mark the edge." The captain clasped his hands behind his back and stared out to sea.

"It's near fifty feet high in some places, sir." Grayson stood in the doorway. "There's a staircase that goes down to the water, and a bit of beach when the tide's out. There was a hedge once upon a time, but the old earl had us uproot it. He thought it cut off too much of the view from the lower floor here." He crushed his hat in his hands. "Your housekeeper is near destroying the kitchen, sir, but she says she'll have tea ready soon. There's another wagon approaching up the drive. Are you expecting more folks?"

"That will be the baggage wagon. See what you can do to help with the unloading. Bring everything into the upstairs hall, and we'll sort it later." The captain sounded tired and resigned.

A frown crinkled the steward's brow, but he bowed and disappeared. Almost immediately he was back.

"Begging your pardon, sir, but that's no baggage wagon coming. It's a coach. We haven't had visitors for weeks, and now folks coming all at once." He inclined his head toward the door. "Shall I send them away?"

"Just what I need." The captain followed Grayson. The front door creaked and complained.

Mamie eased open the drapes to look out onto the front lawn. "How long will we stay?"

Sophie had the urge to wrap her hair in a kerchief, grab a mop and bucket, and get to work. The house might be neglected, but the bones were good. A little effort would bring it back, she was sure. "I think the captain feels like he's fallen out of his boat and into the ocean. Perhaps we could bide here for a few days, until he finds his feet?"

Mamie nodded. "That would be nice."

"I wonder if the captain has any idea what it takes to run an estate."

"He can run a ship. Those skills will aid him now." Mamie leaned toward the window glass.

"Perhaps we can be of some help to him, to say thank you for bringing us south. We're not unused to doing the odd domestic chore, are we, pet?" Sophie could name five things right now that needed doing sooner rather than later. Hiring competent staff and a thorough audit of the estate accounts topped the list. She smiled. If Marcus's friends, the Whitelocks, were here, Diana would be writing out lists upon lists. And if Marcus and Charlotte were here, Charlotte would be searching through books on household management and design to plot her attack on the manor.

Sophie recognized the strengths of their particular methods, but she tended to rely more on instinct when it came to running a house. Of course, Primrose Cottage was much smaller than Haverly or White Haven or Gateshead.

"That's very like you, dear. To want to help. You're always pitching in somewhere. I don't think it will hurt us to stay a few days. After all, I wanted to see the ocean again, and here it is in all its glory." Mamie gestured to the blue water reflecting sunshine in a million points of light.

Sophie joined Mamie at the front windows. A yellow coach, shabby and travel worn, with mismatched horses neared the curve around the fountain. A mail coach. Perhaps someone had sent a letter or parcel to the estate.

The carriage stopped, a swirl of grit whirling up from around the wheels, and the driver leapt from his perch. He yanked open the door. A girl, almost a young woman, alighted, a pensive expression on her face. The wind fluttered the ribbons of her bonnet and the sleeves of her spencer. She had barely touched ground when another girl, younger, shorter, jumped down. Hatless, her hair blazed red in the sunshine. Finally, a smaller face peered from the doorway of the carriage. A little girl of maybe five summers with a cluster of chocolate curls about her head. The eldest young woman reached for the child and swung her to the ground, smoothing her hair. The child studied the house, tugging on her earlobe as she took in her surroundings.

"Well, that's no letter or parcel."

Captain Wyvern stood on the front steps, his back to the windows. The captain's hands, clasped behind his back, fisted. Grayson hovered by his side, mauling his cap. The young woman said something. The captain jerked as if he'd been slapped.

"I don't think this is good news," Sophie said. Burning with curiosity, she told Mamie, "Wait here, love. I'll be back."

She slipped out as unobtrusively as possible. The steward scuttled away a few paces to make room for her on the top step, and the captain sent her a bewildered, half-angry look.

"There you go, guv." The coachman touched his hat brim. "Your girls delivered safe and sound."

"There must be some mistake. I don't have any girls," the captain protested. "You'll have to take them back wherever they came from. You've brought them to the wrong place."

"Oh, but he hasn't, sir." The eldest of the three girls spoke rapidly. "This is our destination. Gateshead. The school has closed. Miss Fricklin had no choice, with so few students and the earl not paying our tuition any longer." She tucked the littlest girl into her side, her arm about her shoulders in a protective gesture. "The headmistress put us on the mail coach and sent us here. She said as we were the old earl's wards, and we were his responsibility, now that he's dead, the chore fell to the new earl."

"Are you the earl? The dead earl was *really* old." The redhead hopped up onto the mounting block and then back to the grass, her hair flopping on her back. "Though you are a bit long in the tooth, aren't you? Penny said maybe you'd be young and romantic." She put her hands under her chin and fluttered her eyelashes. Then she stuck her tongue out at her older sister. "Guess you can give up on the idea of the earl falling in love with you, Pen. He's old enough to be our dad. Maybe older."

A bewildered cast overtook the captain's features, even as a fierce red crept up Penny's cheeks.

"Oh, do be quiet, Thea. You've got a mouth like a leaky bucket," Penny scolded.

"Maybe, but at least I don't fall in love with every pair of trousers that crosses my path," Thea shot back.

The coachman had climbed aboard once more and now threw down three identical bandboxes. Grayson stepped up to retrieve them, setting them on the grass.

"No returns. They're yours now, guv." With a flick of the reins, he set the horses into motion.

As the clatter of hooves faded, the three girls faced off with Captain Wyvern. No one seemed to know what to say.

Sophie stepped forward, her heart going out to these little strangers. "Perhaps we should go inside. The girls must be tired from their trip. There's much to discuss, and I'm sure everyone has questions, but it would be better done in the house, don't you think?"

The captain seemed to come to himself. "Yes, of course." He stood back. "See to their bags, Grayson. Put them in the upstairs hall with the rest when it arrives."

The littlest girl's eyes were wide and wet, and her lower lip trembled. She reached up and tugged on her earlobe. Thea crossed her arms, one foot forward, her chin out in undisguised skepticism. And Penny looked about to cry.

Sophie couldn't help but put herself in their slippers. What uncertainties had they suffered? How far had they come, not knowing what would greet them at journey's end?

"Come, girls. Welcome to Gateshead. I'm sorry we're all at sixes and sevens. We've only just arrived ourselves." She held out her hand, guiding them up the stairs. Thea, the redhead, regarded her from the corner of her eye as she passed, then hopped on one foot up the steps. The baby put herself on the far side of Penny as they went by, sheltering in the protection of someone she knew.

"This place is filthy." Thea tilted her head way back to look at the coffered ceiling three stories above, where cobwebs wafted in the sunlight from a large fan window. "That's a cracking banister, though. Miss Fricklin wouldn't let us slide on the one at the school. She said we'd break our heads, and then where would she be? I always thought she wouldn't be half as bad off as we'd be with broken heads, but she still wouldn't let us." She shrugged, her narrow shoulders lifting beneath her plain yellow frock.

"And neither will I. Keep your feet on the deck." The captain frowned, his tone dry. "Into the parlor."

Mamie smiled welcomingly from the bench seat beneath the front window as they trooped in. "Who are these delightful young ladies?"

"I've no idea, but I intend to find out. Sit." Captain Wyvern pointed to a sofa, and the girls lined up and sat, the smallest one in the middle. The captain took up station before the fireplace, his hands clasped behind his back. He sent Sophie a look of pure frustration.

Sophie bit back a sigh. He looked quite forbidding, every inch the commanding officer. How would she have felt as a young girl confronted with such a stern visage? "Perhaps we should start with introductions? My name is Lady Sophia Haverly, and this is Lady Richardson. And you are?"

"Penelope Pembroke, and these are my sisters, Dorothea and Elizabeth."

The redhead scowled. "Why are you being so grand and snooty? You aren't the lady of the manor. You're Penny, I'm Thea, and she's Betsy."

Trying to stop a fight before it began, Sophie smiled. "Those names suit you perfectly. I'm known as Sophie, myself. Now, how old are you?"

Penny put her arm around Betsy. "I'm sixteen."

Thea straightened and opened her mouth, but Penny rolled her eyes. "Well, very nearly. I'll be sixteen in two months. Betsy here is five. She was really too young to be at Miss Fricklin's, but there was nowhere else for her to be, and the old earl paid extra for Miss Fricklin to keep her."

"I'm eleven." Thea pointed to her chest with her thumb. She twirled one red curl around her finger. "Are you married to him? He looks like he just kissed a sour pickle. Still . . ." She shrugged. "If you're going to be grumpy, at least we're used to it. Miss Fricklin was a grump herself."

Laughter bubbled up in Sophie's chest, and she fought to keep it down. She saw herself in the outspoken Thea. How many times had she aired her mind with no thought to how it would be received?

"No, I am not married to the captain . . . I mean the earl. Lady Richardson and I are his guests for the next little while." She leaned forward and lowered her voice. "The captain—earl—isn't grumpy. He's just surprised. It's not every day you come to live in a new house and then get three young ladies delivered by parcel post. Perhaps you might offer him a bit of grace and remember your manners. You are a guest in his home." She kept her tone gentle but firm.

Thea's mouth twisted as she gave it some thought before nodding. "Fine."

"Where are your parents?" Sophie asked Penny. "Why were you sent to Gateshead rather than to them?"

"We're orphans. The earl was our guardian. Our father worked on the estate, and we lived in a cottage near the cliff. Father's job was to tend the boathouse and sail the earl's boat for him." She toyed with a fold of her dress. "Nearly two years ago now, the boat went down in bad seas off the coast. They managed to salvage the boat, the *Shearwater*, when it washed up ashore near Lyme Regis, but they never found our father." She kept her eyes downcast.

Betsy stared at Sophie, as if the story meant little to her. The child had beautiful, round brown eyes and a sweet dimple in her chin. Her slippers dangled several inches from the floor, and she tucked her hands under her thighs. When she caught Sophie looking at her, she smiled shyly, and one hand crept up to tug her ear.

"And your mother?" Sophie asked.

Thea bounced up and moved to the window. Every line of her little body was taut, and she crossed her arms over her chest, her gaze fierce.

"Our mother never recovered from the loss. A few months after Papa died, she passed away." Penny feathered her fingers through Betsy's hair, and the little girl leaned into her older sister. "We had never met the earl, but for some reason, he took it upon himself to become our guardian. He sent us to Miss Fricklin's School for Young Ladies. It's a small school in Mousehole, down in Cornwall. He paid our fees, and Miss Fricklin kept us there, even over the holidays. But when the earl got sick a few months ago, the money stopped. Miss Fricklin wrote to the steward several times, but she never heard back. There were only a handful of girls at the school, most of them day girls from town, and when our tuition money stopped coming, Miss Fricklin couldn't keep the school open. She accepted a position in another school, and she sent all the girls back to their homes."

"So I guess we don't have a home now." Thea turned to face the room. "'Cept here."

"Are there no relatives?" The captain asked. "No one to care for you?"

Penny shook her head. "The earl and the vicar searched right after—" She broke off, as if she didn't want to say it again. "They weren't able to find anyone. If the earl hadn't paid for us to go away to school, we'd have been sent to an orphanage and probably separated." Her brow knitted as if she realized this was still a real possibility.

Sophie's heart wrenched. No family, no one to look after them, and the prospect of being torn apart and sent away from each other?

"You have no idea why my uncle became your guardian?"

At his abrupt question, Penny flinched. If only the captain wouldn't glower and stand so rigidly, as if he were addressing some miscreant in his crew.

"No, sir. But we're glad he did." Penny hugged Betsy. "What we also don't know is what will happen to us now. Are you going to be our guardian?" The hope in her eyes was undeniable.

The planes and angles of the captain's face sharpened. "That's something I can't decide right this moment. I have no provisions for children, nor the desire to have any thrust upon me. Bad enough that I have the title and estate to look after. I'm a sea captain, for pity's sake, not a nursemaid."

Crestfallen, Penny looked at Sophie.

Sophie's hand had risen to cover her mouth at his harsh words. While they might be true, they were painful to receive. She wanted to temper the wind to these shorn lambs. "You must be tired and hungry. I propose we introduce you to the most important person in the house, Mrs. Chapman. She was rustling up tea for us, and perhaps we can get her to include you in the plans." Sophie rose and held out her hand to Betsy. "Let's leave the captain in peace for a while."

The child blinked, tugged on her ear, and squirmed around to look at her older sister. At Penny's nod, she scooted off the couch and put her little hand in Sophie's. Something warm surrounded Sophie's heart at the trusting look in Betsy's eyes. She had been dealt a bad hand, orphaned so young, sent away from home, and now with an uncertain future and a rather stern new guardian, but she was safe in the love and care of her sisters.

Sophie wanted to scoop her up in a hug and promise her that she would always feel loved and secure.

But she couldn't, because the little girl's future was in the hands of Captain Wyvern, who hadn't exactly made glad-eyed offers to welcome the girls to Gateshead.

His life was pitching about like a ship's deck in a typhoon. He'd lost his command and been cast ashore. He'd tried to fulfill at least part of his promise to Rich by visiting Lady Sophia and Lady Richardson, and he had been drawn into escorting them to the coast. He'd been landed with the earldom and estate his uncle never wanted him to have. And now three little girls had washed up on his shore, looking for a home.

What was next? An earthquake? Pestilence? Fire?

God, what are You doing to me? I had such a simple plan laid out, and at every turn, I am thwarted.

He stood in a corner room off the upstairs hall, in an alcove created by a turret. Surrounded by windows, he looked out on the sea, his heart as restless as the ever-moving ocean.

The room must have served as the old earl's study off the master suite, and the proportions and location pleased Charles, the first thing in the house to do so. If he had been going to stay here, he would have made it his sanctum. A place of refuge. He would be half tempted to paint the entire room pale blue to remind him of the captain's quarters aboard a naval vessel. He smiled ruefully. Wouldn't his old uncle throw a tirade at the thought of his house being taken over by a limey?

Charles heard—of all things—giggling down the hall. As unfamiliar to him as Mandarin. Giggling made him uneasy, with no way to predict an outcome.

Little girls. He had no experience of them. In fact, if he was truthful, they scared him. Laughing one moment, crying the next. And the small one watched his every move.

The middle one, if she had been a boy, had the makings of a powder monkey. She was never still, hopping, skipping, and moving all the time. And with a tart tongue to her as well.

Charles tugged at his collar. Something Thea had said lingered in his mind. That her older sister had hoped the new earl would fall in love with her?

Preposterous.

Girls were as unreliable as gunpowder.

How thankful he was for Sophie—Lady Sophia, he corrected himself. What would he have done had he turned up at Gateshead on his own, with only a steward in residence, and been faced with the arrival of three little girls?

He might have abandoned ship and left the entire place to them.

At the moment, Lady Sophia and Lady Richardson were engaged in the task of putting the girls to bed, a reef he was glad to be clear of.

A tap on the door, and Lady Sophia leaned around its edge. "There you are." She stepped all the way in. "The girls are just about settled, but would you believe that the little one, Betsy, refuses to go to sleep until you come and say good night? It seems she's quite taken with you." A bemused smile played on her lips, and her eyes glowed in the candle flame of the glass lamp she carried.

Charles frowned. "Me?" The little girl had studied him all through dinner. With the upheaval of the household, they had opted to dine all together in the breakfast room, and for the duration of the meal in those cozy quarters, he had felt her brown eyes regarding him. She had scarcely blinked as she nibbled her food. Had she thought he was going to turn to a sea monster and devour her?

And now she wanted him to bid her good night?

Girls were definitely unpredictable.

Of course, Thea had done her share of staring as well, but from her it seemed frank curiosity rather than wariness. He could deal with that, since he had a bit of curiosity about the girls himself.

For instance, he wondered what had prompted his crusty, uncaring, unforgiving uncle to take on the responsibility for three girls of whom he was no relation, when he had turned his back on his own sister and refused to budge?

And what was he, the new earl, supposed to do about it?

Charles followed Lady Sophia to the room she had selected for the girls, his enthusiasm for the endeavor hovering somewhere around nil.

"This was the nursery once upon a time, so it seemed fitting, though it doesn't appear to have been used since your mother's generation. Mrs. Chapman has offered to sleep in the nurse's room until you can sort out a governess for the girls."

Sort out a governess? Charles stopped in the darkened hallway, his mind framing a refusal. He wasn't the girls' guardian. Beyond a bit of Christian charity, giving them a bed for a night or two, they weren't his responsibility. They certainly couldn't live here alone once he received his new command.

Lady Sophia disappeared into the nursery and then stuck her head out the door to see where he'd gone. "Coming?"

He entered the room as he would an ambush. The two youngest girls leaned against pillows in one bed, while their older sister stood near the other bed, clutching a wrapper about herself. With her hair uncoiled and falling in a braid over her shoulder, she looked even younger than she had at dinner.

At his appearance, she scuttled under the covers and pulled them to her chin. "This is most improper, a gentleman coming into a lady's boudoir." Her eyes were round as portholes.

"Stop putting on airs," Thea scoffed. "The place is full of people. Nothing 'improper,'"—she rolled her eyes—"is going to happen."

Mrs. Chapman carried a tray with three water glasses and set it on the table between the beds, and Lady Richardson drew the curtains against the night.

Lady Sophia set the lamp on a shelf and beckoned him closer.

Betsy stared at him with those brown eyes, the lamplight making shadows and highlights on her curly hair. Thea wriggled, thumping her pillow and tugging the blankets until she was comfortable.

"What am I supposed to do?" Charles whispered to Lady Sophia.

Surely she was smothering laughter at his expense. Did she expect him to be experienced at such maneuvers? One didn't "tuck in" cabin boys and powder monkeys. One tossed them into their bunks or hammocks and blew out the lamp.

She took his hand, drawing him toward the bed, and for a moment he couldn't think beyond the contact. Soft as down, her small hand fit into his like a pocket watch. Her fingers were cool but insistent. His heart skipped like spinner dolphins over the water, and he swallowed against the tightness of his cravat.

When was the last time a woman had voluntarily taken his hand? Some officers' dance once upon a time? All he knew was that it was long ago, and even then it didn't affect him the way Sophie's touch did. He took hold of his thoughts and forced himself to pay attention.

"Sit here." She guided him to the edge of the bed.

Out of habit, he went to adjust his sword at his waist, but his hand hit empty air. She let go of his hand, and he quelled his disappointment.

Betsy, instead of cringing away as he'd anticipated, sat up and held out her arms. "Good night, Cap'n. I hope you have happy dreams." They were the first words he'd heard her utter, and before he could catalog them, her little arms went around him, and she buried her head in his waistcoat.

Startled, Charles held his hands away from his sides, looking to Sophie for help. What on earth was the girl doing? Sophie made a small hugging motion, smiling, and he gradually lowered his arms to embrace the child.

She had small bones and a warm, sweet fragrance. Completely foreign, and yet not unpleasant. So fragile and vulnerable.

When she turned him loose, she lay back on the pillows, a satisfied smile on her little bow lips.

"Why'd you do that?" Thea asked her sister, her red brows arrowing down.

Betsy shrugged. "He looked like he needed a hug. I don't think captains get hugged enough."

She spoke so matter of factly, Charles wanted to laugh. It was probably true. Ah, the wisdom of babes. He patted her shoulder awkwardly and rose.

"I bid you good night, ladies." He bowed. "Rest well."

"Don't know how you expect us to rest well when you won't even say if you're keeping us or not," Thea muttered loudly enough to be heard, flipping onto her side and turning her back on the captain.

Such insubordination should probably be dealt with, but he didn't know how or if it was his duty. Making his way to the door, he motioned for Lady Sophia. "When they are settled, perhaps you will join me in the room I was in previously? Bring Lady Richardson if you like. There are things to discuss."

A quarter hour later, she came into the alcove. He'd left the curtains open, and the only light in the room was near the door so as not to pollute his view of the stars and the water. She had been correct in her earlier surmise that the vista was even better on the upper floors of the house. He gave in to the preposterous notion that on a clear day he could almost see to the Channel Islands.

If only his feet were firmly on the deck of a ship, he would be at rest in his spirit.

"They're finally settling down. Mamie wanted to stay with them until they're asleep." Lady Sophia came to stand beside him, breathing in the fresh air through the open window. "She's quite taken with the girls, for all they've only been here a few hours."

"Is that all it's been?" A wry tone seeped out.

She laughed softly. "They certainly add a bit of noise and commotion, don't they? They're sweet. And worried."

"I suppose they've a right to be anxious." He was anxious himself.

"Their lives have been turned upside down multiple times in just two years. Losing their parents, being sent away to school, and now shuttled back here. They're not sure what's coming next." The question stared at him from her blue eyes.

What was he going to do? Every way he turned, he was hemmed in by new responsibilities. If this continued, he'd never untangle his ratlines enough to get away.

"If it would help . . ." She paused.

"Yes?" He was willing to grasp any lifeline.

"I've spoken with Mamie, and she agrees. If it would help you, we could stay on a bit, until you decide what you're going to do with the girls."

His heart leapt, and the muscles of his chest and arms tensed. For days he'd dreaded parting ways with the ladies, and here she was offering to prolong their contact.

"I don't even know my options as far as the girls are concerned," he admitted, rubbing the back of his neck.

She turned and sat on the broad windowsill, silhouetted by the moonlight. "You have three options that I can see."

He clasped his hands behind his back and paced the small space, head down. "Yes?" The alcove was hardly big enough for a proper stride, but it would do for the time being.

"One, you could send them to an orphanage or poorhouse, where they will await adoption, indenture, or growing old enough to be turned out to fend for themselves. In each of those cases, they will most likely know depravations and be separated from one another."

Though the words she chose were objective, the passion in her voice told him what she thought of this option.

He remembered Betsy hugging him with minuscule strength, and the softness of her curly head against his chest, and couldn't imagine tendering the child into the keeping of an orphanage.

"Two," Lady Sophia continued, holding up two fingers. "You could follow in your uncle's footsteps and continue as their guardian. You could find a suitable ladies' boarding school and send them there. Out of sight, out of mind. Duty fulfilled, at least to the letter of the law. They would be housed, clothed, fed, and educated, all far away from the place of their birth. There are any number of schools in England, Scotland, Wales. You would only need to pay tuition and provide transportation to the school." Again her voice held no censure, but no enthusiasm. "Assuming that you wish to continue as their guardian?" She spread her hands.

This option appealed to him. It would salve his conscience that the girls were together and cared for, and also free him from any direct responsibility. Far better that they be under the supervision of a competent headmistress than left to his untutored abilities.

"And the third?" He had an inkling based upon what she'd said earlier, but he would give her the opportunity to spell it out.

"Keep them here at Gateshead with a proper nurse or governess. Give them a home here, a sense of belonging and family. A private education, security, and affection." She stood, putting her hand on his arm and halting his pacing. "Take them on as part of your crew, as it were."

He looked down on her white hand against the dark blue of his naval coat. Make the girls part of his crew. The terminology resonated with him, but how could he let them stay here when he had no plans to remain at Gateshead himself? The moment a command of any kind came through, he would be away to sea. It would disrupt the girls' lives once again if he told them they could stay here and then he received word that a ship was available. They would be shunted off to a school after all. Better to send them away now and avoid the upheaval. Part of being a good captain to your crew was making hard decisions that might be unpopular at the time but in the long term would prove best for all involved.

"I do appreciate your willingness to stay on until I decide what to do. I should refuse your kind offer and fulfill my promise to see you installed in a cottage with all speed, but I cannot deny that having you here will make everything easier." And so very pleasant. He cleared his throat, daring to cover her hand on his sleeve with his own. "Will it discomfit Lady Richardson not to find her cottage by the sea immediately?"

Her hand didn't move under his, but she looked down as well. "I think Mamie will be delighted to stay on and be with the girls. She was already planning a walk to the beach with them tomorrow." She withdrew her hand, stepping back, though her expression was untroubled. He didn't think she censored him for his boldness in clasping her hand.

A walk on the beach. He imagined strolling along the firm sand with Sophie by his side, the breeze blowing her hair and skirts, the birds calling, and the waves scraping in and out like the heartbeat of the ocean. A pleasant memory to have tucked away when he was once more on the ocean.

"You will give the options some thought? About the girls, I mean?" She turned away, heading toward the door.

"Of course." Though it seemed plain to him what the correct course should be. He was not some sentimentalist, and he had a career to consider. "I'll do what is best for the girls and myself. Do you have personal knowledge of any good schools for girls? Perhaps even one here in Devonshire that would keep them closer to home?"

She stopped, and her shoulders lowered. Without glancing back, she nodded. "I'll make some inquiries in my next letter home. Mother and Charlotte will surely know of some."

When he was alone once more, he resumed pacing. Discontent sloshed like bilge water in his middle, and he scowled.

He was used to making unpopular decisions, so why did Lady Sophia's disappointment rankle so much?

Things were simpler at sea. The rules of engagement were clear, and the chain of command set in stone. Feelings and opinions didn't enter into the equation, and total obedience was expected.

Yes, things were definitely simpler at sea . . . but lonelier, too, if he was to be completely truthful.

Chapter 7

Sunshine, waving grass, and the brilliant blue of the sea greeted Sophie as she threw the window sash open and leaned out, inhaling the fresh coastal air.

Gateshead was an impressive home. With a bit of polish, the luster could be brought back to the house, and the views were unparalleled. A trickle of adventure went down her spine, an altogether refreshing feeling. One that she used to get often, a desire to embrace what the day might hold.

Well, she could certainly do that. Three young girls who had been starved of happiness for far too long now resided under the same roof as Sophie, and she was going to see that they had all the joy they could handle while she had the chance.

She could hear them down the hall, laughter, movement, the squeak of the bed. It sounded as if someone—Thea, probably—was jumping on the mattress. Was that child ever still?

Dressing quickly, Sophie pondered the captain's options regarding the girls and the heavy indication he'd given last night as to where his thoughts lay.

Boarding school.

She winced. It wasn't as bad as an orphanage, but it was a far cry from a home where they would be wanted and loved. Sophie had lived in a house where all the attention was lavished upon the eldest son, the next two children in line afterthoughts. She'd lived away at boarding school, an average student who only wanted to go home. And she'd lived at Primrose, secure in the knowledge that both Rich and Mamie wanted her there and that they loved her. Though her dreams of the future had changed, she had known that sense of calm surety of her place in the world and that someone cared about her.

She wanted that for these girls.

How could she change the captain's mind? Should she even try? It wasn't her affair to meddle in, yet how could she not help when she saw a need?

The moment she opened her bedroom door to step into the hallway, she was greeted by two eager faces. Betsy and Thea had clearly hurried with their own dress. Thea's buttons were askew, and Betsy's collar was half tucked into her neckline.

"Good morning, girls. Don't you look bright and ready to conquer the day?" She smoothed Betsy's curls. "Come inside. I have something for you."

Returning to her dressing table, she drew a pair of ribbons from her traveling case. "Hop up here." She lifted Betsy to sit on the stool and reached for her hairbrush. In a moment she had the ribbon tied in a band over Betsy's hair, letting her sweet brown curls frame her chubby cheeks. She straightened the child's collar and pronounced her perfect.

"What's this?" Thea squatted beside Rich's sea chest at the foot of the bed, her arms wrapped about her knees. "Who is Major Richardson?" She wrinkled her freckled nose as her finger traced the stenciled name.

A quick stab went through Sophie, and she forced a smile. "He was Lady Richardson's son and the man I was going to marry. That's his sea chest, and it holds his belongings." The words were hard to say but not as achingly painful as they had been a month ago. Perhaps she was beginning to heal.

Guilt flickered like a candle flame in a draft. Did she want to heal? Was healing forgetting?

Before she could sort it out, Thea asked, "Where is he then?"

"He's in heaven with Jesus. He was a soldier, and he passed away."

"Oh, he's dead like our folks." She straightened, matter of fact in her speech and movements. "We don't have anything that belonged to them. The old earl had the vicar clean out our cottage and sell everything off.

You must be glad to have that stuff, to remember him by." She frowned. "Sometimes I can't remember what mum and da looked like, even though I try really hard."

Sophie nodded. "I know." She was grateful to have a miniature of Rich to keep his likeness alive for her. It was twin to one painted of her that she had gifted him before he'd left for the war. Perhaps she should find that painting and put the two together. They could rest on her bedside table. But that would mean opening the sea chest, and she wasn't ready to do that just yet. "Talking about what you remember can help keep those memories alive for you. Perhaps you can speak to Penny about it. She might be able to help you."

Thea shook her head, drumming her fingers on her crossed arms. "Penny doesn't like to talk about our folks. She tries to shush me up when I ask. She says it was a shameful thing that mama drank all that laudanum and left us on purpose."

Suicide? No wonder Penny didn't want to talk about it. Poor girl.

"Let me fix your hair, Thea." She didn't know what to say to someone young about such a heavy topic. Thea seemed quite accepting of it, but there would come a time in her life when the ramifications of taking one's own life would become apparent.

"You can try, but Penny says my hair always acts like it's been pulled through a thicket backward. It isn't curly, and it isn't straight. It just does what it wants. And Miss Fricklin was forever complaining about the color. She said it was an 'indication of my temper.' Do you think that's true? That all people with red hair have terrible tempers? Maybe it's people talking about their hair all the time that gets them riled?" She spoke the entire time Sophie brushed and braided her hair, tying the ends together with the second ribbon.

"I've no idea, but if someone talked about my hair as a bad thing all the time, I'd get angry too. Rest assured that you have beautiful, thick hair that is destined to draw attention for the rest of your life. I can only imagine your first village assembly. The young men will be tripping over themselves to dance with you."

Thea's face twisted in a horrified grimace. "You sound like Penny. She's all atwitter about boys and wearing her hair up and dancing." She batted her eyelids and pretended to swoon. "But boys are foul, and I don't know why she goes on and on about them."

"Well, perhaps someday you'll feel differently. Let's go find Penny and see what Mrs. Chapman has arranged for breakfast. Have you seen Miss Mamie this morning?"

They headed down the staircase, Betsy holding Sophie's hand and the banister, taking one step at a time, while Thea bounced down like a fox-hound puppy let off the leash.

The breakfast room was deserted, but laughter came from the kitchen. Mrs. Chapman stood at the fireplace, a griddle in her hand, while Mamie sat at the table slicing day-old bread. Penny emerged from what Sophie assumed was the larder with two glass containers in her hands.

"These are labeled strawberry preserves, but I don't think they're still edible. The tops have gone all furry."

"Absolutely not. We'd all be sick before morning tea." Mrs. Chapman made a sweeping motion with her spoon. "Put them in the washbasin. I'll clean them out and scald the jars."

A fair few pots and crocks sat in the washbasin already, testament to Mrs. Chapman going through the pantry herself.

Penny looked at her sisters. "What happened to your hair?" she asked Thea.

"Lady Sophie brushed it, and it didn't even hurt. Not like when you do it. And she likes red hair."

"You must have stood still for her then, which is more than you do for me." Penny chucked Betsy under the chin. "Mrs. Chapman is making pikelets, and then we're going to help her clean house. Without complaining. After we clean, we can go for a walk to the beach."

Thea's face grew stormy, and she crossed her arms, but before she could protest, Mrs. Chapman leveled a stare her way. "Work first, then you get the reward. We won't tackle the entire house in a day. In fact, we won't even get out of this room, I shouldn't think. There's enough to do cleaning and sorting and taking inventory to keep us busy until lunchtime, if we all pitch in."

"A sound plan." The captain spoke from the kitchen doorway. "Until I can hire a replacement, Mrs. Chapman, are you willing to continue to take charge of the kitchens? If so, you will be paid for your work, and you will have sole command of the victuals and the larder."

Sophie could not stop staring. It was the first time she'd seen him dressed in anything other than his uniform. He wore a tailcoat of forest green, buff breeches, and a golden waistcoat. His linens were snowy, but he hadn't bothered with a cravat. He looked very much an earl in his non-naval clothing.

If Cilla had seen him attired thusly, she might have described him as more than just dashing. Sophie shook her head. She had always preferred men in uniform, hadn't she? And here she was noticing a man in civilian dress?

He still moved with military precision, however, and though he had no manservant—probably why he'd opted not to wear a cravat—his presentation was faultless. One could catch one's reflection in the shine of his boots.

Betsy stood before him, staring up, hands clasped behind her in a miniature copy of his stance. He looked down at her, unable to come farther into the room unless she moved or he bowled her over.

The captain raised one eyebrow and looked about for assistance.

"She'll stand there all day." Thea dropped into a chair and inched it to the table. "If you want her to move, you have to say good morning." She reached for a slice of bread.

"Indeed?" He bowed slightly. "Good morning, Miss Pembroke."

"Good morning, Cap'n." Betsy beamed and turned on one toe to return to Penny's side.

Mrs. Chapman slid a plate of pikelets onto the table. "Good morning, sir. Breakfast is ready, such as it is."

"Mrs. Chapman, you are on the payroll as of yesterday. Make a list of what supplies you need to keep the place going. I'll send Grayson into town once we've gone over the books, and he'll bring back provisions." He took the seat next to Sophie. "Good morning, Lady Sophia."

This close, she could see flecks of green in his blue eyes. They were the color of the sea, which she supposed was fitting. She helped Betsy into her chair, and Penny found her seat as well.

Betsy took Sophie's hand and then reached across the table to Penny.

Penny clasped her sister's fingers and reached for Thea's, and Thea took Mamie's.

"You're s'posed to hold hands for the blessing." Betsy clambered to her knees so she could reach better. "You forgot last night."

Sophie swallowed and put her hand into his. He threaded their fingers together, pressing palm to palm, and warmth seeped up her arm.

He cleared his throat. "I only know naval graces. I could say Nelson's Grace, but it's rather short. Perhaps . . .

Bless, O Lord, before we dine
Each dish of food, each glass of wine
And make us evermore aware
How much, O Lord, we're in Thy care.

"Amen," Betsy declared.

"We don't have wine. We have water," Thea pointed out. "Still, your prayer is better than the graces said at Miss Fricklin's. Those went on forever and always talked about what sinners we had been that day." She poured a bit of treacle on her bread. "I could never figure out what we did that was so awful. She wouldn't let us do anything fun, just study and keep quiet all the time."

"That must have been excruciating for you," the earl said, his tone wry. "Perhaps her prayers were in the way of preventative medicine."

"What does that mean?" Thea asked, licking her finger.

"Stop that and wipe your hands properly," Penny said. "It means she was hoping to use guilt and dire warnings to keep you from being naughty. Not that it helped much. You were in trouble the moment your feet hit the floor in the morning."

The back door opened before Thea could fire back, and the steward, Mr. Grayson, slipped in. When he saw them all eating in the kitchen, he stopped. Bobbing quickly, he snatched off his hat. "Morning, guv. Ladies. Sorry to intrude."

"Come in. Have you brought the ledgers?"

He tapped the book under his arm. "I brought my records. The old earl wasn't in his right mind there at the end, and he wouldn't let me work on the books. Kept them in his sleeping quarters and scribbled in them from time to time. I can't make out anything from the last few months, though I did my best. I kept a tally of new lambs and calves, and how many acres were planted, and the crops that went in."

"Very well. Perhaps you'd like a cup of tea, and then we can begin. The ladies have their duty assignments, and I suppose I have mine." The earl speared a pikelet and put it on his plate. "Have you broken your fast?"

"Aye, milord. The wife makes a good thick porridge." He patted his lean middle. "Sticks with a man all day."

"I didn't know you were married."

"Aye, getting on for twelve years now. She's anxious, waiting to hear if we'll be staying on." He raised his brows in that beseeching way he'd adopted last night.

The earl lowered his knife and fork. "Perhaps you'd like to wait in the study. I'll be along shortly."

Grayson bobbed again and all but scuttled through the kitchen. He had to be frustrated to have his future unsettled.

"Are you thinking of not keeping him on in the position?" Sophie asked.

"I cannot say just yet. I don't like to be rushed into decisions." The earl cut his pikelet into even squares and ate rapidly. "Of course, in the heat of battle, you must make quick decisions, but that is where training and planning come to the fore. However, I've had no training or planning for managing an estate. Therefore, I will take as much time as prudent before making determinations."

Which method she also assumed covered his decision regarding the future of the Pembroke girls. Penny looked thoughtful, Betsy unconcerned as she licked a bit of treacle off her spoon.

Thea, however, appeared more than willing to plow in where angels feared to tiptoe. "So I guess we have to wait to hear what you're going to do with us until you have a good long think about it?"

The question landed in the middle of the table with a thud.

"That's correct." The captain ate the last bite of his breakfast and excused himself.

"Thea, why can't you keep your mouth closed once in a while?" Penny scolded. "You do realize that not every single thought you have has to be uttered?"

"What? What did I do?"

"If you want the earl to like us and possibly continue to look after our welfare, perhaps you shouldn't accuse him of neglecting you by taking time making decisions. The entire world doesn't revolve around you."

Sophie had wanted to intervene, but Penny was doing a fine job. No doubt she'd had plenty of practice as a stand-in mother to her younger siblings. A pity such responsibility had fallen to one so young.

"Ladies, enough talk. It's time to work. For this morning, Mrs. Chapman is in charge, and we will follow her lead." Sophie reached for a tea cloth on the sideboard and bent to wind it around her hair. "I would suggest you protect your hair as well. This is bound to be dusty."

The cleaning went as well as could be hoped for considering that the crew was mostly youngsters. By the time noon arrived, the kitchen and pantry were spotless, and Mrs. Chapman had a list of provisions to keep house for the next fortnight or so.

"I know we might not be here that long, but I thought I would lay in enough for the captain for the coming days." The housekeeper tucked her pencil into her gray-streaked hair. "I've added a few cleaning supplies like beeswax, lye, and vinegar. I hope the captain doesn't mind. But what we really need are a few maids, a laundress, and a footman or two." She pointed to the final row of jugs and baskets lining the table. "Penny and Betsy, be loves and put those in the larder, baskets on the floor and crockery on the shelf by the door."

"Do you think it would benefit to write to Charlotte and see if any of her girls in training would want to try for a position here?" Sophie unwound her hair cloth and handed it to Thea, who was tasked with taking them outside and giving them a good shake.

"If you were going to stay, I would say yes, but I don't know how it would eventuate unless you had a reliable housekeeper to continue their training. Not to mention, would the captain—I mean the earl—wish to hire women with, shall we say, checkered histories to staff his manor house?"

"That's always going to be the challenge, isn't it? Will people give those women a chance to move on from their pasts and make new lives for themselves?"

"What's a checkered history?" Thea asked, bringing the wadded tea cloths inside.

Sophie looked to Mrs. Chapman for help.

"It means someone who has done something they wished they hadn't." The housekeeper took the cloths. "And now they want to change and do things differently."

"Oh." Thea pulled a face. "I thought it was something bad." She sounded disappointed. "Everybody's done something they wished they hadn't."

Sophie pondered that. Thea was correct. Everyone had regrets of one sort or another, and it could be hard to get past those regrets, to forgive yourself, and to receive forgiveness in order to change and move on.

Like the captain regretting his part in Rich's death. He had said he was unable to forgive himself, and Sophie had not said aloud that she forgave him, because she wasn't certain she had forgiven him in her heart.

She was willing to forgive the prostitutes who came to Charlotte for help, because their sins didn't affect Sophie. What they did had cost her nothing. But when someone had come to her admitting fault in something that had cost Sophie her dearest love, Sophie had withheld words of forgiveness.

Her conscience prodded her, but she forced it to quiet down. She wasn't ready to face such thoughts, nor to act upon them just now. When she'd had some time to think, when she had spent some time in that cottage by the sea and gotten some distance on both the grief and the captain, she would work through her feelings about forgiveness.

"Let's see about washing ourselves up. We've earned some lunch, and then we'll see about going down to the water. How does that sound?"

If Halbert Grayson had been on a ship under his command, Charles would be sorely tempted to bring the man up on charges of incompetence and dereliction of duty. These ledgers were a disaster. Great amounts of information were missing, and much of the rest was illegible.

"His lordship took the books from me about six months before he passed, and he did all the recording himself. He wouldn't even let me look at them, just called me in sometimes to give a report. I don't think the guv even understood me half the time."

What about the weeks since? Surely Grayson could have made a start on cleaning up this mess once the old earl had died.

The man lacked initiative, which would not bode well for leaving him in charge when Charles went back to sea. For all his supposed experience, the steward seemed at a loss when it came to making decisions on his own.

"Without knowing what the new earl would want, and with the magistrate telling me I should wait until someone in authority arrived, I bided my time. As I said, I kept track of the lambing and calving and crops, but everything else stopped."

"I assume you collected rents?" Charles ran his finger across the columns of the ledger, trying to decipher the headings. "How often do you do that?"

"Supposed to be twice a year, but I didn't collect this spring because the earl hadn't fulfilled his part of the bargain. No repair work got approved for the tenant cottages, and no firing got provided for the first half of the year. With most of the trees gone from this part of the country, his lordship had been forced to haul coal and peat. He brought in a shipload of peat last year from Ireland, but he refused to let me lay in another supply midwinter. He was out of his head, but I didn't have leave to release the funds without his permission. I didn't think it right to charge rent when folks were having a hard time keeping fires lit."

Charles nodded. The man really had been hard-pressed and in a difficult position, and he supposed Grayson's heart had been in the right place. Still, it was bothersome that the steward had so little fortitude and sense of leadership. He would probably make an excellent second-in-command as long as someone was on hand to give him orders.

"That's enough for today. Thank you, Grayson. I'll tour the buildings and grounds this afternoon. Tomorrow morning we'll meet to create a plan of action."

"Would you like me to go with you? I can meet you at the stables to ride 'round the property."

Charles refused to admit to his steward that he'd never sat on a horse in his life. "That won't be necessary. I'll reconnoiter on my own first. I'm sure I'll have plenty of questions for you tomorrow."

"Very good, sir." Grayson stood and began gathering the ledgers.

"Leave those. I'll peruse them more thoroughly tonight."

"Are you certain, sir? Now that I have your leave, I could begin to fill in the entries that are missing. At least as much as I can." He kept his hand on the leather-bound books. "It would be no trouble, sir."

"No, thank you. I'd like to spend more time with them as they are. And I am of a mind to begin a new ledger once we establish where things stand currently."

The steward had begun nodding before Charles was even half finished. "An excellent idea, sir. There is a blank ledger book in there." He indicated a cellaret, originally built to hold wine bottles but now stuffed with rolled papers and piled with stacks of books.

"Captain Earl?" Betsy's face peered around the study door. The ribbon holding her hair had slipped backward and looked in danger of falling off, but she beamed at him, tugging at her earlobe. "Sophie asks if you are ready for your lunch. We're going to take a walk after. Are you coming?"

Her smile and eager words spread a bit of warmth through his chest. She was an appealing child, and for some unknown reason, she seemed to want his company. And she'd called him Captain Earl. An engaging mistake.

Lunch was a hit-and-miss affair, provisions running as low as they were. The kitchen was spotless, a testament to how the ladies had spent their morning. Lady Sophia's cheeks bore color, and her hair was a bit mussed from being wrapped in a towel. It pleased him that though she was a highborn lady, she wasn't above pitching in and working when needed. During the meal, he perused Mrs. Chapman's list.

"I'm sorry luncheon is so paltry," the housekeeper apologized. "Most of what was in the pantry was spoiled."

He took a bite of the poached egg on toast. "If you had seen some of the things we had to eat at sea, you would realize this is bounty."

"What did you eat? Fish?" Thea asked.

"Upon occasion. But the worst was the ship's biscuit. It's a cracker baked so hard you must soak it in your tea or coffee or grog in order to be able to chew it. It had plenty of nicknames, but the one I found most accurate was 'worm castle.' Weevils liked to bore into the crackers, and you had to bang the biscuit on the table in the hopes of dislodging them."

"Ew," Thea protested. "That's nasty."

"The only thing worse than finding a worm in your biscuit is finding half a worm."

The girls shuddered, and Penny pushed back her plate.

He caught Lady Sophia's glance and remembered that he wasn't in a wardroom.

"I beg your pardon, ladies. Being so long at sea has robbed me of my manners."

"I like it. You talk different from anyone I ever met." Thea propped her elbows on the table and her chin in her fists. "I bet you have some great stories."

Penny gently pushed Thea's elbows off the table. "Did you have lots of men on your ship?"

"The *Dogged* is a thirty-six gun frigate, and at full capacity carries two hundred men." Charles crossed his knife and fork on his empty plate. "Twenty officers, two dozen Royal Marines, and the rest able or ordinary seamen."

"That's enough men even for you, Pen." Thea laughed. "Surely you could find one to fall in love with you out of that crowd."

Penny glared, leaning back with a huff and crossing her arms. "You're impossible. Your tongue is hung in the middle, and both ends flap constantly."

"I'd rather be known as a chatterbox than a—"

"Let's take that walk now, shall we?" Lady Sophia interrupted. "Thank you, Mrs. Chapman. Lunch was excellent."

Charles rose as the ladies did. "I'll send Grayson into the village to purchase the items on your list."

"I'd best go with him. No man of my acquaintance has ever been able to shop from a woman's list and get it right." Mrs. Chapman tugged at her apron strings. "If you are agreeable, that is."

The woman was probably used to operating without much oversight, having run Primrose Cottage for so long. He admired her initiative, wishing some of it would rub off on his steward.

"Very well." He reached into his pocket and withdrew several gold coins. "Use what you need, keep an account, and return the rest to me."

Mrs. Chapman's brows rose, and she took the coins, letting then clink in her hand. "Surely this is far too much?"

"I'll confess I have no idea of the cost of provisions. I left all that to my quartermaster and victualing officer, and the navy paid for it all."

"Don't you wish me to hand this over to Mr. Grayson to keep an accounting?" She stared at the coins as if she'd never seen so much money in one place before.

"No. I trust you to see that it's well spent."

"Would you also do me a favor, Mrs. Chapman?" Lady Sophia withdrew an envelope from her pocket. "Would you take this letter to the village and post it for me? I promised to write home regularly. If the duke doesn't hear from me soon, he'll be down here to investigate."

"Of course, milady. I'll do it first thing."

Charles felt a bit like a herding dog, getting everyone outside. Mrs. Chapman set off with Grayson in a trap pulled by a shaggy gray horse with feet the size of portholes. The housekeeper wore a proud, determined look as she clutched Lady Sophia's letter in one hand and her reticule in the other. Grayson seemed a bit down at the mouth being forced to run errands in the village rather than accompany them about the estate.

After being cooped up inside all morning, Charles wanted to strike out briskly across the open grass, but with the women along, particularly Lady Richardson and Betsy, he was forced to shorten his steps and reduce his speed. He'd elected to go bareheaded because the only hat he possessed was his naval bicorn complete with cockade, which would look ridiculous with his civilian garb. If he were forced to be on land for very long, he'd have to consult a haberdasher.

Please, God, don't make me stay on land. Perhaps even now a command was opening up and Admiral Barrington was drafting his orders. Might he be back aboard a ship within a fortnight? Or at the very least, in Portsmouth seeing to the preparations needed to get his ship seaworthy and provisioned?

A sense of urgency dogged his steps, and he organized his tasks in his mind.

First, he needed to get the estate on a solid footing with a reliable man in charge. It was not looking as if Grayson would be that man. Should he inquire in the village, or should he send farther afield? He cast his mind to officers he had served with who were now retired. Might one be suitable?

While searching for the right man, he also needed to sort out the situation with the Pembroke girls. Should he take on the duty as their guardian in his uncle's stead? If so, he would be responsible for providing them with an education and a safe place to live. The well-being of three young ladies was a serious task for which he felt totally unequipped. Still, with the proper boarding school, they might well flourish.

Lady Sophia stopped to listen to something Betsy was saying, reminding him that he had another responsibility. He had promised to see Lady Sophia and Lady Richardson installed in a cottage by the sea. It was a debt he must pay as quickly as possible. They had already sacrificed enough for him. He felt as if a clock ticked in the back of his mind, held by Rich. Beyond a certain date, Charles would officially be considered lax in fulfilling his promise to look after Sophie.

Debts delayed were debts betrayed.

As helpful as it was to have Lady Sophia, Lady Richardson, and Mrs. Chapman here at Gateshead taking care of the house and the girls, he mustn't presume upon them any longer than he had to. He must be careful, because the longer he spent with Lady Sophia, the more his heart was in danger.

God, what is it You require? Each time I think I cannot possibly bear up under yet another responsibility or change, one leaps at me like a fish from a net. I long for order and clarity, but both elude me. Why won't You make Your demands plain to me?

Thea quartered like a ship tacking against the wind. She was as restless as the sea. Had he ever possessed that much energy? His sailing masters had probably thought so once upon a time. He felt ancient beside Thea's youthful vitality.

Penny and Lady Richardson walked side by side, the older woman's arm tucked through Penny's elbow. Charles had never known his grandmothers, but if he could pick one, he would make her just like Lady Richardson. Kind. Wise. Gentle.

Young Penny made him uneasy. If Thea could be believed, this girl on the cusp of womanhood was much enamored of the male gender. Returning her to an all-girls' school took on a new urgency.

As they neared the cliff, he put his fingers to his lips and let out a piercing whistle. Thea skidded to a halt and looked over her shoulder.

He beckoned her.

She jogged back, eyes full of questions. Sunshine highlighted the freckles on her face, and wisps of red hair played about her temples and cheeks.

"Until I've had an opportunity to investigate the stability of that cliff and the staircase leading to the beach, I want you to stay away from the edge."

"But we are going down there, aren't we?" She turned so the breeze would blow into her face. "Sophie promised we could go down to the ocean."

"That is my intention, but not until I am certain it is safe." He put his finger under her chin until she was looking right at him. "You will stay here until I give you leave to move, understood?"

She lifted her chin from his touch and snapped a cheeky salute. "Aye, aye, Captain."

Someone really should curb her insubordination. When it came time to choose a school, perhaps he should inquire into their discipline regimen. She needed to be taken in hand.

He approached the cliff, wary but unafraid. The ground seemed stable enough here, with a worn path cutting toward the edge. Some sort of daisylike flower danced on the breeze in the tall grass, and he was reminded of the unkempt garden behind Primrose Cottage.

Sophie's favorite place.

Why did it please him that his new property exhibited some of the same traits as the place she loved? God willing, he wouldn't be here long enough to enjoy it, which meant Lady Sophia would not either.

At the cliff edge, a wooden platform and staircase jutted out. The staircase turned back on itself three times before ending on the sand far below. Charles had a good head for heights, having learned to climb the ratlines of a sailing ship at a young age, but he approached the first landing with care.

Like everything on the estate, the steps were in need of repair. They cupped and curled, separating from the nails holding them to the stringers. Salt air and sunshine were hard on wood. The railing seemed sturdy enough, but a thorough inspection and restoration were in order for the entire structure. Hopefully, the small village would boast a carpenter fit for the job. Finding one would be a task for his new steward.

The cove lay before him, two long arms of land arcing out in an embrace. At the base of the cliff, in the center of the arc, a long pier jutted into the water, and a sloop rocked gently alongside. The boat he'd been told about. She would bear some investigation. Near the foot of the pier, a covered shed listed, in worse condition than the staircase. Charles made his way down to the beach, pausing for a moment to listen and inhale. Brine, wet sand, fresh air, seabirds, the slap of water against a hull.

Peace.

Remembering the ladies waiting atop the cliff, he studied the rough face. He found several places where the rock had given way and crashed to the beach, leaving piles and shards of rubble. Closer to the water, the shore was smooth-packed sand with a few pebbles. No evidence that the rock falls reached the sea. Ribbons of seaweed marked where the tide had pushed in. The ladies should be safe enough as long as they stayed away from the cliff face.

When he reached the top once more, he found the girls seated in a circle on the grass. Lady Richardson showed Betsy and Penny how to braid daisy stems into a wreath. Thea lay back on the grass, limbs askew, like a rag doll.

"That one looks like a badger." She pointed to a cloud. "And that one looks like a squashed pillow."

"I rather thought that one looked like the Prince Regent." Lady Sophia shielded her eyes against the afternoon sun. "How was your climb? Are we permitted to go down?"

"The stairs are safe enough, though we'll have to take care. Once we're on the sand, you must all stay away from the cliff itself. There have been a few rock falls, though I don't know how recent." He offered her his hand and helped her rise. "Miss Thea, you will go down with me, holding my hand the entire time. Lady Sophia, if you will take Betsy?"

Penny helped Lady Richardson to her feet and nodded to Charles that she understood that she would aid the elderly woman.

Thea talked the entire way, asking questions and not waiting for answers before heading in a new direction with another query. He was reminded of her sister's claim that Thea's tongue was hinged in the middle. Once they were on the sand, Charles let go of Thea's hand, and she made straight for the water.

"Can you swim?" he asked.

"I don't know. I've never tried." Her words drifted back over her shoulder.

"Then until you learn how, don't get wet. I'm not in the mood to rescue you." Swimming lessons. Girls who lived by the sea should know how to swim in case of an emergency.

He paused. These girls didn't live by the sea. They were merely guests here until he could find a school to take them.

"Can I at least look for shells?" She planted her fists on her skinny waist, tilting her head as if exasperated with his strictures.

"As long as they're on the beach and not in the water, be my guest." With the rest of the ladies now safely on the sand, he headed toward the boat. At last, an environment in which he could feel at ease. Being with women, regardless of age, was well outside his comfort.

The sloop, the *Shearwater*, named after the seabird, he supposed, rocked gently on its mooring lines, stern facing the shore. Someone must care for the boat, because it was the first thing on the estate in decent repair. The sails were furled tightly and tied properly, and the ropes all looked fairly new. Someone had spent some time sanding and caulking the deck. The lines fastening the boat to the pier were long enough to allow the boat to rise with the tide when it came in. Whoever the caretaker was, Charles sensed it wasn't Grayson. Nothing about the man spoke of ability around boats.

Burlap bags filled with straw or grass lined the edge of the dock to keep the boat from hitting the pilings. He hauled on a mooring line and pulled the sloop close before stepping over the padding and onto the deck. Tight, well-kept rigging and a sturdy mast, and when he looked into the bilges, very little water sloshed around. A trickle of excitement went through him. Perhaps if he were here long enough, he could take her out for a quick sail, just to get the feel of her. It had been a long time since he'd handled the tiller on a boat of this size.

The seas were calm, and the boat rocked only slightly, but he had no trouble keeping his balance. She was a trim little craft. He would enjoy sailing her in the coming days.

The boat shed looked a different situation. Listing slightly, with rafters showing in places where the shake shingles had blown or rotted off, the weathered boards looked fit for a bonfire. He climbed out of the sloop and headed back up the pier. The door to the boat shed creaked and dragged in an arc along the floor. Shafts of sunlight poked through the holes near the peak of the roof, but the corners and under the eaves remained in shadow. The smell of dank burlap and wet rope greeted him.

So did a pair of yellow eyes. He froze, adjusting to the gloom, trying to make out what it could be that stared at him so intently.

From a perch high in one corner, a large owl studied him. Two tufts of feathers stood up on his head, looking like ears and giving him a decidedly stern visage.

Charles exhaled. He would give the fellow a wide berth. No point in disturbing him. A quick poke around the shed told him that whatever it had been used for in the past, it was empty now. The floor had several wear patterns and grooves, but they were old and filled with sand.

If it weren't for the owl, he'd have the building torn down. For now, he'd leave it. The bird had clearly been using it as an abode for some time, if the condition of the floor beneath his perch was any indication.

Emerging into the sunshine, he nearly ran over Thea.

"Can I go on the boat? What's in there? It looks ready to fall over." She tried to edge around him, but he moved a half step to the side.

"The place is ready to fall down—therefore it isn't safe for little girls. There's nothing of interest in there." He hesitated. "No, that's not correct. I'll let you look inside, but you have to be quiet. Not a peep, understood?"

Her brown eyes widened, and she nodded, clamping her lips shut. He guided her to stand in the doorway. Without a word, he pointed to the corner.

The golden eyes blinked, and the bird shifted a bit on his perch, his wings spreading a few inches from his body as he resettled himself.

Thea exhaled silently, her cheeks puffing out. Charles eased her back and shut the door gently, lifting it so it wouldn't dig along the pier boards.

"That's the biggest bird I ever saw." Thea hopped from one foot to the other. "He's big enough to carry me away."

"Probably not that big."

"What kind of bird is it?"

"It's an owl of some sort. Let's go see the others. You can tell them about the bird, and you can let them know he's not to be disturbed." He started when she put her hand in his, as trusting as . . . well, as a child, he supposed. The contact felt companionable.

Lady Sophia and Betsy walked, heads down, looking for shells, and Lady Richardson and Penny were well down the sand to where the cliff curved toward the sea, but they were on their way back.

When the group was assembled, Charles produced a handkerchief for the seashells. "You'll want to boil these for a while. Otherwise, there's a chance that whatever called it home might still be in there, and they'll begin to stink. I'll carry them for you, if you like."

Sophie handed the shells over, dusting the sand from her hands. "Thank you. I've never gathered shells before. It's a delightful pastime, don't you think?"

"If you want the best shells, you should come as the first tide goes out in the morning. However"—he raised his voice so everyone could hear—"no one is to come down to the beach without an escort. Girls, you are not to come without an adult. The cliff isn't stable, the stairs are in need of repair, and while the ocean looks calm and inviting today, it's nothing with which you should trifle."

"We'll stay away from the cliff," Penny assured him. "And we know how dangerous the sea can be." Grief flitted across her pretty young features, and he was reminded that their father had been a boatman.

Wherever the *Shearwater* had gone down, it couldn't have been too bad a wreck. The boat had been salvaged, repaired, and now looked seaworthy.

"It's beautiful here. I hope we can come again before we have to leave." Sophie turned to look at the horizon.

Betsy's eyes glistened, and she buried her head in Sophie's side. "I don't want you to leave. And I don't want to leave either." Her arms came around Sophie's legs. "I like you. Why can't we all stay?"

Lady Sophia bent and hugged the child. "I like you, too, sweetling."

She looked up at Charles, and he felt lower than a seabed. He needed to move on with his plans for what should happen with these girls. It wasn't fair to leave them drifting. He knew what they wanted, but how could he give it to them?

"The tide is coming in. We should return to the house."

Sophie sent him a troubled look, but she clasped Betsy's hand, indicating that Lady Richardson and Penny should go first. The ladies trudged up the stairs with much less enthusiasm than they'd gone down. When he would have taken Thea's hand for the return trip, she avoided him and reached for Sophie's other hand. Her little back was stiff, and her shoes made a defiant thump on each tread.

Charles lingered to look out to sea, waiting until the girls were on the second landing before he put his foot on the bottom stair. The kerchief of shells dangled from his fingers. There was no way to make everyone happy, and he should let them know his decision sooner rather than later. God had made him a sailor, not a father figure, and it was best everyone understood that. Then he could see to fulfilling his debt to Lady Richardson and Sophie by finding them a nice cottage for the remainder of the summer.

He'd sit the girls down tonight and explain things, and he'd ask Sophie for help drafting letters to send to the best boarding schools. At least he had the money, and now the social standing, to demand the best care and education possible. God had provided the means, and Charles would employ them to see the girls cared for properly.

He paused to look once more out to sea.

He heard the rocks as they gave way, and he'd turned halfway, to look up, only to catch a rock on the head that sent him tumbling to the sand. Blackness enveloped him as the seashells slipped from his hand.

Chapter 8

"He's too big to carry. Penny, go back toward the house. Try the barn. Or the nearest cottage. See if you can find someone to help us." Sophie held her monogrammed handkerchief to the cut on the captain's brow. It was right at his hairline and already swelling. She tried to straighten his limbs while not moving the handkerchief, but it was awkward. Her hands shook.

"How did this happen?" Mamie asked. "It wasn't one of us climbing the stairs who dislodged the rocks, was it?" Her hands fluttered in distress. "The poor man."

"No, the rocks came from higher up on the cliff face." Sophie tried to recall the exact sequence. "It was most unfortunate timing for the captain, standing in that spot when the cliff decided to give way." She checked the wound, turned the handkerchief, and pressed it to the cut again. There was a lot of blood, but she didn't know if that meant the wound was severe. Head wounds tended to bleed. She was more concerned with whether the stone had broken Charles's skull.

What would she do if God took Charles too? That thought brought her up short. It wouldn't be the same as losing Rich, but she wished Charles no harm.

"Is he dead?" Thea squatted, her arms wrapped around her knees. "He looks dead."

"Hush, child. He's not dead. He's been knocked senseless." To satisfy her growing dread, Sophie checked to see that he was breathing. His chest rose and fell in a comfortingly even manner.

Betsy bent at the waist and patted his cheek with her chubby palm. "Wake up, Captain Earl. It's not time for a nap."

Mamie pulled a small vial from her purse and handed it to Sophie.

Uncapping the silver and glass container, Sophie waved it beneath the captain's nose. Even from this distance she could smell the sharp *sal volatile.*

Charles groaned and stirred, his hand coming up, but Sophie grabbed it. "Don't. You've taken a bang to the head. Lie still." She handed the smelling salts back to Mamie with a grateful smile. Now that the captain was conscious, she felt as if a giant fist had let loose of her ribs.

Footsteps clattered overhead, and Sophie tried to shield the captain from the shower of sand that accompanied the noise. Penny leapt down the last few treads, and a somberly dressed man with wispy white hair followed at a careful-yet-still-fast rate.

"I didn't have to go all the way to the house," Penny panted. "This man was coming across the grass toward the cliff."

"I'm the vicar. Dunhill's my name. I was making a call upon the new earl, and when I found no one at the house, I thought I'd see if you were at the shore." He knelt beside Charles. "I'm afraid you've found out the hard way how unstable the cliff face is." Gently he lifted the edge of Sophie's handkerchief. "If you'd been wearing a hat, it might have cushioned the blow."

Charles stirred. "Let me up. I feel like a sea turtle lying on his carapace."

"Are you sure?" Sophie asked. He must be in a great deal of pain. His face was pale, and lines of strain deepened the grooves around his mouth.

"Most definitely." His lips thinned.

"Then sit up slowly. If you get dizzy, lie down again." She put her hand beneath his shoulder, feeling again the whipcord strength of his muscles.

Once in a sitting position, he squinted. "I feel like I got hit by a sack of cannonballs." He touched the swelling on his forehead and winced.

"Do you think you can stand?" the vicar asked. "The tide's coming in. We need to get you up the stairs, or at the very least to the pier, or you'll soon be afloat."

Between Sophie and the vicar, they tugged Charles to his feet. He swayed, and she pressed her hands to his chest to stop him from going over forward. "Do you need to sit on the stairs?"

"No." He closed his eyes, keeping the handkerchief against his head. "Let's get moving."

Thea gathered the scattered seashells, and when she had them tucked into the captain's hanky, she said, "Now you're the one who needs to hold someone's hand."

Betsy's lower lip quivered, and two enormous tears spilled over her lower lashes.

"Oh, sweetling, don't worry. It's just a bump on the head." Sophie motioned for the child to come near. "It would take more than a paltry hit with a stone to fell the captain." She hugged the girl into her side.

"I don't like blood," she hiccupped.

"Neither do I." The captain winced. "Especially my own. But Lady Sophia is right. I've been hurt much worse and survived. I suppose it's a good lesson to all of us to be careful around the cliff." He bent a look at Thea. "Right?"

She shook the shells in the handkerchief and shrugged. "Right."

"Where is Miles?" the vicar asked. "He's never far from the *Shearwater*. I would have thought he'd have turned up by now." He put his hand under Charles's elbow. "Take it slowly and rest if you start to feel dizzy. Better to get there late than not get there at all."

"Who is Miles?" Sophie asked as they climbed. The stairs were too narrow for three abreast, so she contented herself with following behind the preacher and the captain. She guided Betsy ahead of her, and Thea came along after, each holding Sophie's hands.

"He's a bit of a tearaway, I suppose. He showed up sometime last summer. He's not yet twenty, I believe. Halbert Grayson lets him stay on because he looks after the *Shearwater*. Though where Miles sleeps is anyone's guess. He pops up and disappears like a woodland sprite."

The captain grunted. "I wondered who looked after the sloop."

"That would be Miles. The old earl seemed to like the boy. Which is more than I can say for how Rothwell felt for most everyone else. Though it's bad form to speak ill of the dead, milord, your uncle was as crossgrained a man as I've ever dealt with."

They finally reached the top of the cliff, and the captain halted. He closed his eyes, taking deep breaths.

Sophie released Thea's and Betsy's hands. "Penny, why don't you take Mamie and the girls to the house? We'll be along presently. If you would put some water on to boil, that would be helpful."

Charles opened his eyes and squinted against the glare of the sun.

"Does the light hurt your eyes, or is your vision blurry?" She put her hand on his shoulder.

"Yes and yes. Give me a moment to get my bearings." He blew out a long breath and walked toward the house.

She'd noticed Charles's gait when they were heading down to the beach. His shoulders swayed, and his stride had a roll to it. A seaman's walk. Even now when he couldn't move as quickly as he would like, he still looked as if he would be more comfortable on a ship's deck.

"I think you should go right to bed, Captain. Sir?" she asked the vicar. "Is there a physician in town?"

"No, the closest is Lyme Regis. We do have a local healer though. Would you like me to fetch her?" The vicar held the kitchen door open.

"I don't need my bed." Charles held on to the jamb for a moment, closing his eyes.

"It's either that or the divan in the parlor, but you must lie down." Sophie took his upper arm and guided him through the kitchen. Penny lifted a worried face, a folded towel in her hand.

"The water's not hot yet."

"That's fine. Bring it when it's ready. And a pitcher of cold as well."

The vicar knew his way through the house, leading them down the hall to the parlor unerringly. The room was still in a dusty state of neglect, but he seemed not to notice.

"Let us help you out of that coat, Lord Rothwell."

The captain's head came up at the use of the title. His shoulders went down as if pushed by a weight. He shrugged, and Sophie and the vicar helped him remove the tight jacket.

"Boots too." Sophie motioned to the vicar as the captain lay on the divan. She found a pillow for his head and peeled away the handkerchief. A lump the size of a hen's egg rose along his hairline, bisected by a rather nasty cut. It wasn't deep though, and the bleeding had stopped.

"How long was I unconscious?"

"Perhaps a minute or so?"

The vicar leaned over the back of the couch. "Do you feel unwell? Are your ears ringing? Perhaps you feel shivery?"

Sophie raised her brows.

"My father was a doctor." He looked into Charles's eyes. "By the daze in your expression, I would say you're concussed."

"What is the treatment?" Sophie had no nursing experience beyond tending Mamie's occasional cold. "Perhaps we should send for the doctor."

"Nonsense." Charles shook his head and then seemed to regret it, slamming his eyes closed and holding his crown as if he feared it might come off. "It's just a knock."

"Rest is the prescription. He should be kept still, and he shouldn't be allowed to sleep too long at a stretch." The vicar pushed away from the couch. "Beyond that it's a matter of managing the symptoms, I suppose, until they decrease."

"I'm sorry to meet under such circumstances, but I am grateful you were here. I don't know how I would have gotten him up that staircase."

"I would have walked," the captain grumbled.

Penny appeared with a steaming bowl of water, and Thea followed, toting a china pitcher. Mamie came in quietly, but Betsy marched in with a stack of tea cloths.

Sophie nearly burst into laughter. Betsy had somehow appropriated the captain's bicorn and wore it sideways, the points nearly touching her shoulders and the brim covering her eyes so she had to tip her head back to see where she was going.

"Thank you, ladies." She drew a side chair close to the sofa and pulled a small table near. "Set the water here." Removing the towels from Betsy's hands, she lifted the edge of the hat and tweaked the child's nose.

"Is he going to squawk when you clean him up?" Thea plonked the pitcher down. "That's a big bump."

"I am not going to be so undignified as to squawk. I shall be stoic and British to the core." The captain frowned at Thea, and she grinned back at him.

"At least you haven't addled your brains. The scully at Miss Fricklin's once told me of a man who fell out of a haymow and smacked his head, and ever after he couldn't talk right or walk right." She lurched around the room with one shoulder high and one leg dragging.

"You are a gruesome child." The captain used the back of the couch to pull himself into a sitting position.

"I know." Thea shrugged, uninsulted.

"You should lie down for this." Sophie dipped the edge of a cloth in the hot water.

"Nonsense. Just clean the cut, bandage it if you have to, and let's be done with it."

"I shall take my leave if you are certain you don't need me for anything else. Perhaps I could call tomorrow or the next day for a proper visit?" The vicar backed toward the door.

"Of course. And again"—Sophie dabbed at the cut—"I'm sorry we couldn't be more welcoming this time."

"I'll see myself out."

When he was gone, Sophie turned to the girls. "The captain needs quiet and rest. I'd like you to go upstairs and dust and straighten up the nursery. Please don't squabble, and don't move any furniture by yourselves. If you could keep watch out the window for Mrs. Chapman's return, you can come down the back stairs to help her carry in the things she's purchased."

Betsy crowded close, knocking the captain's hat askew on her head, and planted a kiss on his cheek. "Feel better, Captain Earl. I will come back and see you soon." She wrinkled her nose in a gamine grin.

The captain had opened his eyes the moment her lips touched his cheek, and he reached for her hand. "You're an excellent nurse, Betsy. Thank you."

The gruffness in his voice warmed Sophie's heart. He wasn't totally indifferent to the sweetness of the girls. Perhaps, if he grew fond of them, he might consider keeping them here at Gateshead.

Mamie put her hand on Thea's back. "I'll go upstairs with them, dear. We'll be quiet as can be." As they headed out into the hall, Mamie gently lifted the captain's bicorn from Betsy's head and placed it on the table beside the parlor door. When she looked back over her shoulder, she smiled.

Sophie wrung out a cloth in the cold water and folded it, laying it gently on Charles's brow. Mamie was flourishing being around the girls. She hadn't had a spell of absentmindedness all day, and she'd managed the shore visit well. Her cheeks had a healthy bloom, and her eyes were bright and aware.

"I feel an utter fool." Charles put his hand to the cloth, his eyes closed. "I'm supposed to be seeing to your well-being and safety, and here you are tending me."

"I don't mind. I'm only sorry you suffered an injury. We were fortunate that Mr. Dunhill appeared when he did." Sophie went to the front windows, pulling the drapes to lessen the light coming in. "Do you think you can rest?"

"I doubt it."

"Is the pain bad?" She returned to his side. "Perhaps I can see if there is such a thing as a medicine chest in the house and rummage up something for headaches."

"That's good of you, but no. I've suffered more pain than this and lived through it." He winced. "I'm sorry. That was insensitive of me."

Sophie gripped her hands. He had undoubtedly suffered great pain with his saber wound, but his words were a blunt reminder that Rich hadn't survived his injury. With all the happenings, getting to Gateshead, the girls' tumultuous arrival, the trip to the beach, and the captain's injury, she had been able to set aside the grief and constant sense of loss for a few days.

"Did he suffer? I know he must have, but he wouldn't let on in his letters." She pressed her hands against her middle. "Why? Why wouldn't he tell me? I'm trying so hard to understand, but it's as if he lied to me. Why wouldn't he talk about his injury, let us know how serious it was? He had to know for weeks that he wasn't getting better. If he had told us right away, maybe there was something I could have done. My brother is a powerful duke. He might have been able to get Rich evacuated from Portugal, brought home. Or somehow gotten me aboard a ship so I could have been with Rich, seen him one more time before he died." The words poured out in a torrent, and she was helpless to stop them. Anger and frustration flared anew in her chest, and hot tears burned her eyes.

So much for setting aside her grief and pain. Here she was letting it all out on an injured man.

"I think Rich didn't tell you for those very reasons. Believe me—I tried to change his mind." Charles let the wet cloth slip into his hand and placed it on the side of the pitcher. He slowly opened his eyes, pain, both physical and mental, showing there. "He was afraid, once peace had been declared, that your brother would use his connections to get you to the Peninsula. I think from the very outset, Rich knew he wouldn't survive his wounds. He hoped, but he knew it was a faint chance. He also knew . . ."

Gently, Charles took her hands as they sat knee to knee. His fingers were damp and chilly from the cloth, but comforting too, as he rubbed his thumbs on the backs of her hands. The connection was more than physical. This man had been there when Rich breathed his last. He, too, had cared for Rich and had agonized alongside him.

"He knew that you would suffer with him if he were to write to you about the severity of his wounds. He knew better than anyone the great tenderness of your heart, and he felt your burdens were heavy enough."

"Why couldn't he understand that nothing about him was a burden? That I deserved the truth? I was prepared to marry him, for better or worse, in sickness and in health." Heartbreak gripped her throat, constricting her airway.

His clasp on her hands tightened. "Please don't blame him. He was doing what he thought best, and in the end, he wasn't thinking clearly. But he was always thinking of you. He spoke of you constantly, and when he passed away, your name was on his lips. He made a hard decision that he felt was in your best interest. If you have to blame anyone, blame me. It was my fault from beginning to end."

Anger flared, and she withdrew her hands, escaping to the far side of the room to compose herself. He should have done his duty. If not for him, Rich would be here now. He should have written to her how serious Rich's condition was. If not for him, she would have found a way to be with her beloved before he died. Even as she thought this, she knew herself to be unjust. He had fulfilled Rich's wishes in saying nothing. Would she think more highly of him if he had betrayed his friend?

She wiped her cheeks with her palms, frustrated at crying in front of him. "I do beg your pardon."

He stood in the middle of the dim room, spreading his hands in appeal. "It is I who should beg your pardon . . . again. I had no desire to reopen your wounds, especially since I bear the blame for them. I will retire to my rooms, and tomorrow I will put out inquiries about cottages for rent. You will recover from your grief much sooner if you aren't forced to remember through my presence and undisciplined tongue."

"But what about the girls?"

His hands went behind his back and he paced slowly, as if each step sent a shaft of pain to his head. "I, too, must make a hard decision in the best interest of someone else. The girls will go to a boarding facility as soon as possible. They will be properly cared for by professionals, and I will resume my naval career knowing they are safe and well looked after."

Her strength deserted her, and she sank onto the closest chair. How could he even contemplate sending sweet Betsy away? And the ever-moving, ever-inquisitive Thea? And darling Penny, who already had so much responsibility on her young shoulders? A boarding school wasn't a home.

But how could he possibly understand? He'd never had a home of his own, at least not after the age of twelve.

"And Gateshead? What about your obligations here as the new earl?" She kept her voice as modulated as she could, but a tremor crept in anyway.

"I'll appoint a trustworthy man to see to the estate in my absence." He stopped pacing. "I do not believe Grayson is the man for the position, but I would appreciate it if you kept that to yourself until I tell him myself."

Difficult and unpopular decisions made for the good of . . . whom? Not for the girls, nor for Mr. Grayson.

No, the difficult and unpopular decisions Captain Charles Wyvern, the Earl of Rothwell, was making were for his own good.

In spite of his lingering headache and lack of sleep, Charles set about his tasks with unwavering determination the next morning. His first was to call Grayson into the study.

The steward slipped through the door like a wraith, hat in hand, shoulders bowed. He barely raised his chin to look at Charles. His entire demeanor confirmed to Charles that he was not the right man for the job of looking after Gateshead without supervision.

Charles paced the area behind his desk. He always thought better when on his feet, especially when faced with an unpleasant or difficult task.

"Grayson, I will do you the courtesy of not beating about the bush. I have decided to hire another man to take the job of steward here at Gateshead. While you have completed a modicum of work keeping the place together in the absence of leadership, your performance lacked the drive I believe the position requires. I think you will be better suited as a second-in-command, as it were, to a new man. It is my intention to continue with my naval career as soon as a new position opens for me, which will mean I will be away from the estate for long periods of time. The man I select for the job needs to be stern, strict, and a good leader of men. He must have an attention to detail and be accustomed to command. I feel the new steward would be better suited to the job if he came from outside the community, thereby being free of any local ties and loyalties that might prevent him from being evenhanded in his judgments." He paused his pacing to see how Grayson was taking the news.

Anger flared in the man's eyes, and then a flicker of . . . fear? He shifted his weight, staring at the rug.

"This will be a terrible blow to my wife." He tugged on his collar. "Are you putting us off the place then?" His dark eyes were stark at the possibility. "Please say we can stay on. I'll do any job. Gamekeeper, groom, even field hand if that's all you think I'm capable of. But Gateshead is my home. Please don't send me away." Desperation wrapped his words, and he mauled his hat in his fists.

What was the man afraid of? His wife's displeasure? Or possibly disappointing her? Or being jobless? Charles could allay at least some of the man's anxiety. "No. I will reward your loyalty to the old earl. You did your best, such as it was. If you are willing, you may stay on as the under-steward, assisting the head man with his duties. And you are welcome to lodge in the steward's cottage for the time being." He would be gracious. It was the Christian thing to do.

For a moment, a flash of calculation lit Grayson's eyes, and an eager smile split his face. "I see. Thank you for keeping me on." He bobbed his head again, this time with more vigor. "When will you be hiring the new man, milord? And when will you be returning to the navy?"

Grayson certainly was taking the news better than Charles had anticipated. Which showed how unsuitable for command he was. He accepted everything too meekly. A true leader would push back, demand explanations, fight for his place at the top.

"I'll fill the position soon. I'm writing to the Admiralty even now." He gestured to the stationary before him. "There are many newly retired officers currently seeking employment who have, I believe, the temperament and abilities to be good stewards on a property such as Gateshead."

"Very good, sir. I'm most obliged. The wife will be as well." Grayson lifted his shoulders, smoothing the brim of his hat.

"Until the new man arrives, you may continue in your current duties. You are dismissed."

Grayson sidled out of the study. Charles stared at the door, unsure what to make of the man. He appeared in turns inept, obsequious, calculating, sharp. Which was the real Halbert Grayson? Or was Charles merely addled from his blow to the head and ascribing motives where there were none?

He had barely settled back into writing when a tap sounded on the door. Was it the steward back, realizing the extent of his demotion and wanting to quarrel after all?

The Reverend Dunhill poked his head around the study door. "Good morning, milord. I just ran into Halbert Grayson in the hall. He looked most relieved. I take it you're keeping him on as steward? Most wise of you. He knows everyone on the estate and how things run here. Not exactly a fireball, but steady."

"Actually, I will be keeping him on, but not in his current capacity. I think a new man in charge is what the estate needs."

"A new man? Are you promoting someone from the estate? One of the crofters?" The preacher's brow furrowed. "I confess, that would be quite a leap in status for a shepherd or farmer. I'm not certain how the other tenants would react to such a move."

Charles set his pen in its holder. He supposed some curiosity about his plans was normal, but why should the local preacher care about who had charge of the estate?

"You'll think me a meddling fool." Dunhill shrugged his narrow shoulders. "It's just that the estate and the doings here affect the village in subtle and not-so-subtle ways. A good steward here has a positive effect on the outlook of the townspeople, and thus my job is easier."

That made sense, Charles supposed. "You may put your mind at ease that I will take care in my selection."

Dunhill pursed his lips. "I see." There was a long pause as the man appeared to digest this information.

"I will choose a man of good reputation who will not lead your parishioners astray or provide a negative impact upon the village." The man seemed overly cautious when it came to his flock.

The reverend jerked slightly, as if coming out of deep thought. "Of course. I would expect nothing less from a man of your character. How are you feeling? You look to be dealing with your injuries well. No lingering ill effects?"

"Other than the fact that it seems as if someone is driving pilings behind my eyes?" Charles held out his hand. "Have a seat." Though he really didn't have time for a lengthy conversation, it would be churlish to expect the reverend to leave too soon.

Shipboard protocols would dictate sending for coffee or tea, and he assumed the same held for manor houses. He started for the door to summon one of the girls to ask Mrs. Chapman if she could prepare some, but Dunhill stopped him.

"I hope you don't mind. I've brought someone with me. He's waiting in the hall." He held the door open. "Come along, Miles. Don't be nervous. The earl is quite kind, as I told you."

A young man stepped into the study, tensed as if to run. He wore a loose tan shirt of some course material and dark-brown breeches tucked into heavy boots. His sandy-brown hair needed a trim, and his eyes were a strange, yellowish gold that reminded Charles of the owl in the boathouse.

Perhaps seventeen or eighteen years? Stocky and keen eyed, like many a midshipman he'd commanded. "Miles? You're the young man who cares for the *Shearwater*?"

"Y-yes, sir."

"Who taught you about boats?" Nobody kept a craft in good trim by accident.

"My granddad, sir."

"And where is he?"

"Dead."

The boy wasn't exactly loquacious.

"What's your last name?"

"Enys."

"Was your grandfather a navy man?"

"No."

Reverend Dunhill elbowed Miles Enys. "Explain yourself, and stop being short with the earl. If you want to keep your position, show some respect."

The young man glowered and shrugged. "My granddad had a boatyard near Falmouth. I lived with him until he died. The boatyard got sold to pay his debts, and the new owner didn't want me hanging about. So I headed along the coast looking for work. I saw the *Shearwater* down by the dock, looking like it had been in a battle. I came up to the house and asked Grayson if he needed someone to repair the boat. Grayson asked the old earl, and they gave me the job. I fixed up the *Shearwater*, and they kept me on to sail her for the old earl." He shifted his weight, flicking his chin so his hair tossed back off his forehead.

Charles considered his story. It made sense. The Pembroke girls' father had charge of the boat before his death, and the girls reported that while the *Shearwater* had been wrecked, it had been salvaged. "I didn't find your name on the employee list in the ledger. What are your wages?"

"Not being paid as such. I have a place to sleep in one of the sheep sheds. Grayson lets me fish in the cove, and I sell the catch in the village. The crofters trade me fish for bread sometimes." His lips flattened in a look of sheer independence. "I look after myself."

"And the boat." Charles stood, clasping his hands behind his back and measured the area behind the desk with his strides. Miles Enys had the type of self-reliance Charles was looking for in a new steward. Too bad he was so young and lacking in experience. "The current arrangement is not satisfactory."

"You're not going to make him leave Gateshead, are you?" The vicar put his hand on Miles's shoulder. "I assure you, he's a good worker."

Miles sent an alarmed look at Dunhill and then at Charles.

Why must everyone assume he was some ogre, determined to clear the property of its inhabitants? "I have no plans to dismiss him." He pivoted on the rug. "What I find unsatisfactory is you working on the estate for no pay. Subsistence living is not something for which I want Gateshead to be known. From today, you will have regular duties with regular pay if that is agreeable to you?"

Miles Enys looked as if he'd been struck on the head with an oar. "You want to hire me for actual wages?" He put his hand on his chest.

"What you mean to say"—the reverend spoke around the side of his hand to hide his smile—"is 'yes, sir' and 'thank you.'"

"Yes, sir. Thank you. What is it you want me to do? Can I still look after the boat?"

"For the time being, your duties will involve keeping the *Shearwater* seaworthy and filling in as help here in the house until I can hire more staff. Keep in mind I will be hiring a new steward to run the estate in my absence, and you will answer to him."

"Yes, sir. I've never worked in a house though. I don't know the job."

"Don't worry. There are several ladies present who have taken it upon themselves to tidy up the place, and I'm certain they could make use of both your height and your strength. Report to the kitchens to Mrs. Chapman, and inform her that you are here to make yourself useful."

When he'd gone, the reverend indicated the chair in front of the desk. "May I?"

"Of course." Charles took his seat, lacing his fingers on the blotter.

The reverend arranged his long limbs, crossing one leg over the other. "That's a good thing you did. I had no idea his grandfather had died or that he'd come from Cornwall, though with a name like Enys, it seemed likely. You got more information out of him in those few minutes than I have managed in months. Not that he gave much opportunity. He prefers to be alone, and I think he has a habit of sneaking off when he spots me on the horizon." Dunhill ran his fingers along the arms of the chair. "How soon do you anticipate bringing in your new steward?"

"Hard to say. Ideally, I'd have a new man here within a fortnight, but that might be pushing things. I could be called away at any moment, and I want things on an even keel here."

"Called away?" He uncrossed his legs and leaned forward. "For how long? Or do you anticipate having your headquarters in London?"

The man certainly was curious. Small village, probably prone to gossip. The comings and goings of the landed gentry would always be of interest.

"I am a naval officer. I will resume my career at the first possible moment. The new steward will look after the estate and report to me."

"I see." Dunhill steepled his fingers. "Please forgive my inquisitiveness. The villagers tend to take their cues from the occupant of this house, and I'm sad to say that your predecessor was not one to darken the doors of the church with any regularity. I hoped you would be a frequent attender, for your own soul's sake, but also as an example to your tenants and the villagers. You are a God-fearing man, are you not?"

Charles supposed it was in a preacher's handbook somewhere that they must ask that question of every new parishioner. "I am. I shall certainly attend when I am in residence, but I hope not to be here often. The title and the estate were thrust upon me, and between inheriting the earldom, recovering from wounds suffered in battle, and the cessation of the war, my naval career is in a bit of disarray."

"Of course. Perhaps I can suggest a good man from the village to act as your steward? I confess that while I am a friend of Halbert Grayson's, and I like him very much, I have always wondered why the old earl appointed him steward in the first place. Grayson isn't known for his decisiveness, nor—I hope you'll forgive me saying so—his stewardship nous. But a new steward, someone already familiar to the tenants and the villagers, might be the most seamless transition rather than bringing in someone from the outside who won't know our ways."

"Do you have a suitable candidate in mind?" He had his own ideas, but it wouldn't hurt to hear what the preacher had to say.

"Will Owens might be a good choice. He's a solicitor, but there isn't much call for that sort of work this far from a city. He came home a few months ago to care for his ailing mother, and he's been scraping for clients. He's a good man with a keen mind."

A solicitor. Charles mulled the idea.

"I'll give it some thought." He glanced at the half-finished letter on his desk, and it must have signaled to the preacher that he had work to do and was being kept from it. The lean man unfolded himself from the chair, and Charles rose as well.

"Perhaps I could send Will Owens along for an audience?"

"I'll let you know tomorrow after church." Charles shook Dunhill's hand, trying to ignore his satisfied smile. He certainly seemed pleased that Charles would be in attendance at church on the morrow. Charles supposed it was important to the clergy that as many people attended as possible, but surely his presence at the services wouldn't make that much difference?

"Oh, I cannot believe I almost forgot. There were letters for you delivered to the coaching inn." Dunhill withdrew two envelopes from inside his coat.

This close up, Charles noted the fine cloth and tailoring of the reverend's clothes. Preaching must pay well in these parts for him to have such fine attire. Perhaps the fellow was vain about his appearance and put most of his salary toward his wardrobe. Charles had known naval officers like that, impoverishing themselves when it came to buying new uniforms.

"Thank you." He glanced at the letters, and a jolt of excitement shot through him. The top one was from the Admiralty.

He saw Dunhill to the door before tearing into the letter in the front hall. Quickly he took in the words. "Yes!" He pumped his fist in the air. "Finally." Rereading from the beginning, he allowed satisfaction and hope to build in his chest.

Charles felt someone watching him and anticipated spying one of the little girls on the landing. Though they had only been at Gateshead a few days, they tended to pop up where he least expected them. But it wasn't Penny or Thea or Betsy. Halfway up the stairs, Sophie stared down. She wore a blue frock, and color rode her cheeks. Sunshine from the fanlight over the door bathed her in golden rays.

His heart knocked against his chest, but he wasn't certain if it was because of the contents of the letter or because she looked so fresh and pretty. Of all the people he knew, she was the one with whom he most wanted to share the news.

"Did you receive a nice message?"

Charles composed himself. He was supposed to be a crusty old sea captain, not a raw schoolboy. He knew now to control his emotions.

"I did. A letter from Admiral Barrington. With Napoleon exiled to Elba, there is talk of placing a blockade about the island, and they will need ships. Ships need captains. The *Dogged* has been proposed to join the expedition, and Barrington will recommend I be given my old command should the blockade be approved."

Her lower lip disappeared for a moment. "No wonder you are celebrating. How soon would this happen?"

"Difficult to say. Bureaucracy moves slowly, but to have any effect, the blockade should be formed sooner rather than later. We might be under sail quickly." He could almost feel the deck beneath his feet, hear a breeze snapping canvas as it unfurled. The ship would need to be provisioned and inspected. She'd suffered some damage in the last battle, but that should have been repaired by now. How many of his old crew would be available and willing? Hopefully, there would be no need of press-gangs. Not with so many sailors without ships.

Sophie came down the stairs, her fingers light on the banister. "So you could be leaving us soon?" Her hand came up to touch the hollow of her collarbone, and he followed the motion. The wistfulness in her voice struck him and made his skin prickle. Dare he imagine she might regret their parting as much as he?

A hint of lemon and beeswax clung to her, testament to the cleaning endeavors underway in the manor house. Here she was, the daughter of a duke, dusting and mopping and scrubbing. What was he doing allowing her to act like a maid in his house? He needed to see about hiring domestic help. The place needed a proper housekeeper and maids and such.

He didn't even know what positions needed to be filled. If Gateshead had been a frigate, he would know the personnel from the cabin boy to the captain, but a country house? Yet another area in which he would have to rely upon Sophie for help.

There was so much to do, not least of which was to get Lady Sophia and Lady Richardson into a suitable cottage. He absorbed the pang that hit his chest. Would it be proper to ask her to write to him?

The parlor door opened, and Penny emerged, looking over her shoulder. "Bring it through here. We can take it out the back and hang it on the terrace railing to beat it." Her voice sounded high and fast. "It isn't too heavy, is it?"

Miles Enys followed, a rolled rug on his shoulder. "No." He bounced it higher in his grip, his biceps flexing.

"We sure are glad you came. Having someone as strong as you will make the work so much easier." Penny pressed against the wall as Miles passed.

Miles nodded to both Charles and Sophie, but Penny seemed not to know they were even in the house.

Was the child actually batting her eyes? For a moment, Charles thought Thea's imitation of Penny flirting with a boy wasn't far off.

An uneasy thump hit behind his sternum. He had the girls' futures to organize as well, and from the look of the doe eyes Penny was casting toward the first young man to cross her path at Gateshead, he should prioritize that task.

"Who is that?" Sophie stared down the hall as Penny followed in Miles's wake.

"An employee." He told her what he knew of young Mr. Enys. "You haven't met him yet, I take it?"

"No. I've been upstairs taking inventory of the linen cupboards." Her tongue darted out to moisten her lower lip, and he found himself mimicking the gesture. What was wrong with him to be so distracted? Before he knew it, he'd be flitting his lashes like Penny. He'd do better to concentrate on the matter at hand and not let his imagination fly free.

"Oh, the Reverend Dunhill brought a letter for you as well." He pulled it from behind his own missive. "Good news, I hope."

"It's probably Marcus with a scold for being lax in writing to him. The letter I sent yesterday won't reach him for several days." She took the envelope, flipping it to study the wax seal. "Oh, it's from Mother."

With her thumbnail, she broke the closure and pulled out the pages. It was a fat letter with small, even handwriting.

"I'll give you some privacy. I must compose a response to the Admiralty. When you're finished reading, would you come to the study? I need to compile a list of girls' schools." He looked toward where Penny and Miles had disappeared. "Quickly."

But Sophie wasn't listening. By the time she had finished the first page, she allowed her hands to drop. Her eyes closed, and she shook her head, tentatively at first, but then emphatically.

"What is it? Is something wrong at home?" He took hold of her elbow gently, in case she was feeling faint. The way the color had drained from her face must have made her light-headed.

"My mother is the absolute . . ." She looked at the coffered ceiling three stories above. "What is she thinking?" Another pause while she raised the letter and shook it, frustration emanating from her tense muscles. "Why can she not leave me alone? I am not a project to be completed or something broken to be fixed. I can take care of myself, make my own decisions, and choose my own path."

By her challenging glare, she seemed to want him to agree with her.

"Of course you can?" He had meant to be reassuring, but the statement came out as a question. He was in uncharted waters here. "What is the germane issue?"

"My mother." She flicked the pages with the back of her fingers, holding the letter up before his nose. "She seems to think that the minute my 'summer of mourning by the sea' is over, I should hurry back to Haverly Manor because she's already preparing invitations for a hunting and shooting party. It appears there will be stalking going on outside, but inside as well. She's listed no less than seven eligible bachelors that she's inviting for hunting fox, grouse, deer, and spinster daughters." She stamped her foot and threw the letter onto the floor. As pages floated down like sails ripped from the mast, she subsided onto the bottom stair and fisted her hands on her forehead.

Charles stood still, unsure what to do. Should he commiserate with her? Ask questions? Promise action? She had always behaved with maturity and calm, but at the moment her reaction resembled something more akin to Thea or Betsy.

What he wanted to do was lower himself beside her, take her into his arms, and assure her that everything would be all right.

Before he could tell himself what a terrible idea that was, he had his arm around her, drawing her gently toward his chest and putting his chin on top of her head. And to his surprise, she didn't shove him away. Instead, she leaned into him.

"Why can't she understand that I have no desire to fall in love again?"

The words were muffled against his shirtfront, and he closed his eyes, inhaling the scent of her hair. She only spoke the truth he already knew, but it still made his heart heavy. It seemed so wrong for someone as vital and vivid as Sophie to chain herself to the past, to a dead man who would not want her to be forever mourning. Rich would have wanted her to live. Not to forget him, but to find happiness once more.

If he had been going to remain at Gateshead, perhaps she could have someday found that happiness with him.

He shoved that thought aside. It was impossible. Not only was he years too old for her and a virtual stranger, but he had contributed to her greatest loss. She might be gracious enough to be civil to him, or even friendly, but she would never fall in love with him.

He was a naval officer. His life was at sea. She deserved someone far better than he. He didn't want her to fall in love with him, he lied to himself.

Which didn't stop him from reveling in the pleasure of having her in his arms, even if it was platonic on her part.

He wished she could stay safely at Gateshead forever.

A spark of an idea crashed through his head, and his arms tightened. No, it was unthinkable. A wisp of a notion that in spite of his best efforts took hold. A way he could perhaps make everyone happy?

Was it possible? It was certainly practical, prosaic at best.

But no. The notion was ridiculous, and he didn't know what made him think it in the first place. He should enjoy this moment, make his plans as he had intended, and let everyone get on with their lives.

At which moment she sat up, smoothing her hair and gifting him a wobbly smile. "I'm sorry. You must think me a complete ninny, making a cake of myself over something so silly."

"You're not silly." He let his arms fall away, turning to face the front door and putting his elbows on his knees. He still held the letter from the Admiralty, his ticket back to the life for which he longed. "Having met your mother, I can see it would be difficult to tell her to mind her own business."

Sophie gave a shaky laugh. "She thinks everything *is* her business, especially her family. I know she means well, but dealing with her is like trying to stuff a draft horse in a reticule. Eventually you're going to give up because it's impossible."

He smiled at her analogy. He knew nothing about horses, but the image of the dowager as a headstrong dray horse tickled him. Trying to remain casual, he put his arm around her shoulders and hugged her. "You're a strong, capable woman. You've got a few weeks breathing room before you have to confront her. Perhaps something will come up."

"Why are you hugging Sophie?" Thea hopped from one stair to the next, descending toward them.

They leapt up as if stung by hornets.

"Seems everyone's making calf eyes at each other. Penny and that new boy, Miles, and now you and Sophie." Thea made a retching sound. "It's nasty. Seems only Mrs. Chapman and Lady Richardson have any sense around here."

Sophie stalked along the path, well back from the cliff edge, trying to walk off her temper. With little success.

A house party at Haverly.

With more than half a dozen "suitable" young men.

God, why don't You stop her? She's becoming a positive menace. I am not in the least interested in finding a man to marry.

Sophie stopped, looking out across the sea. Afternoon sunshine winked off the waves in diamond points, and a gentle breeze carried the scents of brine and freshness. Daisies danced on slender stems, and grass blew in ripples that mimicked the water far below.

What a beautiful place. She had never thought anywhere could rival Primrose Cottage in her heart, but if there ever was such a place, it would be Gateshead. The house begged for someone to care for it and bring back its former glory. The wide, gentle, grassy slope that led down to the cliffs spoke to her need for a less-structured landscape. She felt as if she could breathe here, without the formality of Haverly House, without all the memories of Primrose.

For the first time in ages, she felt as if she was returning to her former self, before responsibility and grief and loneliness had stifled her customary exuberance.

She would be sad to leave Gateshead.

The girls would too. They were already calling the nursery "their room," and every day they explored some new corner of the house and reported back the treasures and nooks and discoveries. It could be a lovely home for them to grow up in, if only the captain wasn't bent on sending them away.

And then there was darling Mamie. Since the girls' arrival, she had enjoyed a clarity of mind and memory that encouraged Sophie to no end. She and Betsy had formed a sweet bond, with the little girl often standing on tiptoe and Mamie bending low as they shared some secret together.

Sophie walked toward the cliff to where a bench had been placed on a patch of gravel. Taking a seat, she turned sideways, raised her knees, and put her feet on the bench, wrapping her arms around her legs in a posture that would give her mother a fit of the vapors if she ever saw it.

But it was how Sophie prayed best.

"God, I don't know what to do." She spoke softly, and the breeze blew her words away on a whisper. "The captain is bent on leaving as soon as possible. The girls are going to be miserable shunted away to another boarding school. Mamie will be confused and unsettled when we leave Gateshead for a cottage somewhere for only a few weeks. And as soon as I return to Haverly, Mother has men lined up for inspection." Closing her eyes, she rested her forehead on her knees. "I don't see a happy ending for any of us . . . except the captain, who will get exactly what he wants, which is to be away from all of us, from all of this."

Could she blame him? He hadn't asked for any of the things that had happened to him. Being wounded, losing his command, inheriting a title, escorting Sophie and Mamie to Devonshire, three little girls foisted upon him.

She had supplied him with the names of three ladies' academies that might take the girls. And the entire time, she had felt like a traitor.

Sophie could only imagine the look in Thea's eyes as she was put on a coach to a destination she didn't know or want. And Betsy. Sweet Betsy wouldn't even truly understand what was going on. She would look to her sisters and to Sophie for comfort and assurance. Penny would try to be brave, convincing herself that she could handle the situation, that she was old enough to act as a mother to her sisters, when in reality, she needed a mother's guiding hand herself.

"God, everything in me wants to offer to become the girls' guardian myself, but would the courts even allow that? Not to mention what Marcus and Mother would have to say if I took on three motherless children without the support of a husband. They barely agreed to allow us to come on this trip in the first place. I would love to ask the captain if Mamie and I could stay on here instead of looking for a cottage to rent. We could look after the girls, at least for the rest of the summer, and put off them having to leave. But we can't impose and invite ourselves to stay when he clearly wants to wash his hands of all of us and get back to the career he loves. I feel so helpless. I used to know exactly how my life was going to go, but now everything is turned upside down, and I can't find my way. If You would just point me in the right direction, I'd really appreciate it."

She raised her head, wiping away the tears that always came when she and God had a heart-to-heart. Though she had no answers, she felt at peace because she had poured out everything to God. It was up to Him now.

Letting her feet fall to the ground, she straightened her dress and smoothed her hair. Scanning the slope up to the house, her heart popped in a quick extra beat. The captain strode across the grass toward her.

He had comforted her on the stairs, and she had enjoyed it. Strong arms holding her, the steady beat of a heart against her cheek, the warmth of human contact. She had missed that, being able to lean on someone else for a little while.

A twinge of guilt pinched in her chest. Was it wrong of her to have drawn comfort from the captain? She had vowed to love only Rich for the rest of her days. But then again, she didn't *love* Captain Wyvern. No, what she felt for him was . . . regard. Admiration. Perhaps the beginning of friendship?

Did that mean she had forgiven him for whatever part he might have played in Rich's death? When he had first told her of the events that led to Rich being shot, she had been eager to have somewhere to place the blame. If the captain was willing to bear the burden, she had been more than willing to let him.

But as the days had passed, and as she'd thought about his account of the capture of the enemy ship, her anger had faded. She was coming to a place of acceptance. That somehow, someway, Rich dying in Portugal had been no one's fault. Death in war had always been a possibility. She had known it even as she had prayed for it never to happen.

In truth, she hadn't forgiven Charles Wyvern, because there was nothing to forgive.

Charles was her friend, and allowing him to comfort her had not been wrong. There had been nothing romantic in it.

Thea's claim of everyone making calf eyes at one another was laughable. The child merely hadn't understood an embrace between friends.

Why was he seeking her out now? To ask her for help in choosing a school for the girls? Or for assistance in hiring staff before he left? She gripped the back of the bench and waited.

But when he reached her, he merely smiled and raised a nautical spyglass to his eye. "I spotted something from the upstairs study, and I thought you might like to see it."

"What?" She looked out to the water, but nothing seemed different. A wide expanse of sea and sky.

"A ship." He lowered the glass and handed it to her as she stood. "At your one o'clock."

The telescope was fine wood and brass and glass, well cared for and heavy in her hands. How many voyages had it been on with the captain?

She raised it to her eye, and the horizon swung crazily, blurry and hard to find. He moved behind her, cupping her shoulders and turning her slightly.

"There." He pointed. She sighted the spyglass along his arm. "Don't touch the rim to your face. You'll see better with it held just away from you."

She followed his instructions, aware of his presence so close to her. If she backed up an inch, her shoulders would brush his chest. The scent of soap and bay rum drifted around her. She swallowed hard and concentrated. In the center of the cylinder, a ship appeared, the sun gleaming off her sails.

"Is it a navy ship?" she asked.

"No." Humor tinged his voice. "It's a merchant ship. If you'll look at her stern, you'll see she isn't flying a naval flag."

At this distance, it didn't appear as if the ship was making any progress at all, but it must be, because her sails were bellied out.

His sigh skimmed the top of her head.

Lowering the glass, she looked up at him. His three-quarters profile was sharp, his eyes keen as he stared into the distance. The cut on his brow had dried, and the swelling had gone down considerably.

The ship was a mere dot on the horizon, but it grew larger as she watched it. "I wonder who is aboard, and what it's carrying, and where it's going."

"I wonder that with every ship I see. And I hope soon it will be me, carrying men, headed to Elba and the blockade." He took the spyglass, collapsing the segments into a compact tube.

"What is it about life aboard ship that you yearn for so much?" She crossed her arms, aware of the freshening breeze and the sun making its way toward the west. What must this coast be like in winter?

"Many things. The camaraderie of the crew, the clear-cut mission and chain of command. The loyalty of the men." He tapped the telescope against his thigh. "It's the sun and the wind and the waves and the sea. The creaking of the rigging and the cry of seabirds. Porpoises leaping out of the water and the jetting spray of a whale as it blows."

She turned to him. His words were almost lyrical. Her scrutiny must have discomfited him, for color crept up from his collar, and he cleared his throat, shifting his weight. His hands went behind him, and he straightened his shoulders. Within seconds he had traversed the area in front of the bench.

"I came to show you the ship, but I also had another reason." He took measured steps, turning on his heel and repeating the distance. "I know you've only been here a few days, but you and Mamie seem to have settled in well. You have been an excellent help with the girls. I don't know what I would have done without you and Mrs. Chapman to organize them."

He stopped pacing and stood before her, back to the sea, his eyes intent. "I have a proposition for you to consider."

Sophie's breath caught in her throat. It could be anything, but dare she hope he might ask her to stay on at Gateshead for the summer?

"I would like you to stay on at Gateshead. I believe your doing so would solve many of the challenges facing us." He resumed his pacing—four steps, pivot, four steps, pivot.

"First, it would allow the girls to remain here. They've had much upheaval in their lives, and I know you are resistant to sending them away to school. If you are here, they will be able to stay. It's a lot to take on, but they seem biddable enough, and you have a good way with them.

"Second, while a reliable steward for the estate is a must, I need someone in charge of the household. I am certain your training included how to run a manor, oversee servants, and the like. I trust you completely, which would be essential.

"Third, I believe Lady Richardson is at peace here. She seems happy enough, especially when with the girls. I don't believe she would be disappointed to remain at Gateshead.

"Fourth, you would not be subjected to your mother's machinations. She would be forced to cease her plans to matchmake for you.

"And finally," he paused in his striding about. "If you were to stay here at Gateshead, it would allow me to fulfill Rich's last request of me. He asked me to take care of you. I cannot think of a better or more permanent way to take care of you than to marry you."

Sophie wondered if the earth had shifted. She gripped the back of the bench to steady herself. "Marry me?" She had thought he was merely asking her to stay for the summer.

His brows traveled toward his hairline. "Of course. What did you think I meant?" He removed his hands from behind his back, still holding the telescope.

She shook her head. "Marry you?" His proposal had crashed down from a clear blue sky. What could she say? Was this what Rich had wanted Charles to do when he elicited his last promise? How could she marry Charles when she still loved Rich?

Comprehension smoothed the lines of Charles's face, and he gave a rueful chuckle. "I've botched this entire enterprise, haven't I? My dear, I intend our marriage to be in name only. I know your feelings for Rich, and you know my feelings about going to sea as soon as possible. Our union would be for the sake of the girls, the estate, and my debt to Major Richardson. You would have a home and safe place for Lady Richardson, and a way out of any marriage plans your mother might concoct."

"A marriage of convenience." She tried to organize her scattered wits.

"Yes, that's it. What do you say?"

What could she say? Would marrying in such a manner be disloyal to Rich's memory? What would Marcus think? And her mother?

She stared out to sea, pressing her lips together. Not ten minutes prior she had been crying out to God for a way out of her situation, for a clear path that would allow her to look after the girls and stay at Gateshead, at least through the summer. And here she was being offered a permanent place.

Once, when she was young, she heard a preacher say that God's children should pray so specifically that when the prayer was answered, they would know it was God who had done it and not coincidence.

Peace dropped into her heart. This must be God's answer to her specific prayer, though she never would have imagined a proposal of marriage.

The captain waited, standing almost at attention, his hands once more clasped behind him.

"Lord Rothwell, I accept your proposal and your terms. I will marry you and stay on as the mistress of Gateshead and co-guardian of your wards."

He relaxed, a slight smile touching his lips. He reached for her hand and, to her surprise, placed a chaste kiss upon her cheek. "I do think it would be proper for you to call me Charles now. My dear, you've made me most happy."

And oddly enough, she felt happy too. Perhaps that boded well for their future. Her fingers touched the place his lips had made contact with her cheek, and for a moment she wished he had given her a proper kiss on the lips to seal their agreement.

Chapter 9

"You're getting married?" Penny leapt up from the rug where she had been leafing through a book of fashion drawings from twenty years ago. "Oh, that's the most romantic thing ever." She hugged Sophie. "You're going to be a beautiful bride. I've never been to a wedding before." Looking down at her plain muslin dress, she made a face. "I wish I had something elegant to wear."

"Why? Why are you getting married?" Betsy tugged on Sophie's dress. "Do you have to? Are you sad? What does married mean?"

Sophie knelt and hugged Betsy. "Girls, I hope you'll be happy about the news. It means you can all stay here at Gateshead with us. No boarding school, no orphanage. Lord Rothwell will continue as your guardian. And yes, Betsy, I'm quite happy to be getting married. It means that the earl and I . . ." How did one describe marriage to a child as young as Betsy?

"It means they promise to love only each other and live together forever." Penny clasped her hands under her chin and swayed, as if overcome by the romance of it all.

Sophie tugged her bottom lip. She wasn't marrying for love but for expediency. But that was the business of herself and the captain, no one else. It was essentially what her mother was goading her to do. Sophie had just taken the decision out of the dowager's hands.

Thea sat up on the bed, then bounced to her feet and jumped on the mattress. "Yes! No more place like Miss Fricklin's." Hop, hop, hop, squeaking the bedsprings. "No more stupid rules, no more oatmeal every morning, and no more boring lessons."

Sophie hurried over and took Thea's arm. "You'll wind up needing a new bed if you continue. I agree, no more boarding school, but you will have lessons, both academic and social. Someone needs to keep you from becoming a complete hoyden."

Thea scowled and plopped onto her backside on the rumpled coverlet. She shrugged. "Lessons here have to be better than lessons at Miss Fricklin's."

Sophie grinned at the girl's philosophical approach to life. Dorothea Pembroke would go far in this world.

"When are you getting married? Will the banns be read tomorrow at church?" Penny asked.

"No, the earl has decided we should marry quickly. Neither of us wants a large wedding. We'll marry in the small chapel here on the property this Wednesday morning. We'll have a picnic wedding breakfast near the cliff, and then we'll take a quick sail on the *Shearwater* to celebrate."

"Oh, won't that be nice?" A dreamy look drifted into Penny's eyes. "Are we all invited? To go sailing, I mean."

"You just want to see Miles again." Thea snorted.

Sophie studied the girl. Penny was only a handful of years younger than she, and here Sophie was, stepping in to act the role of mother. How did one guide a boy-crazed girl through adolescence and see her safely launched into adulthood?

"What did Miss Mamie say?" Thea asked, dangling her feet over the edge of the bed and kicking randomly.

"I'm going to tell her now." Sophie's stomach muscles tightened. She hoped Mamie would understand and not be offended. It was only a quarter year since Rich had passed away. "I'd like you girls to make a list of your belongings, your clothes and shoes and the like. Write it neatly in columns, and bring it to the parlor when you're finished, all right?"

She left them dragging dresses and nightgowns out of the wardrobe and headed to the parlor.

"Hello, darling Mamie. What are you making there?"

Mamie tugged a length of fine wool from the ball in her knitting basket. "Stockings for Rich. The air is so damp at sea, I worry about his feet getting cold and him falling ill." She sighed, but her needles never stopped.

Sophie's heart sank into her slippers. Mamie had been having such a good day. She knelt before the older woman and put her hands atop the knitting. "Mamie, dear, you know that Rich is dead, right?"

Mamie's lips trembled, and doubts crept into her faded-blue eyes. "Of course. I would know whether my son was alive or not." She looked at her hands, then back to Sophie.

"I've come to tell you some exciting news, and I hope you'll be happy." She sat beside Mamie, taking her hand. "Captain Wyvern, Earl Rothwell . . . Charles . . ." She almost laughed, trying to sort out what she should call him to help Mamie understand. "Charles has asked me to marry him, and I've said yes. You and I are going to stay here at Gateshead and make this our home. You will get to live by the sea forever, and the girls will stay here with us. Isn't that wonderful news?"

Please, God, help her comprehend, and help her not to be upset.

"Married. To the captain?"

"Yes. And soon. This Wednesday. There's no need to wait."

"But, my dear, what about Rich? He's coming home soon. Won't he be upset if he finds you married to another man?"

Tears burned the backs of Sophie's eyes. "Mamie, darling, Rich isn't coming home. He died, remember? He's buried in Portugal. We had his memorial service, and the captain came and brought Rich's things?" Things Sophie had yet to unpack.

"He's dead. He's not coming home."

"That's right, darling. I'm so sorry."

"You loved him."

"Yes, and I always will, just like you always will."

"But you're marrying Captain Wyvern?"

"Yes."

Mamie patted Sophie's cheek. "You're a good girl, Sophie. Always looking after everyone else. I hope you remember to look after yourself."

"I'll do my part in looking after her as well." Charles spoke from the doorway. He came in and pulled a chair alongside Mamie's knitting basket. "You'll always have a home here with Sophie and me." He took Mamie's other hand between his. "You'll be revered, as a mother should be."

Mamie looked long into his face. "Do you care for Sophie?"

His eyes met Sophie's. "Yes, I do. I have long had a fine regard for her, first through her letters and Rich's stories, and then meeting her myself. She's a woman of rare beauty, inside and out."

Warmth spread through Sophie at his words and his intent look. She knew he was only trying to reassure an old woman of delicate mind, but the words sounded so nice, she half wanted to believe them.

"And, Sophie, dear, do you care for the captain?"

Aware that Charles listened intently, Sophie told the truth. "I have a great respect for the captain. He's a good man, and he's doing a good thing making sure we're all taken care of. I am most happy to accept his proposal."

Mamie assessed Sophie, and she tried to stay still under the scrutiny. She hadn't exactly declared an eternal love for Charles. Was that what Mamie wanted?

Finally, Mamie released her hand from Sophie's clasp and patted Charles's knee. "Then I give you my blessing. Treat her well."

Sophie exhaled slowly, meeting Charles's eyes over Mamie's head. The look there made her heart race.

Sunday morning saw them climbing into the estate carriage, a fine vehicle with the Rothwell crest on its door, to attend church in the village. Betsy sat on Penny's lap to ease the crush of seven occupants. Sophie gave up trying not to lean into Charles on every turn, and he raised his arm and put it around her shoulders to make more room.

"I suppose someday I'm going to have to break down and learn to ride a horse." His breath tickled as he whispered in her ear. "Either that or I'll need to buy an omnibus to get this crew from here to there without packing us in like salt cod in a barrel."

"You don't ride?" Sophie winced when she realized how loudly her question had been posed. The girls, Mamie, and Mrs. Chapman all stared, and Charles shifted on the plush seat. But it was odd, a grown man not having such a basic skill. Sophie had been given riding lessons as a matter of course, as had every other young person of her acquaintance.

"I don't know how to ride either." Betsy leaned forward and patted his knee.

"There isn't much call for equestrian prowess aboard a ship."

"But you're not on a ship anymore. You live at Gateshead now," Thea pointed out. She looked angelic. Sophie had helped style her hair, crossing her braids atop her head and pinning them into a coronet.

"For the moment. When my new commission comes in, I'll be aboard ship with no horses to ride and no place to ride them."

Thea struggled to sit forward. "You're still leaving us?" Her eyes narrowed from shock to mistrust. "But I thought you were marrying Sophie."

"I am marrying Sophie. You don't need to worry. You will remain with her at Gateshead, even when I'm away at sea."

"I thought married people wanted to be together all the time." Thea crossed her arms over her thin chest. "If you leave, who will look after all of us?"

Charles didn't have to answer, because the carriage pulled to a stop at the church steps. He was out before Grayson could climb from the driver's seat and open the door. The poor captain. His life aboard ship had not prepared him for being trapped in a carriage with six women.

The beadle escorted them to their pew and unlocked the gate with one of the keys on his belt. The seats were right up front, and the Rothwell crest had been carved into the gate. Sophie felt all eyes upon them, but she forced herself not to turn around. Her bonnet shielded her face, but she could still hear the whispers.

When the vicar took the pulpit, satisfaction shone from his expression when he looked down at the Rothwell pew. Sophie folded her hands in her lap, eager to hear. It had been far too long since she had been to church, and her soul needed feeding.

"Hear the word of the Lord from Ephesians. 'And be not drunk with wine, wherein is excess; but be filled with the Spirit; Speaking to yourselves in psalms and hymns and spiritual songs, singing and making melody in your heart to the Lord; Giving thanks always for all things unto God and the Father in the name of our Lord Jesus Christ; Submitting yourselves one to another in the fear of God.'"

His voice reached the back of the church, and his eyes were so intent, he appeared to be speaking to someone personally.

"When a man gets drunk and becomes belligerent, he does a disservice to those around him. When he demands his own way and doesn't submit himself to what is best for the collective, he puts his own petty wants ahead of others."

A stir went through the congregation, and Sophie looked at Charles. He raised his eyebrows. Everyone in the sanctuary seemed to understand the pointed remarks and to whom they were directed.

Perhaps, after she got to know the villagers, she would understand too. But even then it would be uncomfortable if the reverend continued to use his sermons as a public admonishment of a specific parishioner. She hoped this was an isolated incident.

After the service, at which the girls had behaved beautifully—even Thea had managed to sit still for the entire hour—there were many new people to meet.

"Lord Rothwell, so nice of you to come." A bookish man with gold-rimmed glasses perched on his narrow nose extended his hand. "Will Owens. Local solicitor. I understand from Reverend Dunhill that you're looking for a new steward?"

Charles nodded. "I am. Dunhill put your name forth for the position. I'm still weighing my options and have sent word to London." They moved away, heads bent.

"Pleased, Lady Sophia. It's all over the village that you're marrying the earl." A blowsy woman with frizzled gray hair and a considerable bosom greeted them. "Grayson was talking about it in the pub last night. Oh, I'm Nan Barker. My husband owns the public house. We hope you'll be happy at Gateshead."

Mamie studied the woman's dress, which was far finer than one might expect from a publican's wife. "That's very lovely lace. I haven't seen the like for years. Where did you get it?" She reached out for Mrs. Barker's sleeve, and the woman's face hardened. She jerked away before Mamie could touch her.

Sophie's protective instincts went on alert. Had Grayson spread any rumors about Mamie and her memory difficulties when he was chatting in the pub last night? People could be so odd about such things. If Mrs. Barker said anything mean to sweet Mamie—

But Mrs. Barker relaxed and laughed, self-consciously stroking the trim at her wrist. "It was on a dress my mother had years ago, and I reused it."

Mamie nodded. "That explains it. French lace is so hard to come by, isn't it? What with the trade embargo going on for years. Still, now that the war has ended, perhaps we'll be seeing more European goods coming to Britain again."

"Perhaps," Mrs. Barker said cautiously. "I understand the new earl isn't planning on staying at Gateshead long. Will you and your wards remain, or will you go back to where you came from?"

Villages like Gateshead were certainly hotbeds of gossip. Mrs. Barker seemed to know as much about Charles and Sophie's plans as they did.

"We haven't decided all the details yet."

"Understandable. I suppose the wedding is all that's on your mind right now." She waggled her eyebrows. "Snagging an earl. Still, I guess, as the daughter of a duke, that's not reaching too high."

They really did know a lot about what was going on at Gateshead. She didn't recall people being so inquisitive about Haverly Manor. She rubbed her arms to quell a shiver. Still, as long as it was mere curiosity, there was no harm in it, she supposed.

The day of his wedding. Who could have imagined he would go from bachelor to betrothed to married in less than a week?

Charles stood before the mirror in his dressing room. He wore his naval uniform, which had been carefully brushed by Mrs. Chapman.

Mrs. Chapman. He smiled as he used his cuff to buff the brass buttons on his coat. When she had received the news that Lady Sophia and Lady Richardson would be staying on at Gateshead permanently, she had accepted the role of housekeeper and told him she would see to hiring the help she needed. Not a single histrionic or ruffled feather to be seen.

If he had a ship's worth of Mrs. Chapmans, he would rule the waves.

He smoothed his coat, his hand hitting something hard. Dipping into his pocket, he withdrew—oh no!

The miniature of Sophie. He'd meant to return it to her, and he'd forgotten about it. He cast his mind back, remembering the invasion of the new Baron Richardson and his wild brood that had interrupted Charles's carefully rehearsed apology. He had told himself to return it at the next opportunity, but he'd let it languish in his pocket.

What to do with it now? This long after the fact, he couldn't claim it was a mistake. It hadn't been a mistake. It had been a deliberate act.

A knock sounded. "My lord, the vicar is here."

Charles opened the top drawer of his bureau and buried the miniature beneath his stockings and handkerchiefs. He'd deal with it later.

"Thank you, Miles." The young man had proven quite helpful. "I'll be down directly."

He stared once more into the mirror. "You're doing the right thing. Rich would approve." Charles only hoped it was true. He was certain Rich's plea that Charles look after Sophie hadn't included marrying her, even if in name only.

Dunhill bowed as Charles hurried down the stairs. "Your lordship. Are you ready?"

"As I ever will be." The grimness in his voice startled him, and he tried to smile. This was supposed to be a happy occasion. While it might not be the epitome of romance, neither was this marriage of convenience a death sentence. He was marrying Lady Sophia Haverly. Many a man would trample him over to get the chance. She was beautiful, kind, sweet of nature, and companionable. A treasure.

"I understand the bridal party will meet us at the chapel. Shall we go?" Dunhill indicated the door.

Miles spoke from the top of the stairs. "I'll fetch the ladies and walk them over."

The estate chapel stood in the fold of a hill about two hundred yards from the main house. A small lych-gate guarded the family cemetery, and ivy grew on the fence.

Charles stepped into the little church, and the scent of flowers greeted him.

"The parish women wanted to do something nice for the happy couple. They've cleaned and decorated the chapel." Reverend Dunhill followed him inside. "From the looks of things, they plundered every flower patch in the district."

The altar was a bower of greenery and blossoms.

Flowers.

He should have sent a bouquet to Sophie. What a dolt he was.

The sound of footsteps on the gravel path outside preceded the arrival of Thea. She wore a dress of sea blue, and silk ribbons fluttered with her movements. She panted, and a fine sheen broke out on her forehead, dampening the wispy red hair. "I ran all the way."

"Why? Is something wrong?"

She frowned. "No. I just wanted to run."

He found himself laughing. Thea was as mercurial as a mermaid.

Penny and Betsy followed at a much more sedate pace, and Miles slipped in behind them, taking up a post in the back corner of the little chapel. Lady Richardson was next, and Charles found his chest going tight.

There was no music, and yet his heart lilted as if someone were playing Handel on a pipe organ.

Lady Sophia stepped into the church, her eyes alight, color in her cheeks. Her dress was pale gold, and she wore a bonnet that framed her face perfectly.

He needn't have worried about the bouquet. She carried flowers that matched those in the church. The parish ladies had come up trumps where he had failed.

With little ceremony, she walked up the aisle and put her hand on his arm. She looked serene, as if nerves were no such thing.

He wondered if his buttons were jumping, his heart beat so hard.

Dunhill moved to stand before them, and in what felt like an indecently short time, it was done. He had promised to love, honor, and cherish. Sophie had promised to love, honor, and obey. They had pledged that from this moment forward, they belonged solely to one another.

Dunhill recited from his Book of Common Prayer. "I pronounce that they be man and wife together, in the name of the Father, and of the Son, and of the Holy Ghost. Amen."

They stood at the altar, hands clasped, looking at one another. Did she feel as stunned and sober as he? They were now married, in the sight of God and the church.

There was no going back now. The enormity of what they had done hit him square in the chest.

Lady Sophia Haverly—now Wyvern—was his wife.

His collar felt unbearably tight.

"Are you going to kiss her?" Thea's voice ricocheted through the sanctuary, and the tension was broken. Everyone laughed, and Sophie blushed delightfully.

Charles raised his hand and touched her cheek, marveling at how soft her skin felt against his palm. Delicate as a rose petal. He raised his brows, silently asking for permission.

She bit her bottom lip briefly and nodded.

His heart clattering like a pebble in a bucket, he leaned forward and brushed his lips against hers. The scent of the flowers surrounded them, but as he inhaled, he caught a brief snatch of her lemon verbena perfume. He felt that no matter where he went in the world after this, the mere whiff of lemon would remind him of this moment.

He stepped back, and she gifted him with a smile.

"Can we have our picnic now?" Betsy slid off the front pew and came to take Sophie's hand. "Are we done getting married?"

"Yes, we are, sweetling." Sophie brushed her fingers over Betsy's curls. "Let's have our picnic."

Mrs. Chapman and Miles had prepared everything ahead of time, carrying baskets of food and cutlery down to the flat area near the staircase to the beach, and spreading a pair of blankets on the grass. Reverend Dunhill joined them. He carried a green bottle with a tight cork.

"To toast your happiness."

Probably some ratafia or local ale.

Sophie helped Mamie ease down onto the blanket, and Mrs. Chapman and Miles offered pillows. Penny stole shy glances at Miles every chance she got, and Thea peeked into the baskets. Betsy popped up and picked daisies in anticipation of another chain-making session with Mamie.

They were acting like a family. His family.

God, You move in mysterious ways. Never did I envision having a family, much less one stitched together like this. Three orphan girls, my best friend's fiancée, and his elderly mother. Thank You, God, and help me be worthy of them.

"What are you thinking about?" Sophie took a seat beside him. She twisted the gold circle on her finger.

"I was just telling God how mysterious His ways are to me." Charles leaned back on his palms and crossed his boots. Sunshine streamed down, and the wind, while fresh, wasn't too brisk.

She nodded, tucking a stray curl behind her ear. She had beautiful ears, shell-like, small, and perfect.

"Mysterious, to be sure. But if He is sovereign and He is good, then what He brings about must be for our good and His glory, should it not? I try to hold on to that truth no matter what."

He nodded, contemplating her words. Did that account for the peace and serenity she displayed lately?

"A fine day for a sail."

Miles tore his attention away from filling a plate for Penny. "The *Shearwater*'s ready, sir."

Charles accepted a plate from Mrs. Chapman, but his mind drifted to the sailing trip. If he was honest, he would admit he was looking forward to being back in his element, to show Sophie—and the girls—that he was capable. His pride had taken a bit of a battering, not knowing how to run an estate and being teased about not knowing how to ride a horse. But aboard ship, any ship, he would excel.

"May I be the first to toast the happy couple?" The vicar lifted his bottle, and Mrs. Chapman reached for glasses.

Instead of ratafia or ale, Dunhill poured champagne. Charles accepted his glass, puzzled. Where had the reverend managed to procure champagne? Not only was it expensive, but with the embargo on French goods, it was impossible to get.

"You wouldn't believe it. When I first came here, nearly five years ago now, the parsonage had been empty for a long time. The church had been making do with a circuit-riding preacher. So the house needed quite a thorough cleaning before I could move in. And what did we find belowstairs but a wine cellar? Jugs and bottles of French wines. The previous parson had been something of a collector, I gathered." He held up the gently fizzing drink. "I gave some to each of the parishioners, and I saved a bit back for special occasions. The marriage of the Earl of Rothwell seemed an appropriate circumstance for bringing out the last bottle."

"We're honored." Charles raised his glass before taking a sip. He refrained from grimacing. He had never cared for champagne.

Thea finished her meal first and bounced up to explore.

"Stay away from the cliff edge," Charles warned.

"I will. You don't have to tell me every time." Her words drifted back over her shoulder as she ran through the tall grass.

"Someone is going to have to take her in hand." He pursed his lips. "I suppose that task will fall mostly upon you now."

Sophie touched her lips with her handkerchief. With the breeze teasing her hair and fluttering the ribbons on her bonnet, she looked much too young for such burdens. Was he putting too much on her slender shoulders, placing her in charge of the girls and Gateshead?

"She's got an independent streak, but she's not really willful and certainly not wicked. Just high spirited. I know how she feels. My mother likes to remind me often that I was quite a hoyden in my youth. There's time enough for her to settle down."

"I find it hard to believe you were ever a hoyden."

The gamine grin that flashed across her face negated what he thought. "Actually, I was, until quite recently." She sobered, twisting the ring. "When word came of Rich being wounded, I sort of drew in on myself. Marcus used to tease me that I could talk the leg off a table when I was younger, but somehow I didn't seem to have much to say during that time."

"The letters you sent to the hospital were still as bright as brass fittings though."

She checked on Thea, the girl's dress a splash of color against the grass. "I forget sometimes that you read my letters. I tried not to let on to Rich that anything was amiss at home. Tried to be breezy and light and interesting."

"You accomplished that and more. All the crew, myself included, enjoyed the bits he read to us." He put his hand on hers on the grass. "I don't want you to think you can't mention Rich. He was dear to both of us."

Her hand moved under his, but as she nodded her understanding, a frown crossed her face. "What's she found now?"

Thea ran toward them, streaming a long piece of cloth from her hand. "Look at this." She twirled, making the narrow strip of fabric coil around her. "I found it stuck in the bushes down there."

"Let me see." Charles held out his hand, and Thea gave him the . . . flag? The cloth was white canvas. About a foot of one end had been dyed or painted bright blue with a red *X*, and the same amount on the other end was vivid red with a blue *X*. "What on earth?"

The vicar chuckled. "That's one of the homemade buntings from our celebration. The village threw a bit of a party when we heard the war was over. The ladies made at least a dozen of these, hanging them from their windows."

Odd that it had wound up out here.

"There was quite a storm the night of the celebration. I suppose the wind caught one of the sashes and carried it along until it caught on the brush." The vicar wasn't looking at Charles when he spoke. "I'll take it for you. Perhaps Miles can dispose of it."

Miles snapped into action. "Of course, sir." He took the cloth, wadding it into a ball.

A feather of unease flicked across Charles's mind at the sharpness of the vicar's tone, but he shrugged it away. It was time to go sailing.

Sophie held Betsy's hand until Charles reached across the small gap of water from the boat deck to the pier and lifted the child aboard the *Shearwater*. Thea hadn't waited for help, leaping aboard like a cat coming home. Sophie tried not to let on how nervous she was. She'd never been sailing before, and the thought of all that water around and under her made her apprehensive.

Which was silly. The boat was sound, and the weather couldn't be lovelier. They were under the command of a naval captain and an able boatman. Nothing bad would happen.

Penny allowed herself to be aided by Miles, and Reverend Dunhill helped Mamie. Then Charles, instead of holding out his hand to Sophie, leaned over and bracketed her waist. Her hands went to his shoulders to brace herself, and his muscles bunched beneath her palms. He swung her aboard in a smooth arc, keeping hold of her until he was certain she had found her footing.

Being held by him made her feel both secure and uneasy. It was as if she stood on solid ground but on the edge of a precipice. Was the fact that she was now his wife, even if in name only, what caused her to be so very aware of his touch?

"Can we go now?" Thea stood with her feet braced apart, rocking with the slight bob of the boat. "Can we go fast?"

"We'll go as fast as the wind will take us. Find a seat. Miles, let's shove off." The lines on Charles's face had smoothed out, and he looked eager and happy and younger somehow.

She tried to get her stomach muscles to relax.

"Are you sure you won't join us, Reverend?" Charles asked.

"Thank you, no. I have some visitations to make before it gets dark. Enjoy your voyage. Miles, perhaps you'd like to head up toward Lyme Regis? Show them the cliffs there?"

"I thought we'd head west, this first time aboard." Charles reached across the gap to shake the vicar's hand. "Anyway, the majority of Gateshead's coastline is to the west, and I'd like to see it from the water."

Mamie took a seat near the back of the boat and tucked her arm through Penny's.

"Can I sit right up front?" Thea asked. "There's a little bench there."

Sophie wanted to tell her no, that she needed to stay close to an adult at all times, but Charles got in first. "As long as you don't mind a bit of spray in your face."

The vicar helped Miles loosen the mooring lines, and using his boot, pushed the *Shearwater* away from the pier. With the tide going out, the boat was soon bobbing away from shore.

"Sir," Miles said, "the wind's running east. The sailing will be easier that way. Are you sure you wouldn't like to take the ladies to see Lyme Regis? The cliffs will look nice in the afternoon sunshine."

"I'm sure. It might require some tacking to head west, but the return trip will be quicker. Look lively now."

Sophie dropped onto the bench beside Mamie, and Betsy climbed into her lap.

"Enys, raise the mainsail." Charles wended toward the stern and took hold of the tiller.

Miles untied the lines holding the sail along a spar, then hauled on a rope. With each tug, the large triangle of canvas inched toward the top of the mast. With a few luffs of breeze, the sail filled and bellied out.

"Raise the jib," Charles called.

Miles headed forward and unfurled another sail.

"What's that called?" Betsy asked, pointing to the long spar along the bottom edge of the sail.

"That's the boom," Charles answered. "It controls the angle of the sail. The tiller and the angle of the boom direct the ship."

They sailed west, and once they were out of the shelter of the cove, the waves increased in size. Sophie half stood to check on Thea. The girl knelt in the bow, hands braced on the gunwales, her hair streaming out behind her, loose from its braids. She looked like a figurehead from mythology.

A splash of uneasiness washed over Sophie, and she swallowed. Nerves. It had been an emotional day, serious at the wedding service, cheerful at the picnic, and now apprehensive. With all the upheaval, she would surely sleep well tonight.

"Is it difficult to sail a ship?" Penny asked Miles as he coiled a rope over his forearm.

"Not if you know what you're doing. I've sailed the *Shearwater* by myself before, but it's better with two or three men." He stowed the rope in a locker. "I'll teach you, if you like."

Those two would bear watching, but Sophie wasn't much worried. Penny seemed to be more in love with love than serious about Miles or any young man. In the coming days, there would be time for Sophie to talk with Penny about appropriate behavior and the importance of guarding her heart until the right person came along.

Mamie looked from the shore to the sky to the waves to the horizon, taking everything in and seemingly content. But then again, she'd been raised by the sea and had sailed often. Sophie loved the pure enjoyment on the older woman's face.

A bit of dizziness swirled behind Sophie's eyes, and she lurched, grabbing the edge of the bench with one hand and tightening her hold on Betsy with the other. Mercy!

Cold clamminess sprang out on her brow, and she gulped fresh air.

Charles had his spyglass out, surveying the coast, his knee hooked over the tiller to hold it still. He lowered the telescope, frowned, and raised the glass again.

"Enys, what's that?" he called, pointing to a discolored gash in the cliff face.

"Oh, that's an old sea cave that collapsed some time ago. Rumor had it that it used to be a smuggling den, but that's a silly old tale. The tide floods the base of the cave. No smuggler worth his salt would store goods in a place where they could get swept out to sea." He shrugged.

"It looks like someone built something in the gash." Charles looked again through the spyglass.

"I think Grayson tried to stabilize the cliff there. He said there was a barn at the top, and he didn't want to lose the building if he could help it. He put some stairs along there, and he lets the crofters use that part of the beach to fish. He said it would keep them from using the earl's stairs."

"I see. I haven't had a chance yet to look over the entire estate." Charles studied the crack in the rock. He looked sober, and Sophie wondered if he would have time to survey all the property before he was called up by the navy.

"Look, white-beaked dolphins." Miles pointed to the south.

Everyone swiveled around, and Mamie inhaled sharply. "I haven't seen a dolphin since I was a girl."

It took Sophie a moment to spot them. Sunlight reflecting off the water made them difficult to see, but once spotted, she could follow them. As the dolphins cavorted, another wave of nausea slopped through her.

Perhaps something from lunch didn't agree with her. She closed her eyes, but the dizziness got worse.

"Are you well?" Mamie asked, resting her hand on Sophie's arm.

Swallowing hard, Sophie nodded. "Fine." The word came out a whisper. Her head spun, and her stomach lurched.

"Sophie?" Charles waved to Miles to take over the tiller and squatted beside her. "What's wrong?"

Bile rose, and with an effort she held it back, but weakness radiated through her limbs. What was wrong with her?

"Sophie, my dear, I think you're seasick."

The humor tingeing his voice did not endear him to her at that moment. Seasick? How humiliating.

"Miles, we'll run for home. Sophie, stare at the horizon and take deep breaths. Here, Betsy, you sit with Penny." He massaged Sophie's hands for a moment and then went to the tiller. "Prepare to come around."

They had been out barely half an hour. Sophie felt bad cutting everyone's enjoyment short, but she wasn't sorry when the cove came into view. Still, drawing up beside the dock took much longer than she would have liked, involving furling sails and applying oars.

"Miles, see that she's buttoned up."

Sophie jerked her head up, then relaxed, realizing Charles was talking about the *Shearwater*.

"Penny, can you look after the girls and Miss Mamie?"

"Yes, sir. We'll be fine. You take care of Sophie."

Thea skipped down the deck, her hair and dress damp with sea spray, her eyes alight. "That was the best fun. Too bad you got sick, Sophie. When can we go again?"

Sophie let the conversation go unheeded. It took all her concentration not to embarrass herself by bringing up her lunch. She couldn't recall ever feeling so unwell. How could it be that only a few moments on the water had hit her so hard?

"Come, my dear. Let's get you back on land." Charles helped her rise and put his arm around her waist. "You'll feel better soon."

Miles leapt to the dock to assist, and Sophie soon stood on the weathered planks. Her head still swam, and her legs felt like jelly.

The girls chattered and clattered toward the staircase, but Charles remained by Sophie's side. "Don't rush. Take your time." He rubbed circles between her shoulder blades. "And don't feel badly. Did you know that Admiral Lord Nelson, England's greatest naval commander, suffered from seasickness?"

Sophie sent him a skeptical look as she concentrated on breathing deeply and trying to stop the rocking feeling in her head.

"No, it's true. For the first three or four days of a cruise, he was wretched. Kept to his cabin and let his first officer run the ship." They made slow progress down the pier and across the sand. "When we get back to the house, you can have a lie down with a nice cold cloth on your forehead. You'll feel better soon."

"I cannot believe I get seasick." She blew out a breath as they mounted the stairs. "I had no idea. We are a mismatched pair if ever there was one, aren't we?"

Once they reached the house, Mrs. Chapman met them at the door. "Lady Sophia? Are you poorly?"

She tried to smile to reassure the housekeeper.

Charles tightened his hold around her waist, and she couldn't say she minded. It felt better to have someone to lean on. "Mrs. Chapman, will you brew some ginger tea and bring it to Lady Sophia's room?"

"Of course. I prepared everything as you asked. I'll be along directly."

Sophia didn't have long to puzzle over what they were talking about. Charles turned left at the top of the stairs, guiding her toward his own rooms. Her steps slowed, and she sent him a bewildered look.

"Don't worry. I've nothing untoward in mind. But as my wife"—he paused, as if pondering how odd that sounded—"you will be expected to sleep in the mistress of the manor's room. Mrs. Chapman reminded me this morning that the room was unaired and had yet to be cleaned, but she assured me she would see to it."

Of course. Mrs. Chapman would not know that theirs was anything other than a real marriage, and appearances must be maintained.

When he opened the door, she sucked in a breath. "Oh, it's lovely." She wished she didn't feel so weak. Perhaps in a while she would be able to truly appreciate the beauty of this room.

"Come lie down. I'll open the windows so you can get a fresh breeze." He tugged on her bonnet ribbon and lifted the hat from her head.

The bed had a set of stairs, and he held her hand until she lay on the pale-blue coverlet. Overhead, the canopy of ruched blue cloth surrounded a golden medallion. Charles disappeared, and Sophie closed her eyes. Her stomach began to settle and the weakness to bleed out of her limbs.

He returned with a pitcher of water and a cloth over his arm. Sitting on the side of the bed, he dipped the cloth, wrung it out, and placed it on her forehead. "I'm an old hand dealing with seasickness."

"Have you ever suffered it yourself?" He had taken her hand, and she liked the way hers nestled in his. She hadn't felt so protected and cherished since Rich went away to war.

Silly thoughts, since theirs was more of a business arrangement than anything. Well, not business exactly, since they were friends, but it was far from a grand romance. Still, it felt nice to have someone take care of her for a change.

"I never have. Not even in the roughest seas. I remember once in the Caribbean we hit a hurricane. Half the crew had their heads in buckets before it blew itself out."

Her queasiness returned with the mental image.

He chuckled. "I'm sorry, my dear. That was thoughtless of me. You'll feel better soon."

Mrs. Chapman arrived with the tea tray, and Sophie scooted up, holding the cloth against her head, then switching it to the nape of her neck. Charles held the cup, but she took it from his hands. "I can do it, thank you." She sipped the hot, fragrant liquid, letting the ginger tea hit her stomach and waiting to see what the reaction would be.

It stayed down, warming her from within, and she dared another dose.

"There you are—you'll be right in no time."

"Shall I serve dinner in the formal dining room tonight?" Mrs. Chapman asked.

Sophie shook her head. "I don't believe I want dinner. You and the girls can eat in the kitchen again, and we'll try the dining room tomorrow."

Late that night, as she lay in the beautiful bed, fully recovered, she pondered her circumstances. She had never intended to marry after losing Rich, but now that she was a wife, she had never considered that she would spend her married nights alone. She had agreed to this arrangement, but she felt an odd yearning now that the deed was done. Her heart longed for something that seemed just out of reach. A marriage of convenience meant . . . forever being celibate. Never being loved. Never being a mother.

Not that she had ever imagined bearing children to anyone other than Rich, but Rich was dead and so were her plans and dreams with him.

The captain had his own plans and dreams, and they didn't involve fathering children with his wife, nor even living much of the time with her.

She would have to content herself with mothering the girls.

Restlessly, she slid out of bed and padded to the window. Brushing aside the curtains, she looked out on the blackness of the sea. Clouds had rolled in, and the moon and stars hid. The sea looked like ink, and it was hard to make out where the land ended and the water began.

Far out on the edge of the cliff, though, a dot of light moved. She narrowed her eyes and leaned forward. Someone with a lantern. The light swung in a tiny arc, matching the pace of the person who carried it. Who would be out walking in the middle of the night?

Was it the captain? Was Charles as restless as she, contemplating their unconsummated marriage?

"Lord, did we do the right thing? I felt at such peace when I made the decision. It seemed an answer to my prayers. But I have to wonder—what does a God-honoring marriage look like? Is it enough that we've come together to parent these children and look after this property?"

The light disappeared, and she jerked. Either the man had headed down the stairs to the dock, or he'd fallen off the cliff.

Chapter 10

One week later, Sophie didn't know whether to bless or curse the arrival of the mail. For days there had been no mail at all, and now a deluge. She had known her mother would have a response to the letter Sophie had sent telling her of her marriage to the earl, but this was ridiculous.

"You are the most vexing child. What of my house party plans? I'm only thankful the invitations hadn't gone out yet. Still, at least this time you've managed to snag an earl, but Rothwell is not a well-considered name at the moment. It has only recently come to my attention that his cousin tried to kill the Prince Regent! This is what I get for allowing you to travel. I knew in my bones this escapade to the coast was a mistake."

The letter went on for some time, but it was the final sally that made Sophie wince.

"Your brother will be there in a few days. He has some business that takes him to Sussex, and he will journey over to see for himself what you've gotten into. And you should prepare a room for me. I will come myself in a few weeks, when I've gotten over my outrage. Cilla and Charlotte send their regards."

Marcus was coming?

And then Mother?

She blew out a long breath, bracing herself for the onslaught of her family. She set aside her mother's letter to see what Charlotte and Marcus had to say. Charlotte had started first.

"Trust you, darling, to leap into matrimony. Are you all right? I hurt to think that you got married with none of your family in attendance, not even Marcus, who would have walked you down the aisle. I wish you every happiness though. Do write and tell me everything. Your letter of announcement was much too terse. I need to know you are well."

The day before the wedding, Sophie had fired off a missive to everyone at Haverly, because there hadn't been time for a longer epistle. And she had kept it brief and sent it at the last moment, because she hadn't wanted anyone to come haring down to the coast to talk her out of it.

Marcus came over very big-brotherish.

"Soph, you bedlamite. What are you thinking? If I were there, I don't know if I would turn you over my knee or pull you into a hug. It's just as well I made inquiries into Captain Wyvern. At least I know the caliber of the man whom you've married. However, such a bold move means I must come and see for myself which way the wind is blowing. Expect me shortly after you receive this letter. And for mercy's sake, don't do anything else rash before I get there."

She set her mail on the corner of the desk. Her brother's chiding made her feel warm and secure in his love.

Charles read his mail at his desk.

"Good news?" she asked. One of the letters had been from the Admiralty.

"Yes and no. Admiral Barrington has taken my need of an estate steward to heart, and he's sending along an applicant who should arrive within the fortnight. One Alistair Lythgoe, former naval first lieutenant. Barrington assures me he is just the man for the job. I hope so. After speaking with the local solicitor, Will Owens, I've decided a man from outside the district would be a better fit."

"That's good, right? So what is the bad news?"

He tossed the pages down on the desk and stood quickly, as if he couldn't bear to remain seated. "Parliament has rejected the naval blockade of Elba. They say there is no danger of Napoleon escaping his exile, and the war has already nearly bankrupted the nation. There is no need for the expense of a blockade. Therefore, there is no command awaiting me in Portsmouth."

He went to the windows, staring out to sea. Hands clasped behind his back, his shoulders straight, muscles rigid, he embodied frustration.

No naval command? What did that mean for them, then? Would he stay here at Gateshead? Or would he take a position with one of the merchant ship companies?

She didn't know her new husband well enough to predict how he handled disappointment. She had seen him surprised, grieving, and perplexed, but not yet disappointed. Should she give him an opportunity to talk about it? Should she leave him alone?

When he turned from the window, he appeared composed, though lines of strain bracketed his mouth. "How much correspondence is left?"

"Just one. Addressed to the Earl of Rothwell."

He pulled a stiff card from the envelope. "Hmm. An invitation. For you, me, Lady Richardson, and . . . Penny."

"An invitation? To what?" She leaned forward as he turned the card around.

"An assembly in the village. Dancing and refreshment. Four days from now."

Sophie hadn't attended a social event in months. "What a nice way to get to know people here. I wonder if there is time to have dresses made? Is there a seamstress in the village?"

Charles didn't reply, his mind far away. He turned the card in his hands, holding it by opposite points.

"Shall I answer the invitation in the affirmative?" she asked, gathering the letters together and putting them in order of importance for responses.

"I suppose. I hadn't thought to be here long enough to take part in local events, but it looks like I will have to be." His tone was flat, accepting but unenthused.

She tried not to take offense, but it hurt to know he was so disappointed to have to remain at Gateshead with her.

Which was silly, because it wasn't as if theirs was a real marriage with emotional involvement. He had laid out his plans and expectations, and she had agreed to them with little reservation. What exactly did she want?

"I'll accept the invitation on behalf of all of us, and if you're called away to duty before then, we'll make your excuses for you."

Penny went into predictable raptures at being invited to her very first dance. "Oh, what shall I wear? This will be so much fun. Who will attend? What happens at a country dance?" She clapped her hands to her cheeks and then stacked them atop her head. "Sophie, I don't know how to dance. What shall I do?"

"Didn't Miss Fricklin's curriculum include dance lessons?" What ladies' academy failed to teach such important things? Sophie sorted through the girls' clothing in the armoire, comparing what she saw to the lists the girls had made.

"Yes, she offered dancing instruction, but not until a student's final year. Only the oldest girls got dance lessons, because a dancing master cost so much. Miss Fricklin always pinched pennies where she could. I was supposed to start lessons next term."

"Well, four days isn't much time, but you're a bright girl, and you can learn some basic steps. For now, we need to go to the village and search out a dressmaker. You've nothing suitable for a party, and I would love to have a new dress too. Thea and Betsy, you can come along. We can put in a gloriously large order and have the seamstress expedite the party dresses." Sophie felt a lightness of heart. Having foregone a debut Season in London in favor of becoming engaged to Rich and staying at Primrose to care for Mamie, she had missed out on grand balls. But she loved to dance. It had been one of her favorite classes at school. Teaching Penny to promenade and dance would be a doddle.

When she asked after a seamstress, Miles shrugged. "There's one in town. I can go and fetch her."

"Oh, no, we'll go to her." *I could do with a bit of an outing. I've barely been off the estate since I arrived.*

"She won't mind, ma'am. Really." Miles shifted from foot to foot. "She prefers to go to her clients. I'll fetch her now."

"Don't be ridiculous. I have quite a list of things I need, and I want to see what fabrics she has on hand and whether we will need to send to a larger town for some things." Sophie frowned. Miles would need some serious training before he was a proper footman. A proper footman didn't argue with his mistress, nor should she have to explain her reasoning to him. Sophie always endeavored to be kind and understanding with her employees, but she also maintained discipline when needed.

When the dowager arrived, Miles had better know his responsibilities, or Sophie would never hear the end of it.

"Fetch the carriage."

Mamie opted to remain at Gateshead. "I have enough dresses, my dear. I'll wear my black taffeta in any case." She patted Sophie's hand. "Now that you've married, you can wear pretty colors again. I love you in light colors that match your disposition."

The town had a quiet charm, with several shops and thatched cottages butted up against one another along the High Street. There was even a stretch of cobbles, unusual in such a small village. The town had maybe three hundred residents? Where had they gathered the money for a cobbled street? Every house looked in good repair, prosperous, and tidy.

As they flashed past the livery, Sophie caught sight of a large, bearded gentleman who reminded her of one of her brother's employees. But Partridge wouldn't be in Gateshead. At least not yet. He was either with Marcus on business in Sussex, or Marcus had left him at home to watch over Charlotte. Partridge was invariably kind and polite to Sophie when they crossed paths, but he was a bit of a mystery as well. This man was so like him, they could be brothers. She craned her neck but lost sight of him too quickly for another look.

Eventually, on the far side of town, Miles pulled up before a thatched cottage with a pretty garden out front. "This is Madam Stipple's. She's a sailor's widow, and she makes her living with her needle. Used to be a seamstress in London, I heard. She'll do you right. Though she won't be best pleased to have you calling. She goes to her clients, like I said." He shoved his hands into his pockets, not exactly scowling, but not happy either.

Sophie knocked, and a youngish woman with curly blonde hair becomingly arranged opened the top half of the Dutch door a few inches.

"Yes?"

"Madam Stipple?"

"Yes." The woman regarded Sophie, a wary look in her eyes. She glanced over Sophie's shoulder to where Miles waited by the carriage.

"I'm Lady Rothwell. I've come to see about the purchase of some clothing for myself and my wards." She held her arm out to where Penny, Thea, and Betsy waited.

"Oh, Lady Rothwell." She put her hand to her throat. "I don't usually . . . I mean, I had assumed if you needed something, I would bring it to Gateshead for you." She kept hold of the half door.

"That's very kind of you, and perhaps we will do so in the future, but as we're here now, may we come inside?" What an odd way for a craftswoman to behave. "Time is of the essence, and we'd like to order new gowns for the assembly in just a few days."

Madam Stipple stood still long enough that Sophie thought she might refuse, but eventually she stepped back and opened the lower half of the door.

The entire front room had been turned into a workroom with a cutting table, shelves of cloth, and baskets of buttons, hooks, and trim. A triple mirror stood in one corner, and a bowl of lavender buds scented the air. It looked ready for patrons. Why had she been so reluctant to let anyone in when she clearly served customers here?

"What an amazing inventory. You must have had quite a shop in London." Sophie let her hand drift over a vivid bolt of red velvet. Imagine finding such a treasure trove in this little village.

Thea and Betsy pressed their noses against a glass case of ostrich feathers, ribbons, and jet beads, while Penny wandered to the rolls of duchesse satin and brocade.

It would be disloyal to Charles and present the wrong face to the village and to the girls for Sophie to continue wearing somber colors, so she had put away her grays and blacks. For this celebration she would choose something light and pretty.

Madam Stipple invited Sophie to have a seat in an overstuffed chair. "I have pattern books, if you would like to peruse them. I really wouldn't mind visiting you at the manor." She drew a pad of paper from a shelf beneath the cutting table. "I can jot down some ideas and bring samples for your approval?"

"That won't be necessary." Sophie had never felt so unwelcome in a retail shop. "Penny and I are looking for dresses for the assembly. Is there time to make two gowns with the dance so near?"

"As long as you don't ask for anything too elaborate that will require much embellishing, and as long as you don't mind them being delivered the day of the party, it should not be a problem." She poised her pencil over the paper. "I have a couple of ladies I can call upon for help with the basic sewing."

"That will be fine then. Once the gowns are completed, I have several other things that need making up." She consulted her list.

Penny held up a length of teal brocade. "What do you think, Sophie?"

"While the color flatters you, the material is both too ornate and too heavy for a dancing dress. Look in the muslins along that wall. You may have anything white, pale pink, or light blue. Those are appropriate colors for a young girl at her first dance."

Penny put the heavy fabric down, reluctance in every slow movement. To cheer her, Sophie said, "You may pick out several yards of ribbon to match the fabric you choose. Madam Stipple can trim the gown, and we can use the same ribbon to thread through your hair."

And in a blink, all was right once more in Penny's world.

"I wish I didn't have to wear dresses," Thea said. "I wish I could wear knee breeches like a boy. I could climb trees and run faster without skirts getting in the way." She stirred a basket of buttons with her finger.

Though Madam Stipple and Penny were shocked, Sophie wasn't surprised. There were times when she had wished the same when she was growing up. What would it feel like to wear breeches and stalk around in boots? Skirts did hamper a girl from time to time.

"Thea, I understand how you feel, but you must remember that God didn't make a mistake when He made you female. If you continue to rue being born a girl, you'll always be blaming God and letting that hold you back. You can and will do amazing things, and being a girl won't stop you if you put your mind to it."

"Can I be a sailor?" Thea asked. "Like the captain?"

Did Charles know the impression he'd made on the girls in such a short time? Betsy followed him everywhere, copying his movements and mannerisms, and if his bicorn wasn't on his head, it was on hers.

And though Thea stated she wished she was a boy, her actions said that what she really wanted was to belong to someone, to be someone's little girl. Someone safe, who wouldn't abandon her.

"Perhaps not in the British navy, but there is nothing to stop you from learning to sail. And aren't you blessed to have a naval captain who also owns a boat as your guardian? Ask him to teach you. I'm sure he'll oblige." And perhaps it would occupy his time until he received a new commission.

Betsy opened a polished wooden box about the size of a tea chest. "Pretty."

Inside, in separate compartments, was a lovely selection of lace. Ivory, white, gold, black, pastels and bright colors. Several of the cards had French inscriptions.

Sophie picked up one spool of lace about four inches across. Where had she seen it before?

Madam Stipple hurried over and took the card from Sophie and replaced it in the box. She closed the lid and set it on a high shelf. "I'm sorry. Those aren't for sale." She sent a stern look toward Betsy. "Don't open things that don't belong to you, miss."

Betsy's eyes grew round, and her bottom lip quivered.

"Never mind, Betsy. It's my fault. I should have told you to look but don't touch." Sophie cupped the child's head, trying to hold on to her temper. The chiding of Madam Stipple had brought out a fierce protectiveness in Sophie.

Sophie's memory clicked. At church. That's where she'd seen that distinctive wide lace pattern. The public house owner's wife had that same trim on her dress. Mamie had asked her about it. The woman had claimed it had come from an old dress and been sewn onto a new one.

And yet here was the same lace in the dressmaker's shop. Sophie could see why the dressmaker wouldn't want anyone poking around in that box. The lace was clearly French contraband. How had she acquired it?

Penny dithered between the pale-blue and the pale-pink muslin until Thea lost her patience. "Close your eyes and poke one with a pin, for pity's sake. You'd think you were picking out clothes to go to court. It's just a country dance."

Betsy had fallen in love with a bundle of rabbit skins used for trimming coats, capes, and muffs, and with Sophie's permission stroked the soft fur over and over. Sophie tucked this knowledge away for future use. Though it was August now, Christmas was coming. Perhaps a hooded cape for Betsy trimmed in fur would be a nice gift.

Thea slumped into a chair.

"Sit properly, Thea. You're not a bag of wheat." The words were out before Sophie knew she'd said them, and she paused. It was a correction her mother had spoken often when Sophie was little.

The child struggled upright and put her feet primly together, folding her hands in her lap, but her jaw jutted at a rebellious angle. Sophie stifled a laugh. She had a feeling that Thea was obeying on the outside but not so much on the inside.

When Penny finally chose the pink, because she liked the pink ribbon the best, Sophie applauded her taste. "You will look like a rose. I'm certain you won't lack for partners for this dance."

For herself, Sophie chose a light-green gown with gold trim. She had nothing like it in her wardrobe, and Charles had a forest-green coat that would look well if he wore it alongside her. Once that was settled, she consulted her list for the girls.

Madam Stipple, when she discovered the size of the order, grew more accommodating. Nightgowns, caps, dresses, petticoats, pinafores, stockings—the items added up. Betsy stood sweetly to be measured, but Thea squirmed.

"She's sticking me," she complained as Madam Stipple pinned pattern pieces.

"If you'd stand still, she wouldn't." Penny had no sympathy. She picked up an ostrich feather, running the barbs through her fingers and then poking the feather into her hair, studying her reflection in the triple mirror. "I can't wait to be old enough to wear all the colors and all the accessories."

Don't rush things, Penny. There's plenty of time to be an adult. Don't miss out on the life you have now hoping for something in the future. But Sophie remembered what it was like to want to hasten her growing up, to have some say in what happened to her.

The door opened, and the vicar came in. "Good afternoon, ladies. What a pleasant surprise. I saw your carriage outside. Doing a bit of shopping, are you?" He spoke to Sophie, but he locked eyes with Madam Stipple.

"Yes, and I must say how happy I am to find such a well-stocked dressmaker's shop here in the village," Sophie said.

Reverend Dunhill rested his hand on the cutting table. "Harriet, I thought you were going to visit Gateshead with your wares rather than put Lady Rothwell out, forcing her to come here?" He phrased it as a question, but an edge to his voice drew Sophie's attention.

"That was my plan, Reverend." The seamstress took a few steps back and put the table between herself and the preacher.

"I'm afraid we stole a march on her," Sophie said. "Penny and I were in such a hurry to procure dance dresses that we decided to come to town." *What was going on here?* Like any village, there were undercurrents in relationships that one couldn't decode until one had been a resident for some time. That must be why there were so many signals being sent that Sophie couldn't decipher.

"I see. I hate to interrupt, but are my shirts ready, Harriet?"

"They are. I finished the last buttonhole this morning." She took a paper-wrapped package from one of the shelves. She held it at arm's length, eyes wary.

"Thank you, madam. I am much obliged. I do hope you won't keep the countess and her charges long. I'm certain they have a busy schedule." He tucked the parcel under his arm, sending a sharp look at the seamstress. "I'll see you at the assembly, no doubt." Touching the brim of his hat, he ducked outside.

Glancing through the window, Sophie watched the reverend approach Miles, who leaned against the hitching rail. As the preacher neared, Miles straightened. Dunhill leaned in, his finger in Miles's face, and whatever he said hit hard enough for Miles to wince and retreat.

Perhaps Dunhill was having a bad day. Sophie supposed preachers were like anyone else, sometimes waking cross-grained and ill-tempered. He'd been so cordial at Gateshead. Was this the real Dunhill, or was it an anomaly?

"He didn't pay you," Thea pointed out to Madam Stipple. "Do you want me to run after him and bring him back?"

The shop owner shook her head quickly, picking up her tape measure and setting it down, smoothing the hair at the nape of her neck. "There's no need. I'll send him a bill."

The vicar jabbed the air once more in front of Miles's nose and stalked away. Miles sagged against the carriage wheel and wiped his brow, staring after him.

Charles wanted to protest he didn't have time for this, but the truth was, he did. He had nothing but time at the moment.

He stood in the ballroom at Gateshead, ruefully contemplating living in a house large enough to boast a room just for dancing. It was all a long way from the captain's quarters aboard the *Dogged*. He had occupied the largest personal space aboard the ship, and it would still have fit in this room several times over.

"Mamie will accompany us. She plays beautifully." Sophie drew back the curtains, letting in sunlight and revealing the seascape outside. One of the new maids hired by Mrs. Chapman ran a dust mop over the floor, while the housekeeper supervised. Mamie took her seat at the pianoforte and played a few keys.

She winced. "It's in need of a tuning."

Charles couldn't tell one way or the other. The only music he'd been subjected to for most of his life was hymns on a Sunday morning aboard ship and sea shanties the rest of the week.

Penny bit her lower lip, her eyes wide as she hovered near the doorway. What was the matter with the child? She looked about to bolt. After going into raptures about being invited to a party, now she radiated nervousness. If she was this strung up practicing, what would she be like the night of the dance?

"Come in," Sophie invited. "This will be painless, I promise. At least for you and me. I can't vouch for the captain. He might get his toes stepped on a few times." She sent a teasing glance his way, and he smiled in response.

Charles found he'd smiled a lot recently, especially at Sophie. Aboard ship he was known for his stern visage and lack of humor, but one couldn't remain stoic around the armada of girls who had invaded his life. What would his crew think if they could see him now?

Betsy strode into the room, his bicorn on her head, her hands behind her back. She took steps too long for her short legs, but it was a fair imitation of his walk, even to the slight roll he'd developed from years at sea.

"Are you taking the watch?" he asked, hiding his laughter.

"Aye, aye, Captain." She snapped a little salute, much to his amusement.

No one had ever told him how observant children were. Nor how much they liked to pretend. He had never imagined he would engender such feelings in any child, much less a girl of tender years. It made him feel . . . paternal?

"I'm glad I don't have to learn how to dance." Thea did a pirouette with coltish grace, her dress belling out. She collapsed onto the floor in a heap of arms and legs. "I'd rather climb trees than dance. Miles let me swing on a rope in the horse barn, until that old grump Grayson ran us out of there. When are we taking the boat out again? I love sailing more than anything."

If Thea had been a boy, he would seek a navy position for her with all haste. She had pelted him with questions each night at dinner about the parts of a ship and how to sail. He'd not seen a keener mind amongst the many cabin boys he'd tutored over the years. She would have made a fine sailor.

Sophie went to the center of the room and put her hands on her waist. Charles tried not to notice how her hips flared gently. She had a striking figure, and her dress touched her in all the right places to garner a man's attention, though there was nothing bawdy or tawdry about her attire. With the discarding of mourning clothes, she now resembled the woman in her letters, lighthearted, adventurous, and inquisitive. He saw new facets of her character all the time, and with every passing day, he felt more and more drawn to her.

"Perhaps we should begin with a country dance. There should be more people, but you will get the general idea. Penny, come stand where you can see well."

Mamie played an introduction, and Charles took his place opposite Sophie. He held out his hands, and hers fit into his nicely. He caught the beat Mamie set, and they were away.

He glided down the room, guiding Sophie through the simple pattern. She had a lightness and grace to her movement and mirrored him flawlessly.

She looked at his face the whole time, unlike some girls who looked at their feet when they danced. The Adriatic under sunny skies couldn't have been bluer than her eyes. As the tempo increased, color came into her cheeks, and she laughed.

"You're very good," she said as she curtsied to him when the song ended.

"Most sailors make good dance partners." He shrugged, but her compliment pleased him. "You're an excellent dancer yourself."

"Hours of lessons. The dancing master at my finishing school was a perfectionist." She brushed back a curl on her cheek and let her fingers trail down the side of her neck.

Charles swallowed, following the movement. She appeared oblivious to the effect she had on him, and he was grateful. Sophie in her letters had been appealing. Sophie in real life was proving irresistible.

"Now, Penny, you take my place." Sophie beckoned the girl to come stand before Charles.

"Oh, I'm not ready yet. May I watch just a little longer?" She twisted the ribbon tie at her waist.

"I'm surprised at you, Penny. I thought you wanted to attend this dance." Sophie put her arm around the girl, drawing her into the middle of the floor.

"I do. It's just . . ." Her voice trailed off, and she bit her lower lip, looking up at Charles with uncertainty.

Was the child afraid of him? He had done nothing to frighten her, had he?

"Penny doesn't like to have to learn anything." Thea knelt on the window seat to see outside, looking back over her shoulder as she spoke. "She wants to be good at something right away. If she can't be good at it right away, she doesn't want to do it."

Her shaft must have hit true, because Penny blushed. Thea had a way of shooting straight to the heart of an issue.

"Be that as it may, she needs to learn to dance. She won't be good at it at all if she doesn't practice." Sophie moved Penny into the correct spot.

Mamie played the introduction once more, and Charles held out his hand, trying to be as innocuous as possible.

"I'll call the steps for you, and you follow the captain," Sophie offered.

"Don't worry about making a mistake. There's no one here but us, and we don't mind. Mistakes mean you're trying," Charles reassured, and was rewarded with a nod and a determined lift to her chin.

By the time Penny had learned the steps to three different dances, everyone was tired. Betsy had abandoned her post and now rested on her tummy in a patch of afternoon sunlight, chin on her hands, feet swinging in the air over her head. Thea had found a stray button, and she lay opposite her sister, rolling it between them.

Miles Enys appeared in the doorway, tugging at his jacket. Though he wasn't required to wear a footman's livery, Sophie had insisted he have new clothes, but he didn't appear to have settled into the more restrictive garments yet.

"Mrs. Chapman's wondering if you want tea now or if she should put it back a half hour." His eyes never left Penny's, and seeing her hand in the captain's, something flared there.

Surely the young jackanapes wasn't jealous? How preposterous. But he dropped Penny's hand.

"Miles, come in. I was just going to send Thea to find you." Sophie smiled. "I thought it might be nice for Penny to perform one set with a different partner and having more people on the dance floor. Do you know how to dance?" she asked as Miles slowly came toward them.

"Yes, milady." He sounded torn between eager and appalled.

"Excellent." She pointed to his spot, and he hurried to do her bidding.

Charles wondered if Sophie realized her own natural leadership skills. She had a way of getting others to want to do what she was asking of them. Even the girls, who could scatter in every direction without notice, fulfilled her requests quickly and with good attitudes.

"Mamie? The minuet?" Sophie gathered her skirt in one hand.

Penny seemed to forget she was ever hesitant, her face alight, her steps sure. Once Sophie saw she was going all right, she turned her attention to Charles. "It's too bad we don't have more people. We could finish the lesson with the Boulanger."

"Or a reel." He stood still and let her circle him before taking her hand once more.

In what seemed a short amount of time, Mamie played the final chord. Thea jumped to her feet. "I'm glad that's over. I'm starving." She headed toward the door with Betsy in her wake, still toting Charles's hat.

Charles released Sophie's hand and bowed deeply. "A pleasure, Lady Rothwell."

Her grin shot heat through him. She dipped a low curtsy, her hand at her neckline. "An honor, Lord Rothwell."

Thea snorted on her way out.

Before Mamie rose from the pianoforte, she said, "Please, just one more. You haven't shown Penny the waltz."

"Surely they won't waltz at a country dance. And in any case, Penny's too young to waltz," Sophie objected.

"Perhaps not, but you make such a lovely couple, and I know you waltz beautifully." Mamie began a three-quarter-time tune. "Please, for me?"

Since they both made a practice of not refusing Mamie anything that was in their power to provide, Charles didn't argue. He offered his hand to Sophie, and she shook her head, placing her fingers once more into his. He barely admitted to himself how he wanted this moment.

Penny and Miles moved to the edge of the dance floor.

"It's a shame young girls aren't allowed to waltz, though I understand why. It's the easiest step to master, I think." Charles drew Sophie in and put his hand at the small of her back, trying to keep his voice casual. Counting off two measures in his head, he swung her into the one-two-three rhythm of the song. The lemon scent of her perfume drifted into his nose, and he studied her face from this new angle. She had long lashes, and her cheeks curved youthfully. He was reminded of the gap in their ages. He was an old seadog married to a stunning young woman.

She was the relic of his best friend. He had been charged with taking care of her.

What had seemed a sensible plan, this marriage of convenience, now seemed absurd. He'd bound her to himself with promises that he would not often be at Gateshead, and she had accepted on those terms.

He moved to the music, exerting slight pressure on her spine, but leading lightly. She might have been a bit of thistledown, she was so airy. She had been made to waltz.

Desire caught him amidships, and he missed a step. Pivoting to cover the mistake, he tried to bring reason to bear on his emotions. The regard in which he had held her up to this moment blossomed into something much stronger, and he realized he wanted nothing more than to stop and cup her face between his hands and taste those rose-colored lips.

Realizing where his thoughts were leading him, he stopped dancing, letting his hands fall away. Sophie's momentum carried her a few more steps, and a startled look crossed her face.

"What's wrong?"

He felt a fool. For all he had been on his guard against his feelings for her, they had ambushed him.

"Nothing. I do apologize. I just remembered something I need to do. Don't wait on me to have your tea." He bowed and made his escape, retreating from the scene like a coward.

His study beckoned, and he made for that personal sanctuary. He ignored the piles of papers on his desk in favor of going to stand at the windows in the alcove.

What a cake he'd made of himself. He needed a brisk walk and a stern lecture. The sooner he had a commission the better. If he didn't hear again from the Admiralty soon, he'd be forced to swallow his pride and apply at a merchant company for a job. For the first time, staying at the estate had a strong pull, possibly stronger than that of the sea. Was his heart going to be a traitor to his calling?

He couldn't stay at Gateshead if he was going to be foolish enough to fall in love with his wife.

It would somehow be disloyal to Rich, wouldn't it? He was tasked with looking after Sophie. Just as he was the girls. He should think of her only in those terms. She might be married to him, but she was like a ward, and he was like a guardian. Right?

In love. What twaddle.

Going away to sea under those circumstances would be both a relief and pure torture. How had Rich managed to keep an even keel, loving Sophie and yet being parted from her for such long stretches?

He pounded his fist on the windowsill. What an idiot he was.

Well, he wasn't going to let it happen. It was a matter of disciplining his mind and heart.

Perhaps a bit of tedium with the estate books would sort him out. There was nothing so unromantic as ledgers. He would be glad when Alastair Lythgoe arrived to take the position of steward. Charles would gladly foist most of the paperwork onto Lythgoe's desk.

The leather of the most recent of his uncle's account books creaked and cracked as Charles pressed it open. In a final protest, the spine gave up the fight, breaking at the hinge and exposing the spine's interior. A small puff of dust rose up, and Charles swatted it away.

What was this?

A roll of paper had been shoved down the spine and now lay on the marbled endpaper. Charles picked it up, mildly curious. His uncle had been a long ways off being in his right mind, and Charles had found similar documents tucked here and there in the old earl's rooms. Spidery notes that made no sense. He'd thrown them into the fire-starter bin each time he'd found one.

Unrolling the paper, which was in remarkably good condition—the hiding place must have sheltered it from wear—he noted that this one was different. It hadn't been written by his uncle.

It was a letter addressed to the former earl.

Rothwell,

The money has been deposited in your account. Your share of the haul was 30 percent, as agreed. The next load will leave Calais on the ninth. See that your boat is on station to receive it on the eleventh. We can't hang about waiting for you. The Revenue cutter has been doing sweeps, and the last thing we want is to get caught in that net. This time light the signal lamp. The flag was of no use to us in the dark.

P.

Charles read the note again, hoping, praying he had misunderstood. But no. There could be no other explanation.

His uncle had played some part in smuggling goods.

Fire burned along his veins. He'd spent the greater part of his life defending England, protecting her borders, manning the blockade, and here his own uncle had been subverting the law and bringing in contraband.

Which meant at least some of Charles's inheritance had been funded by illegal activity. The fat bank account his uncle had amassed had come through breaking the law.

He examined the note again. No date. No way to tell when it had been written or when it had been received. The paper hadn't yellowed or cracked, nor had the ink faded. It looked as if it could have been written yesterday.

His uncle's boat had been used in the crime. Which meant that someone else knew about it, because his uncle, as old as he was, hadn't been running the *Shearwater* out into the channel to pick up contraband alone.

Miles?

Grayson?

Someone else?

Who was "P"? Pembroke, the girls' father?

Two questions were paramount: Was the smuggling still going on, and what should Charles do about it?

He folded the paper and slipped it into his pocket. He would need to deal with this before he took up a captaincy. Lawbreaking had no place at Gateshead, not while he was in charge.

At least this new problem had gotten his mind off Sophie.

Chapter 11

The night of the assembly, Thea stood by the front door, face reproachful. "I don't see why I can't go."

Sophie checked her appearance in the mirror one last time as the carriage pulled into the circular drive. She had to stand on tiptoe and crane her neck, because Penny primped and tried different expressions before her reflection, taking up nearly all the space in front of the looking glass.

Without turning around, Penny scolded her sister. "You've done nothing but poke fun and chide me for being excited to go, and now you want to come?" She made a little pout at her reflection, lowering her chin and batting her lashes.

Thea crossed her thin arms. "I don't like being left out. I'll miss everything if I have to stay here. I don't see why you got invited. You're not that much older than me."

"Nearly five years, darling." The eldest Pembroke sister was too consumed with her own excitement to worry about how her middle sister was faring.

Going to Thea, Sophie cupped the child's cheek. "I know. I felt the same way when I was your age. But you'll get to go soon enough. And I promise to tell you everything tomorrow morning."

"Can I come to your room first thing?"

"Absolutely." Sophie hid her wince. Thea was known for rising before the rooster, and tonight they would be late returning. She would jump into Sophie's bed at first light with questions and wiggles and opinions galore. Still, one night of short sleep in exchange for making Thea feel safe and loved? A bargain.

Mamie waited patiently in her dark gown with the jet-bead trim. Sophie had styled her hair in pretty curls and loaned her a bandeau of black velvet to wear. Sophie wanted to hug her, she looked so sweet.

"Where are we going?" she asked.

"A village dance, Mamie. There will be food and music and new friends to meet." Sophie spoke with confidence, but a tickle of unease went through her. Today hadn't been a good memory day for Mamie, and she'd needed reminding several times about tonight's event. Here at Gateshead, her good days had outnumbered her bad, but the bad ones hadn't disappeared altogether.

Charles hurried down the stairs. "Sorry to be late. Are we ready?"

Feathers of excitement brushed Sophie's skin. He looked so distinguished in his formal attire. Though she liked his naval uniform, Charles Wyvern in civilian tailoring with snowy linens was enough to take a girl's breath away.

She covered her surprise by checking that her reticule and fan hung just right from her wrist.

When had she begun to think of him as handsome? Austere, yes. Commanding. Even a touch dashing, as Cilla had commented . . . but handsome?

Her tastes lay in a different direction, didn't they? Charles looked nothing like Rich. Rich had been shorter, stockier, with chestnut hair. More blunt of features with a strong jaw and broad brow. And in Sophie's eyes, perfect.

And yet the captain's appearance made her heart bump against her stays in an odd manner. *Careful, Sophie. You would be unwise to take more than a bit of notice of him. Don't let your head be turned. Yours is a business arrangement only, and the last thing you want is to be attracted to a man who will never be content at home. You had enough of that with Rich, forever waiting for him to return to you.*

Charles offered his arm. "I'll be the envy of every man there, escorting such beauties." His words were proper and flattering, but he had a distracted look, as if he had much on his mind. Something had put him on edge ever since they had waltzed together a few days previously. He'd been reticent, and he'd taken a long walk at dusk every evening, refusing company, even Sophie's.

Was he getting restless about not hearing anything more from the Admiralty? He had been so disappointed when the blockade of Elba had fallen through. They hadn't spoken of what his plans would be, though she recalled him saying a captaincy of a merchant ship would be a last resort.

Once inside the carriage, excited tension radiated from Penny and she flicked open her fan, then clicked it shut, fidgeting and unable to sit still.

Mamie hummed quietly to herself, content enough to be with them, though Sophie wasn't certain she fully grasped where they were headed. Sophie only hoped the villagers would be kind.

Sophie smoothed her skirts and tried to lighten the mood. "I haven't attended a dance in a very long time. When I think of the dances we had at Haverly House, the weeklong party we had to celebrate my brother Neville becoming engaged to Cilla, we danced every night. I wasn't much older than Penny is now. I met Rich that week. Do you remember, Mamie?"

"I remember that night." Mamie's voice had a faraway quality. "You were everywhere, chatting and laughing, and Rich couldn't take his eyes off you. He came home that night and declared he was going to marry you someday."

"That's so romantic. And tragic." Penny sighed. "But look how things turned out. Now you have the captain, and you're a countess. You got a happy ending after all."

Sophie nodded, and Charles shifted on his seat. She wouldn't . . . couldn't . . . explain to Penny the true nature of their marriage. But it was an answer to prayer, for both of them, she hoped.

Almost as if Mamie had read her mind, the older woman said, "I prayed very hard for you, Sophie, when Rich died. I was afraid you would mourn him until you were old and gray like me. You loved him very much, but he would never have wanted you to stop living. I'm glad you two made a match of it. Your marriage was the answer to my prayers."

Sophie had thought so at the time, but how she wished she could talk to Rich just once more, to get his blessing, to explain her reasons.

"I'm grateful that you pray for me, Mamie." Sophie leaned across and patted her hand. "I only hope that Marcus and Mother think this marriage a blessing when they arrive. I did tell you they were coming? Marcus first, and then the dowager will descend. I feel Gateshead should brace itself as if for inclement weather."

"You do talk a lot of nonsense, child. You love your mother, and she loves you. Beneath all that bluster is a woman who cares for her children so much, she doesn't realize how forceful she sounds. I've always gotten along with Honora Haverly, in spite of her being a duchess and putting on airs."

The carriage stopped before the public house, and Penny could barely contain herself. Light spilled from the windows, and people arrived on foot all around them, chattering and laughing.

When they climbed out, a path opened for them to the door. Men bowed, and women curtsied. Charles took Sophie's elbow, herding Penny and Mamie before him.

Inside, they were led upstairs to the assembly room. A long table stood at the far end, laden with food. Miles, who had driven the carriage, came in behind them and placed Mrs. Chapman's contributions to the feast, jugged hare and apple compote, with the other dishes.

When Reverend Dunhill spied Sophie, he smiled, coming to her side. "Lady Rothwell, you're looking very well tonight. I see you brought your charges, young and old." He favored Penny with a smile and Mamie with a brief handclasp. "I hope you won't be disappointed in our rather provincial entertainments."

"I'm sure we'll have a delightful time," Sophie said.

"We'll begin soon. The musicians come from Lyme Regis, and they're quite good."

A fiddler, a flautist, and a harpist gathered in one corner, and the publican, Mr. Barker, brought a small table to set near their chairs. Mrs. Barker followed him, holding three pewter mugs and a pitcher. Sophie smiled. The musicians would be well lubricated this evening.

Penny had eyes for everything, bouncing on her toes, tapping her fan into her palm. "How are they going to fit everyone inside?"

A good question, since the room was nearly full, with more people arriving each minute.

"I imagine a large number of the gentlemen will head to the taproom." Charles tugged at his cravat, his eyes narrowed as he looked from one face to the next, as if weighing people up.

"Mamie, let's get you settled." Sophie guided her to where some pillows had been placed on benches along the wall. Several older ladies in lace caps had gathered there.

"You go and enjoy yourself, Sophie. I'll be fine here. I'll see you when they take the supper break." Mamie seemed to have gathered herself and to be aware of her surroundings again.

"Ladies and Gentlemen, assemble for the promenade." A stout little man with a shiny bald head and fringes of hair sticking out over his ears stood on tiptoe. His voice was strikingly loud for such a short fellow.

"I forgot to find a partner for Penny. I'll be back to check on you, Mamie. If you need anything, I'll be nearby."

She hurried through the crowd, but she needn't have worried about Penny. The girl was surrounded by young men, and Charles was at her side, frowning. The reverend was making introductions, and Penny looked flushed and overwhelmed.

"This is Ulrich Fields. His father is the blacksmith here, and Ulrich helps out in the forge." Reverend Dunhill drew forward a sturdy young fellow with blazing-red hair that would rival Thea's. "I can vouch for his character."

Charles gave a short nod, and the transaction was done. Ulrich bowed, held his hand out, and led Penny away like a prize.

The rest of the potential partners drifted away. The reverend chuckled at their dispirited looks. "You will find yourself besieged with men asking to partner Miss Pembroke tonight. The young men will flock, and the other young ladies will pout and glower."

Charles took Sophie's left hand in his left. "We've been asked to lead out." He put his right hand on the small of her back. "I'm told it's a simple promenade, twice around the room."

A ripple of heat radiated on her skin at his touch, traveling up her arm to her chest. If she closed her eyes, she could feel each of his fingers spread on her back. She wasn't supposed to feel this way, was she? Not for the captain. A flush gathered momentum, surging into her cheeks. She prayed he wouldn't notice, and that those looking on would think her merely feeling the heat from the crowded room.

She and Charles stepped out together, and the onlookers clapped along to the lively tune. Some folks stared and whispered behind their hands as the earl and countess went by, but Sophie kept her chin level and a pleasant expression on her face. It was to be expected that they would be the objects of curiosity. That was part of the reason they'd come, to make the acquaintance of their new neighbors and settle some of the questions the villagers would no doubt have about the new residents of Gateshead.

Charles matched his steps to hers, but he still seemed distracted. His hand was firm against her back, maintaining contact, but she might have been a stranger for all the attention he paid her. His composure irked Sophie. How could his mere touch have her at sixes and sevens, and he remain unaffected? And yet he was in the right, wasn't he? Maintaining an even disposition, keeping things on a formal, business footing as agreed. She didn't *want* to feel like this, did she? Especially if she was the only one.

The moment the music stopped, villagers surrounded her, drawing her away from Charles, asking questions, introducing themselves, being so very nice. She hoped her answers were coherent, because her emotions were most certainly not.

Penny wasn't the only one with a queue of potential dance partners. Sophie danced every set. Will Owens, the solicitor, led her through the allemande, and Mr. Barker, their host for the evening, partnered her through a reel. Of Charles she saw nothing, though she kept watch for him.

By the time intermission arrived, Penny had pink cheeks and eyes filled with stars. She clasped Sophie's arm.

"This is the most fun. I've met ever so many people, and I haven't stepped on anyone's feet yet." She laughed, flicking open her fan and stirring the air around her face. "I've had no less than three offers to sit with gentlemen at supper, and Mr. Fields even declared he was going to send me a memento on the morrow."

"Really? What did the captain say about that?" Sophie asked, searching yet again for her husband in the crowd.

"I haven't seen him for some time. You don't think he would disapprove, do you? Surely Mr. Fields only means to send a posy or perhaps some chocolates?" Penny lowered her fan. "That wouldn't be too forward, would it?"

"Fields?" Miles Enys spoke from behind them. "You wouldn't take a gift from him, would you?" His hands fisted, and he scowled.

Sophie wanted to roll her eyes. Surely she hadn't been like this at their ages? No, she had fallen in love with Rich and never even thought of loving another.

Until now, her heart whispered. *You're thinking about someone else now.*

Shoving that thought away, she went to one of the open windows. The room seemed unbearably crowded and noisy. Leaning on the sill, she caught sight of Charles in the middle of the road. Who was that with him?

They stood just outside the circle of a lantern on a pole. Charles faced away from her, but she had no doubt it was him. He stood stiffly, tension in every line of his body.

He shoved a scrap of paper into the other man's face, stabbing the page with his finger.

The other man backed up a step, put his hands up, and shook his head. The light fell upon his face, even as his obsequious gesture revealed his identity.

Grayson.

The argument was growing quite heated. Perhaps Charles had discovered some discrepancy in the estate books? Had the steward been swindling? His bowing and scraping had always seemed at odds with the calculating look in his eyes.

The reverend strolled out the front door with his hand up, as if to calm the men.

Sophie's shoulders relaxed, and her breath eased.

Reverend Dunhill would sort things out. Nothing made men behave better than the arrival of the pastor.

Charles noted the interested stares as he led Sophie in the promenade. They were definitely going to provide the *on dits* for Gateshead Village for the next little while.

Sophie would stand out in any crowd, and he was proud to have her on his arm. Her green dress with delicate gold bits showed her excellent taste. Her citrusy scent filled his head, and his mind swirled with familiar and unwanted thoughts. He shouldn't allow his attention to be diverted. He needed to concentrate on the business at hand, which was pinning Halbert Grayson to one spot long enough to confront him about the note.

But Sophie made thinking about anything other than her difficult. She smiled up at him, her cheeks rosy, and his heart lurched like it had hit a reef. When she moved in step with him, her hip brushed his, and his knees felt odd. None of the reasons he had for keeping his emotions out of their relationship seemed important in that moment.

The first set ended, and they were separated by the crowd. When he next caught sight of her, she was being escorted by Will Owens onto the dance floor. He seemed quite happy with his prize, grinning like a gargoyle and keeping hold of Sophie's hand much too long when they pivoted.

Owens was younger than Charles. Closer to Sophie's age than to his. The ratio of men to women was fairly even, possibly even weighted toward the men tonight. A handful of young bucks stood along the wall near the refreshment table, whispering and elbowing, watching the dancers—particularly Sophie. He clamped his teeth until his jaw ached.

Penny went by on the arm of Miles Enys. Uneasiness sloshed through Charles. What did he know about raising girls? He was thankful Sophie had stepped up to help him, but she seemed to think he should be involved with the decision-making required for the girls' welfare too. He didn't want Sophie to become too reliant upon him, because when he left, she would have to shoulder that burden alone.

Which somehow had seemed logical a week ago but now wasn't sitting well.

He finally spotted the man he had been looking for all evening. His steward, Grayson, caught his eye and made a quick dart for the stairs.

Just as well. The taproom or the yard would be a better place for their discussion than the crowded assembly hall. Charles wended his way around the perimeter of the room to the steps. When he reached the taproom, half full already of men who would rather drink ale and talk than dance, Grayson was disappearing through the front door.

"Good evening, Lord Rothwell. Fancy a drop?" The man tending the bar leaned over with a full tankard. "Best in the county."

"No, thank you."

Another man scooted his chair back and stepped in front of Charles. "Milord, let me introduce myself. I'm Porter MacFie, and I own the butcher shop." He tucked his fingertips into his waistband. "I understand you're not planning on staying around these parts? Hiring a new steward and leaving us, eh?" He scratched the hair over his ear. "Not that I blame you. Not much of a life for a fancy gent like yourself."

"I apologize—there's someone to whom I must speak." When he moved to go around MacFie, the man edged into his path once more. "Oh, I beg your pardon."

They swayed and swerved, bobbing in front of each other until Charles finally lost patience, took the man by the upper arms, and moved him out of the way. If he didn't know better, he'd say these men were conspiring to keep him away from his quarry.

Finally, Charles made it out into the night air. Where had Grayson gotten to? The man's actions were certainly suspicious.

A large man with a beard leaned against the front of the public house, arms crossed. Charles gave him a glance as he went by, but since he wasn't Grayson, paid him no mind.

Grayson had crossed the road, but he stopped dead when a man wearing a hooded cloak stepped out of the shadows. Turning around, Grayson looked for a way of escape, but Charles had caught him up by that time.

The hooded man stepped back into the shadows, but not before Charles caught the glint of a blade. The hair on his neck stood up, and he grabbed Grayson by the sleeve and hauled him toward the middle of the road.

"I want a word." He looked into the darkness behind them, but the hooded man had disappeared. Charles pulled the paper from his pocket. "What do you know about this?"

"What? I haven't done anything." Grayson cowered, putting on his best hang-dog air. But Charles wasn't having it.

"Smuggling. I want to know who is involved and how long it's been going on." He rattled the paper. "If my uncle was smuggling goods, he was doing it with someone's help."

"Smuggling? I don't know what you're talking about." Grayson struggled, but Charles hung on.

"If you don't know smuggling has been going on right under your nose, then you're the most inept steward in the history of estate management."

Grayson jerked, as if stung. "You can't pin this on me. I don't know anything about that letter or smuggling or anything else."

Charles dropped the steward's arm. "I'm going to get to the bottom of this, with or without your help."

"I don't know what you're on about. Even if I did, I wouldn't tell you. Sailing in here and demoting people when you don't know the first thing about running an estate. Hiring outsiders and pushing people out of their jobs." The cowed, bumbling steward act was gone. In its place, defiant anger. The true man at last.

"You're finished. I want you off the estate tomorrow."

"You can't do that."

"I can. If you're not out by noon tomorrow, I'll have the bailiffs in. I'm sure you won't starve. You'll have all your ill-gotten gains to live on until you can find another position, though you won't be getting a reference from me."

"Gentlemen, is there a problem?" Reverend Dunhill's voice cut through the darkness. "Tonight is supposed to be one of enjoyment and celebration, not confrontation."

"He fired me. Thinks I've been helping the old earl smuggle goods into the country." Grayson jabbed a finger under Charles's nose.

"Is that so?" Dunhill stepped close. "I'm sure that can't be true. Not of Grayson here, nor of the late earl."

Charles held up the paper. "This says otherwise. I feel I'm being taken for a fool, but I assure you, that is not the case. Tomorrow, I consult the authorities. If the smuggling is still going on, it stops now."

The preacher took the page, turning it to the light. His face grew grave, with deepening lines bracketing his mouth. "This is serious indeed. Halbert, you had no notion of this activity?"

"No. And if he says so, he's a liar."

"There's no way," Dunhill said, slowly, "to know when this note was written. It might have been years ago. Perhaps even meant for your grandfather. Smuggling happens, of course, but not here. I'm sure I would know of it."

That gave Charles pause. Was it possible he had it wrong? Was the note older than it looked?

"Gentlemen"—Dunhill's tone was both placating and parental—"I suggest we leave the topic for tonight. Don't spoil the evening's entertainment letting anyone know of the issue. We can sort it on the morrow, I'm sure." He took Grayson's arm, leading him away and talking into his ear with every step.

Charles balled his fists. He hated waiting, and he didn't trust Grayson.

Chapter 12

"Did you dance every single dance?" Thea burrowed under Sophie's covers as the sun peeped over the horizon. "What did you eat? Did Penny flirt with all the boys? Did the captain dance too?"

Pelted with questions, Sophie grimaced, pulling the pillow over her head. "Do I know you?"

Thea was having none of it. "You promised, Sophie." She pulled the pillow off.

Another little body climbed into bed, and Sophie cracked one eye to see Betsy in one of her new nightgowns and sporting Charles's bicorn.

"Permission to come aboard?" Betsy clambered over Sophie and collapsed in giggles. "That's what the captain says you have to say when you want to go on someone's boat."

"Good morning, lovelies." Sophie sat up, stretching. For having such a short night's sleep, she felt refreshed and ready for the day. She tickled Betsy and pulled Thea into a hug.

"Penny's still asleep. I didn't even hear her come in last night, though I tried to wait up." Thea crossed her legs and leaned her elbows on her knees. "When did you come back?

"It was very late. And to answer your questions, I danced almost every dance, we ate all sorts of foods, Penny behaved very well, and the captain danced the first dance. Beyond that, he had business to attend to, and it was a good opportunity for him to meet some of the community leaders."

"Was your dress the best?" Betsy asked.

Sophie could only see one of the girl's eyes, the other being hidden by the forepeak of Charles's hat. "There were many pretty dresses there. Madam Stipple must have sewn a lot of them, for I recognized some of the fabrics from our visit to her shop." The variety and quantity of new gowns had caught Sophie's attention. Did they have assemblies very often, or was this such a rare event that new dresses for most of the ladies in attendance were to be expected? The village certainly seemed better off than others she had passed through on their journey here.

A faint pounding came from downstairs. Who would knock on the front door at this hour?

"Girls, go back to your room and get dressed. Mrs. Chapman will have breakfast for you." Sophie swung her feet over the side of the bed and grabbed her wrapper. Heading into her dressing room, she nearly tripped over Rich's sea chest. She'd forgotten that she'd pulled it out to use as a step stool last night to reach the hatbox that held her evening fans and reticules.

With a shove, she sent it back along the wall. She really should go through his things one of these days.

Noises came from the adjoining dressing room, so she assumed Charles had heard the knocking too. With chilly fingers, she buttoned her day dress.

A tap sounded on Charles's bedroom door, and Miles said, "Milord, there's a bunch of men downstairs. They say they're from the Revenue. They have a warrant."

Sophie wrenched the connecting door open. "A warrant? What for?" She spoke around the hairpins clenched in her teeth, her arms high as she finished styling her hair.

Charles stood in the doorway of his dressing room, in breeches, with his shirt on but unbuttoned, his boots in his hand. She noted the muscled planes of his chest and the taut skin of his abdomen before she realized she was staring and averted her eyes.

"They wouldn't tell me, milady. Said to fetch his lordship, or they'd be coming up to get him." Miles shifted uneasily. "Looked like half the village was with them."

Charles stomped into his boots and buttoned his shirt. "Tell them I'll be down directly. I was going to contact the Revenue Office this morning anyway."

Sophie returned to her room to find her shoes and hurried downstairs. Miles had not exaggerated. Half a dozen men stood in the front hall, and through the open door, many more clustered.

"Sir, I have a warrant to search the Gateshead estate for violations of the Orders in Council concerning trade with France and her allies. We have reason to believe you have been engaged in the illegal importation of goods from France and have been avoiding paying the excise tax on goods imported from Belgium." The well-dressed man in front of the pack held up a paper complete with a wax seal and red tape binding. "If you resist, we will be forced to restrain you."

"I have no desire to resist. I was planning to speak with you today about this. I haven't been involved in smuggling, but I believe there has been smuggling activity connected to this estate." Charles's ability to speak calmly reassured Sophie that he had everything under control.

Smuggling. That might account for some of the oddities she had noticed. But it was preposterous to think Charles had anything to do with it. He hadn't been at Gateshead a month.

"We have this communication, delivered to us last night." The Revenue officer unfolded a piece of paper. "It is a letter written to you, acknowledging your part in the illegal activities, receiving money, providing transportation, both signaling and meeting ships carrying illegal goods."

Charles tried to snatch the paper, but the officer was quicker. "Sir, that is evidence. You are not allowed to have it."

"I found that letter stuck in a book in my office. It's not addressed to me. How did you get it? It was in my possession last night."

"So you admit that it is yours. The note is addressed to 'Rothwell,' sir. You are Rothwell, are you not? We've received intelligence over the past few days that directs us to a certain building on the property, and I believe we should start there." With a self-important nod, the officer turned on his heel. "If you will come with me, sir."

"Charles, what is this?" Sophie hurried after him. "What's happening?"

"We're going to get to the bottom of a crime that's been taking place at Gateshead for a long time." His face was grim. "I suspect someone is trying to blame me for breaking the law, but it won't work. The idea is preposterous."

His strides were long, and she had to trot to keep up.

The crowd moved with them, and Sophie recognized many of the faces from the assembly last night. How could they have offered friendship and hospitality one day and now looked to blame an innocent man?

"Sir," she addressed the back of the man in charge. "You are on a hiding to nothing. There are no stolen goods here."

They approached a stone building attached to the south end of the stables. A well-worn path led to the door.

This was ridiculous. Her husband was no smuggler. There was something sinister going on. Someone had taken a letter from Charles and was using it to have him charged with crimes. Well, they were in for an unpleasant surprise if they thought there were stolen goods on this property.

Sophie positioned herself where she could see both inside as soon as the door was opened and the faces of the crowd when they got the news the building was empty. Then she would blister this Revenue man for listening to rumors.

The oak door had a large padlock hanging from the hasp. "Where's the key?" the officer asked.

"I have no idea. I've never been inside this place before." Charles stood between two burly men who were no doubt tasked with preventing his escape.

"I'll break it." Mr. Fields, whom Sophie had met last night, stepped forward. He was the father of the young man who had danced with Penny first, and he carried a heavy hammer. He'd come prepared? This smelled more and more like a trap.

With one mighty blow, he smashed both the hasp and the lock, and opened the door.

Sophie peered into the gloom, expecting cobwebs and dust.

Which there were in abundance.

But there was also a pyramid of crates, each labeled with contents illegal to possess in England.

"Your Lordship." The Revenue officer scowled. "You're under arrest for smuggling goods into the country in violation of the Orders in Council governing the possession of French wares, specifically cognac, champagne, and other spirits."

Charles stood in the doorway of the stone barn, staring at a mountain of cases of French liquor. The hypocrisy and thoroughness of the job someone was making to pin this crime on him were staggering.

"The contraband is clearly on your property, and"—the Revenue man held up the letter once more—"with the information delivered to our offices in Lyme Regis during the night, the evidence is clear. You've received payment for stolen goods, you've provided a boat to bring in the goods, and through the use of stealth and signaling, you have sought to evade anyone from the Revenue Office apprehending you."

This was a nightmare. He was innocent, the charges were trumped up, and the real villains were going free.

One of the officer's men produced darbies and clapped them on Charles's wrists. "Come along, sir, if you please."

That letter. How had the Revenue man gotten it? And with such speed? Charles's head whirled. They had arrived at Gateshead just past first light with a warrant in hand. Someone had ridden during the night to the closest Revenue Office and gotten the authorities out of bed.

His eyes sought Sophie's as he was pulled roughly out of the barn.

"Charles? What should I do?" she asked, her eyes wide and her face pale.

"Get me a solicitor." He tugged back on the manacles to force them to stop. "Where are you taking me?"

"Lyme Regis jail, sir. To wait for the magistrate."

The letter was at the crux of their claims. It had been in his pocket when he'd arrived at the assembly room last night. He had shown it to Grayson . . . and then Reverend Dunhill. What had happened to it after that? He'd been so angry and frustrated . . . Had someone heard him confront Grayson in the street last night? He hadn't exactly been whispering. The man in the hooded cloak perhaps? Or the bearded giant just outside the public house?

Had someone lifted it from his pocket after he'd returned to the dance? They had been speaking rather loudly in the street. Anyone could have overheard and learned of the note's existence.

They reached the front steps of Gateshead, where a box wagon with iron bars on the openings awaited him. They had come prepared to haul him away.

The girls stood on the gravel drive, Penny in the middle, her arms around her sisters. Mamie hovered in the doorway, her face scrunched in worry. Sophie went one step toward them but stopped, as if reluctant to leave his side.

"Sophie, get me a solicitor. Not Will Owens. Someone from outside Gateshead. And contact Barrington at the Admiralty."

"I will." She went to the girls, cupping Betsy's head for a moment and squeezing Thea's shoulder. "Don't worry, girls. We'll sort this out."

"What are they doing? Why are they taking him away?" Thea's voice rose. She tried to get around Sophie, but Sophie held her back.

"He broke the law. He's going to jail," someone in the back of the mob shouted.

Charles's gut burned at the injustice and humiliation, especially in front of the girls. The minute he was proven innocent and released, he would mete out a bit of justice of his own on the real culprits.

Sophie's encouraging smile as they shoved him into the wagon gave him heart, but Thea's look pierced him to the core. She didn't understand that he wasn't guilty. This thing had the stench of conspiracy all over it. But Thea's look had been both accusatory and angry.

Sophie would have to set her straight. Or he would, once he was free.

The ride to Lyme Regis was intolerable. The closed wagon had no springs, and they were tossed about like loose cargo in a storm. Charles was pinned between two large jailers who showed no sympathy. If anything, they seemed to take great joy in arresting a titled gentleman. They spoke about him as if he weren't there, laughing and joking.

Charles ignored them. He could only think of all the clues that had been right in front of him from the moment he'd arrived at the estate. They jumbled together in no particular order, but each one was a plank, fitting together into a whole deck.

The banner Thea had found during their picnic. It had to be for signaling ships from the cliff.

The excellent condition of the *Shearwater*, even after it had been wrecked once. No wonder his uncle had been eager to salvage it and get it back into service.

The apparent affluence of the villagers, from the vicar's nice suits to the extensive inventory at the dressmaker's that Sophie had commented upon. Each person seemed to have more and better things in their possession than their circumstances would indicate.

The rather healthy look of the estate books, in spite of the steward being less than adequate and his uncle being out of his mind in the last months.

The second path from the shore to the cliff top where the so-called "smuggler's cave" had collapsed that Charles had spotted on their brief run up the coast aboard the *Shearwater*.

The French champagne the vicar had brought to the wedding breakfast.

The imported lace Mamie had mentioned seeing on a woman's dress at church.

Even further back, the death of the Pembroke girls' father. No wonder his uncle had taken on the guardianship of his boat captain's children. The man had lost his life in the service of the earl's illegal work.

Was the entire village in on the smuggling? Or were some unwitting accomplices? Were only a few guilty, but many drawn in through unknowingly purchasing illegal goods?

He had known smuggling was a widespread problem. Admiral Barrington had mentioned that the Home Secretary had requested naval involvement in stopping the flood of illegal goods into the country.

But right on his own doorstep? With his uncle providing the funds and ship and warehousing?

Charles felt like an idiot.

God, how could I have been so blind? What if I can't prove my innocence? What will happen to Sophie and the girls and Mamie and Gateshead? How are You working here? Are *You working here? Nothing has gone right. Everything was going to be so simple. I had a plan, a reasonable plan, and now it's wrecked.*

He should be captaining a naval ship right now. And yet if he had gotten his way, he would have left Sophie in a precarious position, with thieves and smugglers all around her. She would have been in danger if she ever tumbled to it, and as smart as she was, she would have discovered it sooner or later.

His chest constricted at the thought of what might have happened. Thus far no one had been hurt, but that didn't mean they wouldn't have gone to great lengths to escape discovery and prosecution.

After what seemed ages, the wagon jerked to a halt, and the back door flung open. "Get out." A burly gray-haired man with a truncheon flicked his head. The jailers inside grabbed Charles by his elbows and shoved him toward the door. Staggering, he emerged into the sunlight, blinking against the glare.

Lyme Regis.

He was escorted into a dingy, dank stone building. Two cages of iron bars stretched across the back of the single room. The darbies were removed, as was his coat and stock, and he was shoved into the left-hand cell.

Musty straw covered the floor, and the only light came from a narrow slot near the eaves.

"The magistrate will have a session tomorrow or the next day. When your lawyer shows up, we'll send him in. Until then, keep quiet." The truncheon-bearing guard slammed the iron door with a clang that went right through Charles.

Tomorrow or the next day? He would be trapped in here while his adversaries were roaming free, building the case against him.

"God, You say You won't let evil prevail over good." He wrapped his hands around the bars and lowered his head to lean against the iron. "Please give Sophie strength, help her to find a good solicitor, and help her not to lose faith."

Chapter 13

Her husband had been arrested and carted off to jail.

Not words Sophie had ever anticipated thinking.

Charles had been arrested, and for something Sophie knew he hadn't done.

After they loaded him into the wagon, she rounded on the onlookers. "How dare you? This is preposterous. You know he isn't guilty. And you know who is."

The crofters, farmers, and villagers looked from one to another, spreading their hands and raising their brows. "You gentry think you can do anything and get away with it. He got what he deserved," someone shouted. Several heads nodded, exchanging looks.

"My dear, you're overwrought." Reverend Dunhill stepped forward, making a gesture as if he would put his arm around her. "I'm certain we can sort this out. Though I am surprised. I never would have believed it of the earl." He sounded distressed and disappointed.

She stepped back, glaring. "I'd like you all to leave now. I have work to do, and I'm sure you all do as well, getting rid of the contraband in your houses and barns. Trumping up more charges to make sure you get away with your crimes."

"We ain't the ones with a barn full of liquor," came a voice from the midst of the crowd. "Caught proper, his lordship is."

A carriage trundled up the drive toward them, and for a moment, Sophie's heart leapt. Were they bringing him back? But no, it wasn't Charles. However, when the horses pulled to a stop, she almost cried. The

Haverly crest decorated the door, and none other than her brother stepped out.

It was all she could do not to disgrace herself by running straight into his arms. Marcus was here. He would help her. He would help Charles.

Such was the power of his presence that people parted to make way for him. He strode through, looking neither right nor left, keeping his eyes on Sophie. When he mounted the steps, he put himself between her and the preacher.

Tears swam on her lashes, and she blinked hard.

"What have you been getting yourself into, Sophie?" His gentle teasing almost proved her undoing. He slipped his arm around her waist, bringing her into his side and turning to face the villagers. "Disperse now. If you're not involved in this debacle, I will expect you to support your mistress wholeheartedly." He stopped, and an edge entered his voice. "If you are involved in this travesty, know that you will face justice. You'd best get yourself on the side of the angels, or you'll find yourself in dock when I sort this out."

He guided Sophie and the girls into the house and closed the door in the face of the reverend when he tried to follow them inside.

"How did you know?" She spoke the muffled words into his waistcoat as she hugged him.

He sighed. "We've got work to do. I've sent Partridge to London for a barrister, though I'm hoping we won't need him."

"Partridge." Sophie straightened. "I could have sworn I saw someone in the village last week who looked just like him . . ." Suspicion raised its head. "Have you been spying on me through him?"

"Spying? Me?" He put his hand to his chest. "Nonsense. It would take someone more clever than I to be a spy. Didn't you get my letter, or Mother's? I told you I would be coming for a visit since I had urgent business in the area. Partridge came with me, as he usually does. I was in Lyme Regis this morning, ready to set out for Gateshead, when a man rushed into the taproom and interrupted my breakfast with news that the Revenue men had departed to arrest the new Earl of Rothwell."

"He's not guilty. The very idea is preposterous." Anger flared in Sophie's middle, causing her to tremble.

"Hello, Mamie. You're looking well." Marcus reached out a hand to clasp Mamie's, his eyes warm. He had always had a soft spot for Rich's mother, and Sophie loved him for it.

"Who is this man?" Betsy asked, coming to stand beside him, looking up a long way. "He has long hair." The captain's bicorn slipped off her head to the floor.

Marcus squatted and picked up the hat, placing it gently on her head once more. "I'm most anxious to be introduced to you as well, young miss." He looked at Sophie. "Care to perform the niceties?"

"There isn't time. I have to get to Charles. I'll tell you everything on the way. Girls, you are to stay with Mamie and Mrs. Chapman and be good. I'll be back with the captain as soon as I can." Sophie picked up her reticule from the table in the foyer and plucked her spencer and bonnet from the hall tree.

Mrs. Chapman bustled into the room carrying a small valise. "I put a few things in here for you, milady, in case you have to stay over."

"You're a treasure. Thank you. I don't know what I'd do without you."

Mamie fluttered her hand. "Go, child. We will be fine."

"I'm leaving a couple of guards here to watch the house." Marcus took Sophie's arm and the valise. "Ladies, I'm going to ask that you remain inside the manor until we return. My men will keep you safe."

Thea predictably crossed her arms and shot her chin out, but Penny nodded. "We'll stay inside. Just help the captain."

In the carriage, Sophie gripped her hands in her lap. She was so grateful for Marcus's presence, she felt weak, but worry constricted her throat and pressed her shoulders like a yoke.

"Who are those girls? The little one is cute enough to eat."

"They're Charles's wards."

Marcus's brows shot up. "How did he come to have wards?"

In halting bits, Sophie told him of the girls' arrival and their relationship to the former Earl of Rothwell.

Marcus tilted his head. "Odd that the old fellow would take on three young females. There's more here, I suspect, than meets the eye. Tell me about the town and what you've observed. Who has more than they should, or who has acted suspiciously? Start at the beginning, and tell me everything that happened from the moment you arrived at Gateshead."

As she spoke, she fit pieces together in her mind, realizing that some of the things she had thought odd but that had been conveniently explained away at the time, actually pointed to the truth.

"The seamstress has a workshop full of inventory. And lace that could only come from France. She said she brought most of it from her shop in London."

"You said you visited the boathouse and shore, and part of the cliff gave way and hit Charles on the head?" Marcus asked.

"Yes. The cliff is very unstable."

"Are you certain it was an accident?" Marcus leaned back against the squabs and crossed his arms.

"Surely no one would do such a thing on purpose. He could have been killed." Sophie blinked.

"The arrival of a new earl must have put the smugglers into a panic. Grayson has to be involved somehow, and Charles was a danger to their operation. Someone tried to stop him with a rock to the head, though they were unsuccessful. But then word got out that the new earl would be leaving soon to return to the navy. Everyone breathes a sigh of relief. It will be business as usual once he's gone."

"But he hasn't received any orders yet."

"And he stumbled upon the smuggling operation. Now he definitely has to go. Therefore the plot to frame him for the crime."

"Would someone like Halbert Grayson be capable of such an intricate plot? I wouldn't have thought he had the intelligence or influence in the town."

Marcus nodded. "No one's off my list of suspects at this point. We're nearly there. I don't know that you'll be allowed in to see Charles just yet, but I can take a message from you if you'd like."

"Will they let *you* in?"

He snorted. "I'm the Duke of Haverly. I'll get in."

The coachman had to stop and ask directions to the jail, and when he pulled up before the stone building, a shiver went through Sophie. A guard with a musket stood before the door.

"Wait in the coach."

"Tell him . . ." She paused, heat swirling into her cheeks as she realized what she'd almost blurted out. With an effort, she composed herself. "Tell him we're doing everything we can, that I know he's innocent of these charges, and that he'll be free soon."

Marcus leaned across the carriage and squeezed her hand.

When she was alone, she let the tears fall.

She had almost asked her brother to tell her husband that she loved him.

"This is a sorry turn of events, Wyvern. Or should I call you Rothwell? It's quite irresponsible of you to marry my sister out of hand and then land yourself in jail a fortnight later."

Charles looked through the bars at his brother-in-law, appreciating the wry humor. The outer door remained open to let in some light and to allow the guard to keep an eye on them.

"You should call me Charles, and this isn't exactly the way I wanted to be welcomed into the family."

When he held his hand out through the bars, the guard barked from his post by the door, "Stay back!"

"How is Sophie?" Charles asked, withdrawing.

"She's outside in my carriage, but they won't allow her in. I had to threaten to go to the magistrate to be let in myself. Now, before they think better of giving me access, there are a few things you need to know. First, a lawyer is on his way from London. I've sent a man to the firm of Coles, Franks, and Moody, and they'll find a barrister and bring him along. This same man will stop by the Admiralty and inform Barrington."

A bit of the tightness in Charles's chest eased. "These charges are false. I've never stolen or smuggled a thing in my life."

Except a miniature of my wife. The thought came unbidden. He still had the painting. Why hadn't he returned that to her and admitted what he'd done? It seemed so silly now that he'd been embarrassed into silence.

Marcus was speaking, and Charles tried to concentrate. "I'm aware the accusations are false, and I've got men investigating. We'll get the charges dropped."

"And then I'm going after the real culprits."

"We're making a list of possible conspirators. I'm afraid this might take some time. If my suspicions are correct, the scope is broad, and it might even extend to buying off local authorities. That warrant was procured with remarkable speed. I'd say the trap was laid some time ago and only sprung last night when you confronted Grayson. There are too many moving pieces for this to be spontaneous. For now, don't talk to anyone but me and your lawyer. You never know who might be listening."

Someone had bribed the magistrate? If that was true, what chance did Charles have? Surely he wouldn't be hung by a crooked judge bought off by his enemies?

Charles halted his thinking. Marcus had quite a bit of information for having arrived just this morning. How had he come by his intelligence?

"I met your wards briefly. The little one was wearing your hat." Marcus put the side of his finger against the seam of his lips, but he couldn't hide the amusement in his tone.

"Betsy." Charles nodded. "She loves that hat, my gloves, my pocket watch. I've even found her wearing my uniform jacket, epaulettes and all. She tries to march around like she's striding a quarterdeck, and any naval jargon that floats her way is captured and fired back at regular intervals."

"You've made quite an impression on her in a short time. And the other two?"

He thought for a moment. "Penny is at turns sweet and baffling. One moment eager to grow up, the next holding on to girlhood. I will say, she has taken excellent care of her younger sisters. It's a heavy responsibility for one so young." Charles paced the small cell, hands behind his back. "Then there's Thea. I've never met a more observant person, child or not. She's perceptive and quick. Smart as can be, and absolutely fearless. She's the one I worry about the most. I fear she's in for some disappointments and futile battles, she's so independent. Doesn't think being a girl should hold her back from doing anything she wants."

"Hmm, that sounds familiar. I am eager to introduce her to my wife.

They sound like twin souls." Marcus crossed his arms. "I will say, I'm glad Sophie married you."

"You are?" Charles asked, stopping his pacing to spread his hands wide, encompassing his bleak surroundings. "I would have thought you would be questioning her sanity."

Marcus smiled. "Actually, I'm quite pleased. I thought Sophie might wear the willow for Rich for the rest of her life. She's fiercely loyal like that. I'm glad she found someone else to love. Much like Rich, when she loves, Sophie will take a bullet for you." Marcus's stare pierced Charles right through. "But she'll also shoot a few on your behalf. She's out in the carriage right now, worried but ready to go to battle. That tells me her heart is fully yours."

Rockets of heat and light burst in his head and chest. Could it be true? Sophie loved him? Enough to fight for him?

"You look stunned. Surely you know she loves you?"

Charles tried to loosen his cravat, until he realized he wasn't wearing one. "Of course. She's my wife, after all." His voice sounded strained. "Tell her . . ." He stopped. "Give her my regards."

"That's a tame way of putting things. It's plain as a pikestaff that you love her in return. Have you never told her?"

Chapter 14

Sitting day after day in that cramped, musty cell, Charles thought he might lose his mind. When his incarceration stretched into a second week, he was ready to dig an escape tunnel.

"It all starts tomorrow." His solicitor, Mr. Coles, set a bandbox on the floor. "The magistrate approved me bringing you this, and the guards have searched it. Your wife sent clean clothing and your shaving kit. Get tidied up and looking respectable before they bring you into the dock."

"Where has Haverly been? I haven't seen him all week." Charles couldn't imagine what had kept his brother-in-law away. He'd come every day for the first five, then disappeared.

"He's working on your case. As am I. His Grace has gone to Portsmouth following a lead. Now, I must go, but Mr. Allard here has a few questions, just to ensure that we're well prepared for the morrow." The bald-headed solicitor bowed and left the jail.

Mr. Allard, Charles's barrister, sat at a small table in the area in front of the cells, quill in hand, in the glow of a small lantern. "Now tell me again where you found the note."

It had been baffling to Charles that he needed two lawyers, a solicitor and a barrister, until Marcus explained that only a barrister could act for him in court. A solicitor handled all non-court-related points of law, but when one was really in trouble—say incarcerated and facing the noose if convicted—a barrister was needed. Mr. Allard insisted they go over everything again. And again. Either the barrister was very thorough, or he was completely out of ideas and just filling time.

Finally, the gray-haired man packed his papers and picked up the lantern. "Oh, I almost forgot. Your wife gave me a letter for you."

Charles snatched the paper. Sophie hadn't been allowed to see him, and he missed her greatly. She invaded his dreams, and when he woke, it was to such longing and emptiness, he hardly recognized himself.

"I'll leave the door open so you will have light." Mr. Allard sent him a knowing smile. "Your wife is quite a woman. Very loyal and staunch in your defense. And, I might add, quite charming. She gave me a thorough examination, wanting to know my credentials, my record in cases like yours, and what I planned to do to get you released."

An excited weakness flowed through Charles, and he could just imagine Sophie putting the barrister through her version of the Inquisition.

Before he could open the letter, Admiral Barrington entered the jail. "Charles, how are you faring? Holding up?"

Resplendent in gold braid and brass buttons, the admiral seemed to take up all the space in the small room.

"I'm weathering the storm, sir." Charles stood at attention, saluting his superior officer.

"Yes, well, I think, under the circumstances, we can dispense with all that. You're an earl now, Wyvern."

"I'm still a captain in the Royal Navy, sir." Charles paused. "Aren't I?"

"We'll discuss that at a later date. For now, I have news. Alastair Lythgoe has arrived and will manage your estate in your absence. He's a top man. I've just been dining with your wife. Well done getting spliced to such a fine young woman. She's got a bit of Tartar in her too, doesn't she? She will accept no other outcome than that you are exonerated with all speed."

"I believe she gets that fierceness from her mother, sir," Charles said.

"I came down the coast on a Revenue cutter, and between the Duke of Haverly, Lythgoe, and myself, we've come up with a plan to scoop up the real culprits the moment this trial is over." Barrington dug in his pocket for his pipe.

"As long as I get to take part." Charles's hopes lifted.

"Very good." He patted his pockets for his tinder case. When he lit the pipe, clouds of smoke wreathed his head, and he blinked. "I cannot believe the Royal Navy, the most powerful fleet in the world, is reduced to hunting petty criminals, but there you are. We'll do the job, and we'll do it to the best of our ability." Barrington tucked his tinder box away. "I'll see you in court tomorrow. And never fear. This case has no foundation, and we'll soon knock it out of the water. That it has gotten this far is a travesty." He headed out into the sunshine, putting his bicorn on his head and scowling at the guard.

The moment he was alone, Charles ripped open Sophie's letter, nearly tearing it in his haste. After reading so many of her letters aloud to Rich in the hospital, this was the first he had received written specifically to him.

"Dearest Charles."

Did she mean that? Was he dear to her? When Marcus had suggested Sophie was in love with him, Charles had at first rejected the notion. But the more he thought about it, the more he hoped it was true.

> First, the girls are well, though Thea is behaving strangely. She's having trouble sleeping, and she's angry all the time. And quiet, which isn't like her at all. I am hoping when this is over, she will return to her normal active self. When we realized you were going to be in that dreadful cell longer than just a day or two, I brought the girls and Mamie to Lyme Regis. They are such a comfort to me. Marcus procured lodging for us in a respectable inn, and we're comfortable enough. Better accommodations than you currently enjoy, I have no doubt. Why won't the magistrate at least let me in to see you? The man is impossible. He maintains that a jail is no place for a woman, and there are no provisions for a proper meeting room. I think this is a lot of hogwash, and he's just being obstructive. It's almost as if he's taking particular pleasure in punishing you.
>
> Marcus has departed, but he wouldn't tell me where. Only that it would help your case. He's left his most capable employee, Partridge, to watch over us. I can assure you we are in safe hands. Partridge's great size deters most trouble, but he can and will act if necessary.

Admiral Barrington arrived by boat. You've got a very loyal friend there. The day before he arrived, the new steward, Alistair Lythgoe, presented himself to me at the inn. He had been on his way to Gateshead and stopped over in Lyme Regis, just as we did on our journey. That seems a lifetime ago, does it not? He stopped at The Crown and Child, and the publican informed him that his new employer was sitting in the local jail. Mr. Lythgoe came right to our lodgings. He seems quite capable, younger than I had anticipated, and indignant about your current circumstances. When I met him, he took my hand between both of his, and he said, 'Lady Rothwell, I know these charges are completely unfounded. Captain Wyvern has an excellent reputation in the fleet, and he is above reproach. It's an honor to work for him.' I was most reassured. He and the admiral and Marcus put their heads together, and then Marcus and Mr. Lythgoe went their separate ways.

Charles read that last paragraph again. Mr. Lythgoe was young, and he'd taken Sophie's hand? It was silly to be jealous, and yet he was. He would love to hold Sophie's hand right now. The age difference, and their history . . . would it always stand between them?

He returned to the letter.

I hope the clothing Mr. Coles brought to you is suitable. I sent someone to Gateshead to procure what I thought you would want. If you would prefer something else, send word and I'll search out a haberdasher here in Lyme Regis. I will be in the gallery tomorrow, and if the magistrate tries to keep me out of the courtroom, I'm going to cause a scene.

The girls will stay with Mamie during the trial. She's been wonderful. I can't thank you enough for the way you accepted her with all her frailties. I know you did it because you wanted to honor Rich's memory, but I think you also did it because that's the kind of man you are.

Betsy wants me to send you her greetings. Actually, she just marched by with her hands behind her back, and said, "Tell him to come home."

Penny has been a bit . . . morose. I think she is just now realizing that while you are not guilty of smuggling, others are, and she's wondering how high and far the smuggling ring reaches. She hasn't asked any questions about her father's possible involvement, but I think she's realized that Miles Enys is almost certainly guilty of collusion at the very least. I don't think her heart is involved, however, because she has managed to notice that the innkeeper's son is quite handsome.

Charles, I do hope you're keeping up your spirits. I have prayed for you so often, that this miscarriage of justice would be righted soon and that you would maintain your integrity and witness. I have questioned so often how any of this can be God's will, and yet I am at peace that His will shall be accomplished in spite of your enemies surrounding you.

I have been reading in the book of Job, and this morning I came across this verse that gave me great comfort.

Job 5:12: "He disappointeth the devices of the crafty, so that their hands cannot perform their enterprise."

I am confident this will be true in your case. Hopefully, by the end of the day tomorrow, you will be a free man, and we will be reunited.

All your girls send their regards. We are thinking of you and praying for you.

He cast his eyes to the signature.

"Affectionately, Sophie."

His throat constricted. As she had done for Rich, encouragement and hope flowed from each line. She had informed him of much he had wondered about, had lifted his spirits, and satisfied him that while he was missed, she was caring for those he loved.

He would have to thank Marcus for seeing that someone was looking after Sophie while she spent her time looking after everyone else.

Who would look after her when Charles went back to sea?

If he got the opportunity to go back to sea, that was. He had to get through this trial first.

Sophie edged into the row of chairs near the back wall. People packed the assembly room. The magistrate, a small man with enormous side-whiskers, marched to the table in the front of the room, chest puffed out, coattails fluttering.

Sophie stiffened. The man had been rude and pompous to her, forbidding her to see her husband. Insisting it was to protect her sensibilities since she was a "mere woman." She clamped her teeth together.

Admiral Barrington sat beside her, drawing glances and whispers. He exuded power and confidence, and Sophie was grateful for his presence. On her other side, Mr. Coles took a chair. He gave her an encouraging smile.

"Have no fear, my dear. This trial is a formality, nothing more."

"What happens if we don't win?"

"The case will be referred to Crown Court, and we'll all go to London. For now, the affair is being handled by the local magistrate, but if things don't go our way—though I'm certain they will—Allard will appeal on the grounds that the case should have been tried in Crown Court from the beginning."

A side door opened, and Charles appeared between two guards, his wrists in shackles. But his head was high, and he wore the clothes she had sent him.

His naval uniform.

She had known he would want it, would feel best if he could wear it. It was such a part of his character, his being a naval captain, and she wanted him to be proud and assured as he defended himself today.

The barristers entered. Mr. Allard carried a satchel under his arm.

The only one not present was Marcus. Where was he?

Charles's eyes sought hers as he was ushered to the chair beside his barrister, and he nodded. His face was grim, determined. In the ten days he had been incarcerated, he seemed to have aged.

The magistrate called the room to order, and the formal charges were read. Knowing they were false made hearing them all the more difficult. Sophie clenched her hands in her lap and pressed her lips together. Barrington shifted in his seat, but Mr. Coles was unmoved.

Then the prosecuting barrister rose.

The case appeared damning. Especially when so-called witnesses were brought in to testify. People Sophie had never seen before saying that they had often seen signals from the cliffs at Gateshead since Charles had become the earl.

Mr. Allard refused to cross-examine any of them, and Sophie nudged Mr. Coles. "Why won't he ask them questions? Why is he letting them tell lies?"

"Not now, milady. Allard has his methods. The defense will have the opportunity to tell their side of things later."

The magistrate frowned in their direction, and Coles straightened.

The Revenue officer took the stand and testified to finding the contraband alcohol on the estate. He also showed the note to the court.

That wretched note. Where had it come from? Had it been written to the previous earl, or was it manufactured and planted to condemn Charles?

Then a man was called to the stand, and he produced the red, white, and blue banner that Thea had found on Sophie and Charles's wedding day. The banner Miles Enys had been instructed to destroy.

"It's common knowledge that this is for signaling ships. I've seen it on the cliffs at Gateshead plenty of times. When it's there, within a few hours a boat usually slips into the cove, or the *Shearwater*, the estate's boat, runs out of the cove to meet up with a vessel anchored offshore."

The magistrate called for a noon recess. Sophie made for the defense table, hoping for a word with her husband before he was escorted out. She had to force her way through onlookers and gawkers. By the time she got to the rail, he had been shackled once more and the guards were leading him away.

"Charles." She elbowed between two rotund men's backs. They turned, frowning, and reluctantly made room for her to pass.

One guard held up his hand. "Stop there. You can't approach the prisoner."

"She's my wife," Charles declared, standing tall and straight.

"I don't care if she's Princess Charlotte herself. We have our orders." The guard tugged on Charles's arm.

Sophie reached out, and her fingers brushed her husband's outstretched ones. "Keep your courage."

"You too." And he was gone, whisked away to his cell.

Thus far, if Sophie had been a disinterested party, she would think Charles guilty. His barrister had put up a paltry defense against the prosecution's lies. Where had they dug up witnesses with such ridiculous stories, and why hadn't Allard confronted them?

And where was Marcus? If he had gone to find evidence to prove Charles's innocence, he needed to hurry.

"You will not let evildoers prevail. You will disappoint them in their crafty ways." She breathed the prayer as she went out of the assembly room. Though it was midday, she couldn't think of eating.

In the afternoon, it was finally Charles's turn to make his case. Mr. Allard rose, adjusted his robe, and addressed the court. "Gentlemen, what you have listened to this morning is a fabrication, a carefully crafted plot to make my client *appear* guilty. It is illusion and subterfuge. Before you is an honorable man, a naval captain of excellent reputation, a titled gentleman willing to take on three orphaned girls with little thought to anything except that it was the right thing to do.

"He never asked for the title or estate at Gateshead, wishing only to remain in the navy, but he understood his responsibility. And he was pitchforked into an impossible situation. Smuggling has long been a problem on our shores, and when he arrived to assume his position at Gateshead, he unwittingly set in motion a chain of events that the real culprits found intolerable. Therefore, they sought a way to get rid of him, even if only for a time, in order to complete their nefarious deeds."

Charles nodded, his hands gripping his thighs under the table.

Mr. Allard rocked on his heels, surveying the room. "At this time, I would like to recall several of the witnesses who have spoken against Lord Rothwell."

One by one, he put the witnesses on the stand. Though some were defiant, his questioning was so skillful, he picked apart their stories as if his words were a seam ripper.

When the Revenue officer took the stand, Mr. Allard was in fine flow. "Sir, who brought you the note you thought condemned my client?"

"An informant."

"His name, if you will, sir."

"I'd rather not say. If folks knew he was an informant, he'd be no use going forward."

"Sir, a man's future and liberty are at stake. You will tell me your informant's name and find another source for your leads. And going forward, as you put it, I pray you will find one more reliable than your current talebearer."

The officer looked at the prosecuting barrister, and then at the magistrate, but there was no help for him there. "Porter MacFie, butcher in Gateshead Village. He brought the note in the middle of the night. Said he'd found it on the floor of the assembly rooms after the social when he was helping to clear away."

Was that possible? Charles had thought and thought about how they might have gotten the note, and he could remember only showing it to Grayson. Then Reverend Dunhill had intervened, and Charles didn't remember seeing the note after that.

"And you assumed without investigating that the note was genuine and that it could only refer to my client?"

"I had no reason to doubt it. We've been watching Gateshead for some time, and this seemed to prove what we suspected, that the estate was involved in smuggling." The officer leaned forward. "All the pieces fit."

"And yet is there a date on the note? Is there any way to know if that note was written to the current earl, his uncle, perhaps his grandfather?"

"The paper looks new," he said, frowning.

"Ah yes. And if you were going to frame a new earl, putting this crime on his head, wouldn't you write the note on newer paper?"

Charles sat straight in his chair, fascinated at this line of defense. It was like watching a drama in a London theater. Or it would be if his entire future didn't rest on the outcome.

Allard commanded the attention of the room, and the witnesses responded to his demands. The audience remained quiet. Charles had to hand it to his brother-in-law. He had brought the best barrister in the country to defend him.

The man who had testified about the flag took the stand.

"Sir, are you a resident of Gateshead Village?"

"No. I live in Seaton, down the coast." His hands were big, gnarled, with swollen knuckles, and his clothes were plain and heavy.

"And how do you make your living?"

"Fisherman."

"I see, and that's how you came to see the flag on the Gateshead cliffs so often?"

"That's right. I fish all along that bit of coast."

"Have you witnessed the *Shearwater* making rendezvous with a ship off the coast at a time when that flag has been displayed?"

"I have."

"Have you ever seen my client aboard the *Shearwater* when she met this ship?"

"No, sir. But I never got too close. I didn't want anything to do with whatever they were up to. I keep my nose out of other people's business, I do. Wouldn't be here now if the bailiff hadn't said he'd bung me into a cell if I didn't show up and tell what I saw."

"When did you first see the flag and the corresponding boat activity?"

He scratched his bulbous red nose. "Don't know exactly."

"Did you ever see this behavior prior to six weeks ago?"

"Oh yes. Been going on a long time. All last summer, and the summer before. Funny thing though—it dropped off lately. Haven't seen those boats together since June, if I recollect."

Charles thumped his fist on his thigh. Allard was making good progress.

"So you're saying you saw this peculiar activity before my client's arrival at Gateshead, but you haven't seen it since he arrived?"

A small disturbance caught the magistrate's attention, and heads swiveled toward the door. Allard stopped and glanced back, as did Charles. It was Marcus, but Marcus unlike Charles had seen him before. Dusty, travel worn, and carrying a disreputable cloak—that somehow looked familiar. Where had Charles seen something like that before? In Marcus's wake, a dignified man of perhaps fifty strode in.

"Sir, if you will give me a moment?" Allard asked the magistrate as Marcus came to the rail. They whispered together, and Marcus produced a folded document and gave it to the barrister. Then he motioned to the austere man beside him.

Allard's brows rose, and he bowed to the stranger, clearly recognizing him. Then he read silently the pages Marcus had given him. A smile spread across his face, and he turned back to the magistrate.

"Sir, I pray you will forgive me. I'd like to introduce to you the Right Honorable Sir Winston Pierpont, president of the King's Bench. Would it be possible to find him a chair near the proceedings? He's come to watch this trial." Allard trod heavily on that last word, as if he thought travesty might be a better name for what the court was putting Charles through.

A ripple went through the room. Charles studied the man as a chair was brought and placed at the end of the defense table. Who was the president of the King's Bench? He must have considerable influence, because the magistrate looked as if he'd swallowed his tongue.

"Also, I'd like to present to the court documents procured by His Grace, the Duke of Haverly. My client has been accused of smuggling French wines and spirits and secreting them at his property. That contraband was discovered by the Revenue officer when executing a warrant to search his holdings. The cases were clearly marked as to their origins. I have here the provenance for that shipment of alcohol. It left the docks in Calais, traveled to Ostend, in Belgium, and was smuggled here aboard the Dutch ship *Adelaar* June twelfth of this year."

He sorted through the papers in his satchel, grabbed one, and marched both documents across the small open space, placing them forcefully on the magistrate's desk. "I also have here my client's service records. On June twelfth of this year, Captain Charles Wyvern, now Earl of Rothwell, was recovering from wounds suffered in the course of his war service. He was in a hospital in Oporto, Portugal, and nowhere near Gateshead. If you need further proof, Admiral Barrington, his superior officer, is in this meeting room and will testify to these statements."

Allard paused, turning slowly and looking from face to face, his expression at once stern and outraged at this miscarriage of justice.

"Sir, that concludes the remarks for the defense. I trust you will rule rightly in this matter and dismiss these ridiculous charges, as they should have been from the beginning."

Charles turned in his chair to search for Sophie. She sat along the back wall with Barrington and Coles flanking her, and he saw hope in her wide eyes. Hope he was beginning to feel himself.

And in only a few moments, the magistrate wilted, whether under the weight of the exculpatory evidence or the scrutiny of Sir Winston. If he had been paid off to find Charles guilty, he couldn't go through with it under the stern eye of his superior. The magistrate said, "I find there to be no evidence that Charles Wyvern, Earl of Rothwell, colluded in the crimes outlined here today." He stared hard at Charles. "However, it is clear that crimes *have* been committed. I'm ordering you to cooperate with the Revenue Office in their efforts to find those responsible." He rose, and everyone in the room followed suit . . . except Sir Winston Pierpont, who remained seated.

Marcus clapped Charles on the shoulder, and Charles shook Mr. Allard's hand. "Thank you. Thank you to both of you. Marcus, I don't know where you got your information, but I'm glad you did."

Then Sophie was worming her way through the crowd. Charles barely had time to open his arms before she dove into them. She collided with his chest, and he was forced back a step. "Oh, Charles, it's over. You're free."

He hugged her, pressing her head into his buttons. "I am free, but this is far from over. I have questions. The foremost is, why? Why go through with this trial at all?"

"We'll answer those when we return to Gateshead," Marcus said. "For now, there are some very worried people residing at a local inn who will be happy to see you."

Charles kept his arm around Sophie as they left the assembly room. Sir Winston declined their invitation to join them.

"I believe I will have a short conversation with our friend the magistrate."

Marcus herded them outside. "I'm glad we arrived in time. When I explained to Sir Winston what was happening in one of his lower courts, he insisted on coming in person to investigate."

"I have another question." Charles stopped on the street. "Where is Grayson in all of this? I assumed he would be called to give testimony. Tell me he hasn't escaped."

"He's hiding in the village. I have an idea as to why he needed you in jail for a while." Marcus shook his head. "We'll talk further when we get you home."

Charles nodded. There would be a reckoning. But first he needed to see to his family.

Chapter 15

Sophie leaned her head against her husband's shoulder, tired to her very bones. The tension of the last twelve days bled away like wheat from a sack, leaving her slack and drowsy.

Betsy insisted upon sitting on Charles's lap the entire journey back to the estate. Awkward, since she also insisted upon wearing his hat.

Thea watched everyone in the coach, eyes tight, mouth pinched. Penny wore a lovelorn expression, sorry to be leaving her latest "attachment" behind in Lyme Regis. The girl seemed to change affections like she changed bonnets. Now that things had been resolved at court, Sophie would need to direct her attentions to giving Penny some guidance. Girlish fancies were one thing, but constancy and faithfulness were traits to be cultivated.

"Admiral Barrington will meet us at Gateshead. He's coming aboard the Revenue cutter and will anchor up the coast out of sight. We've some matters to discuss." Charles smiled. "He invited Marcus to travel with him. They will arrive before our evening meal."

"It must bring you happiness to have someone from the navy here. You must have missed being able to speak of those things with someone who would understand without explanation." Sophie braced as the carriage jounced. Charles tightened his hold on Betsy, who giggled as he added an extra bounce with his knees.

"I saw the admiral's boat." Thea spoke for the first time. "If it's coming to Gateshead, can we go aboard?"

Charles shook his head. "I shouldn't think so. That cutter is an official vessel, not a pleasure craft. You'd need the permission of the captain. I'm not certain he'd want a little girl climbing over every inch of his boat."

The thin arms crossed, and she sagged into the corner of the seat once more.

"It feels good to be going home." Mamie sighed. "I never thought I would call anywhere but Primrose home, but Gateshead has become just that. Home is where your family is, and as long as I'm with you and the girls, Sophie, I can be happy anywhere." Her voice held wonder and realization, as if just coming to accept that fact. "I don't even worry about Primrose and what might be going on there. I will remember it as it was, and I will keep the memories I made there . . . at least as long as the Lord lets me." A little frown crossed her face. "I don't always remember the best."

Penny, who sat beside her, took her hand, and leaned into her shoulder a bit. "We love you, Mamie. You're like the grandmamma we never had. Gateshead has become our home too. Thanks to the captain and Sophie and you."

Warmth spread through Sophie at the bond that had formed there. Though they hadn't gotten to spend time at a seaside cottage, just Mamie and her, they'd been given something much better. A family. The family Sophie had thought they would never have after Rich died.

She stole a glance at Charles.

He'd come to mean so much to her. In spite of her intentions, she had come to love him. But before that path could be taken and she was free to give her heart, there was something she must do.

The carriage rolled through the village and headed out onto the peninsula, passing through the iron gates and winding around the swales and curls of the landscape until the manor house and the point came into view.

Pulling to a stop outside the front doors, Sophie noted that the fountain now splashed clean, clear water in bright spurts that caught the sunshine.

The new steward greeted them at the door.

"Welcome home, Lord Rothwell." He bowed and trotted down the stairs to help the ladies from the carriage. "Alastair Lythgoe at your service."

"Lythgoe. You have met Lady Rothwell?" Charles helped Sophie himself and kept hold of her hand.

"It is good to see you again. Are you responsible for the fountain?" Sophie reveled in the feel of Charles's handclasp.

"Yes, milady. It seems a shame to have such a pretty piece and not have it in use." He set Betsy carefully on the gravel and handled Mamie as if she were made of Venetian glass. Penny alighted and sized him up, evidently assuming he was too old at somewhere around thirty to be considered in the game of suitors, and moved toward the front door.

Thea stood in the carriage, hands braced on the doorjambs, looking up at the house. Without waiting for aide, she leapt to the ground, red hair bouncing, and clattered up the steps.

"I'm pleased you were released, milord. As per the admiral and duke's wishes, I've not toured the estate, keeping mostly to the house. I've noticed a few things, though, by using your spyglass from the upper stories." Something in Alastair's tone lent the matter urgency, and Sophie squeezed Charles's fingers.

"Go ahead. I've things to attend to as well." She preceded them into the manor and headed toward the kitchen to search out Mrs. Chapman. Charles led his new steward upstairs to his study.

She found the housekeeper in the servants' dining room polishing silver. "Oh, milady, welcome home. The girls pelted right inside to see me first thing. Wasn't that nice?"

"It was. They think the world of you, Mrs. Chapman." Sophie untied her bonnet ribbons and lifted her hat away. "You've become an anchor for them. They count on you being here, as do I. Where are they now?"

"Penny took Betsy upstairs, and Thea hit the back door with a couple of tea cakes in her hand and mayhem on her mind." Mrs. Chapman smiled indulgently at her reflection in a serving tray as she buffed the metal. "That one is too restless to stay indoors on such a beautiful day."

"We'll have guests for dinner. My brother, and an admiral, and Mr. Lythgoe. Oh, and though I know it's not the custom, since this is by way of a celebration, please set places for the girls too."

Mrs. Chapman nodded throughout. "I'll see to it. Do you have a menu preference? I've managed to fill several of the positions here at the house while you were gone—subject to your approval, of course—and the maids and laundresses are working well. I haven't found a cook yet, but the scullery maid will assist me." She set down the rag and picked up a red brick, scraping it with a knife to grind a bit more powder into the polishing dish. A dip of the cloth into a bowl of water and then into the dust, and she rubbed again at the hints of tarnish on the silver. "The dining room is clean and ready to use, and the parlor for after dinner as well."

Sophie broke protocol entirely. She dropped her bonnet onto the table and embraced the shocked housekeeper. "You are a pearl of great price. I can't tell you how much it put my mind at ease that you were here watching over the house while I was away. I don't know where I would be without you."

After a frozen moment, Mrs. Chapman returned the embrace and then stepped back, flustered and bustling about her work. "It's my duty, and I'm glad to do it. I'm glad the captain was released. Load of codswallop those charges were."

"I heartily agree. There are a few things I must tend to upstairs, and I would appreciate some privacy. If the girls come down, please keep them occupied. And Mamie too." Sophie paused. "Where is Mamie?"

"She went with Penny and Betsy. Betsy asked Lady Richardson to read her a story. I believe both of them will nap for a bit before dinner."

"They do tend to keep the same hours, don't they?"

Sophie went upstairs, noting that the driver had deposited the bags inside the front door. Had Miles left their employ then? Perhaps it was for the best if he was embroiled in the smuggling. Though it made her sad. He was young enough to be reformed if he wanted to be. She would speak to Charles about it.

But first there was something she must do, and she'd put it off for far too long. She entered her bedchamber and closed the door, and for the first time, turned the key in the lock.

The chest sat just inside her dressing room, pushed back under the bench. Grabbing the leather handle, she tugged it out into the middle of the bedroom rug. She sank before it, placing her hands on the stenciled name. Major Richard Richardson, Royal Marines. And in small letters beneath his name, Baron, in parentheses.

"If I'm going to move forward with my life, I need to lay to rest my past." She whispered the words. "I need to say goodbye."

She fetched the key from the reticule in her bedside table and returned to the trunk. The lock stuck for a moment, then snicked open.

When she raised the lid, a musty, foreign smell emerged. The contents were a jumble, but that should be expected, considering how far the sea chest had come. She lifted out a red tunic with the high blue collar, trimmed in white. She held the cloth to her nose, hoping to catch a hint of Rich's scent.

But it had been too long stored. It smelled of must.

Sophie laid the uniform aside and drew out first one tall boot, then a second. And a sword, a canteen, a lantern. At the bottom was a bundle of books lashed together with a leather strap, and Rich's wooden traveling desk.

She ran her hand across the scarred and battered top. How many places had this desk gone? It had been Rich's when a boy at school, then a Royal Marine, and finally a patient in the hospital in Portugal.

The latch was tiny and loose, and she had no trouble opening the lid. A cut-glass ink bottle, quills, and even an ink pen with a metal nib were fastened by loops to the underside of the lid, and when raised into place, stood upright before the writing surface.

The blotter was a collage of ink spots, blotches, and lines. "Rich Richardson" had been carved into the writing surface with a boyish hand. She touched the name briefly.

Seeing his things brought an ache, but not unbearable. Not the crashing grief of before. A longing to see him again, but not soul-crushing agony and an inability to imagine life going on without him.

"What would you tell me, Rich? What would you say to me if I asked for your blessing for what I've done, marrying Charles and wanting him now to be more than a convenient, absent husband? Would you feel betrayed? Angry? I wish I could speak to you for just a few moments."

At that thought, her eyes burned and her throat tightened.

She opened the drawer where the stationary was kept, and two things lay there. A wallet and an envelope.

The wallet was empty, cracked leather that had dried out from disuse. But the envelope bore her name in Rich's familiar hand.

Her hands trembled, and she set the desk on the rug, took the envelope, and moved to the window seat. For long moments, she held the letter to her chest, overwhelmed with love and loss.

Finally, she opened the pages.

Dearest Sophie,

This is the letter I should have sent you right away when I awoke in this hospital. I should have sent it when I first realized I was not going to recover from this wound. Each day I feel more of myself slipping away, and I know now that I will not be able to keep my promises to you.

How I long to walk with you again in the back garden at Primrose in the setting sun. I long to smell your lemon verbena perfume even above the riot of pansies and peonies. How I wish I could hold your hand, touch your cheek, or let your silky hair slip through my fingers.

Above all, I wish I could hold you against my heart one last time."

Sophie paused to let fat tears drip down her cheeks. She dug for her handkerchief in her sleeve, not wanting her tears to mar the handwriting.

There is so much I need to say to you, heart's darling, and this letter cannot hold it all, but I must try.

I will rest easily knowing Mamie is in your care. You have loved her as a mother, and you honor her. I will always be grateful for your generous heart.

Though I have no desire to burden you with anything more than what you have taken on already, there is one thing I would ask of you when you receive word of my passing. It might come hard to you at first, but I am trusting that generous, big, giving heart of yours to come through in the end.

The favor I beg of you involves my friend Charles Wyvern.

I plan to ask him to come see you when he returns to England.

To tell you what happened to me, and that I loved you with my very last breath.

But when he comes, he is going to be in great pain. Physical pain, possibly, because he was wounded in the same battle where I was shot, and he is still recovering, lying in the cot next to mine. He's asleep even now and does not know I am writing to you. He improves daily, and he will soon be discharged.

But more than his physical pain, Charles is going to be suffering, because he feels responsible for the injury that has led to my coming death. He is taking a burden upon himself that he doesn't deserve. He was not at fault, and it is I who should apologize to him. If I had been thorough in my duty, he never would have suffered that saber wound. I have tried to tell him, but he does not believe me. Make him understand. Absolve him of the guilt he doesn't owe to me or to anyone.

Sophie, darling, I know it is a tremendous thing to ask, but for me, and eventually for yourself, I beg you to be generous with Charles. He is a man of integrity, and he feels great responsibility, especially to his crew. While he may seem remote at first, it is just that he is wary when making friends, cautious in his dealings with others. I am going to ask him to come to you to deliver my belongings and to tell you in person how much you are loved by me.

And it is my hope that in your mutual grief—I am vain enough to think you will both grieve for me—that you will find comfort together.

Yes, Sophie, I am asking that at some point after I've gone, you will give yourself permission to love again. You try to take care of the whole world, and I wanted to be the one to take care of you, but that is not to be. Instead, I hope you will allow yourself to be cared for by Charles.

If I have to give you into the keeping of anyone else, I hope it is my dear friend. I feel you will need each other in the coming months, and I know he will treat you well.

But also know that if Charles isn't the one for you, you must follow your heart. My prayer is that you let your heart be free to remember me fondly but not hold you back in loving again.

Give my love to Mamie and share my regards with your family.

There was a space, and then the writing continued, but in a weaker, more spidery hand.

Dearest Sophie, my strength is fading, and this will be the last I write. Charles has offered to take dictation in the future, and I will communicate through him.

When you read this, I hope you will know all that I cannot put into words and that you will go forward with your life knowing yourself to have been greatly loved.

God bless, my darling,

Rich

Sophie leaned her head against the windowpane, letting the tears fall. Not giant sobs, but a quiet release that cleansed and healed.

And freed.

The last vestige of guilt at loving someone other than Rich drifted away with her tears. She had, in his own handwriting, his wish that she love again. And his hope that she would come to love Charles.

And she *had* come to love him, but what to do about it? He had been forthright with her that theirs was not a conventional marriage. She would live at his estate and care for his wards. In exchange she would be free to nurse her broken heart forever and escape her mother's matchmaking efforts. She would have a home, Mamie could stay with her, and Charles would give Sophie his protection, his provision, and his name.

It had all seemed so simple mere weeks ago.

Before her heart got involved.

A noise from her dressing room drew her attention, and she looked up, but no one was there.

Wiping her eyes, she folded the letter, tucking it into the envelope and returning all the things to the chest. When she finished, she locked it.

Like Mamie had said about Primrose, she would keep the memories, and the rest she would let go.

Charles strode along the cliff edge, grappling with his emotions. She still loved Rich. In spite of what her brother had said, in spite of what Charles had hoped, Sophie was still so in love with her dead fiancé, she wept over his belongings.

He had gone to her room, intending to speak with her, to bare his heart, to ask if she might consider changing the terms of their marriage agreement. He had planned to tell her everything, about how he had fallen in love with her, first through her letters and then by being with her day after day.

He had gone through his dressing room in order to retrieve the miniature, hoping to explain to her that in a moment of weakness, he had kept the likeness and to ask forgiveness.

He had been prepared to make himself vulnerable, something that came hard to him.

He wished he had never gone to her dressing room door. Never seen her tears.

Finding her trapped in the past, holding fast to her loyalty to Rich, communing with his memory and weeping for him, had jolted Charles back into reality.

She would never weep like that for him. He was too old, too reserved, too wrong for her. She could never love him, because he could never measure up to Rich.

At least Charles hadn't revealed his folly in falling in love with her. He had his pride, after all.

Pride was a cold companion on long nights at sea with nothing to do but remember the warmth of her smile.

Blinded by his thoughts, he nearly tripped over Thea sitting in the grass.

"What are you doing here?" His tone was sharp, and she jerked.

"I live here, remember?" Sarcasm coated her tongue, and her eyes narrowed. "At least for now."

"What is that supposed to mean?" Why was he being so brusque when she wasn't the one who had wounded his heart?

"I heard the admiral talking to Uncle Marcus in Lyme Regis. He said he had a new ship for you." She wrapped her arms around her up-bent legs, barely taller than the waving grasses when she put her chin on her knees.

A concussion of surprised gladness shot through Charles. A command. At last. The thing he wanted most in the world.

Or at least the thing he had wanted, before he'd fallen in love with Sophie.

But with that door firmly closed, a command waited? It was exactly what he needed.

"I am a naval captain. That's my job." He squinted toward the horizon. To the east, a sail appeared. Patting his pocket, he realized he'd left his spyglass at the house.

He glanced down at Thea. She held his spyglass to her eye like some long-practiced pirate. "Borrowing things, are we?"

She had the grace to blush, collapsing the glass and handing it up to him. "Sorry. When you said the admiral and Uncle Marcus were coming by ship, I wanted to watch it sail round the point."

"You're getting as bad as Betsy taking my things. When I get back to sea, at least my possessions will be my own once more." He put the telescope to his eye. It was the Revenue cutter, her distinctive sails full and blazing white against the haze of the ocean and sky behind her. She would run in close to shore, furl her sails out of sight of the pier and the *Shearwater*.

"Why do you want to leave us?"

He didn't. Not exactly. He sought to divert the conversation. "Why are you so crotchety?"

"I'm not crotchety. I'm sad. My owl is gone." Thea put her forehead on her knees. "I went to check on him, and he's gone. He's always been there in the daytime before."

"You went to the shore? You've been told on more than one occasion to go nowhere near the stairs, the boathouse, or the beach without an adult." She might have fallen on those rickety stairs, or caused a rockslide, or decided to go wading and gone in too deep. All the dangers lurking on that particular stretch of sand loomed up and made Charles angry. Not to mention there were smugglers about that still needed apprehending. "You will return to the house and tell Sophie our guests have arrived. After that, you will go to your room and stay there."

"For how long?" Her jaw set, and her eyes glared hot.

"Until you learn to obey commands without question."

The fire went out of her eyes, replaced by resignation. Thea rose to her feet slowly and trudged toward the house. What was wrong with that child? Up to this point she had been full of high spirits, yes, but she'd never countermanded an order of his.

Frowning, he watched the cutter's approach. The admiral had a mission for him. Once more to be a captain of men, to command a ship of his own. Would it be the *Dogged*? Or would he have a new vessel to learn? Each ship, be she rowboat or frigate, was unique with her own foibles and quirks and abilities and charms.

Like women.

Charles snapped the telescope shut and jammed it into his pocket. It was high time he was away from Gateshead and all the females that surrounded him. He was losing his reason.

That evening, when Sophie entered the parlor before dinner, Charles could barely get to his feet, his knees felt so weak. She was stunning. A dress of pale lemon with blue trim that brought out the clarity of her eyes, and a blue ribbon threaded through her complicated hairstyle. How long had it taken her to fashion such perfect curls?

He looked closely for signs that Sophie had been crying, but she looked calm, even radiant, as if a newfound confidence bubbled just under the surface. Perhaps she had heard Charles was to be offered a command soon and looked forward to his departure.

Penny followed Sophie into the parlor, with Betsy and Mamie in tow. Thea remained upstairs. He had decided that missing dinner with guests would be her punishment for disobeying his orders, relaying his wishes through Mrs. Chapman. He regretted having to discipline her, but she must learn that rules were established for her safety and breaking them had consequences.

Marcus, Admiral Barrington, and Alastair Lythgoe arrived, and they went in to dinner. Sophie took Charles's arm, and he tried not to think of her acting the dutiful wife merely for appearances' sake. Being near her distracted him. Thankfully, she sat at the foot of the table, so he could think clearly.

Halfway through the first course, the admiral finally shared his news.

"Charles, I've finally gotten the word for which you have been waiting." He tugged a document from his pocket. "The Prince Regent has appointed several new diplomats who need to be delivered to their positions in the Caribbean. The navy is assigning the *Dogged* to the task, and the ship will leave in ten days' time. I don't envy you traveling with civilian passengers, but hopefully having a command again will make up for that drawback. You'll transport the new men to their posts and bring the replaced civil servants back to England."

A trip to the Caribbean. He did a few basic sums. At least seventy days there and back, depending upon several factors. Possibly as many as ninety days if the trip required much interisland travel or the weather didn't cooperate. Three months. That would put him back in England just before the first of December?

Christmas at Gateshead. With a family. He hadn't celebrated Christmas with family since he was a boy. Visions of Christmas with Sophie and the girls filled his mind. He would bring back gifts from the islands. That should please them.

"I had to fight hard, what with your family history and then these charges being filed against you. But I was adamant. The *Dogged* is your ship, and you were just the man for the job. The council said if the charges proved false, I could offer you the position." He patted the document. "These are your orders."

Charles glanced at Sophie. For once he couldn't read her face.

"How long is a voyage like that?" Marcus asked, also looking at his sister.

"Three months, give or take." The admiral helped himself to more fish.

"You'll be enjoying a warm climate while the rest of us brace for winter." Marcus smiled. "I'm heading home in a couple days, Sophie. I've been away too long as it is. Of course, you have Mother's visit to anticipate. When Charles sails to Kingston and Nassau, you won't be lonely."

Sophie nodded, but she didn't smile. She toyed with her fork. "I hate to think of you being gone so long, Charles. Three months. We will miss you."

If only he could believe she meant that.

"Are you leaving?" Betsy's voice quivered. "You just got home. I don't want you to go." She flew off her chair, past Lythgoe and the admiral, and threw herself into Charles's arms. "No. You're my captain. I don't want you to leave." Her wails produced real tears, and she clung to him.

Sophie and Penny rose at the same time, each coming around the table from opposite directions.

Sophie arrived first and knelt to console the child. Charles sat frozen, unsure what to do.

Betsy continued to cry, but she transferred her grip to Sophie, wreathing her neck with her little arms, burrowing her head into Sophie's shoulder. Sophie's perfect curls pulled to the side, but she didn't seem to mind. She stood, lifting Betsy with her, whispering in her ear and holding her close.

The wailing stopped, but Betsy continued to cling to Sophie like a barnacle.

"I apologize, gentlemen. I'll just be a moment. Penny, perhaps you could help Mamie with the hostess duties?"

As she passed through the door into the hall, Sophie looked back over Betsy's head at Charles.

Did she want him to follow her? When he pushed his chair back, she shook her head and motioned for him to remain seated.

Her reaction to his new posting puzzled him. Was she sad? Was she relieved? Did she want him to turn down the offer?

She had wept when rereading Rich's letters.

She would be eager for Charles to leave, and Betsy's outburst notwithstanding, the girls would be well enough left in her care. He and Sophie had made their agreement, and he was foolish to want to change the terms of their marriage. He owed her too much, and Rich too. He would pay his debts with honor and not look for anything more.

"I appreciate the command, Admiral." He took the orders and set them beside his place. "As long as we've rounded up the smugglers before the *Dogged* is scheduled to depart, I'll be happy to go."

Chapter 16

He was leaving them. He said he would be happy to go. That part hurt. Would he miss them at all, or was he giving thanks for the escape? Sophie had known this day would come, but she dreaded it. Part of her wanted to react like Betsy, throwing herself in his arms and begging him not to go.

Three months? At least he would be home for Christmas. Or would he? She didn't know how the navy operated in peacetime. Would they issue orders right away when he completed this mission, or would he have some leave time?

Betsy, at five years old, was really too big for Sophie to carry, but the urgency of her embrace and hiccupping tears made Sophie loathe to put her down.

"It's going to be all right, Betsy. He won't be gone forever. We should be happy for him. He's waited a long time for this." She was saying all the right things, but it still hurt. "We will miss him, but we're going to be strong women, taking care of Gateshead until he comes back."

They reached the nursery door, and as she pushed it open, she said, "Maybe you and I and Thea can have a snuggle in Thea's bed. She's not been herself lately either. I will pop down to the kitchen and get us some cups of chocolate, all right?"

The room was dark except for the faint light from the windows. Even that wasn't much, because just before dinner, a squall had moved in, sending down fitful gusts of windblown rain. Was Thea asleep?

Sophie put Betsy on the bed. "I'll be back, love. I just need to fetch a light from the hall." She hurried out and removed a candle from a wall sconce, bringing it in to light the lamps. When she raised the candle near Thea's pillow . . . it was empty. Her dinner tray sat beside the bed, only crumbs on the plate.

"That child. She's probably snuck down to the kitchen to talk to the maids and perhaps get some apple tart. Betsy, love, do you want to come with me, or do you want to start getting ready for bed while I fetch Thea?"

"I . . . want . . . to come with . . . you." Her voice jerked, though she'd stopped crying.

"That's fine, but I can't carry you this time. You're getting to be such a big girl, you'll have to walk." Sophie held out her hand.

The scullery maid and Mrs. Chapman bustled in the hot kitchen between the preparation table and the fire.

"No, milady, I ain't seen her." The new scully was fresh-faced and young.

"I'm sorry," Mrs. Chapman shook her head, the lace fringe on her white cap fluttering. "Thea was upstairs when I took her tray. I haven't even thought of her since." She transferred pastry to a tray.

"Botheration. Betsy, you stay here, and I'll find your sister. If the captain finds out she's disappeared, he'll be rightly upset." Sophie hurried out to check first in the captain's study, which held fascination for both the little girls. Thea loved to use his spyglass at the windows to search for ships.

Not there.

Should Sophie raise an alarm? Thea had been punished for going down to the beach without permission. Surely she wouldn't do it again. And in this weather?

But alarm bells rang in her head. Better to be sure than have regrets later.

Hurrying into the dining room, she interrupted the conversation, not worrying about manners. "Charles, I'm so sorry, but I cannot find Thea. She's not in her room."

Penny tossed her napkin down. "That girl. She'll be hiding, angry about being punished. She did this once before at Miss Fricklin's."

Charles pushed his chair back. "Gentlemen, if you'll excuse us."

"We'll help you look." Marcus stood. "We've got time yet."

"Penny," Sophie said, "please fetch Betsy from the kitchen and get her ready for bed. Search the nursery, dressing room, and schoolroom, then stay with Betsy."

They had barely moved into the hall when a heavy pounding started on the front door. Without Miles, who still hadn't made an appearance, to perform his duties as footman, Charles took it upon himself to open the door.

Partridge stood there, streaming water from his hat and canvas cloak. "Boss," he gasped, looking past Charles to Marcus. "They came early. They're loading the boat, and . . ." He gulped a gout of air. "The little girl, the red-haired one, she snuck past me and went down the stairs to the shore. Went right into the boathouse. Boss, they saw her, and they've snatched her. I'm ashamed. I don't know how she managed to get by me. They're preparing to shove off with her aboard."

Ice ran down Sophie's spine. "Who has her? What's going on?"

"We'll get underway now. Signal the cutter to round the point, and send a boat to the pier to pick us up," Marcus ordered. He opened a chest by the front door. Sophie hadn't noticed the box before. Partridge vanished into the dark rain without another word.

Marcus whipped out a scruffy cloak and a brace of pistols. He tossed another heavy cloak to Charles, who didn't seem surprised at the contents of the chest. Mr. Lythgoe took a sidearm and a coat as well.

"What are you going to do? Who has Thea?" She gripped Charles's arm.

"We planned this action this afternoon. While I was in jail and Marcus was scouring the countryside for evidence to exonerate me, he also left some men here to watch the real culprits. We thought they would probably try to move the smuggled goods tonight, and when Partridge gave the signal, we'd spring the trap we've laid."

"And somehow Thea has gotten entangled in this?" Sophie let go of Charles's arm and yanked her cloak off the hall tree. "I'm going with you."

"No. This will be a sea chase, and there could be violence. Not to mention that you get seasick in calm waters, and the sea tonight is choppy at best." Charles strapped on his saber. The admiral armed for battle behind him. "This won't be a pleasure cruise."

"I'm going, and that's final. Thea is my . . ." Her voice broke. "She's our daughter, and she's in danger. I won't get in the way, but I'm going with you."

"Soph—" Marcus began.

She held up her hand. "Don't start. I'm going. Now stop wasting time."

Cold rain splattered her face when she stepped outside, and she pulled her hood up. They ran through the long, wet grass to the staircase leading to the pier. Marcus carried a lantern, and his strides were long. Water soaked her skirts, making them heavy. When Sophie fell behind, Marcus and Charles each grabbed her upper arms and helped her hurry.

"Nearly there." Charles sounded grim. But focused as well, which was what Thea needed him to be.

They reached the cliff edge, and Marcus raised the lantern. A light flared below, and he moved to the side. She could only see a few feet of the staircase before darkness swallowed the rest.

Sophie's head spun. She wasn't fond of heights or this rickety staircase even in broad daylight, but in the darkness, with rain making each step slippery . . . Her heart jumped into her throat and lodged there.

"I'll go first. Hurry." Charles stepped onto the platform. "Send Sophie next so I can guide her."

Marcus ushered her onto the wet planks, but after that, Charles took command. "One step at a time, Sophie. Keep one hand on my shoulder and the other on the rail."

He spoke over his shoulder all the way down, his voice calm and reassuring. "Revenue officers have kept an eye on the village, making it difficult for anyone to move the illicit property quickly or openly. While the officers were being overt in town, Marcus's men were moving in the background to confirm the main persons involved. When they had that information, we decided to lay a trap for them. Yesterday the Revenue men were withdrawn from the town in the hopes that the smugglers would feel safe enough to gather and stockpile the goods in one location here on the estate before moving them to the *Shearwater*. Our hope was that if word spread that I had returned to Gateshead, they would move quickly. We've been waiting for Partridge's signal all evening."

She was so focused on what he was saying, she forgot to be scared. His shoulder was firm under her hand. The sound of the surf grew louder, and before long her shoes hit the rough sand. The cutter rounded the eastern point and entered the cove. By the time Marcus, the admiral, and Mr. Lythgoe arrived at the bottom of the steps, she could see the splash of the oars digging into the water from the smaller boat that would ferry them to the cutter. A clattering above announced Mr. Partridge's descent. He leapt the last half flight, his boots puncturing the sand.

"The *Shearwater* is nearly out of sight to the west." His chest rose like bellows.

The dory arrived at the pier. Marcus jumped in first and held his hands up for Sophie. Charles put his hands on her waist and lifted her over the gunwale into Marcus's grasp.

Her hair hung in rattails, and she had barely caught her breath when Charles landed in the boat beside her. His arm came around her waist, and he anchored her into his side on the seat. His cloak covered her, providing her additional protection against the rain and wind, and she buried her head on his shoulder, closing her eyes and willing herself not to become dizzy or sick.

The rowers shoved off, and in seconds the small craft lurched over the incoming waves as the men bent the oars. Almost immediately dizziness swirled through Sophie's head, and her gorge rose. If only she had skipped dinner. The few bites she'd managed threatened to make a reappearance.

Just the thought of the fillet of sole she'd eaten made her feel pea green and clammy.

Thea. Focus on Thea. She needs you.

Oh, God, please protect that child. Don't let evildoers escape.

After that she could only pray that God would help her survive this rescue mission, as crest after crest of nausea poured over her. She clung to Charles, trying to stay out of the way of the brawny rowers.

Finally a hulk loomed out of the darkness, and the boat bumped into the side of the cutter. Sophie had only to stand, bracing her feet on the bottom of the dory. Partridge and Charles lifted her up to strong hands that brought her over the side.

"Come with me. We need to let the men do their work and stay out of their path. The *Shearwater* has quite the head start." Admiral Barrington took her arm. "Captain Wyvern has command of the ship!" he shouted to the crew.

Charles headed to the bridge. Marcus lurched with the pitch of the ship, but Charles walked as comfortably as if on land. Probably more so.

"Ma'am?"

She allowed the admiral to lead her toward the stern.

"The cutter is lean and fast, built that way to aid in catching smugglers' boats, but there isn't much room, no luxury, and almost no privacy." The admiral spoke above the sounds of men running and the constant patter of rain. "But there is a bit of an alcove where we might remain until we intercept the *Shearwater*." He led her into a corner formed by a set of steps to a raised deck. A small overhang got them out of the worst of the rain. "I could escort you below." The admiral had to shout as the noise increased. They were moving out of the shelter of the cove and into the open sea. "You'd be drier there."

Sophie shook her head. She needed to stay topside. If she went into a dark hold, both her sickness and her fear might overwhelm her completely. She recognized Charles's voice, shouting commands. He seemed firmly in control.

"He's one of the best captains in the navy. I've watched his career for more than two decades." The admiral braced himself against the roll of the deck and gripped Sophie's arm as she lurched. "He'll find them, even in the dark."

"Do they know where the *Shearwater* is going?"

"Toward Plymouth."

"How can you be sure?"

"That young boatman of yours, Enys? The boatyard his grandfather used to own? Marcus discovered that the warehouses have been used as a depot for smuggled goods for a long time."

Her heart pinched. "So Miles is with them?"

"Yes. He's sailing the *Shearwater*. He's been helping them ever since the father of your young wards was killed. He took Pembroke's place, helped them raise and repair the *Shearwater* after the wreck, and started running stolen goods up and down the coast with the old earl's backing and blessing."

Though she had no time now, she knew she would mourn the poor choices Miles had made. He had seemed a nice young man with great promise.

Men swarmed over the cutter, following orders, and as the sails caught the breeze, they filled and lifted the vessel higher in the water. The wind slapped at Sophie's wet clothes, and her teeth chattered. Quite an odd sensation when coupled with her desire to be sick.

After what seemed forever, huddled as she was with nothing to think about but Thea's peril and her own seasickness, someone finally shouted from the bows, "Sails ahead."

Sophie grabbed the rail and pulled herself upright. She had to see what was going on. Her head swam, and she swallowed too much saliva, gulping in as much fresh air as she could. *Please, Lord, not now.*

How anyone had seen a ship in this squall, she didn't know. She couldn't see a thing. Charles stood behind the helmsman, giving orders. Marcus hung on to the rigging to keep from being buffeted about. His hair had come out of its queue and lashed his face and neck, making him nearly unrecognizable. The hood of his cloak whipped behind him. The pistols he'd taken at Gateshead were crossed in his belt.

Sophie went to her brother, and he clamped his arm about her waist, helping stabilize her. The deck pitched and rolled, sometimes feeling as if it were dropping away altogether. She tucked into his side, and the hilt of a knife dug into her ribs.

"If you throw up on me," Marcus yelled into her ear, "I'll toss you into the sea."

Somehow his jesting made her feel better, as she knew he intended.

"Come right twenty degrees," Charles shouted.

The helmsman twisted the wheel.

Sophie stared through the sheets of rain and finally saw their quarry. The sails were barely lighter than the surrounding darkness and occasionally disappeared from view as spray shot over the cutter's bow.

"Those lights are Seaton." Marcus pointed.

Seaton, the coastal town west of Gateshead.

A sailor hurried from the bow. "Sir, there's something amiss with the *Shearwater*. She's spun like there's no one at the helm."

Charles held out his hand, and one of the men slapped a telescope into it. The rote nature of the gesture surprised Sophie. Charles looked and acted as if he could never be anything but a ship's captain, and the crew followed his lead. He raised the glass, searching the sea ahead of them.

"The headsail's come loose. It's flapping like a flag." He lowered the telescope.

"Sir," the helmsman shouted. "There's a shoal not far ahead. If they don't get her straightened out, she'll hit it."

Marcus put Sophie's hand into the rigging. "Hold on. I'm going forward." He plunged away from her. Spray flung up, and the cutter rolled, plowing into each wave. Sophie hung on tight. She tried to pray, but no words formed. *Please, Lord*, was all she could muster.

"We're closing on her."

Sophie opened her eyes. The *Shearwater* was maybe a hundred yards ahead, and her sails flapped like clothing on a line. The sail in front—what had Charles called it?—the headsail, whipped and fluttered, and beneath it, two men tried to grab the loose ropes to haul it down.

A flash of lighter cloth appeared, someone small darting on the deck. That had to be Thea. She was alive. Sophie's breath snagged in her throat. She let go her hold on the rigging and staggered toward Charles. "I see Thea!"

The cutter leaned with the wind, taking the buffeting of the waves three-quarters on her bow, and gave a sudden lurch. Sophie crashed into Charles, and he grabbed her to keep them both from skidding to the deck.

"Hold on." Charles anchored her into his side, clamping his arm around her shoulders. He gave the order to reduce sail. The *Shearwater* was only fifty yards away, but it heeled over as the boom swung and dipped. The mainsail gave a shudder and began to sink toward the sea. The flash of pale cloth scampered over and around the boxes lashed to the deck.

"Thea's sabotaging the rigging!" Charles shouted. "Prepare the dory!"

Men leapt to lower the small boat. Charles ordered the helmsman to hold their position as best he could, and along with the rowing crew, Marcus and Charles jumped aboard the dory. Mr. Lythgoe followed, but the admiral stayed aboard the cutter.

"No, milady. You're to stay here." The admiral took her arm. "Let them do their work."

Please, God, keep them all safe. Sophie fought her fear and her nausea. *Bring them back to me.*

Charles felt no satisfaction that their trap had worked. He could only think about getting Thea back safe and sound.

The dory bobbed in the surf. At least the tide was running in, taking them toward the *Shearwater*. "Row, men!" If they could get to the wallowing *Shearwater* before she hit the shoal, they might be able to keep her from grounding.

Charles moved to starboard, ready to leap aboard the moment they were alongside. A shout rang across the water, and a man charged across the *Shearwater*'s deck in pursuit of a small drenched figure.

Thea!

She eluded the man chasing her, only to run into the grasp of another of the smugglers coming around a stack of net-covered and lashed crates. Her scream rent the air.

"Faster!"

Marcus had drawn one of his pistols, but he held his fire. The danger of hitting Thea was too great.

Just feet before the two boats made contact, the *Shearwater* shuddered. A ripping, grinding noise rumbled up. She'd hit the shoal. Her occupants were tossed to the deck Charles lost sight of Thea as the dory hit the side of the now immobile sloop.

Charles grabbed the gunwale of the *Shearwater* and scrambled aboard. Marcus was right behind him.

Thea scrabbled on hands and knees toward the stern, with one of the men grabbing at her ankles as he rolled to his feet. "Get back here, you limb of Satan."

Reverend Dunhill.

The vicar had hold of her for a moment, but she jerked, and her shoe came off in his hand. Charles tackled the preacher, trusting Marcus to handle Grayson. Dunhill writhed, lashing out, but Charles settled the preacher's aggression with a well-timed elbow to the jaw. The reverend staggered into the arms of one of the cutter crew, dazed and bleeding.

Marcus held Grayson by the arm, a pistol hard against his temple. The *Shearwater* groaned, taking each broadside wave harder than the next. The sails slapped and rippled, sagging and flying with the gusts.

More of the cutter crew climbed over the side.

"Thea?" Charles shouted. "Where are you?"

She bounced out from behind a shifting stack of cargo and launched into Charles's arms, clutching him hard. Her drenched, slight form trembled, whether from cold or fear or both, he didn't know. Wrapping her in his arms, safe beneath his cloak, he breathed a grateful prayer.

Then he froze. A sinking feeling hit the pit of his stomach as a memory of another ship flashed in his mind. "Fan out. Search the ship."

He would not make the same mistake twice.

The men from the cutter headed toward the bow, staggering and clinging to any handhold they could as waves buffeted the *Shearwater*. Within minutes they had marched two sodden, downcast men forward.

Will Owens, the solicitor, and Porter McFie, the man who owned the butcher shop in Gateshead Village.

"Where's Miles?" Thea raised her face from his collarbone. "Those men wanted to throw me overboard, but Miles argued with them, and that man hit him." She pointed to McFie. "Miles fell down like he was sleeping." As she spoke, Miles emerged atop the shifting pile of crates, knife in hand, panic in his eyes. Blood ran from a cut on his head, mixing with the rain.

"Get back. Get back or I'll cut someone!" he shouted.

"Stop!" Charles lowered Thea and pushed her behind him. He drew his pistol, fighting to keep it aimed on the young man as the deck pitched. He flashed back to that terrible instant when the French sailor had raised his sword. "Don't make me shoot you, Miles." His finger trembled on the pistol.

Miles hesitated, looking from Charles to the other men. Charles kept his focus on his erstwhile footman.

"You turncoats. Bashing me on the head." He glared at his coconspirators. "I'll have your lights and livers." He bared his teeth, crouching atop the cargo, staggering and adjusting with each heave of the boat.

"Make up your mind, Miles. We have to get off the *Shearwater*. She's breaking up in this surf. If you're coming peacefully, then come. You tried to save Thea, and I won't forget that."

For a long moment, Miles didn't move. The boat groaned, grinding along the shoal. In increments, clinging to the ropes lashing the crates, Miles descended, but a gleam in his eyes raised warning flags in Charles's mind.

"There's no way to escape. You have your whole life ahead of you. Don't do something even more foolish."

"My whole life? You know what will happen to me. I'll be tried, and if I don't get hung, I'll be shipped to Botany Bay." His knife hand shook.

"I'll do what I can to help you, Miles, but you have to come peacefully." Charles kept his tone reasonable and kind, but he remained alert, ready to shoot the young man if he so much as twitched in Thea's direction.

Miles seemed to realize he'd reached the end of his road. The blade lowered.

"Throw it overboard." Marcus, having turned Grayson over to the crew, stepped forward, pistol in one hand, knife in the other. "Charles, get Thea aboard the dory. I'll be right behind you. If this young jackanapes doesn't want to come, he'll have to take his chances going into the water with a pistol ball in his guts."

Charles's brows rose. The bite in Marcus's tone sounded odd for an aristocrat. His brother-in-law continually surprised him.

Miles pitched his blade into the waves. As it hit the water, the *Shearwater* creaked and slipped on the shoal, careening at a wild angle. "Everybody off!" Charles picked up Thea and made for the dory.

They had rowed partway back to the cutter when the *Shearwater* capsized. Her hull didn't disappear completely, being stuck on the shoal, but the wood cracked and splintered under the fury of the waves, and the cargo, so carefully hoarded by the smugglers, bobbed and wobbled, breaking open and sinking.

When they reached the cutter, Charles turned Thea over to a weeping Sophie, and resisting the urge to gather them both into his arms, he made his way to the helm.

"Come about," Charles called. The wind and rain had slackened somewhat. As the cutter turned back toward Gateshead, streaks of moonlight broke through the thinning clouds.

He'd nearly lost her. How Thea had managed to escape her captors' control and wreak such havoc on the *Shearwater* was baffling. If he had thought about it at all, he would have assumed that a girl in those circumstances would have cowered in fear until someone came to rescue her.

But not his Thea. She was as brave as any sailor he'd ever commanded.

And stubborn. If she hadn't been out of her room and down at the dock, none of this would have happened.

His hand tightened on the rail.

They would have a reckoning once they got home.

He paused. Never in his adult life had he called a house a home. His home was the sea and whatever ship he happened to be aboard.

But if it was true that home was where the heart was, then his was firmly at Gateshead with Sophie and his girls.

Chapter 17

Charles put Sophie and Thea into the capable hands of Mamie and Mrs. Chapman. They were soaked through and shivering, but there were things to tend to before he could deal with Thea's disobedience.

He hurried through putting on dry clothes and made his way downstairs. The prisoners had been left aboard the cutter, to be turned over to the authorities when the boat returned to Portsmouth. All was quiet on the ground floor, and only Marcus occupied the parlor. His longish hair was still damp, but he warmed himself in front of the fireplace.

"It's been quite a night, hasn't it?" His brother-in-law moved to a sofa and collapsed on it in a most un-aristocratic sprawl.

Charles could see where Sophie got some of the insouciance that vexed their mother so much.

"Everything went exactly to plan, except for Thea." Charles subsided in the chair opposite. He scrubbed his hands down his face.

"Have you noticed that the inclusion of the female of the species in any endeavor is fraught with complications?" Marcus chuckled. "I had my entire life planned out pretty well, before God knocked all my plans into a cocked hat. I actually thought I could consign my wife to the margins of my life and go about my business as if nothing had changed."

Charles studied his hands. He had thought the same. He had laid out his future and expected God to just go along with his plans. He had laid out his plans with and for Sophie and the girls, and he had thought they would cooperate just as well.

What a fool he was.

"I don't know what's going on between you and Sophie, but it's clear as crystal that you're pulling against each other. You need to talk. If Charlotte and I had talked, we wouldn't have wasted so much time at cross-purposes. Don't sail away without resolving your differences. Nothing gets better with neglect." Marcus straightened, his eyes kind. "Sophie deserves some happiness, and so do you. I think you can find that with one another."

Nodding, Charles looked away. Marcus was a good man, and he was only trying to help, but he didn't know what Charles knew.

Charles was in love with his wife. His wife was in love with a dead man.

The admiral entered, his hands cupping a mug. "That housekeeper of yours is worth her weight in Spanish gold. She brews coffee the navy way, with salt." He gave an exaggerated shudder. "Now I remember why I like being posted to the Admiralty. There's something about a storm at sea that seems colder than anything else. The chill goes right to my marrow. I'm surprised you want to go back to that life, Charles, after being given all this." He waved to encompass the room.

Charles nodded. He should be jubilant. His name had been cleared, they had broken the smuggling ring, and the *Dogged* was waiting to whisk him across the ocean. Here he was on the cusp of getting everything he had wanted, of accomplishing his goal of returning to command at sea, and he could barely muster any enthusiasm for the prospect.

Well, he wouldn't be the first man to take to the sea to get over a broken heart.

The door opened, and Sophie ushered Thea in. The men all rose to their feet.

"Admiral, I believe there are some orts left from the dinner we didn't get to finish. Suppose we launch a raid on the larder?" Marcus headed toward the hall, with the admiral in tow.

Thea had her head down. She looked fragile and vulnerable in her nightgown and wrapper, with a towel over her shoulders to keep her wet hair off her clothes. Freckles stood out like pepper flakes on her pale face. He readied himself for her apology, taking his seat and reminding himself not to be too harsh.

Then she raised her chin. Instead of repentance and remorse, her eyes blazed hot.

"Thea," Sophie warned. "Say what you need to say."

She started to cross her arms, but one glance at Sophie had her dropping them to her sides. Sophie seated herself and drew Thea onto the sofa beside her. Thea tucked her chin into her chest.

"I'm sorry."

"I don't believe you." Charles stood and moved around the chair to pace. He put his hands behind his back. "I don't believe you are truly sorry." He glanced at her mutinous little face. "A person who is truly sorry does not give their apology to the floor in a defiant tone. A person who truly regrets their actions looks the person they have offended in the face and asks for forgiveness. I don't believe you feel sorry."

"I don't." She shrugged. "I'm mad at you."

Sophie remained silent, but her brow bunched and she bit her lower lip.

"I could claim the same. You were ordered to stay in your quarters this evening." He continued to pace.

"You wouldn't listen to me. I told you my owl was missing, and you didn't even care enough to go look." At this, her chin came up and she dared him with her glare to deny it. "I went down there this afternoon, and he was gone, and the boat shed was full of crates. When I saw the lights going toward the cliff tonight, and Miles sneaking out of the house, I followed him to tell him to get that stuff out of the shed and leave my owl's home alone."

Before he could respond, she hopped up. "I thought we were your crew. You said a captain is always loyal to his crew, and he would never leave a crew member behind. But you are. You can't wait to get away from us." This time the arms crossed.

He stopped pacing, considering her. To his horror, two fat tears formed on her lashes and spilled down over her freckles. She swiped at them, as if disgusted to be caught crying.

Charles closed his eyes, feeling the pain and confusion radiating off her. He opened his eyes, rounded his chair, and sat down. "Thea, come here."

She reluctantly crossed the rug, her feet dragging with every step.

Gently he lifted her and set her on his thigh. At first she was rigid as a mast, but then she drew a deep breath and sagged against his chest.

"Why do you want to leave us? Is it because you don't like us? I'm sorry I'm so bad. If I try really hard to be good, will you stay?"

His eyes locked with Sophie's, and her hand went to her lips. Thea's plea hit him in the chest like a harpoon. He rubbed a small circle between her narrow shoulder blades.

What should he say? He had a feeling this was a crucial moment in their relationship, but he was at a loss. He'd never dealt with young girls before the Pembroke sisters landed in his life, and on a good day with them he was barely treading water.

Sophie threw him a lifeline. "Dorothea Pembroke, you silly goose. Where do you get your ideas? The captain not only likes you, I suspect, if you ask him, he will say he loves you and only wants what is best for you." She sought confirmation from Charles without words, inclining her head toward Thea.

He cleared his throat. "Of course. You, Penny, Betsy. You're mine now, and I look after what's mine. If I didn't care about you, I wouldn't have become your guardian. I wouldn't care how you acted or what you did or what happened to you." He tightened his arm around her. He would have to say it. Nothing else would calm her fears. "Thea, I love you."

Other than possibly his mother when he was a small boy, he'd never said those words to anyone. It was at once terrifying and freeing.

"And Penny and Betsy too?" she asked, her voice muffled against his collar.

"And Penny and Betsy too." He shifted, and she raised her head. Cupping her cheek in his palm, he used his thumb to swipe at her tears. "I don't want you to worry about your future. You will always have a home at Gateshead. I'm sorry I didn't listen better to your concerns about your owl. If I had, none of this would have happened. Now, I want you to go to bed. We'll talk more in the morning."

She scooted off his lap, took two steps toward the door, then turned back to fling her arms around his neck. "I'm sorry I disobeyed and went to the pier when I shouldn't have." She kissed him on the cheek and slipped out of his hug. Just as she reached the door, she looked back over her shoulder. "You said you loved me and Penny and Betsy. Do you love Sophie?"

Heat blossomed in Charles's chest and made its way up his neck. "Good night, Thea."

And then he was alone with his wife.

Charles looked as bleak as a winter pond. He'd been magnificent with Thea, giving her the assurances she needed.

Sophie wished he would do the same with her. Open his arms, take her on his lap, and assure her of his love.

She was being foolish, but she couldn't help it.

"I'm sure Thea will understand someday." She blushed. "I mean about why you want to go back to sea." Time she was going to bed. She was too scattered and raw from all that had happened, and if she didn't leave, she might make a fool of herself and beg him to stay.

She didn't hear him come up behind her as she made her way to the door, and she jumped when he took her hand.

"Come with me."

With purposeful strides, he led her into the hall and up the staircase. Where was he taking her? All sorts of thoughts crashed in her head. The nursery was upstairs. Perhaps he had something else to say to Thea and the girls? Her bedchamber was upstairs, so perhaps he was merely leading her to her door to say good night?

His bedchamber was upstairs too. Her heart bumped wildly at that thought, but she dismissed it.

They turned left at the head of the stairs, so he wasn't taking her to the nursery.

And they went right past her bedchamber door.

And his.

With a quick twist, he turned the knob and gently pulled her into the room he had made his study.

Deflated, she waited in silence while he lit the lamps.

"Come." He beckoned her into the alcove where he liked to watch ships traveling along the coast. The curtains were all open, and moonlight twinkled on the water. The sea was calm, as if the tempest earlier had never happened.

She wished she was as calm. He looked out over the ocean, and she studied his profile. How had she ever thought it severe or forbidding? She knew each line and angle, and she loved every one. The creases beside his eyes bespoke years of sunlight reflecting on water. The lips rarely smiled, but when they did it took years off his countenance. The set of the jaw said he was a man of strong convictions and able to lead.

He turned to her and took her hands. "Sophie, tonight your brother said something I recognized as very wise. He spoke of his regret that he wasn't open with his wife early on in their relationship, and as a result, he felt they had wasted time with their lines snarled when they could have been sailing through calmer waters." He twisted his mouth, as if rueful. "He didn't put it in so many words, but you understand my meaning."

He squeezed her fingers. "Sophie, there is something I must confess to you. Actually, two somethings, but they are two cords of the same rope. I don't want you to feel badly. I understand you are a loyal person, and you have a right to your feelings."

She frowned. "What are you talking about?"

"I am making a snarl of this, aren't I?" He shrugged. "Please bear with me."

"A snarl of what?"

He closed his eyes, as if gathering himself. Fear trickled through her. Whatever it was, it must be momentous to affect him so.

"Sophie Wyvern, I love you. I have loved you for . . . months? Years?" He shook his head.

She blinked, and the blood rushed from her head, leaving dizziness behind. "What?"

"I know, and I'm sorry. I didn't mean to. It was your letters. I fell in love with you through your letters to another man. I'm not proud of it. I can only beg your indulgence, because I never intended for such a thing to happen to me. I think I was more in love with the idea of you, because I would never have acted upon those feelings. You belonged to Rich heart and soul. I knew that then, and I know that now. I looked forward to the mail boat, and I hoped every time there would be a letter from you and that Rich would share something from it." In the moonlight, his face darkened. He let go of one of her hands and reached behind him to his desk. He took something from a drawer, holding it in his fist.

"I've tried several times to return this to you, but I either lost my courage, or I was interrupted. But no interruptions this time. When I brought you Rich's sea chest, I took something from it." The look in his eyes was so remorseful, so tortured . . . He laid the object in her hand. "My only excuse is that I wanted something to remember you by. I had no right to it, and I apologize." True to what he had told Thea, he looked her in the eyes when he made his confession.

She opened her palm. The miniature of herself lay there. She had noted it was missing from the sea chest and had assumed it lost or buried with him.

Charles had fallen in love with her through her letters, had taken a memento when he thought he would never see her again.

"You love me?" It was too much for which to hope, but she asked anyway. "The real me, not the letter me?"

His laugh was sad. "Sophie, I love you. The real you. The you who sees joy everywhere, who takes care of everyone around you as if they were the most important person in the world. The you who brings laughter and security to the girls the same way you do for Mamie. I love you more each day, which is why I have to leave Gateshead. I know you could never love me in return, but I wanted you to know my feelings. You agreed to this paper marriage and the things I offered you, and one of those was the ability to continue to love Rich without my resenting it. I know you love him still and that you always will. I know I could never take his place, and I would never try. He was a better man than I, and if it weren't for me, he would be with you now. I'll take command of the *Dogged*, and I'll leave you in peace. I'll require nothing of you but that you care for the girls when I'm away."

He released her hand and turned back to the windows.

She studied his silhouette, the lean frame, the broad shoulders, the way he stood as if on the deck of a ship with his legs braced and his hands clasped behind his back.

"Charles?"

"You don't have to say anything. I didn't tell you in order to burden you. I just wanted you to know." He sounded as if he were already preparing for his lonely future.

"Charles." She spoke more sharply.

He turned. She pressed the miniature into his hand. "I'm giving this to you, to take with you aboard ship. But before you depart, there's something I need to show you. Wait here, and do not move from this spot." She ordered him about in the tone her mother used when she was adamant about something. "Not an inch."

On light feet, Sophie sped down the hall to her room. He loved her. He loved *her*. Her captain loved her.

Is it possible, God? Have You taken the ashes of my mourning and turned them to something beautiful?

She went as fast as she could, imagining Charles's misery, and she ran all the way back.

And she made certain the door was closed behind her when she reached the study. He'd followed orders and stood exactly where she left him, his fist closed around the painting.

"Charles, I forgive you about the miniature. And I forgive you for what happened to Rich, though I do not believe there is anything to forgive. But I want you to know Rich forgives you too. Here. Please. Rich says it better than I ever could." She handed him the letter. "I found it among his things when we came back from your trial. I should have looked at it sooner, but I couldn't make myself go through his belongings when you first brought them to me, and then I was afraid of opening a wound that was healing."

She stopped talking so he could read Rich's words. He opened the envelope slowly, and her heart constricted when his hand trembled. Holding the pages toward the light on his desk, he read silently. Sophie laced her fingers beneath her chin, biting gently on the tip of her tongue behind her lips.

When he finished, he lowered the paper, his eyes meeting hers. She smiled.

"There is no debt. There is no guilt. I loved Rich, and you are correct—I will always cherish his memory. But, Charles . . ." Her voice went soft as the full weight of what she was going to say hit her. "I love you. I don't know when it happened or how or even why. I just know that I do. I love your walk and your dependability, and I love the way you take on responsibility, shouldering each new challenge without complaint. I love that you can deal with my mother and have her eating out of your hand. I love that you let Betsy wear your hat and that you teach Thea about boats and that you give Penny such a great example of what a good man should be. But aside from all of that, Charles, I just love you."

She barely had the last word out when he dropped the letter and the miniature, and his hands came up to hold her face. An instant later he was kissing her. His lips moved over hers, and she threaded her arms around his neck. His hands lowered to her back, clasping her to him, and he deepened the kiss. A growl formed in his throat and vibrated on her skin.

The power of his desire thrilled her, and she clung to him, trying to say without words everything in her heart. He broke the kiss to scatter more on her cheeks, her forehead, her temple. She gasped for air, her heart thudding against his chest.

"Sophie." He breathed her name as if hearing it for the first time, full of wonder.

She put her cheek on his chest, listening to his heart, as he rested his chin on her hair. "I understand who and what you are. I will miss you so much. But I will write to you. I promise. Just please return to me safe from time to time."

A ripple went through him, and he put his hands on her upper arms, standing her away from him a few inches. "What are you talking about?"

"When you take command of your ship. I understand. You were made to be a sea captain. It's all you've ever wanted to be. I know you didn't want to be an earl, didn't want to have wards dependent on you, didn't want a wife. I promise we won't do anything to keep you on shore or make you feel like you shouldn't leave. I'll talk to Thea and make her understand."

A smile quirked the side of his mouth, and he shook his head. "Sophie, my darling girl, now you are the one with odd ideas. You're right—I was a seaman, and I will always feel the pull of the sea. But if you think you're getting rid of me that easily, well, you have another long think coming. I realized recently that I wanted to stay with you at Gateshead, but I didn't know how to tell you, how to stay without violating the terms of our marriage agreement. Tomorrow I will tell the admiral that I am resigning my commission. My place is here, with you and our family."

Waves of wondrous happiness threatened to topple her. To cover the tears she knew were coming, she sent him a sassy grin. "So am I to understand you are amenable to renegotiating the terms of our agreement?"

The air rushed out of her lungs as he crushed her to him, covering her lips with his. When she could finally listen once more to anything beyond the singing in her heart, he said, "I believe we should continue this conversation in a more intimate setting."

With no argument from her, he scooped her up and marched to the connecting door to his bedchamber. Sophie felt as if one chapter of her life closed, and she joyously embraced the opening of the next, free of guilt, free of debts from the past. She prayed that Charles felt the same. No ghosts, no guilt, no debt.

Epilogue

Gateshead Estate
October 1814

"Poor Mother. It seems none of her plans are coming together exactly as she would want." Sophie let her mother's lengthy epistle fall to the bedcovers and took the small plate Charles offered, grimacing at the crust of dry bread that had become her morning routine. "Her leg is healing, by the way, but slowly. I cannot imagine what Charlotte and especially Cilla have been through as she convalesced this fall."

Charles stretched out beside her, atop the coverlet, stacking his hands behind his head. "What's got her ratlines in a snarl this time?" He crossed his boots at the ankles, the epitome of relaxation.

Sophie nibbled the edge of the bread, chewing slowly. "She's decided to alleviate her boredom, and her disappointment in me foiling her plans for a fall hunting party, by inviting us to Haverly for the Christmas season. And from the sounds of things, since I had the temerity to marry you out of hand and foil her matchmaking, she has switched her focus to finding a suitable husband for Cilla."

"Poor Cilla. From what little I know of the dowager, when she fastens onto a notion, she's harder to remove than a barnacle."

Sophie shrugged back the lace cuff of her bed jacket and reached for her tea. The bread had stayed down, thankfully, but she wasn't going to press the matter.

"Can we come in?" Thea asked as she traipsed across the rug, not waiting for an answer. Betsy followed, her favorite doll tucked under her arm. The captain's naval hat dangled from the other hand, one of the peaks bouncing on the floor with each step. The poor bicorn was tattered and well loved, and Charles had given up thought of getting it back.

Penny drifted into the room, her nose in a book. Herrick's *Hesperides*. Reading poetry seemed to satisfy something in her romantic little soul at the moment, for which Sophie was grateful.

"Did you flash the hash again this morning?" Thea asked, lacing her fingers around the bedpost and leaning back to swing side to side. "Why do you keep doing that? You don't look sick."

"I'm not sick." Sophie looked to Charles. "Where did she learn such a vulgar phrase?"

He grinned and shrugged. His naval lingo *would* creep in now and again.

"Charles, the time has come to tell the girls, and I will write to the dowager this afternoon, declining her invitation. I won't tell her why just yet. Not when she should be focusing her attention on Charlotte's upcoming confinement and now this Christmas party."

"Tell us what?" Penny looked up. "Thea, stop swinging like a pendulum. You're shaking the entire bed."

Betsy had rounded the footboard, dropped her possessions, and clambered up the steps to sit by Charles. He lifted her to lean back against the pillows between himself and Sophie. Thea, not to be outdone, hopped up to sit cross-legged on the coverlet.

"Ladies." Charles continued to grin. "The time has come to announce that we're adding to our crew." He looked from one young face to the next, and Sophie thrilled to the pride and love in his eyes.

He reached across Betsy to clasp Sophie's hand.

"For the new sloop? Why? We don't need but two crew for her, and you hired a boatman just last month." Thea scratched her temple. "When are we going to name the new boat, anyway?"

Penny dropped her book on the bed and came round to hug Sophie. "Are you sure? Oh, how wonderful." She turned to Thea. "No, not crew for a boat, you bird-wit. Do you ever think of anything besides boats? Sophie is going to have a baby."

"A baby?" Thea's face screwed up. "Why?"

Charles caught Sophie's eye, and he gave her a wicked wink. She smothered a laugh.

"Do babies make you sick? Is that why you have to eat dry bread every morning?" Thea looked skeptical. "I don't ever want to have a baby. I hate being sick."

Sophie nudged Betsy. "What do you think, sweetling? Would you like a new baby brother or sister?"

Betsy thought about it so solemnly, Sophie grew concerned. Then the little girl nodded emphatically. "Yes. I will be a good big sister."

Sophie's eyes grew damp—something that happened far too easily these days. "You will all be good big sisters. Let me get up and dressed, and we'll go tell Mamie, shall we?"

The girls scampered out into the hall, and Charles called after them, "Don't tell her until we get there."

"We won't," Thea's voice drifted back.

"I'd lay you a shilling to a ship's command, she's sliding down the banister right now." Charles rounded the bed, and as Sophie slid to the ground, she also slid into his embrace. "Feeling all right?"

She rested her head on his chest, content to steal a few moments in his arms. She would have never thought that God could bring such great joy out of her grief when her captain had walked up the steps of Primrose Cottage a few short months ago. "Never better. Let's go tell Mamie, and then let's take the girls down to the shore."

"Aye, aye." Charles brushed a kiss on her head.

About the Author

Erica Vetsch is a *New York Times* best-selling author and ACFW Carol Award winner, and has been a *Romantic Times* top pick for her previous books. She loves Jesus, history, romance, and watching sports. This transplanted Kansan now makes her home in Rochester, Minnesota. When she's not writing fiction, she's planning her next trip to a history museum and cheering on her Kansas Jayhawks and New Zealand All Blacks. Learn more about Erica at www.ericavetsch.com.